PLATINUM TINTED DARKNESS

TIMOTHY WOLFF

ISBN: 979-8-9867655-2-5 (Paperback)
ISBN: 979-8-9867655-1-8 (Hardcover)
ISBN: 979-8-9867655-0-1 (eBook)
ISBN: 979-8-9867655-3-2 (Audiobook)

Any references to historical events, real people, or real places are used fictitiously. Names, characters, and places are products of the author's imagination.

Front cover image by Alejandro Colucci
Edited by Jonathan Oliver
World map by Chaim Holtjer
Title page image by Apex Infinity Games
Book design by Lorna Reid

First printing edition 2023.
TimWolffAuthor@gmail.com

MAP

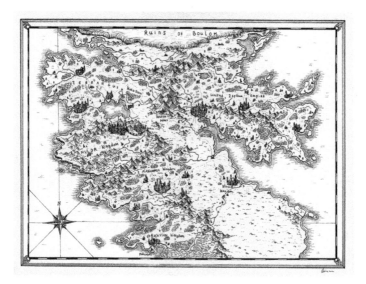

CHAPTER I

NO MERCY

erenna Morgan stood from the Mylor capitol balcony beside her father, gazing out onto the war-torn lands of their mountainous kingdom. Smoke drifted into the morning skies from the occupied bastion, mercifully hiding their vision of the horrors below. But no smoke could block out the screams, or the foul aroma of their fallen. That stench had never faded from the first day. It had followed Serenna through the Mylor gardens; it had followed her to the balcony; it had even stalked the bed of her chambers, an endless reminder of the consequences of inaction. *To hell with the Guardian Pact. I could stop this all. Today.*

Now.

"From the moment you send that first soldier out to die," Charles said, stroking his gray beard, "you lose the privilege to ever look away. This view is my burden, not yours."

Foolish words from a tired old man. She loved her father, but Senator Charles Morgan hadn't the slightest clue on how to wage war. One month into the Terrangus siege and their people were empty. They were never expected to win, but they *were* expected to retain hope until the rest of the southern kingdoms arrived. Except they weren't coming. "Not my burden, Father? Am I not of Mylor?"

He sighed. "My dear, you *are* Mylor."

His words were rooted in kindness, but they stung all the same. As the runt of the Southern Alliance, finally having a Guardian from Mylor was a treasured rarity. Mylor *did* have plenty of crystal mages, but only one had full platinum hair. Only one wielded the Wings of Mylor, the bright white staff with the Mylor insignia—the pale owl with ebony eyes— forged onto the top of the shaft. Serenna's staff represented the kingdom's pride, a promise that in the darkest of days, the bright wings would protect them all.

In the darkest of days, the grand staff leaned against her bed, collecting dust until the next Harbinger of Death threatened the realm, which could be any day now that a year had passed. To enforce the pact protecting all major kingdoms from such threats, the six Guardians were forbidden to participate in war or politics to ensure they could always unite when the time came.

So again, Serenna watched. Watched and did nothing. *My people must despise me.* If they did, they never openly expressed it. Even after the most brutal of days, all sorts of her people would smile and cheer, donating their hope as if it weren't already lost. She took a deep breath and headed towards the exit.

Charles turned to her. "Serenna, I know how you feel, but please don't go down there. I already lost your mother; I cannot live with losing you too."

She stopped in front of the doors. "This isn't living. You have no plan, no experience. Where are our allies? Alanammus isn't coming; it figures the most powerful southern kingdom is the most useless in our time of need. Enough. I have sat here for weeks and done *nothing*."

"My dear, waiting is a strategy. Not a popular one," he

said with a small grin, "but a strategy all the same. Sometimes, it takes courage to do nothing. Honor the Guardian Pact and believe in your people. Our day will come yet."

"Our day comes *now*." She slammed the door behind her, then dashed towards her chambers. Meeting eyes with the owl staff leaning across her bed, this was always the point where she would say no. Something would deter her, whether it be recalling Guardian leader David's orders to stay neutral and uphold the pact, her father's words, or the real reason.

If she went back down, the God of Death would speak to her again. Death wanted her to be his next Harbinger: a mortal vessel for the deity's wrath who would willingly sacrifice everything to become a demonic version of their former self. Such a fate had only been for the most pained and desperate of souls, a fate that, before the war against Terrangus, would be unheard of for Serenna.

Reality and time had taken their toll.

She left the room with staff in hand, refusing to meet any of the wide eyes stalking her as she left the capitol building and navigated towards the bastion. Her white mail armor was already strapped across her upper body and down through her legs, with a matching white cape flailing in the wind. *If you hear the deity's voice, don't respond. Never respond again.*

Her heart pounded as she rushed through the streets of Mylor, ignoring the wave of injured soldiers and mages limping away. *Gods, is that a child?*

"Serenna!" the boy yelled, replacing his empty gaze with a giant smile.

It's too late to turn back now. Running away is worse than doing nothing at all—

A hand grabbed her, filling her with a frigid chill. "Guardian Serenna, my brother is out there. Please, we need you."

She pulled back and kept marching ahead. Cold sweat poured down her forehead. Tranquil winds had enveloped her back on the balcony, but the warmth of safety was absent down here. A mountain of eyes were upon her. It was impossible to focus on any of them, with the whispers and voices in the air carrying her name from all directions.

Serenna entered the massive bastion hall—the only entrance to Mylor from the plains to the high mountains—and stumbled as dizziness caressed the back of her head. Too much death. Men in white Mylor uniforms lay cold on the stone floor, with groups of young mages huddled behind pillars, covering themselves in crystal shields.

Counting only a handful of Terrangus soldiers gave her a flicker of hope. If the enemy hadn't gotten this far through, the true battle would be farther down the vast, open hallways. Closing her eyes, both hands grasped her staff. With the world dark, everything made sense. The cacophony of war silenced, and it was just Serenna and the void. *It's time. Justify their faith. Never let them see how weak you truly are.*

Her eyes shot open, filled with ethereal streams of platinum light drifting off her body. She could only hold the empowered form for a few minutes at best from the pain, but a few seconds was all it would take to fill her people with hope—and the *other* people with fear.

The squad of Terrangus soldiers slowly backed away, likely conflicted over whether they had any authority to engage a Guardian. That was the least of their problems. She surrounded herself with a lucid crystal shield in the form of a sphere—the most basic of crystal sorcery's arsenal—before tapping into her true power and creating a vivid, glasslike barrier that blocked their exit. They could see freedom behind them if they chose to look, but such a life was gone forever. A surge of adrenaline coursed through her as their eyes descended to terror. *Gods, forgive me for enjoying this.*

She raised her staff, drawing energy from her body and channeling it into the form of six individual crystals, shaped into translucent spikes that would pierce through any armor ever crafted.

The large spikes floated in front of her, shimmering with prisms of light, reflecting the glow of flames from the corner of the open hall. "Soldiers of Terrangus," she said, her voice deepened by her empowered form. "You were fools to trespass upon my home. Mylor has never fallen. Her mountains are stained red from the blood of those who tried."

She pointed her staff forward with one hand, launching five of the six spikes towards the men. The spikes tore through their flesh so quickly they died in silence—an unintended mercy. She drifted towards the remaining soldier, levitating the sixth spike by her right side. "Who leads your forces?"

He scowled at her, his eyes screaming murderous intentions well beyond his ability. "General Nyfe sent us to scout your last remaining hold on the bastion before the final push. Not even you can beat him; he is favored by the God of Death."

She froze. Nyfe was supposedly the one with the dagger—the Herald of Death, as her people had called it.

"Am I free to leave? Is the dishonor of breaking the pact not enough? You weren't supposed to be here…"

He will alert them. "No mercy." She launched the last crystal spike through his skull, painting her armor and pale face red with fresh blood. After facing Harbingers and the wrath of gods, it was easy to forget how fragile human frames were. An icy gust of wind blew through her, which should not have been possible inside the bastion halls. A throbbing migraine pulsated as a familiar, deep voice entered her thoughts.

"Serenna…Serenna, Serenna. Is this violence all in the name of Mylor? Or is there a deeper desire? You yearn for the ecstasy of their destruction. All of them. Together, we can make that happen.

Nyfe is ahead—kill him and take my dagger for your own. I want you. I will have you. I need you.

"*Harbinger of Death Serenna Morgan will end them all in my name.*"

She gasped, gazing at the disfigured corpse in front of her. *No mercy? What is happening to me?* Rushing through the barrier, she refused to look at any of her people behind her. What horror would she find in their eyes?

The next room was more compact, with brown pillars closer together and a desk by the window—likely a war room abandoned earlier in the occupation. A young Terrangus soldier in loose ebony armor with his sword sheathed stood above a child holding a staff. Not noticing Serenna, he helped the girl stand, brushing the rubble off her shoulders and smiling. "Don't cry; I would never harm you. The safest way out of here is—" He met Serenna's blue eyes, losing his smile.

"Serenna!" the child yelled, leaving the man and rushing to her side.

"Girl, the room behind me is secure. Be gone from here and find safety." Serenna cringed at the realization the child would find the remnants of her violence, but at least she was safe.

A new voice filled the air. "Did I just hear that correctly? *Serenna* is here? I knew this would happen; the Guardian Pact has always been a joke. Just like I told you, Zeen, but no one ever listens."

He entered the room, with pale white hair and heavy dark circles under his eyes. His right hand grasped a glowing dagger, emanating dark energy that shadowed the pale walls. General Nyfe appeared younger than the rumors, but an alliance or whatever it was with the God of Death had taken a harsh toll.

Grasping her staff, she refreshed her crystal shield. The glasslike sphere distorted her vision before reverting to its natural, lucid state. She then formed a single crystal spike, levitating it in front of her.

A wicked grin crossed Nyfe's face. "Ah, straight to violence. Just my type. Death was right: you're a monster like me, aren't you?"

The younger soldier grabbed Nyfe's arm. "No! She's a Guardian; we must stand down. I gave David my word that no harm would come to her."

The grin faded to a snarl, filling Nyfe's fatigued eyes with a surge of anger. "You know what I think of your word, Zeen?" He ripped his arm back and swept his dagger across Zeen's face. Groaning, the boy fell over as blood poured from the wound.

Nyfe's eyes turned towards Serenna. "Duels like this are what decide the fate of kingdoms. Don't worry, after you're dead, I'll tell them you put up a battle for the ages." His grin returned as he approached.

At least this one deserves to die. Are all Terrangus leaders unhinged?

She launched the spike, aimed at his chest, the largest target. It flew with absolute precision, but the hit didn't have to be perfect—any contact with flesh would be the end. Nyfe swung his glowing dagger through the air, shattering the spike into a rain of multicolored fragments as if he broke a mirror.

She stumbled back. Anxiety smothered her, diminishing the platinum glow of her aura. *I need more power, no matter the cost. Take your toll, magic.* She screamed, forcing anything that resembled crystal energy to flee her body. Agony wretched her sides as her legs wobbled, but the pain was nothing compared to the temporary energy emitting from the Wings of Mylor.

I could still try Prison. It had failed when I tried it against the Harbinger in Nuum, but what other options do I have—

Nyfe's dagger interrupted her thoughts, crashing through her crystal shield and knocking her to the ground.

Do it! NOW!

She unleashed everything, creating a crystal sphere around Nyfe. Not the usual shield, but a prison. He banged against his barrier, yelling something that was muffled by the glasslike sphere holding him in place. He then slammed his dagger against the barrier, causing a large crack to form where the blade hit. It wouldn't survive another blow.

As much as she wanted to shield herself, offense was her only available defense. She raised her staff, hovering Nyfe several feet in the air. Her dizziness returned from the tension in her upper back, but she stomped her foot to regain balance. She then turned her staff towards the window, exhaled all her energy, and sent the sphere—with Nyfe inside—crashing through the window onto the steep, jagged hills of the Mylor outskirts.

Maybe the fall would be enough to kill him; she didn't have the energy to check. She wiped the sweat from her face, then gasped as her hand returned with blood. *Too much. I'll destroy myself if I—*

The world went dark.

"Serenna...Serenna, Serenna. For a moment, I thought you would die. You cannot do that to me. Not yet, at least. Why do you tolerate the limitations of mortal sorcery? Accept my gift. With our powers combined, we could fill the void. Force the Time God to start over. He sleeps. I want him to wake to an empty world."

"Guardian Serenna? Are you okay?"

"You have opened the gateway to a lifetime of war. I will be waiting; maybe I will even be kind enough to offer a taste of my wrath in a desperate moment. The void awaits all those you strike down. Resist if you must, but you will be mine.

"I am nothing. I am forever. I am the end."

Her eyes opened, finding Zeen kneeling beside her, examining her wounds with his faint amber eyes and disheveled brown hair. Up close, she figured he was in his early twenties, at least a year or two younger than her. Blood still poured down his tan face. "Don't touch me!" she yelled, rising and grasping her staff. She formed a spike—a pitiful one—then launched it at his chest.

In the blink of her eye, he drew his sword to block the crystal, but the force knocked it out of his hand and sent him stumbling back, banging his head against a pillar. "I understand," he said, groaning. "If it were my home, I would do the same thing. Your people deserve better than us." As his smile descended to a frown, the despair replaced her rage with the same sentiment.

Not this one. I am a Guardian, not a murderer. I cannot become the monster Death expects of me. "You spared the child, now I return the favor. If we ever meet again, you will not be so lucky. Farewell...Zeen, was it?"

His smile returned and she resisted the urge to smile back. "Zeen it was. Thank you, Guardian Serenna. You are a kind soul."

Foolish words from a hopeful young man. Heading towards the exit, reality set back in. She wasn't a kind soul, even if she wanted to be. Death's words played in her head, over and over.

I am nothing. I am forever. I am the end.

CHAPTER 2

HONOR AND APATHY

ONE YEAR LATER

Standing in the middle of the trade district, David Williams sighed as the cold Terrangus rain poured down his bald ebony head. His hair had stopped growing back in his thirties, so he'd cut it all off and left it that way after forty. He missed his hair—particularly when it rained—but when you're destined to lose, it's best to lose on your own terms.

He was out earlier in the morning than usual, unable to sleep from the anxiety of his upcoming meeting with the emperor. He didn't fear the man, but his old friend was a shadow of the warrior he had grown up with. How much of that had been attributed to a decade of loss—and how much to the God of Wisdom showing up—was anyone's guess. David's own guess was that some men simply lived too long. It would happen to him too, if it hadn't already.

It rained so often in Terrangus that the people didn't care. Countless city-folk drifted through the streets, bartering with merchants and yelling across alleyways. Everyone always yelled—causing everyone else to yell—competing against themselves, the rain, and pure ignorance. *Gods, if only they could collectively agree to shut the hell up.*

They wouldn't.

The only time the streets went silent was when a Harbinger arrived in the kingdom. One of these days, silence would fall upon Terrangus and it would remain that way *forever.* Hopefully, he would be dead before then…

There you are.

He smiled as fellow Terrangus Guardian Melissa Euhno approached from the weapon shop, likely restocking her gadgets. After twenty years of facing Harbingers together, she was more beautiful every day that passed. The rain dripped down her curly hair, and the pale glow from the Terrangus sky highlighted her flawless, dark skin. It was as if one of the gods had torn the radiance from the void and used it to craft an angel. The perfect woman.

The only one.

"Look who's up early!" she said, snickering. She was close, but nowhere near as close as he would prefer. While there was no official Guardian rule against it, she had opted to keep their affection out of the public eye. Such a waste.

"Not by choice. Today is my meeting with Grayson."

"Ah. I'm surprised you didn't cancel; he isn't going to withdraw from Mylor. You're wasting your time and putting yourself in danger."

"A waste of time, perhaps, but I'm certainly not in danger. As bad as Grayson has become, he wouldn't dare harm a Guardian."

"Oh? Would Serenna agree with that?" The words stung, but she ended with a disarming grin that lit up her green eyes.

"No. She would likely call me a fool to my face, and maybe she would be right. I begged her to honor the pact and avoid the war; our purpose is strictly defeating Harbingers. The next one is overdue... It should be any day now." His gaze grew lost in the clouds above. *Two years without a Harbinger? What are Death and Fear planning? Are they waiting for Serenna to die?*

Melissa shook her head. "David, that's her home. Her father is the senator, for god's sake. It's a lot easier to honor the pact when nothing is on the line. What would you do? If Terrangus was under siege from the southern kingdoms or the zephum, am I expected to believe you would do nothing?"

"Honor and apathy sometimes travel the same road. I stopped caring ages ago. Pact or no pact."

"Well, that's a stupid thing to say. Why bother to wear the uniform then?" No grin followed those words. She had always hated when he spoke callously about Terrangus, but why lie? What had these people ever done to thank them?

"Forgive me, I'm just...it's been too long since the last Harbinger. What happens if Serenna dies? We *will* lose eventually; I can't shake the feeling this could be the one."

She smirked. "Silly boy, how can we lose when we have you?"

Gods, I love her. "Perhaps that's true," he said, meeting her grin. They left together towards the military ward. He considered reaching out for her hand, but she had a tendency to swat it away.

"We need a sixth Guardian. Are you still set on the boy?" she asked.

Zeen Parson. "Yes. The soldiers revere him, and the rumors are that he stood against Serenna and lived. Nyfe hates him, and that's about the best test of character for a man I can think of."

"Really? Another Guardian from Terrangus? David...that sounds good and all, but none of those qualities suggest he could actually battle a Harbinger. He sounds a lot like Thomas—"

He froze. "Don't...*please.*"

"I have to say it because no one else will. They all fear you. Thomas was too fresh; we need a seasoned veteran and not another young man with a good heart. Also, we could release some of the tension against the southern kingdoms if you invited a new Guardian from Xavian or Nuum. Their senators are particularly upset no action has been taken with the pact shattered."

Another young man with a good heart. Thomas died for the realm and those words are his only parting gift. The burdens these people place on me are unfair. I just want to rest.

Rest forever. "And what am I supposed to do? Disown her and face the realm without a seasoned crystal mage?" he yelled, too loud, based on Melissa's flinch. "Forgive me, my love...We will discuss this later. We're almost there."

"Shall I join you?"

Yes. Please, gods, yes. "No. If for whatever reason I do not return, the Guardians are yours. May you lead them better than I have." He held back a tear; part of him welcomed the idea of not coming back. That part overtook him just a little more each day.

She gave him a light kiss on the lips. "Make it quick. Talk to our Grayson, then come back to me. Since you're up early for once, we can spend the entire day together!"

It was rare—but wonderful—to receive a kiss in public. What triggered it? He had never discussed despair or emptiness with her. It was easier to say nothing and decay over time, but "over time" had come faster than he'd hoped. Maybe she knew. Maybe twenty years of love shattered the veil.

Maybe not.

Unable to find the words, he nodded goodbye and headed towards the castle. The closer he got, the more Terrangus banners of the Ebony Blade flapped in the wind. They were all over the ward, an unnecessary reminder of which kingdom you'd stumbled into, as if the noise and stench weren't enough. None of the Terrangus soldiers in the military ward greeted him or paid any respect, particularly after Serenna involved herself in the war. He was one of them once—Captain David Williams—but his cold demeanor had planted the seeds of isolation.

At the end stood Terrangus castle. Rain poured down the giant stained-glass window on the east end, with the slightly out-of-place miniature tower popping out of the top. He had only entered that room once—ten years ago—when the emperor's Harbinger daughter drew her last breath.

Vanessa Forsythe had surrendered to the deity, and gods, David had taken no joy from it, but he had been the one to get the final blow after she was defeated. No one else would do it. Grayson had screamed at him, begging to find some way to reverse the demonic form, some way to make everything right again. Such a way had never existed. David took a deep breath.

Everything had changed after that.

Guards held the enormous doors open as he walked through. Whoever had designed the castle had been a simple man. There were many doors and corridors on the sides leading to grand halls, chambers and whatever else, but the throne room was straight ahead, lit by torches on the walls. They never lit the hallway properly, or at least nowhere near as efficiently as the kingdom Alanammus, or gods help him, the zephum empire of Vaynex, but the shadows of darkness were a harsh reminder of the shadows of men awaiting him. One mortal—one worse.

With one hand on the throne room door, he took a deep breath. He used to be thrilled before meeting Grayson. David—a man from common birth—had ascended to lead the Guardians as the emperor's most trusted advisor. Better days that no longer existed. *Enough. Get us out of Mylor. Prepare for the next Harbinger.*

It's coming.

He opened the doors harder than intended, creating a loud thud as they clashed against the throne room walls. The room was relatively empty, filled only by Emperor Grayson Forsythe and the God of Wisdom. A weak crack of sunlight from a storm break beamed down from the window on the right side, showering the stairs in front of the throne with an amber tint.

Grayson rose from his black throne, towering over David from his higher vantage point above the stairs. If it were ten years ago, the man would have run down to hug him as a brother. The years had not been kind. His once blonde hair had faded to moonlight; his old emerald eyes somehow colorless. The more he had aged, the more he became a physically imposing version of Nyfe. "Welcome, Guardian. Quite some time has passed since you decided to *bless* me with your presence."

This was a mistake. "Good morning, Grayson. Forgive me—"

Grayson's hand rose to cut him off. "No. You refer to me only as Emperor now. You lost the privilege to use that name many years ago."

David sighed. "Of course, Emperor." For a moment, his eyes shifted to the God of Wisdom. The floating deity with a sun mask for a face and a gold and red cloak attached to nothing filled David with unease. "I suppose you can guess why I'm here."

The emperor crossed his arms. "Have you come to apologize for murdering my daughter? Or have you finally taken responsibility for the Guardian Pact? So far, you have favored inaction, not accepting that inaction in itself is an act."

This was a mistake. "Gray…Emperor, I picture Vanessa's face every night as I lie down, unable to sleep. She deserved better, but I assure you there is no coming back from becoming a Harbinger—"

"You *don't* know that!" the emperor yelled, his voice echoing off the empty seats where the senators normally sat. But David did know that, everyone did. Maybe, deep down, Forsythe knew it too.

"My dear Emperor," Wisdom said in a man's voice, with a distinct accent David couldn't place—which was odd, considering he had been to every kingdom. "It is too early in the morning to shout. Raising the volume of one's voice does not inject words with truth."

That thing is on my side? David watched Wisdom intently, trying to decipher meaning in the deity's face, but there was no face. It *did* have two bulging eyes that moved on the mask, but only a black frown and a platinum smile were engraved into the design, offering nothing of value.

"Ah," Grayson said, "my Divine Jester speaks. I imagine you two will get along famously."

"Indeed! My dear David, it is *quite* an honor to meet you! I do my best with this brute of a man, but there is oh so little to work with."

He's toying with us both. What is he truly after? "Deity, do not speak ill of my friend."

Wisdom chuckled. "Taking his side—a bold move. Unfortunately, not bold enough to change his mind. Mylor will soon fall, and the consequences could lead to another Boulom."

David resisted the urge to stumble back. Boulom: the fallen kingdom. It was much worse than he'd feared. "What do you know?"

"Not as much as I prefer," Wisdom said, floating around the room, "but I *do* know this. The reason for Death's delay is that he targets your Serenna as his next Harbinger."

No...

"More reason for her to die *now*," Forsythe said, scowling.

This is madness. "Emperor, this skirmish threatens the entire realm. You would risk *everything* over tariffs? Tariffs?"

"An old man's greatest strength is knowing he won't outlive his mistakes. Anyone who plays brinkmanship with me can rot in the void."

"What would Vanessa say if she could see you now?" David's heart pounded; the words rushed out before he could regain himself.

After an agonizing pause, Forsythe walked down the stairs, then placed his hand on David's shoulder. "Ah, look at us now. Leadership and age have taken a harsh toll. I don't just blame *you* for slaying my daughter; I blame myself too—her fate was ultimately my fault. Patience was supposed to mend the wounds, but every day is worse. They say time is fleeting, but gods, it seems to be all I have left." He eased his hand away and paced back. "Listen, if Serenna is destined to become a Harbinger, it is best to end her now and save the girl from a terrible descent. You know I am right in this."

"No…no, it's all wrong. Grayson, call off the siege. Bring our troops back; we'll prepare for the next Harbinger together. It can be like the old days."

Forsythe stopped pacing and actually smiled. "Sorry, old friend. The old days are no more. I have no family, no heir— no *purpose*. All these senators and generals are vultures, circling a wounded old man and waiting to pick at my bones. I cannot afford the luxury of admitting mistakes. I'll see this through, wherever it takes us."

That part about no heir would be a serious problem after Grayson. The southern kingdoms had long used elections, but Terrangus refused to adapt with the times. "And what if it takes us to the void? If Serenna becomes a Harbinger, that is our fate."

"Then I'll see you there. Perhaps, in a different life, our families could have been happy."

I won't convince him. I'm speaking to a man already gone, he thought, before an odd chill covered him.

"Do not react," Wisdom said through his thoughts, *"just listen. This man is useless. Any specter of friendship is less alive than the young demoness you pierced through the neck. Secure your sixth Guardian, then we need to get this oaf off the throne. Serenity is coming, my friend. I cannot heal your past, but allow me to cradle you into the perfect future only I can create. Ah, how marvelous it will be…"*

David took a deep breath. "Grayson, your deity is actively plotting against you."

"Oh, I know," Grayson said, snickering. "I find it rather amusing. The tariffs were actually his idea. Consequences be damned, Terrangus has never had more gold. It's no wonder Alanammus cast him out, but it *is* a wonder that it took so long."

Wisdom sighed. "Alas, who am I to fault brutes for being brutes? You both linger like plants by the windowsill, watching it rain, wondering why you still thirst. As much as you deserve to lose, I hope for all our sake it doesn't come to pass. I cannot mold paradise if everyone is dead."

The god faded, lifting some of the tension, but nowhere near enough. "No words will persuade you to withdraw?"

"The only words I will accept are 'we surrender.'"

"So be it." They met eyes; not in disdain, but in acceptance. "Then farewell, my friend. It pains me that our journeys have drifted so far apart. No matter what horrors lie ahead, I will never let go of the memories we have created together."

Forsythe walked up to his throne, then looked not at David but through him. "Let them go. The men of our pasts are as gone as the Guardian Pact you left to dust. Now, remove yourself from my presence."

I need to find Zeen. Now.

CHAPTER 3

BE KIND AND LOVE EACH OTHER

Zeen Parson lay in his tent, book in hand, drowning out the noise from his fellow Terrangus soldiers outside by the Mylor portal. It would be another brutal afternoon, but that didn't matter right now.

His heart pounded. The final page. *Tales of Terrangus: Rinso the Blue – Volume III.*

The pain of family is unique, Zeen read, *like water flowing down the stream of a river. We crash into the rocks, jagged fragments of earth, molding us into a storm of lost dreams and expectations. Our loved ones know where to strike, where the pain lies, for they knew us when we were children—when we were too young to hide our weaknesses away into the shadows of safety and denial. No pain is created equal—and thus no pain tears like the father's gaze, screaming without words that I am a failure.*

He will never love me.

Rinso opened his eyes, then flung his legs across his unicorn, mounting the proud beast and preparing to ride out into the gray, Terrangus storm break. Death would return with a new Harbinger—and he would be ready.

Zeen sighed and closed the book. This volume was his favorite yet. The sex scenes were still odd—Rinso would "mount his woman" and "roar with the might of a zephum warlord," but the message always resonated: be kind and love each other.

The realm was too dark to live any other way.

"Zeen?"

Glancing up, he found a familiar soldier inside his tent. The boy had a mix of fear and slight annoyance, as if he had been trying to get his attention for a while. Zeen got up and shook his hand. "What can I do for you, Oliver?"

The boy's eyes lit up. "You...remember me?"

"Of course," Zeen said, holding his chin. "Two weeks ago...mage ambush. You were the soldier that dodged the flame blast gracefully, yes?"

"You tackled me out of the way after my ankle shattered. I never got a chance to thank you."

Zeen smiled. "That was all you. I'm glad to see you looking better; is it safe to assume you're rejoining my squad?"

"No, sir. General Nyfe placed me with Marcus. I just wanted to say good luck, and I hope we cross paths again today."

"As do I. Farewell, Oliver." Zeen's smile ended. A year ago, he'd been an up-and-coming soldier, a squad leader—the rank just below captain—at twenty-four. A year later, he was a squad leader with a scar on his face. In the army of Terrangus, there were too many Nyfes and not enough Olivers.

Alone again, Zeen patted his loosely fitted leather armor, making sure everything was intact before the next battle. The crest of the Ebony Blade was on his right shoulder, an insignia he used to wear with pride.

There wasn't much to be proud of these days.

His sword was set in his sheath, much longer and thinner than a standard Terrangus blade. Too many of them favored power over speed. If you swung faster and more precisely, the damage would exceed a poorly swung two-handed axe. Especially here, where most of their opponents were mages. Such a burden to wield a slow weapon in a kingdom where your opponents launched fire and ice spells from all corners of the bastion. He took a deep breath—it was time.

He stepped outside, welcoming the cool breeze and mild sun. Four days in a row without rain—such a miracle would never occur in Terrangus. The joy of green grass, fresh lilies, and vibrant life enchanted the mountains and hills of the Mylor outskirts, but the man waiting for him had none of those qualities.

"You're late," Nyfe said, staring into his eyes. He was in full black leather, holding his dagger and caressing it with his fingers. The blade was never sheathed; he grasped it as if he feared that at any moment, Death would take it away.

Being under the command of a general that preferred Zeen dead had several disadvantages. Apparently, Nyfe acting cocky and getting tossed out of the window had been Zeen's fault. "Good morning, General. Usual plan today?"

"I'll be honest, Zeen. I'm actually impressed you're still alive. Most men die their first day at the front, but no matter how many times I send you out there, you always come back. If you weren't so naive, you could have been a great soldier."

"Am I not a great soldier now?" he asked, smiling.

"Don't be a fool. Great soldiers are the ones like Serenna and I. She is *single-handedly* costing us this war, and by Death's name, it exhilarates me. She dies today. Serenna's blood will pour down my dagger, then I'll throw her broken corpse on the throne room stairs and demand my ascension to emperor."

"Right…good luck with that." He'd been concerned the first five or six times Nyfe gave him this speech, but the empty words dug further down the hole of delusion. A year into the war, Serenna's power grew immensely. She'd shielded entire squadrons, launching spikes and imprisoning men left and right. Maybe one day, they would fight together, side by side against the forces of Death and not on opposite ends, warring over tariffs, whatever the hell those were.

I think about her every day. Does she even remember me?

Zeen flinched as Nyfe grabbed his hand. "This war is a fucking joke; I look like a fool as they press us back. We can only win if she dies. Help me get the kill, and there will be a place for you in my empire. Otherwise…"

Zeen ripped back his arm; he retreated a step and placed his hand on his sheath. "Otherwise what? If you want me gone so badly, just kill me yourself."

"The next scar will be on your neck. You won't feel a thing."

Nyfe rushed off as several onlookers drifted away. More concerning than his threats were the barrage of leers from soldiers all over the outskirts. "Be kind and love each other" didn't seem too popular these days.

*

None of the vibrant features of the outskirts could be found inside the bastion. Hopefully, Terrangus's next war would be against a kingdom *not* entrenched high up in mountainous terrain, with a single fortress choke point forcing an absurd conflict of armies battling in giant open halls and smaller barracks-like settings with tables, chairs, and weapons scattered about.

Maybe—in better days—the fortress had been a sophisticated structure with luxurious rooms and windows gazing out to the endless mountainous terrain of Mylor, but it had progressively got worse in the past year. It was more mazelike than strategic. Doors led to empty rooms and giant grand hallways could be found seemingly at random, filled with pillars that stretched to the high ceilings. Bodies littered every room after the entrance—a mix of white and black uniforms coated in red. It was somehow worse than the Koulva mines, but at least this war wasn't against the zephum. Those reptilian beasts *still* haunted his nightmares.

Nyfe wasn't in the war room, so Zeen approached Captain Marcus, who was reading a crudely drawn map that sat on a shattered desk. "Morning, Captain. I imagine it's off to the front for me."

"Ah, Zeen. Not today; Nyfe wants you to locate a lost scout team in the west corridors. Take those three. Oliver...that guy, and...that one."

Come on, Marcus. You stopped learning their names? Really? "Not that I'm complaining, but I only get three?"

Marcus snickered, rubbing his goatee. "My orders were just Oliver. Whatever you said this morning really got the boss man riled up. Don't rat me out, kid; I want us both to make it home alive."

"Well, your chances are better than mine," Zeen said, smiling. "Who exactly am I looking for?"

"Zeen...you know I have no idea. Just bring someone back and say it was a success. Be alert, my friend. We haven't seen *her* all day."

Zeen saluted, then turned to his squad. Oliver brushed his blonde hair back, drawing his sword and nodding at Zeen. "That guy" looked bored, scratching his back while a giant axe hung from his shoulder. He was far too tall and bulky to be an efficient scout; this man would be dead before the hour. "That one" wore an eye patch, and blood already trickled down his arm.

Great. "Soldiers, what are your names?"

"Private Oliver, sir."

"Rowan," that guy said, drawing the axe from his back.

"Fuck you is my name," that one said, words slurred.

Zeen walked over and slammed his fist into the drunken man's face, sending him crashing to the ground. "Marcus, I'll need a new one."

Marcus spit on the ground. "Hayden, you're with Zeen."

"Dammit," Hayden said. "Tell my wife I love her. Tell her I died a hero, and not a pawn in some petty general's grudge."

The three of them lined up before Zeen had to ask and, to his surprise, they all saluted.

"I'll lead—stay by me and the four of us will survive. You all ready?"

They nodded, nearly in unison.

Zeen drew his blade and headed out the west doorways. The key battle was in the center of the bastion, but the far sides had endless skirmishes of smaller scout teams, with neither army making any actual progress. "Stay close," he whispered, slowing down to soft steps once he entered the next room—much larger than the war room, but half the size of a grand hall, despite the corner pillars.

From here on out, they were out of Terrangus's territory.

"Can't we just grab some corpses and go back in an hour?" Rowan asked, far too loud.

"Shh," Zeen whispered. "No, some of our people are out here, let's make the most of this."

Wait—what is that? Steps?

He held his hand up, signaling the three of them to stop. They did, and the sound of steps continued.

"Find a pillar and make it yours; we'll need cover to engage these mages. Remember, platinum hair means crystal mage. Target them first—"

Rowan roared, wielding his axe and rushing into a small team of Mylor soldiers. His axe slammed down on a mage's face, filling the air with screams and splashing fresh blood on his uniform. Zeen sighed as the rest of his team rushed straight through, ignoring cover, strategy, or any other tactic that would keep them alive.

Following standard Mylor strategy, Mylor's melee stood upfront while the three mages fled to the back. The woman had a streak of platinum in her otherwise red hair, a clear sign of a crystal mage. The male mages were bald, a growing annoyance, which had started a few months back once Mylor had realized their crystal mages were always the first targets.

The woman clutched her staff and shielded herself before Zeen lunged his sword through, shattering the shield in a single thrust. He slashed across her neck as she stumbled back; he then immediately dove to his right behind a pillar as a ball of flame crashed down where he once stood. Taking a deep breath, he glanced around the pillar. Rowan's body lay motionless on the ground, but Oliver and Hayden still clashed with the melee.

Clutching his sword, he dashed out towards the two remaining mages. The closer one met his eyes and began glowing a deep blue, channeling an ice spell. Fire was the most brutal of the elements, but ice was the most dangerous. For a man that relied mainly on speed, getting rooted in ice would be a death sentence.

The mage launched his arms forward, sending the blast of ice—for some reason—aimed at his face. Zeen slid underneath the blue wave and jabbed his sword into the mage's leg. Zeen then kicked himself up, slashed his sword downwards and across, and tore a fatal wound through his pale cloth armor.

A loud *crash* broke Zeen's focus and his eyes shot to his allies. The burning Hayden flailed through the center of the room, letting out a horrifying scream as flames scorched the man to the point where leather fused to his skin. Oliver huddled against a pillar, sobbing uncontrollably. The boy deserved better. His ankle had healed, but his heart would be wounded forever.

Even the mage stood motionless, gazing into his devastation as if he had never seen such a thing. Zeen rushed towards Hayden, then slashed his sword through his neck. It ended the man's pain, but there was nothing in his arsenal that would end the man's stench. Nothing was worse than burning flesh. For a brief moment, he regretted the misconception that Koulva had been worse. Nothing was worse than this.

I'll tell your wife you died a hero. Terrangus only exists because of soldiers like you.

"Get up!" he yelled at Oliver. Zeen then dashed towards the fire mage, who just stood there, trembling with staff in hand. His orange aura faded and he closed his eyes as Zeen spun around and swung his sword, aimed at his throat. Right before the blow could land, Zeen's blade crashed against a lucid crystal shield.

It cracked but did not shatter.

The force knocked them both to the ground in opposite directions. Zeen froze, his eyes lost on the brown ceiling.

Serenna.

Oliver darted towards him, reaching out his hand to help Zeen stand. He slapped his hand away. "Get behind a pillar—NOW!"

Oliver gave him a confused glance, then turned to his right. "Oh, no—"

A crystal spike pierced his mouth mid-sentence, launching his neck far enough back to cause a loud crack. The boy's body crumpled to the floor. Too young, but at least this one didn't suffer.

Zeen immediately rose, gazing at the Crystal Guardian and meeting her blue eyes. Her white armor was covered in blood; her unkempt platinum hair slumped down her tired face. He took a deep breath and held his sword. *With all these pillars, I have the advantage. Mylor works against you.*

She created a crystal spike and hovered it in the air, studying him as if he were vaguely familiar. She pointed her owl staff at him, launching the spike in his direction. Zeen swung his blade up, deflecting the spike to send it crashing behind him. The vibration burned his hand, but the thrill burned his chest.

I won't lose again.

"Hmm," she said, never breaking eye contact. After a moment that could have been eternity, she turned around and dashed out of the room.

"I'm sorry," Zeen whispered to Oliver, before rushing after her into one of the open, grand halls where the true battles took place. She stopped in the middle, shielding herself and staring through him. Remnants of Terrangus and Mylor forces fought at the other end of the room, seemingly oblivious to the fact Serenna was there. *I can't engage her in the middle; it's too open. She knows exactly what she's doing—*

"Zeen!" a voice yelled. He turned towards the pillar across from him to find a wounded older man in his black Terrangus uniform hunched against a pillar. He waved him over.

Dammit.

Without checking, Zeen sprinted to the man's pillar, sliding to cover and barely dodging a spike that flew above his head. "You okay?"

"No, sir," the man said with a weak smile. "The Pact Breaker killed my entire squad. Just her. What are you doing here?"

"Actually, I may be here for you. Follow my lead, we'll make it through this. She could never defeat us both."

The man chuckled as blood trickled down his mouth. "It's kind of you to lie. Listen, I'm dead either way. Let me rush in first; maybe it will buy you enough time to get a fatal blow."

"I swore to David I would never kill her. Defend yourself; if I can get close enough, maybe I can knock her out. It's...not a terrible plan."

"For Terrangus?"

"No, for us."

CHAPTER 4

PLATINUM TINTED DARKNESS

erenna stood in the center of the grand hall, watching *that* pillar intently. The skirmish behind her didn't matter; a quick glance reassured her that Mylor would eventually win. What *did* matter was finding another soldier who could deflect her spikes. So far, only Nyfe had accomplished that feat, but he had the Herald of Death. What did this one have?

Who is that boy? He looks too familiar—

The older man from the squad she had vanquished earlier yelled, drawing his blade with one hand and rushing out of cover towards her like a fool. Several of the older ones had gone out this way. Maybe that last act of defiance gave them peace, an assurance that serving Terrangus wasn't all for nothing. His wounds made him sluggish, so she closed her eyes for a moment and surrounded him in a crystal prison—a spell that had slowly become a favorite. She rose the sphere to slam him neck first into the ground until quick steps stalked from behind.

Diversion? Nice try.

She turned around to find the same boy, then clutched her

staff to capture him. A year of experience had given her the ability to keep several prisons active simultaneously. The outline of a crystal sphere surrounded him, but he side-stepped quickly enough to avoid her grasp.

She froze, giving way to all the fatigue and anxiety pent-up after yet *another* grueling day in the bastion. There was no such thing as a moment of weakness. Once she accepted any trickle of doubt, all the pain would pour out at once, smothering her—a reminder that Mylor would crumble if she fell. She yearned to scream, but they could never see her that way.

Everything depends on me. It always did.

Not always. Less than two years ago, she'd feasted in the gardens with her father, laughing and saying random, inspiring words to the small children that cheered and called her a hero for slaying Harbingers. They still called her a hero, but none laughed. None smiled. She would pay any price to end the war and return to those days.

Any price, other than *that*.

She flinched as the soldier's blade slammed into her crystal shield. It cracked, but he didn't lose his composure this time. He swiped again, shattering the shield but avoiding her face.

She swung the Wings of Mylor across at him as he stumbled back from the broken shield, knocking him to the ground before he rolled away. It was always a delight to slam her staff into a soldier—the shift in their expression from pure shock to throbbing pain never ceased to amaze her. Most mages had no backup plan when soldiers closed the gap, but most mages weren't the Guardian of Mylor.

As the boy rose, she dove forward with her staff high above her head, then slammed it down towards him. He parried at the last second, but lost his footing, crumbling to both knees. There it was: pure shock. His familiar eyes studied her, likely wondering if this was the end.

In a few moments, it would be.

Pressing her staff against his sword, she leaned forward, then drove her right foot into his face. Sandals weren't much, but they would always win against flesh, and there it was: throbbing pain. She'd cut open the scar on his face and blood flowed out as he backed away and clutched his sword. One clean crash against his skull would end him, so she sprinted forward and jumped again, slamming her staff with all the strength her broad shoulders could muster. A sharp pain shot through her arms as her staff pounded the ground, missing the soldier, and leaving her vulnerable.

He dodged with a quick spin, then held his sword against her neck.

The blade was bitterly cold; the icy touch from the point flowed down her entire body. With all her shields, nothing had touched her in so long. *Kill me... I deserve this. I'm sorry, Father. I'm sorry, Mylor.*

"And now we're even," he said, smiling.

It was him.

Up close, Zeen's amber eyes and brown hair were exactly the same as a year ago. The man she had spared, now here to punish her foolishness. What a miserable end.

"You..." she whispered, shivering as the chill in her chest amplified. It wasn't from his sword.

"Serenna...Serenna, Serenna. Together, we could kill this one. You would enjoy that, wouldn't you? No one smiles in the void."

Not even in winter's storms did her body shiver with such force. It was one of the few times she had ever considered saying yes. She closed her eyes, blocking out reality and controlling her breaths. *Don't panic; unleash your power. Today needs to end, one way or the other.*

She yelled, unleashing her platinum aura, which knocked

him back. The pale room glowed with the fury of her light, drawing attention from the skirmishing forces at the other end of the room. The Terrangus soldiers ran off, followed by the new bravado of her Mylor forces. Two men remained, one of them already in a prison.

"You should have killed me, Zeen. For whatever it's worth, you will die with my respect."

He drew his blade and took his battle stance, chest forward and legs back. To her surprise, he didn't lose his smile. What a ridiculous temperament for a soldier. "It means more than you know, Guardian."

Grasping her empowered staff, she summoned a dangerous amount of magic from her body, ignoring the pain, forming four crystal spikes. She launched one by itself as a test; he deflected it and fell to one knee before regaining his stance. *He swings up to block them. Nyfe did the same thing. Let's see how you handle three.*

She launched the rest, with momentary delays between them. He deflected the first, flinched away from the second, ducked at the third—but not low enough. The shard grazed his skin, tearing the leather off his right shoulder and opening a large gash. An inch lower would have killed him.

Letting out an awful shriek, he fell to both knees before taking a deep breath and clutching his shoulder. His eyes filled with terror, but he stared off behind her—into what?

She turned to find his horror, and there it was: General Nyfe, with at least twenty men behind him. They entered from the doorway her forces had rushed through earlier, all of them now covered in blood. *No. No, no. Not him. Anyone but him.*

"Yes!" Nyfe yelled. "It's finally happening! I have waited an exceptionally long time for this, sorceress."

Her power was already draining from fatigue; the form wouldn't last more than a minute. Between Zeen, Nyfe's forces and the soldier trapped across the room, her mind raced for options.

She had two, and both were terrible.

Unleashing whatever was left from her platinum form, she shielded herself, then created a larger crystal barrier surrounding herself to buy some time. The barrier wasn't lucid, covering her vision in a faint platinum hue. She sat, bringing her legs to her chest and allowing trickles of tears to flow as hostile forces surrounded the barrier. She wouldn't dare weep in front of the enemy, but the mix of fatigue, thirst, and an unwavering fear took their toll.

I should've never left that balcony.

Nyfe jabbed against the outer barrier, his grin growing as it deflected his dagger. "I wouldn't call this losing with dignity, Guardian. The harder you make me work, the more you'll suffer before it ends."

She looked over at Zeen, but he was huddled against a pillar with his hand on his wounded shoulder. He had no reason to help her, anyway. The only one who would offer aid ripped through her thoughts.

"Serenna… My offer still stands, but my patience is ending nearly as fast as your life. Take my gift; kill them both. Kill them all. Turn this bastion into a Terrangus graveyard. The void grows hungry; it's either them—or you."

Any chance at killing Nyfe was tempting. Maybe if she wasn't in Mylor. Terrangus deserved to suffer. Her southern allies deserved to suffer for abandoning them. Die weak, or die a monster? She couldn't do it here. Harbingers had devastated whichever kingdom was unlucky enough to host them, and no revenge was worth losing her home.

Nyfe grunted as his blade finally shattered the outer barrier. All that stood before them was her lucid shield and that wouldn't last three hits. "It's almost over, Pact Breaker. I'll drag your cold body through the bastion halls, then I'll make sure your father sees you before I kill him next. All glory to Terrangus. All glory to *Nyfe*."

"I won't do it," she said, trembling. "I would rather die here than become a monster. Maybe my death will rally the South. A martyr is a noble end… I can accept that."

"Oh, Serenna. Your defiance makes me want it that much more. Here is my final offer: a small taste of the void. I will grant you a test of annihilation, a chance to see what we could accomplish together. You have until you're dead to give me an answer."

Nyfe thrust his blade into her shield, opening a large crack. She couldn't stop staring at his grin. He looked so *damn* happy to murder her; the Guardian who had saved Terrangus from a Harbinger of Fear just four years ago. It was an easy decision.

"Just a taste? I accept…"

"SAY THE WORDS! YOU GET NOTHING UNTIL YOU SAY THE WORDS!"

She froze. The words had run through her head every day, but she had never dared speak them out loud.

Until now. "I am nothing. I am forever. I am the end."

Nyfe's grin vanished. Whatever came from this decision, that alone made it worth it. "No," he whispered, stepping back. "You promised me. This can't happen."

He kept speaking, but the world went mute. All she could hear was her own heartbeat; it echoed over and over as a mythical force flowed through her body. Thirst remained, but fear and fatigue were gone, perhaps forever. The power filled her to the point where she couldn't breathe. It kept flowing in; she had to release it, but how?

She screamed, launching a nova of pure black energy that emanated from her body. Zeen dove behind a pillar, but the nova tore through Nyfe's troops, literally crumbling most of them into dust, with a few unfortunate stragglers shaking on the ground. She would consume their lifeforce soon enough. Nyfe's dagger glowed and protected him from the blast, but the force still sent him flying across the room. The terror in his eyes as he crawled behind a pillar was a beautiful sight. Such insignificance. His dagger was the only way to tell it was him.

From the harrowing gaze of platinum-tinted darkness, gods, generals, and men all appear the same on their knees.

Ethereal void wings sprouted from her shoulders; she instinctively channeled them to levitate in the middle of the room. The thirst got worse, but not for water. She held her hands to her face—her pale skin now radiated with a dark energy. Even the Wings of Mylor changed, with the once ebony eyes now glowing a dark crimson. Startling, but not intimidating. She was too powerful to entertain the idea of fear.

"Children of Terrangus," she yelled in a deep rumble that in no way resembled her old voice. "Look upon your Guardian. Look upon *your end*!" The words came naturally, from where she couldn't guess. *I have to stop this thirst. One of them must die.*

You.

She ascended the imprisoned man into the air, meeting his insignificant eyes, unworthy of the goddess before him. How many of her people had he killed? She wished she could see them all for evidence to judge his torment. No suffering would be enough; all these invaders would look upon her and die screaming. Every last one.

She roared, creating a void-imbued scythe out of the air. The spell came naturally through her thoughts, despite her never learning such magic. Casting her hand down, the scythe tore through his sphere, shattering the prison into a rain of dark fragments. The remnants of man and sphere were indistinguishable; the void ended all matters of life equally.

A green essence gravitated to her body from the corpse.

She naturally let it enter her—calming the thirst and increasing her power. *More. I need more. I'll tear the life from every being in this bastion.* "Nyfe!" she screamed. "Where are your threats? Your god has forsaken you. He is mine now."

She formed a spike, using void energy instead of crystal. The shape was the same, but the color radiated darkness, losing the translucent shimmer of her old, inferior sorcery. This was true power; everything made sense for the first time. She was Serenna Morgan, Harbinger of Death and slayer of men.

Pointing her staff at Nyfe's pillar, she launched the projectile into the middle of the structure. The pillar crumbled as fragments of the ceiling rumbled and collapsed. A chill came over her, the first one since her awakening. *Something* flowed out of the hole in the ceiling, led by an ineffable entity of darkness with the same glowing crimson eyes as her staff— except *much* larger.

The God of Death laughed, in its real voice and not through her thoughts. "Your taste is nearly up, little girl. You better kill them before I grow bored."

She struggled to breathe; air entered, but did nothing. The thirst diminished her to a fiend. If she couldn't kill Nyfe, Zeen had to die. Something had to die.

What is happening to me?

Zeen stepped out from behind his pillar. He glanced at her with a deep frown before turning towards the God of Death. He rushed at the entity, tears trickling down his face as he yelled. Soldiers didn't rush to find peace—they rushed because they were scared. She was scared too, and the moment filled her with a brief clarity.

I would never harm him.

"You *dare?*" Death yelled. "Come then, boy. Come face an infinity of torment. You will suffer *forever* in the void."

She nudged her staff, capturing Zeen in a crystal prison.

No matter how fast he was, he would never dodge a spell from her current form. He banged against the sphere, yelling something over and over as tears rolled down his cheeks.

The thirst returned. *He can't move. I could tear off his limbs, burn him alive, shatter him into fragments of dust. I want his essence; it needs to be mine.* She gasped, meeting the sorrowed eyes of Zeen. He likely thought she was a monster—and he would be right.

Death's presence filled more of the room, covering the entire half of the hall with its encompassing nothingness. "Kill him, and the power is yours forever. I have waited too long for violence. TOO LONG!"

Taking a deep breath, she hovered his crystal shell safely away from the God of Death. "No…"

Death roared, shattering Zeen's prison and enveloping his weapon in a cascade of void energy. The simple blade now pulsated with the madness of a lost god. "You *spit* on my gift? I will make this easier for you. The soldier is free; his blade now blessed by my wrath. One of you must die. At this point, I do not care which one."

It will be me. And I accept that.

To her relief, Zeen grasped the abomination of a sword and rushed towards her, his eyes filled with a crazed determination. The idea of today ending forever, of not facing any consequences, was wonderful. Let it all end. *I'm glad it's him. I wish he would smile at me one last time.*

She threw her staff to the ground and closed her eyes.

CHAPTER 5

HIDING A DANGEROUS TRUTH WITH A CHAOTIC LIE

Zeen rushed forward, his empowered blade burning the tips of his fingers. He had always prided himself on being quick, but true power was nothing he had ever expected to wield. What would his father say if he could see him now? Maybe it was best to never have that answer.

He kept his eyes on *her*, avoiding the visage of the monstrosity above them. The Rinso novels had always described Death as a "black cloud of nothing but crimson eyes," and it was eerie how accurate that vague interpretation worked. *How does he know? Who writes these books?*

Her staff fell to the ground with a clang. *She's still in there. I can save her.* Still, he kept alert. She seemed…unhinged, and if she went back to bloodlust, he would be dead in the open hallway of the bastion—likely in a brutal matter.

Death continued screaming, making unintelligible sounds that would haunt the rest of his days. That *thing* shouldn't have a voice. "DROWN IN THE GRAVES OF YOUR FAILURES! TEARS OF THE TIME GOD WILL BURY HIS FORGOTTEN CHILDREN!" The threats grew louder and less comprehensive the closer Zeen came. It may not have been wise to defy the ancient deity, but he was never more certain he was doing the right thing.

He stopped in front of Serenna, accepting the frigid chill that emanated from her demon form. He took one last look at his new sword, then threw it to the ground by her staff. His hands eased to her shoulders. "Serenna, everything will be okay. We'll get through this."

Her eyes gently opened, and she met his gaze with her soft blue eyes. In that fading moment, he met the true woman, and not the Pact Breaker nemesis of Terrangus. In a better realm, it could have always been this way.

"Thank you, for everything," she whispered, before losing consciousness and collapsing into his arms. The darkness dissipated off her body; Serenna was no longer a monster.

With his left hand, he grabbed her owl staff—much heavier than expected—and placed it through his sword sheath behind his back. It hung out awkwardly, but it didn't seem right to separate a Guardian from her weapon. His own sword still lay on the ground; it was easy to leave it there as vapors of void energy tapered off the blade.

He lifted her, stepping towards the exit. She was like air in his arms; he had never considered that such a tiny frame held the power to crush entire kingdoms. The entity kept rumbling, but Zeen never glanced up. Was the art of bravery to just ignore fear? *Stop shaking. Don't let it see you this way.*

"You will *never* be free of me. Neither of you. I will look upon you one last time in the void, before I forget you ever existed at all. I am nothing. I am forever. I am the end. I AM THE END!" It faded from the room and left an icy chill in its wake.

Zeen passed Nyfe by the broken pillar, who was still breathing but unconscious. *That will be a problem tomorrow.*

Terrangus soldiers stared at him in shock, with no one saying a word as he navigated through the next room. *How in the hell will I explain this? David will know what to do.*

Marcus gasped as he entered the war room. "No fucking way... I send you on a suicide mission and you kill their Guardian? Is it finally over? It's a miracle!" The captain laughed, rolling up his map and throwing it to the side—he then froze when he saw her breathe. "*She's alive?* Are you fucking serious, Zeen? What are you doing?"

What am I doing? "I need to bring her to David. Despite everything, Serenna is still a Guardian. He'll know how to work out this mess with the broken pact and the God of Death..."

Marcus's jaw dropped. "You're bringing her to Terrangus? Are you mad?"

"What other options do I have?"

"Kill her! This... All of this is because of *her*. I should be slamming wine and feasting with whores, but I'm stuck here with people like Nyfe! People like that guy!" he said, pointing at the drunken man Zeen had struck earlier. That felt like days ago.

Surprising words from the married captain, but if a normally well-tempered man reacted with shock, this was almost certainly a mistake.

I should've just given her to Mylor. No, we would be right back in the same spot tomorrow. David will know what to do...right?

Right? "I'm taking her to David. Please, let me do this; I gave him my word she would be safe. You saw the last Harbinger of Fear...we need her alive."

Marcus sighed, rubbing his balding head. "Zeen, I swear... Alright. I'll escort you to the portal so they don't murder you in cold blood. No more—whatever happens beyond that is your problem. If she wakes and kills us all, then fuck you in advance."

Zeen smiled. "Thank you, Captain."

He followed behind Marcus, to gasps and leers as they made their way through the outskirts. It was difficult not to snicker. If "be kind and love each other" wasn't popular this morning, it would be despised by late afternoon.

They stood before the Mylor outskirts portal, a mammoth structure of tan rocks and old magic he would never understand. Some sort of technology from Boulom, apparently. There was a faint ebony shimmer in the center, crackling at random and buzzing at the portal mage's oak staff.

Marcus snapped his fingers at the portly young girl. "Marcy, open it back to the Terrangus outskirts. Now."

She squinted her eyes at Serenna, then dropped her staff with a gasp. "What have you done? I want *no* part in this."

"Just do your job, girl. It's the easiest job here. Why do the gods always bless the most useless people?"

She snagged her staff off the ground, then pointed it at the portal. The dim shimmer erupted into a cataclysm of a faint, yet powerful darkness. "Whatever. Good luck, *Captain*."

"Oh, not me—I'm sure as hell not going in there," he said with a snicker, patting Zeen on his undamaged shoulder. "Good luck, Zeen."

Zeen forced a smile; he had never trusted these things. They had never let him down, but there were old soldier tales of men entering and being torn to shreds, or worse yet, appearing in the middle of the Vaynex citadel, ending up face-to-face with the zephum warlord. "Thanks, everyone. Well…here we go."

*

Zeen opened his eyes, sighing in relief as the familiar grass on the Terrangus outskirts flattened under his boots. The portal rang with a sharp buzz before going dull, then the glow diminished to a faint white. Serenna was still in his arms; her eyes closed, likely no idea she had entered enemy territory. His shoulder ached, but at least the bleeding had stopped. A handful of soldiers guarding the portal approached.

It's not raining for once. That's surely a good sign.

"Zeen? What are you doing here? You're not deserting, are you?" the lead guard asked with a smile. His smile faded as he noticed Serenna. "Oh, shit."

"Yeah…It's been an interesting morning. I don't suppose you would escort me to David?"

"David? No! We have to report this to the emperor. *Now.*"

"I…would rather not."

I should not have said that.

The guard waved his soldiers closer, creeping his hand to his blade with the subtlety of a fat zephum. "Something is off about this. You're coming with us. I think Nyfe was right about you."

Sweat trickled down his forehead. *Five of them—the leader looks competent enough, but the rest have likely never seen a battle. If I take him down first, I might be able to…*

I don't have a sword. "Alright then, lead the way."

One guard grabbed a wooden cart, pushing it forward and nodding to the leader. The leader took Serenna from Zeen's arms, then threw the most powerful woman in the realm into the cart like she was a sack of meat.

Zeen grimaced, then walked over and placed the owl staff by her side. "You guys *do* know this is the Guardian of Mylor, right?"

The guard shrugged. "Yeah, figured she would be taller. With the way our men talk about her, you would think she was a seven-foot beast. At least David and Melissa *look* like Guardians." It was likely for the best that Serenna stayed unconscious. Whenever she did wake, he would make sure to leave these details out.

They approached the gates of Terrangus with the massive steel doors already open—as they always were—during the afternoon. The men serving the kingdom had their flaws—many of them—but the kingdom itself would always be beautiful. Despite the constant rain; despite the poverty; despite the traders already brawling in the streets over the price of bread.

It was home.

The guards noticeably picked up their pace as townsfolk began to stare and follow from a distance in the trade district. Murmurs stalked them, but once a random voice yelled out, "It's Serenna!" the murmurs ascended to yells and some shrieks. Even by Terrangus standards, it was too loud. The five guards by his side would be no match for the unruly mob building behind them. Fortunately, they seemed to know that, picking up the pace until approaching the military ward gates and then—

Silence.

The emperor himself stood on the other side of the gates, with…the God of Wisdom? Rinso *never* wrote about that one. It was common knowledge the deity "advised" the emperor after getting cast out of Alanammus, but it never showed itself outside the castle. An anxious nausea filled Zeen's chest.

He knows. Wisdom told him everything. He'll kill us both right here.

The emperor lowered his hand, staring directly into Zeen's eyes. "Ah, I had to see it for myself. Truly, the gods bless this day, offering not only sunshine, but the Pact Breaker. People of Terrangus! Rejoice! For the war is over—and victory is ours!"

What? I don't think it works that way.

The crowd roared as Zeen's guards backed away. If the emperor was pleased, they had no reason to change that. Bottles smashed in the streets, with people hugging and sobbing at the spectacle. The war wasn't won—or lost—but apparently it was over. What of the tariffs? Did they ever matter?

Silence returned as the emperor raised his hand. "Who are you, soldier?"

We met twice already. "Squad Leader Zeen Parson, my lord." It was unsettling to hear his own voice so clearly this deep into Terrangus. Everyone was watching him.

"Ah! You're the one Nyfe always complains about. On that note, where is he?"

"Still in Mylor. He was wounded in today's battle; I wish him a speedy recovery." He would never wish the man dead, but some non-threatening wounds *would* buy him some time.

"I see...well, it would appear the *better* man has prevailed, would it not? Come, you will be properly rewarded." He whispered some words to one of his personal guards, who opened the gates and pushed Serenna's cart into the ward. "People of Terrangus! Look upon this man! Know this man! Zeen Parson is a hero of Terrangus, and there will be a grand feast tomorrow in his honor!"

The crowd—and his anxiety—roared in unison, ascending the once ignored soldier into their new hero. *This is surreal. I wish Dad were here. Gods, he would never believe me.*

Zeen followed the cart into the military ward, then the guard closed the gate behind him. The emperor had six masked personal guards, each wearing red mail instead of the standard Terrangus black. They pointed to an open spot by the emperor's left. Zeen drifted to the spot, then the guards made a circular formation around them and began walking towards the castle.

Zeen's smile grew bright at the wonder. "Thank you for this, Emperor."

"Silence, fool," he said, scowling. "I was prepared to execute you on the spot for bringing *her* here, but you finally gave me an excuse to end this miserable war."

Zeen's frown grew dim at the reality.

"You're lucky, boy; Wisdom convinced me you're worth keeping around. You can be their hero while I figure out how to use this to my advantage." The entourage stopped as he placed his hands on Zeen's shoulder. "I *do* have a question, though. How did she turn back to normal? What did you do? I *must* know this."

"Honestly, I don't know. Everything happened so fast. I rushed to her, we met eyes, then she just sort of…fell into my arms and the darkness faded. Death kept screaming threats; it wanted us to kill each other, but we refused."

The emperor eased his hands away. He smirked, but it was the most sorrowful smirk Zeen had ever seen. "Ah, I was right. All these years and I was right. Thank you, boy. Your upcoming days will be grand."

They continued their approach to the castle as an odd chill entered his thoughts.

"Do not react—just listen. How wonderful it was to see Death fail. He is quite the brute; the empty soul has been a god far too long, completely without empathy, love, or any emotions or drive whatsoever. My dear Zeen, understand this: Death is bored. All of this madness stems from boredom, and you mortals are his plaything. Can you believe such a concept? Your realm teeters on the brink of annihilation because a powerful fool is too simple-minded to entertain himself."

Zeen cocked his head and gazed at the sun mask of the bizarre god. That voice was Wisdom, right? Its eyes shifted, but not towards him.

"You fool! Don't look at me! Oh no, are you dense? I always find the dense ones…oh well. My simple friend, listen carefully. This emperor plans to kill your sorceress, but Fear and I prefer it doesn't happen yet. While Fear happens to share your dense nature, she at least respects the natural order of things. There will be a Harbinger of Fear in the west section of the military ward

tomorrow evening, a disgruntled mage who will soon discover his son died in some pointless Mylor skirmish. Oh, how mad he will be!"

The emperor rubbed his chin. "Interesting; none of us seem to be speaking. Zeen, what is Wisdom saying to you? The fool never shuts up, and right now he isn't speaking to me, so I assume you're stuck listening to his nonsense."

I can't tell him that. But I'm a terrible liar. What if he already knows and this is a test? Hmm. Rinso would try some deception.

"My Emperor, he is telling me to kill you."

Everyone froze. The emperor's guards drew their blades, all pointing at Zeen. The emperor drew his own weapon, a royal two-handed sword with a golden hilt. Perhaps deception had not been the best idea. "I'm curious how you expect to accomplish such a thing? Choose your next action carefully, Zeen. No one writes songs about heroes that die on their first day."

At least he'll remember my name after this.

"Emperor, I am a loyal soldier of our kingdom, merely repeating what Wisdom said to me. I am not your enemy—I don't even have a sword."

The emperor scoffed, sheathing his blade. "How fitting that such a foolish child defeated the Pact Breaker. Tomorrow, you will enjoy a warm bath and some proper food, not the garbage they serve in Mylor. Do not be so quick to join the losing side; you will find my allies enjoy *several* advantages."

He is worse than the rumors. I need to get away from this man and find David. "Of course, Emperor. Thank you."

"Oh my, that was arrogant. Hiding a dangerous truth with a chaotic lie; how utterly rogue of you. My dear Zeen, you are still dense, but at the very least, I prefer you to this charlatan of an emperor. I hope you survive the upcoming horrors. Men like you

usually don't, but don't be alarmed. After you die, I'll find someone better to usher in the paradise of Serenity.

"I always do."

CHAPTER 6

TERRANGUS'S FINEST

David wiped a trickle of sweat from his forehead. Terrangus castle was refreshingly cool this afternoon, but stress heated his body like a summer night in Nuum. Melissa never stopped her smile as they walked to the grand hall; the destination for the feast in honor of Zeen Parson—a fool beyond words. An ignorant child who had brought Serenna to the doorstep of an unhinged emperor yesterday.

Melissa chuckled. "Dear, try to relax. This may actually work out for the best. A Terrangus prison cell is no more dangerous than a battlefield."

He stopped and rubbed his hands down his face. "I *cannot* handle this right now. Why can't anyone act rationally? I wish the Guardian team could just be me and five of you."

"What fun would that be? Could we at least split it up as three and three? I doubt you could handle five of me."

A joke, but the idea of actual relaxation was haunting. It had been easier to deal with problem after problem in his younger years, but patience had faded long before his last strand of hair.

"Zeen failed me; he is damning us before even joining the team. I just cannot pick Guardians anymore; it used to be easy. Francis, Pyith… I would kill to have another one of them." *I left out Thomas and Brian. Rest in peace, my friends.*

She smirked. "He's young, give him a chance. Honestly, what did you expect him to do? The fact that he got her out of Mylor alive is a miracle."

Trickles of sweat turned to streams. *How will I address Serenna? Do I punish her? Do I remove her from the Guardians? No—any harsh action may push her farther away.* "Ugh, I don't know what to do. If Serenna becomes the next Harbinger, all is lost. This is a delicate situation, and delicate is *not* my specialty."

"Leave that to me. We're like sisters; I can talk her off the ledge. Make sure Grayson leaves her alone, then give some guidance to this kid and get him ready. I'm sorry I doubted you. You obviously see something special in Zeen; I'll support him as one of our own."

He held her hands. "Never apologize for doubting me. I need that second voice to balance out the one in my head. You are as brilliant as you are beautiful."

She giggled as he kissed her hands.

Outside the banquet entrance, yells and the aroma of fresh turkey swept through him. The thick scent of smoke was an indication it was all burned, as it always was. It had never bothered him until his first visit to Alanammus. The idea that chefs could actually cook for the proper amount of time and serve a turkey without charred lines had been a startling revelation. Oh well. As long as Terrangus still had wine, everything would be okay.

They entered together and David sighed at the chaos of drunken soldiers yelling and stumbling about. *Why do they always have to yell?* Wooden tables were scattered across the open hall with barrels of wine stacked in the back being served by a handful of soldiers out of uniform. The second floor hosted the emperor and God of Wisdom, and Grayson's eyes immediately met his own. Grayson scowled at him with a fiery rage David had not seen in years.

He's going to kill Serenna.

Several soldiers approached Melissa, saluting and offering her chalices of wine. She wore a casual variation of the standard Terrangus black, making several adjustments to account for her weapons. A sword across her back, elemental-detonators on her belt, knives scattered along various sheaths by her legs. Every man in the room wanted to be hers, but she had chosen David. Gods, for some reason, she had chosen him.

You're the only one that ever loved me.

He grabbed a chalice of wine, then navigated to the north corner with the fewest number of people. While everyone approached Melissa, no one ever bothered him. Fear smothered any possibility of small talk long before the words were born. He took a large swig, sighing in relief as the harsh burn formed in the back of his throat.

Very few things in life were better than that delayed numbness that always caressed his senses. A simple drink could calm the fear of their eventual loss, of ending up alone, of dooming yet *another* young kid to their death, or even the idea that if he slept one night and never woke up—that would be okay. No matter how much he drank, that one had never fully faded.

He finished his chalice, then grabbed another off a table...

Oh no.

Zeen stumbled in the middle of the room, waving a wooden sword to the cheers and laughter of his peers. A random soldier staggered up to him. "Zeen! Face me! Show me the skill of Terrangus's finest!"

As if he were a child, Zeen obliged, and the two of them clashed their toy swords to the delight of the crowd. He was surprisingly efficient, despite his intoxication, blocking when necessary, but showing constraint with his counters. These soldiers were too ignorant to see it, but Zeen allowed him to lose with dignity, tripping his opponent and never wounding his face. The defeated soldier got up and bowed, first to Zeen, then the emperor, who gave a nod and a light clap.

A new idiot stepped forward, wielding two practice swords and twirling them around. Instead of making another grand challenge, the soldier roared and dashed forward. He swung both swords at once towards Zeen's face, who did a spin move to close the gap, then held his sword to the man's neck. "I yield!" the idiot yelled, dropping his weapons and doing the same bowing procedure.

The cheers amplified David's anger and he glanced at Melissa to see her "I told you so" smirk. *This is my choice for the next Guardian? I look like a fucking fool. Is there no end to this shame?* He pounded his chalice and grabbed another. It was clearly someone else's, but he *dared* them to confront him today. While alcohol normally dulled the senses, it would take all the wine in Terrangus to subside his rage.

Yet another fool stepped forward, so intoxicated he couldn't stand without leaning and stumbling all over. "Zeen... You are die...for the emperor!" This one had a polearm with the sharp end removed. Odd—such a weapon was more standard for Alanammus gold cloaks. The man charged forward, tripped on his own feet, then collapsed in front of Zeen. Everyone— Grayson included—laughed at the humiliation.

Zeen grabbed a new chalice, drank it in one gulp, then held his wooden sword in the air. "Anyone else? Taking on all challengers!" The words slurred, but the people cheered all the same.

David took a deep breath before turning to the closest man sitting down. "Your sword. *Now.*" Whoever it was immediately rose, standing at attention and drawing his blade. He handed him the weapon without words and sat back down.

David met eyes with Melissa, who frowned and mouthed something. Likely, "don't you dare," but he *had* promised to give the potential recruit some guidance.

Today's lesson was fear.

An empowering silence smothered the halls as David approached the center. The more onlookers that noticed his presence, the more they found they were done speaking. Zeen turned around—and *smiled*. "David? Finally!"

"So, I hear you're the best. Are you better than me?"

Zeen kept smiling. "I've been looking all over for you. We have so much to discuss."

David drew his own sword—a real sword—and fixed his gaze on his opponent. "That clearly isn't important to you right now. You said you're taking on all challengers. Now, you face the leader of the Guardians."

Zeen drew his wooden sword, finally losing that smile.

"Get that *ridiculous* thing out of my sight. We aren't children; we don't duel with wooden toys." David threw the soldier's sword in front of Zeen.

Sweat dripped down his face as Zeen picked up the blade. Alcohol had a funny way of abandoning people when reality set in. "I'm ready, David."

"So be it. Show me your violence."

Since Zeen wouldn't dare make the first move, David rushed forward, swinging away from his head, ensuring not to cause a wound if the boy had no reaction. To his surprise, Zeen parried high, pushing his sword back and entering a somewhat dignified battle stance.

There you are. Show it to me.

Zeen swung at David's chest, far too slow to be of any real threat. David stepped back, avoiding the strike with minimal effort. "You *dare* hold back against me?"

"I...don't want to hurt you."

Intentions be damned, he would suffer for that insult. David swiped his sword across his shoulder, opening a cut that had been covered by poorly wrapped bandages.

Zeen groaned, stepping back and grasping his blade. His eyes filled with anger. "You would target my injury?"

"If you don't bother to hide it, Harbingers will always target your weakness." David swung again at the same shoulder, meeting Zeen's blade. *Good.*

Zeen swung at his upper chest at a respectable speed, finally causing David to block and take a step back to regain his footing. Zeen followed through—again targeting the chest—and David blocked his blade, then struck him in the face with his elbow. Blood poured down Zeen's nose; David made sure not to break it, but it would certainly sting.

David drifted towards him, slicing at his shoulder while Zeen tended to his wound. Shrieking, Zeen fell to one knee, which caused several groans from the onlookers. "Terrangus turns against you," David whispered.

The wounded boy rose, clutching his sword and finally staring into David's eyes with a *deep* anger. Zeen swung wildly at his face. David blocked what would have been a fatal strike and stepped back.

The real duel had begun.

Zeen's next strikes were too quick to dodge, but David held his own by staying close and blocking them all. His speed had declined in his later years, but he'd found he could keep up by fighting close quarters. Quick ones like Zeen would overwhelm him if they used open space, but David would never allow that advantage.

The more David blocked, the sloppier Zeen's strikes became. The boy wasn't used to losing, but as his skill yielded to desperation that was the only possible result. *He goes low, low, high. One more and it's over.*

He respected the tactful ruthlessness of targeting an older man's legs. For all his smiles, Zeen knew how to kill a man better than he would reveal. David blocked the strike towards his left leg, turned to avoid the follow through, then rushed forward as Zeen's blade came up, dodging the strike and holding his blade to his throat.

Zeen frowned, his eyes on the ground. "I yield." The crowd booed, and the emperor and his deity left their post.

"There is no surrender. Rest only comes when we meet the darkness. For you, that moment is *now*." He slammed his fist into Zeen's face, dropping him to the cold floor. The room dissipated, with no one coming to help him up.

Melissa remained, wielding a frown, with her hands on her hips. She had never appreciated the necessity of breaking down a future Guardian. The more arrogant ones—Francis, Pyith and now Zeen—would either learn their humility in a controlled environment, or when a Harbinger sent them to the void. *This is for the best. They will never thank me, but I accept that—*

Bells rang.

Loud, haunting bells.

Bells he hadn't heard in two years.

Melissa rushed over. "You get Serenna; I'll get the rest." She glanced at the fallen Zeen. "Is he in?"

Despite all the commotion of panic and yelling, the world was deaf other than Melissa's voice and those damned bells. Hmm. This Harbinger's timing seemed a bit...convenient with Serenna's fate in Grayson's hands.

David nodded. "We have our sixth Guardian."

CHAPTER 7

THE BELLS RING

erenna gasped awake from the clashing of bells. She rolled out of her hard bed—wherever it was—and fell to the ground. *The bells ring. They're coming for me. I'm going to die.*

"Oh, you're finally awake?" a distant voice asked. An older man approached.

Prison bars. Terrangus uniform. Damn it.

"Soldier," she said, grasping the bars. "What is happening? How did I get here?"

"Relax, I'm an ally. My name is Landon Bennett; Zeen called on me to be your prison guard to keep you safe. Unlike you, I won't break my pact. You could say…I now guard the Guardian." He snickered, rubbing his white beard and looking her over. "How do you feel? You won't burn me to ash, will you?"

"Landon, I need my staff. The bells ring…they haven't rung in so long." *Where do I stand with the Guardians at this point? Will they even let me battle beside them? I never thought I would yearn to face a Harbinger…*

If this is Terrangus, I should just let the Harbinger win. Let them find a crystal mage who will stand by the pact as their kingdom burns.

I don't have to save anyone.

"Yes, I hear them too. Odd timing that they ring the night after you arrive. I suppose it's for the best that crystal mages are powerless without their staff, but I'll do my duty and get you fed and cleaned up." He offered a frown and left the room.

Night? It's been a full day? Her body shook, yearning for water. Tears trickled down her cheeks as she relished her freewill from a prison cell. Every memory was too vivid: every soldier reduced to ash, every moment of yearning for Zeen's death. Her heart sank.

Father. By now, he knows. I wish Zeen had killed me. That would have been merciful.

Focus. "If there truly is a Harbinger, and it isn't me...who is it?"

A soft, yet frigid gust of wind passed against the back of her neck despite being indoors.

"Oh, Serenna. This one isn't mine. Fear grew jealous of our fun and wants to unleash her own havoc. I hope you lose—even if it isn't by my hands, watching the Guardians wither and die will be a sight of pure wonder. Fear has no standards, but I only want the best...

"I only want you."

She took strained breaths and clutched the prison bars. As her grip tightened, she fought against the rising thirst. Even if it was truly for water, that feeling would always carry a taint; a reminder that somewhere inside her was something *terrible*.

Landon returned, holding a plate of food in one hand and a rather large jug of, hopefully, water in the other. "Start with this, I'll be back in a moment." He placed it down and left again.

What if it's poison? If it were a week ago, she would have dwelled on the fear longer, but now she poured the water down her mouth, gasping in relief as the dryness in her throat faded. Her stomach rumbled from the aroma of burned turkey. With no fork or blade, she ate it with her hands like an animal. *Can life get any worse?* Landon returned—now with a pot, bucket of soapy water, and a thick towel.

Apparently, life would get much worse.

"You're serious? You expect me to wash up and... that...here?"

"Girl, I have five daughters; I've seen everything. Do you have any idea how hard it is to get soap in Terrangus? You young ones have no respect. Now Guardian Everleigh...*that* was a true Crystal Guardian. Ah, they were so much better back in my day..."

To her relief, Landon turned away and kept complaining while she freshened up. Her armor was still a mess, but if she was going to face a Harbinger, cosmetics weren't important. Heavy steps approached after she finished.

Landon stiffened up and bowed. "My lord."

The emperor stood in front of her cell. Forsythe was a shadow of the man she remembered—almost literally—with his decrepit face and colorless eyes.

He has my staff. The emperor of Terrangus holds the Wings of Mylor...

Forsythe's eyes stared through her. "Soldier. Open the door then leave us."

Landon obliged, doing a quick bow, then rushing out of the room.

"It has been quite some time, Guardian Serenna. Last we met, you were saving my people, not murdering them. How it pains me to see you become a Pact Breaker."

"I did what I must. If the South invaded Terrangus, I have no doubt David and Melissa would do the same. No one with any dignity would yield to the Guardian Pact while their home burned."

He snickered. "*Dignity?* Melissa, maybe. David, no. I actually respect what you did. The way I see it, if my soldiers can't kill you, they deserve to die. But that is not why I'm here."

"Why *are* you here?"

"I must know. Wisdom told me you were a demon. How did you turn back? *How?*"

She fought to block out the memory but that made it worse. *Just a taste? I accept.* "Would you believe me if I said I really don't know?"

"Of course not, and if I'm not satisfied with your answer, I'll kill you."

His eyes were too empty and cold to consider calling his bluff. He would shrug away the demise of Terrangus, just as he had shrugged away an unnecessary year of war. Was there any harm in being honest? "I refused to become a Harbinger, so Death offered temporary access to his power. Right before Nyfe would kill me...I accepted the offer. I figured my life was over, but Zeen didn't finish me after I surrendered. He held me and said everything would be okay."

For all my failures, I said I would never harm him—and didn't. Gods, I hope he's safe.

After a long pause with Forsythe staring into nothing, he threw the Wings of Mylor down at her feet. "Nobody held Vanessa. Nobody told her everything would be okay. Defend my kingdom, Pact Breaker. You owe me that much."

She picked up her staff as Forsythe walked off. Would her father descend the same path because of her actions? *Loss is painful, but perhaps nothing is worse than losing someone not yet gone—*

More steps? Who is it now?

David hesitated when they met eyes, then rushed over to

Serenna. "Are you okay? Did he harm you?"

She'd been dreading this reunion. Not only had she broken the pact against his orders, but accepting the aid of Death was certainly some mortal sin in Guardian law. Hopefully, quick, vague responses could delay the scolding that would soon come. "I'm fine."

"I understand. Come, other than Pyith, the others are already here." They left together towards the Terrangus Guardian room. David walked with an awkward quickness, actively avoiding eye contact. "I'm glad you're safe…"

His behavior was strange; this wasn't the Guardian tyrant that had berated her in public for being slow with a crystal shield, or the man that had punched Pyith's zephum snout with such force she'd collapsed into a table. The only one that could make him this uncomfortable was…

Ah. Melissa told him to back off. I certainly owe her a drink.

"Thank you, David. I'm not going to say it…but thank you."

"Stop," he said, shooting her a stern glance. "That talk *is* coming, but let's deal with our Harbinger first."

Damn. "Fair enough. Is it strange that I'm more excited than afraid? I haven't seen everyone in so long. Oh, did we ever get a sixth?"

He flashed a rare grin. "Potentially, but I imagine you will be *very* angry when you see who it is."

Serenna followed David into the Terrangus castle Guardian room and took a deep breath. It had been four years since she last stood in this hall. The Guardian portal still hummed in the back with the large wooden table in the center. Swords, daggers, even elemental-detonators were a scattered mess, thanks to Melissa. *That woman loves her weapons.* Despite the miserable standards of living in the western kingdom, they had kept this room bearable—for Terrangus at least—avoiding the city stench that had never managed to pass through those doors.

Melissa was the first to meet her eyes, and Serenna walked up to give her a warm embrace. Melissa was the closest thing to a mother for the Guardians, a tranquil presence to balance out the cold aura of their leader.

"Thank you," Serenna whispered in Melissa's ear.

Melissa kissed her cheek and giggled. "You look so good! Has it really been two years?" It was a kind lie. Terrangus didn't have any mirrors for whatever reason, but Serenna was happy to avoid the reflection of the disheveled mess that would stare back.

"Somehow, yes. Though after last year, it feels like a lifetime."

"It's okay. Let go of your pain, we will handle all of it—*together*." It was difficult not to cry as her hug tightened. For all the horrors of the realm, the fact Melissa kept her glowing outlook was a true blessing. Part of Serenna was thankful a Harbinger had finally arrived, if only to reunite with her. She would never, *ever* admit that out loud.

Who am I kidding, I would do anything for this team. Any of them. Well, maybe not…

They let go, and behind Melissa was Francis Haide—the Alanammus Guardian—standing in the back. As a fellow mage—elemental instead of crystal—he favored soft white robes that complimented his dark skin but were far too large for his smaller frame. Now in his late twenties, he had taken on many of the facial features of his mother: the late archon of Alanammus. All he was missing was that silver-tinted hair. Serenna had almost believed he would come to her aid during the war, since they were both mage Guardians from the southern kingdoms.

He did not. No one did. "Hello, Francis. It's been a while."

"Hmm," he said, extending his arm to shake her hand. "A while indeed. Don't worry—it won't be easy, but I may eventually grow to forgive you for breaking the pact."

He's still such a prude. "You forgive *me*? Maybe if your people had bothered to help, I wouldn't have been left to die in the middle of the bastion."

"Oh, spare me. Your father basically begged for war by not standing down to the tariffs. If snails ever learned the common tongue, perhaps one could offer your kingdom better leadership. I mean, what were you thinking? A full-blown war—for Mylor's pride? Preposterous! If Alanammus got involved, *thousands* on both sides would be dead."

He's been sitting on that snail line for months. "I assumed your excuse was the Guardian Pact, not that Alanammus is a kingdom of cowards. I'll let the rest of the southern kingdoms know the proper course of action is to just yield to any and all demands. Apparently, only a *fool* would defend themselves—"

They both jumped as David slammed his fist on the table. "Both of you shut the fuck up. We don't need this right now."

Francis sighed. "After two years, I fooled myself into thinking perhaps there would never be another Harbinger. Gods, why is it Terrangus *again*? Other than the God of Wisdom, there is nothing of value here." Interesting words, considering his archon mother had cast the deity out of Alanammus, but one fight was enough for today.

"Wait," Serenna said, looking around. "You said we had a sixth?"

After a few seconds, the Guardian door creaked open, revealing Zeen, holding a large jug of water. The top of his left eye had a swollen bruise—David's doing, most likely. She *forced* herself not to match his smile as their eyes met. *Zeen. Of course it's him. I'll never get away from this man...*

Stop staring at him. She turned away towards Melissa, who was already grinning at her. *You stop that.*

"Everyone's in favor of it," David said, "but based on your history, I offer you the chance to object."

"No objections," she said, *maybe* a little too quickly. "I vouch for Zeen's skill and temperament from firsthand experience. We are lucky to have him."

Zeen nodded, hopefully accepting her words as a truce for that whole Harbinger of Death thing. It was kind of him to lie with a smile. He had seen the void-touched Serenna laying waste to his fellow men, the woman who had accepted aid from the God of Death rather than accept her end.

Before anyone could respond, the Guardian portal erupted with a harsh, ebony glow. The outline of a massive green reptilian form with a snout and tail began to materialize, revealing Pyith Claw, the zephum guardian from Vaynex.

The heavily armored Pyith clashed her enormous sword on her shield, letting out a roar and observing the room. Her eyes stopped when she found Serenna. "TO ARMS! I found the Pact Breaker!" She tore off half the wooden table, launching it well over Serenna's head. Everyone stumbled back, but Pyith let out a guffaw.

"Relax, humans," she said, laughing. "Everyone is so fucking tense. Is Francis whining about his *destiny* again? Or is David brooding and whispering veiled threats? Just grab a drink and let Serenna and I do all the work." She pointed her sword at Zeen. "Now who the fuck is this?"

Zeen hesitated, then slowly approached and offered a handshake. "My name is Zeen Parson. It is an honor to meet you."

She ignored his offer and stared at David. "Are you serious—have you learned nothing? Ah, whatever. I have three-to-one odds this one dies like Thomas. Who's got me? Gold upfront."

"Pyith!" David yelled. "Stop…" He drifted towards her,

filling the air with a silent tension. David then laughed and embraced the larger zephum. "Too long, my friend. You are the only Guardian uglier than me."

"Nothing alive or dead is uglier than you," she said, jabbing him in the chest. He kept laughing, but lost his breath, dropping to one knee for a moment, then rising. "Welcome to the Guardians, Zeen. Don't mind me, I'm just excited to be away from the warlord and his useless son, who happens to be my life-mate. A word of advice, don't marry a powerful leader's not-so-powerful son."

For all the anger towards Serenna, no one seemed to care how little the zephum had regarded the Guardian Pact. Instead of keeping Pyith out of war or politics, the warlord had arranged a marriage to his son to increase his influence. Tempest Claw was, well—not exactly his father.

Zeen smiled. "I know all about you. I believe you're the inspiration for Cympha in the Rinso Saga."

"No! You *read* that garbage?" Pyith said, laughing. "Okay, I'll make you a deal: survive this Harbinger and I'll introduce you to the author."

What the hell is the Rinso Saga?

His smile grew large, much larger than any he had offered to Serenna. "That would be wonderful. You have a deal."

She was happy for him, but envious of his charisma. Two minutes into being a Guardian and he was already more beloved than her. He wasn't a "pact breaker" apparently, or a warmonger, nor an unstable child needing protection from the Guardian matriarch.

If I wasn't powerful, I would be alone.

"Guys," Zeen said, rubbing the back of his head, "when I arrived in Terrangus, the God of Wisdom spoke to me through thoughts…or whatever that was. I don't really trust him, but he mentioned this was Fear's plan to prevent the emperor from killing Serenna."

Ah, so it was more than dumb luck that a Harbinger of Fear arrived at the time of my capture. Wait, why in the realm would Fear prefer me alive?

Francis's eyes grew large. "The God of Wisdom spoke…to *you*? What did he sound like? Did he mention me at all? I have so many questions!"

"Ignore him," David said, sighing. "None of the gods are our allies. Wisdom in particular treats us as playthings on a board to be manipulated. The zephum God of Strength is the only honorable god, and I'm not just saying that because Pyith is standing there."

Pyith scoffed. "I would *love* to see you act so bold in front of the warlord."

"Well, Sardonyx isn't here," David said with a chuckle before walking to the center of the room. "Enough. We have a job to do. Take an hour to prepare yourselves, then meet outside the castle. This is the finest Guardian team ever assembled—I trust each of you with my life. We do this not for Terrangus, not even for the realm, but for each other. No one else deserves it."

CHAPTER 8

SOMETHING WORSE THAN FEAR

Zeen finished his jug of water and approached the castle doors from the inside, ignoring the sharp sting in his left shoulder that was far worse than the soreness pressing against his face. For a man about to face a deranged deity's empowered demon, he wasn't off to a great start. At least the wine had worn off, although that would have helped with the anxiety creeping through his gut.

It had been an awkward hour alone; he figured at least *one* Guardian would spend that time with him, giving him guidance, encouragement—or anything. He would have preferred Serenna but she had actively avoided his gaze in the Guardian room. She'd seemed…annoyed?

I'll keep my distance. It's going to be tricky for a while after our battle. Gods, she must hate me.

Oh well, no time for such thoughts. Today would be monumental: accepting his role as a Terrangus Guardian and fulfilling a childhood promise. *I wish Dad were still here.* His father had just shrugged anytime Zeen boldly claimed this day would come.

Back then, he didn't even want it.

It had just been something to bring a spark of joy to a dead household, an empty attempt to inspire a man plunged into war and drink after losing his wife during Zeen's birth. Seeing him sign up for dangerous roles in campaign after campaign, Zeen had adored his father as a hero until the truth became obvious: Zachery Parson had sought his end and, like all men that do, eventually found it.

Zeen took a deep breath and nodded to the Terrangus guard to open the massive steel doors of the castle, who shrugged in disbelief at the request to go out *there*. Zeen stepped outside, smiling at the darkness, allowing the cool breeze and rain to caress his wounds as the bells continued to ring. This was how epic battles should be fought. Anytime Rinso had faced a Harbinger in Terrangus in the Rinso the Blue novels—which was often—lightning would crack through the skies while rain patted down at a rhythm that could sync to his rapid heartbeat. The rest of the Guardians were already waiting.

David nodded him over. "Come." The team left towards the familiar military barracks, just east of the castle, opposite the noble district. "Had I known a Harbinger would arrive today, I never would have harmed you. I apologize for that, but it's *imperative* you obey my instructions from here on out. Do you have any issue with my command?"

"I can follow orders. After being under Nyfe for the past five years, I'm accustomed to abuse. You were Terrangus military, you know how it goes."

"*Never* compare me to Nyfe," David said, sighing. "With Fear, there are three main enemies. Crawlers, colossals, and the Harbinger itself. Crawlers are quick little bastards that prioritize mages. We need to defend them, so I'm putting you and Melissa by Serenna. I'll stick with Francis; Pyith will engage the colossal while we take out the crawlers. When that's done, we collapse on the colossal and bring it down together.

The Harbinger should reveal itself at that point. Any questions so far?"

Too many questions ran through his head to just pick one. Zeen could sense David's frustration at his delay. "You're sure Pyith can keep the colossal's attention? How does that work?"

Pyith smirked as rain poured down her green reptilian snout. "Well, it's an art form. I'm going to run in, swing my sword, and call his mother a whore." Her smile faded, and for the first time, Zeen felt an icy chill run down his neck. "Listen, kid, that beating you took from David could save your life today. You must survive. The way these fights go, if more than two or three of us drop, it's probably over. And when I mean over, I mean that's it; kingdoms fall, empires crumble. If you survive tonight, you will understand why I laugh and David broods."

"Why?" Zeen said, stuttering. "Why do we only have six when the stakes are so high?"

Calm yourself. Rinso the Blue never acted this way in any of the books.

David nodded. "Harbingers of Fear grow more powerful by absorbing fear, so it's a disadvantage to have a larger team. That's how Death took Boulom… There is debate on whether six or seven is the most efficient, but six is the number of old, and I stick with that."

Zeen struggled to breathe until a warm hand eased onto his shoulder. Serenna smiled at him, offering a moment of tranquility he wished could last forever. "You stood against Death to protect me and, tonight, we stand against Fear. I, for one, am excited to finally battle on the same team."

After a year at war in Mylor, it was surreal to see her up close as an ally—maybe even a friend. His heart pounded from her smile and blue eyes. Gods, if the men who despised her could only see that deep, sapphire gaze.

Maybe being a Guardian wouldn't be all that terrible. "Thank you; I won't let you down."

"Oh, Zeen," Francis said, "after the Harbinger learns our fears, it will yell them out to throw us off. We have a rule: no matter what gets said tonight, we let it go."

Well, my fear should be boring. I am woefully unprepared and will probably die a horrible death. That shouldn't startle anyone.

What could David possibly fear?

Melissa approached. "Seriously," she whispered, "whatever you hear tonight, don't bring it up again. *Especially* Pyith—just don't go there. For me, I'm afraid I'll grow old and never raise children with David. Every year solidifies that fate and pushes him farther away. I wear it proudly, so Fear can't harm me. Whatever demons you have, be honest with them. Stay by me. I know I'm adorable, but I've killed tons of these things."

My demons... I never wanted to be a soldier. I fought a war against good people in the name of a tyrant. My actions have made the realm worse off than if I were never born. "I...am afraid that I wasted my life."

"A wise fear," she said with a nod.

Francis's warning must have struck a nerve; it was silent as they progressed through the military ward. The bells still rang as people—soldiers and civilians alike—rushed in the opposite direction. They all yelled, but it wasn't the way men yelled in war. These screams were pure terror, an unconscious act to reminisce over in shame later. *It's just like four years ago, except I'm going the other way.*

He stopped and gasped, finding a crystal barrier scaling into the dark night and blocking off an entire section of the military ward. Likely a hundred or so mages stood around the barrier, holding glowing staffs that resonated vibrant gray. He was used to the lucid shields that would surround and follow, but he had never seen anything at this magnitude. What he assumed was the lead mage walked up to David.

"Ah, you're here," she said, wiping rain and sweat off her face. "We have secured the perimeter. Whenever you're ready—it's all yours."

"Thank you," David said. "Your team saved many lives today. If we don't return, I leave the realm in your hands."

"As much as I would enjoy a promotion, feel free to come back." They both snickered as the mage opened a door-sized hole in the barrier. Zeen was the last to enter.

The military ward—his home—was never supposed to be so...empty. Behind him was civilization, frantic people still fleeing, while mages energized the containment barrier. In front of him could have been the void itself. The large black barracks blended into the night, with shattered fragments of stone and steel from collapsed structures all over the ground. Rain splashed down the crystal ceiling of the barrier, creating an unnatural echo. The cool breeze ended, replaced by the chill of fear.

They stood in ruins, as if they had already lost.

David and Pyith went to the front, and it took every ounce of constraint not to grab Melissa's arm as a *hissing* noise filled the air. "What the hell is that?" Zeen asked, eyes growing wide.

"Crawlers," Serenna said, grasping her staff and casting individual crystal shields on everyone. Zeen's sphere came last, and the vibrant platinum filled his vision before going invisible.

For the brief moment in his view, the shell had a strong *thickness* to it. Terrangus barely had any crystal mages of note; he had once had a shield shatter after he sneezed. *I'm glad you're on my side for once.*

David raised his arm, waving them to follow as he trekked farther into the ward. "Stay close, stick to the plan. They're out there..."

Zeen drew his blade—the unlucky sword David had thrown at him before his beating. *I should've picked up my sword in Mylor. Damn, do I regret that—*

Did something move on that barracks? He squinted his eyes, and something rushed away from the corner of his view.

Don't panic.

He drifted closer to Serenna, using his instincts as a soldier to avoid tripping on the jagged fragments of stone littering the ground. Glancing to the building to his far left, there was definitely a *thing* latched onto it—some spider, maybe reptile-looking creature.

He focused on the crawler to comprehend its shape before it turned around and hissed at him, then scuttered off behind the building. He took a deep breath, clutching his blade as several of the shapes rushed down the buildings, surrounding them.

"*They killed my son...*" a demonic voice echoed through the air, nearly drowning out the hissing as the ground rumbled.

That must be the Harbinger of Fear. Wisdom did mention the other day that Fear targeted some mage who had lost their son in a recent Mylor skirmish. Were they all formed this way?

A yellow essence hovered away from Zeen's body, drifting to the unknown darkness farther down the ward. He wondered why David didn't press ahead until a roar went off.

Melissa stepped forward, grabbing two of the elemental-detonators from her belt: both round objects coated in steel with a lightning insignia on them. She threw the first one and it erupted with a bright light, illuminating several crawlers that scattered away. She threw the second detonator and it erupted to reveal something *much* larger hunched awkwardly.

Damn, that thing is big. I guess that's what David meant by a colossal.

Pyith let out a roar of her own, grasping her shield and

rushing at the enormous demon. The colossal stood twice her size, with crooked horns coming out the side of its head. Red bulging veins coursed through its muscular arms, highlighted by the monster's silver tinted skin. It suddenly made perfect sense why all the Guardian teams had favored using zephum in the engager role.

David stared into Zeen's eyes and yelled something, but there was too much chaos to make out the words. *My job is Serenna. Stay by her.*

One crawler finally lunged at Serenna, only to meet Melissa's blades as she dashed in front. She wielded small one-handed swords in each hand, immediately slashing for the throat and opening wounds all over as the demon collapsed. A second crawler dove forward; Melissa sheathed one sword, grabbed a detonator from her belt and threw it. The detonator erupted into an ice spell, freezing the top half of the crawler before she shattered it with the hilt of her sword.

Serenna rushed closer to Pyith, refreshing her crystal sphere as the colossal slammed down with another blow. As large as Pyith's iron shield was, there was too much force to get clean blocks.

"They killed my son," the Harbinger's voice echoed from afar.

Zeen watched in awe as Pyith stood toe-to-toe against the abomination. Gasping, he turned to Melissa and Serenna, who were farther ahead and not waiting for him. He took a deep breath and ran to the team, before something tackled him into the darkness.

His body tumbled down an alleyway between two buildings, barely illuminated by Melissa's detonator. The hissing was *deafening*. He grabbed his sword and held it with shaky hands, struggling to breathe and too paralyzed with fear to rise. Something moved out of the corner of his eye.

GET UP! As he rose, the crawler screeched, swiping its bladed claw by his face. He flinched and stumbled back as the crawler crashed against his crystal shield, illuminating a crack before fading out of his view. The *thing* was a mix between a spider and scorpion with a jagged tail flailing behind. It had two main "arms," with smaller ones coming out of its body, all ending in vicious claws.

I'm better than this. I survived an entire year in Mylor with Nyfe trying to kill me. This is just a demon; I stood against the God of Death itself. I…can't be so weak.

He entered his battle stance and clutched his sword, studying the creature and waiting to counter. It screeched and dove again—as expected—so he stepped forward and slashed high-across, using its downward momentum to maximize the damage from the swipe. It stumbled back and screeched before reverting to the same strategy. The next cut was a perfect cross-slash, sending the demon limp and, more importantly, silent. *I can do this, just have to get back to the team.*

The Harbinger's voice rumbled again, this time far clearer than the distant echo it had been. "Francis Haide. I have read your fear: you despise your role as a Guardian and believe this life is beneath you. You were gifted the advantage of being an archon's son, but avoided your destiny and joined the Guardians out of spite. All these mistakes linger well past her death, but what will Alanammus do without Wisdom? History will curse the Haide name as your kingdom faces another dark age."

Three crawlers scuttered to the end of the alley, blocking Zeen from rejoining the team. *No one is coming to help. I have to do this alone.* Waiting for a counter wouldn't be viable against three, so he rushed at the crawler to his left, going low, low, high. That combo always came naturally, and for the briefest of moments, he didn't consider he was facing demons. The other two dove at him simultaneously and he rolled forward to dodge. He turned to face them—his exit from the alley open behind him—but this was a chance to deny his fear. *I deserve to be a Guardian!* He dodged the first strike, slaying the demon in one blow, before doing a spin move and slicing the remaining demon in half.

I can do this—

A hidden crawler rose towards his rear, slamming against his crystal shield and sending him to the ground. His body skidded on fragments of stone and his lost confidence amplified the pain seething all over his body. He tried to rise but fell, against his will, to both knees. The crawler towered above him, preparing its claws and eyeing the killing blow.

The Harbinger's voice rumbled from afar. "Pyith Claw. I have read your fear: Vaynex falls to madness, a relic of shame and useless traditions. The warlord is a tyrant, and your life-mate Tempest? He would be heralded as a savior in a better world, but you don't live in a better world. Weakness will crumble him; leadership will be your burden as he tears himself apart. All will hail Warlord Pyith."

Blades slammed against Zeen's crystal shield, finally shattering it as multicolored fragments scattered around him. The crash staggered the demon, giving him an opportunity to rise and clutch his blade. A vicious *rage* coursed through Zeen as he held his sword with both hands and plunged it through the crawler's stomach. The demon screeched, but Zeen kept pressing the blade through, letting out a scream as warm blood splattered on his face. Until now, he had avoided anger. Losing composure in battle was a sure way to get sloppy and die, but anything was better than fear.

He left the alleyway, using Francis's blue glow as a beacon to rejoin the team. As he got close, another crawler jumped in front of him and screeched, returning the paralyzing fear. The crawler got a swipe across his face, opening his old scar, and new rage. He slashed across, taking another open swipe against his chest, before finishing the crawler by tearing across its neck.

The rumbling voice returned as he ran up to Melissa and Serenna. "Zeen Parson. I have read your fear. You fear your own weakness: a helpless boy swinging his sword in a world of mages, gods, and Harbingers. Your father despised you in his dying moments, and nothing can ever change that. Even if you slayed Death itself, you could never slay your father's despair. The same thing will happen when Serenna descends to the void. You will die alone—hated and miserable."

Zeen's rage subsided, giving way to something worse than fear.

CHAPTER 9

WHERE REALITY FAILS, DREAMS ARE ETERNAL

David slayed another demon next to Francis before turning towards Zeen. The boy had empty eyes, clearly not ready for the truth unleashed upon him. The mind had an odd way of protecting the heart for as long as reality would allow. Francis and Pyith had no reaction; Guardian life had molded them to stoic vanguards of the realm—empty husks who served, then tried to pretend life was normal afterwards. Hopefully, they didn't realize normal was already lost forever. He had realized it the first time he'd told Melissa, "I love you." She'd said it back—stared into his eyes— but life didn't change…it just continued.

Despite the two-year hiatus, this battle was going well. Maybe *too* well. It was difficult to send Melissa to the other side, but it was the only way to ensure he could focus. Francis continued his radiant glow, shifting from blue to yellow—an indication lightning spells were coming. The boy had grown so much since first joining. The wide-eyed mage who couldn't hit the Xavian Sea with an ice blast now composed himself and planned every spell with the tactfulness of an archon.

David thrust his blade through a crawler, forcing it to the

ground and stomping on its head to finish it off. Part of him hoped the demons were sentient enough to know fear, to know they died by his hands. A bright flash from lightning blasted in his vicinity, incinerating a crawler that approached from his blind spot. *Well done, Francis*—

Pyith screamed out in pain, taking a massive blow to her shield that collapsed onto her right leg. She crumpled to the ground, releasing her weapons and clutching the wound.

"Melissa Euhno. I have read your fear: your endless life as a Guardian. You want to settle down, but there will never be a family. There will only be David. You cling to the reality of a man too far gone to ever hold a child; hope fading as you descend the shadows of obscurity."

She was too perfect to show a reaction, but David's hands shook. *I swear to you, this Harbinger will die by my blade.* It wouldn't change reality, it wouldn't give them a family, but violence was all he could offer. David's heart froze as the colossal came down at Pyith with a fist.

Serenna erupted into her empowered form, cleansing the darkness with platinum streams of light. She shielded Pyith with a dense sphere, just before the colossal's arm crashed down and cracked its top. Zeen dashed past David, sheathing his sword and sliding down to Pyith. Serenna refreshed Pyith's shield, then Zeen's, stumbling back as she laid a square-like crystal barrier on top of them both.

The colossal roared, lifting its arms high above its head, then slammed down with an enormous force, shattering the barrier and cracking their spheres. The colossal wasted no time swinging the other arm down. Zeen covered Pyith with his body—as if that would do anything—and turned away. Serenna cried out in pain and refreshed their shields right before the arm crashed against them. She collapsed, then Melissa rushed over to help her stand.

The battle was no longer going *too* well.

With Pyith injured, options were limited. David cut through another crawler before grabbing Francis. "Go back to ice. If you can freeze an arm or a leg, we can immobilize it. We need time to regroup." To his relief, Francis nodded and channeled his blue form. A sign of maturity; he had flat out ignored him last time.

Zeen wiped blood off his face and set his battle stance. He stood in front of the colossal, eyeing it as if he had any chance in the realm to stand his ground. It was possibly the most foolish thing David had ever seen and yet it was *beautiful*. This is what Melissa didn't understand about "a young man with a good heart." Zeen set his fear aside upon seeing his new allies fall, just as David had done twenty-two years ago. He yearned to join him, but crawlers kept rushing towards Francis.

"Serenna Morgan. I have read your fear. It's not a matter of if, but when, you surrender to Death. The god only targets the most desperate of souls, and what does that say about you? Look upon me, Serenna, for we are the same. When reality cannot be fixed, we have no choice but to burn it to the ground and start over."

The colossal flung its fist down at Zeen, who side-stepped and countered with a quick slash across its arm. Blood poured out, but the colossal just roared and attacked again, barely missing as Zeen dove away.

He's going to die. Just like Thomas. Just like Brian. Why do I keep doing this to people?

Zeen dodged another crushing blow, then countered again at the same arm. The colossal actually stumbled back, before flinging its other arm wildly and knocking him tumbling through the rubble. The colossal then gazed at David, who was fighting off two crawlers.

It began to charge. *So be it. Show me your violence.*

A crawler finally broke his first crystal shield as he was distracted. David tore it in half with a brutal swing, his eyes darting back and forth between the final crawler and the charging monster. His eyes then went to the blue haze of ice that flew above him, landing on the demon's neck and freezing it solid.

Dammit, I said an arm or a leg. That doesn't help me—

A crystal spike flew above David, piercing the frozen neck and shattering it. The colossal plummeted with cold, dead eyes.

He turned to find Melissa tending to the exhausted Serenna. Blood trickled down her face; she'd used far more energy than was safe. She always hovered too close to the edge, but it was difficult to blame her after saving them. What a terrible burden to have access to such power. *If it were me, I would have died years ago…*

Or worse.

Everyone converged on the wounded Pyith. "Dammit," she said, groaning. "I can't stand on this leg. What a load of shit. Zeen, I'll give you credit; you have some giant, golden balls to duel a colossal. Tell Sardonyx he owes you a barrel of zephum ale."

"Did we win?" Zeen asked with a weak smile, leaning against Melissa.

"David Williams. I have read your fear: the overwhelming emptiness that smothers you after a lifetime of service. You don't trust any of them to lead after you're gone. Francis doesn't care, and Serenna is too unstable. You have reached the point where you hope to die, just to avoid living in a realm where Melissa leaves first. There is no salvation. You recruited her. You damned her. Everyone who gets close to you suffers."

Nothing I don't tell myself every day. "Slay the Harbinger," David said, "then we go home. This one is mine. Serenna, do you have anything left to shield me?"

"I…will try," she said, closing her eyes and covering him

with a crystal sphere. It was dim, barely flickering in his view, before going lucid.

I ask too much of her.

The Harbinger approached: a balding man with void energy emitting from his tall frame, giving the appearance of hazy, ebony wings sprouting from his shoulders. He wielded a simple oak staff radiating the same glow with an aura so harsh, David shivered. The Terrangus emblem of the Ebony Blade was still strapped to his shoulder and David nearly smiled at the irony.

Another mage. Fear always empowers the mages. For as long as I've done this, I've never figured out why.

"Melissa, stay by Francis and Serenna," David said. "Zeen, be careful. Aid me if you can, but don't strain your injury. You will *not* fall today." He rushed forward, clutching his blade and studying the Harbinger. Francis's yellow glow illuminated from behind as hissing began, but David couldn't turn around anymore. The fear about his lack of trust was a legitimate issue, one he had to let go.

The Harbinger's crimson eyes stared through David as it channeled a yellow aura. One advantage of facing mage Harbingers was the aura predicted the spell type. David prepared to side-step as it erupted, lighting the sky with a bright flash.

The crash hit…behind him? He glanced backwards to find Francis thrown to the air, his staff flying in the opposite direction. As bad as that was, the fact that he wasn't incinerated meant his crystal had saved him from the brunt of the blast.

David closed the gap, swinging his blade at the Harbinger's neck. The empowered oak staff blocked his sword as if it were the Wings of Mylor. The Harbinger pushed him back, then swung the staff towards his face. *I'm ready for you.* David allowed the staff to bash into his head as he plunged his sword through the mage's chest.

"A bold move, Guardian," the Harbinger said, "but not enough. It will never be enough. Your fear makes me invincible."

David spit blood from his mouth, clutching his sword and not allowing a gap to form. He had expected Serenna's shield to block *some* of the attack, but she had nothing left. "For all my faults, fear has never been one of them." He clutched his sword, meeting the crimson eyes, prepared to finish the battle one way or the other—

The Harbinger shrieked, falling to one knee.

What? Is this a trap?

"My sweet David," the same Harbinger said as it rose, in a woman's distorted voice, one he had never heard before. "Do me a favor and kill this one. I would hate to see you fall before we meet face-to-face. The man you have become…is the man I *need*."

"What…the fuck is going on? Who are you?"

It grabbed David, lifting him as if he were weightless. Harbingers were always powerful, but the strength of its grip now seemed *limitless*. "The threat of destruction is the only way to ensure peace. I am the Legacy of Boulom—the first one to fight back. Remember my mantra: Where reality fails, dreams are eternal. Never forget—"

Zeen's blade thrust through its mouth from behind, the bloody sword dangerously close to David's face. The crimson eyes faded as the Harbinger crumbled to the ground. Zeen pulled out his sword, swinging at the corpse over and over as if his blade were a hammer. The hissing ended; all he could hear was the gruesome splatter from Zeen's blade and the rain tapping against the top of the barrier. It was as close to silence as tonight would allow.

"Zeen," David said, drifting towards him. "Enough. Well done…you made me proud today." David embraced him like a son. The one he would never have. "I've made terrible mistakes, but you were not one of them. Not this time. Thank you." He let go to check on the others.

Several injuries, but everyone lived. By any fair measurement, tonight was a success, but it didn't feel like a success. That voice... Was it Fear? There was no other explanation. The words haunted him, preventing him from reveling in another victory for the realm.

Where reality fails, dreams are eternal.

CHAPTER 10

NEVER MIND

The next morning, Serenna stood in the healing ward outside Terrangus castle, awake much earlier than after her battle against the Nuum Harbinger two years ago. That novice version of Serenna no longer existed, replaced by the *true* Guardian of Mylor, the woman who would let crystal energy tear off all her flesh for one last spell. Her durable body had recovered with ease. Only David had awoken before her today. He'd probably never slept at all. Whatever he had seen at the end shook his core; that expression of *pure* terror was more haunting than any words—lies or truth—the demon had spoken.

The Guardians had their own reserved spot in the corner of the massive hall, with rundown beds and...were those the same tattered banners from last time? What an awful stench. A handful of men near the middle were *clearly* dead, but they appeared to be a low priority with only five older women tending to the entire ward. *Forsythe doesn't care about any of them. I'm surprised he even bothers with us.*

Since everyone had survived—unlike last time—there was no mental anguish. Gods, that silence the next morning after

Thomas's death. Not today; this had been a clean victory. No temptation from Death; no screams from her people. No casualty reports read to her father, who would stare blankly and nod. Would David commend them for once? That would complete the miracle.

Even after everything, I helped save Terrangus. There is still some good in me. I...may actually be happy.

Zeen was the only one still asleep. The heavy-set healer mage shook her head as she moved her wand over his face—again—but the scar wouldn't fade. *Was that really a year ago?* "Excuse me, miss," Serenna said, "that's an old wound, you won't be able to heal it—"

"Silence, child. I've been doing this longer than you've been alive. Maybe if we didn't spend so many of our resources tending to the men you *murdered*, I could get this off."

Alright then. She took a last glance at Zeen; of course he would smile as he slept. His messy hair lay above his eyes; his tattered armor stained red. What a wonderful boy. A boy with *terrible* fears apparently, but a wonderful boy. *And to think I nearly killed him.*

Hopefully, he would wake before she left. It would be...unwise to linger here. Terrangus would see their nemesis of war, the Pact Breaker that had shattered their brothers to dust. She eased her hand to his shoulder. It had drawn a smile before the battle; if Zeen wouldn't wake, maybe she could give him sweet dreams. *Damn, I really wanted to say goodbye. I thought maybe...*

Never mind.

She headed towards the exit. It was best to avoid eye contact with any of the wounded. *Maybe* the healer had a fair point about how several of them had gotten there. She stepped outside, closing her eyes, allowing the cool rain to soak through her hair. For all the kingdom's flaws, the way the constant rain made her platinum hair shimmer always brought a warm smile to balance the chilled air.

On the other side of the castle lay the ruins of the military ward. Countless soldiers scrounged through the rubble, piling up rocks, steel, and bodies. That part of victory had always eluded the bard's tales. It was odd to gaze upon the piles and feel…nothing. War had changed her. There *was* still good in her, but it had to compete with the other traits that had risen from battle after battle.

Serenna drifted towards the castle, grinning at all the Terrangus people who shot their eyes down immediately. *Not a single "thank you." These people will never know what we did for them—what I did for them.* More reason to leave as soon as possible; it would only be a matter of time before the daggers in their eyes manifested to their hands. Still, she relished the idea of walking freely through her enemy's kingdom. Stop her? They wouldn't dare. The soldiers at the castle entrance murmured to each other as she entered.

She froze.

Forsythe stood past the doors, shooting the same murderous gaze from their meeting in the prison cell. He had such a vivid presence, despite his lifeless figure. "Ah, Serenna of Mylor. Terrangus thanks you for fulfilling your Guardian oaths and defending my kingdom. I will consider this when we decide your sentence." The doors closed behind her.

The harder she clutched her staff, the faster any remnants of joy faded. Forsythe had a large entourage of guards in red mail by his side, while armed soldiers took a position behind her. "My sentence? What nonsense is this?"

"The war may be over, Pact Breaker, but judgement yet remains. One act of heroism does not excuse a scoundrel's past."

"Unless I missed your surrender, the war isn't over."

"Oh, but it is. I have already begun to recall my soldiers. With you in our custody and the Harbinger slain, I am feeling rather *bold*."

The war...was over? Her hands lost color as her grip tightened. *I can't take them all, but I'm certain I could kill him. I could impale him, or tear his wrinkly skin right off. No...that would doom Mylor to another war. Everything was supposed to be okay.*

Why is this happening?

"I saved Terrangus...after *everything* you did to my people. You would truly do this? Have you no honor?"

"Don't act surprised, girl; all of you Guardians have a difficult time accepting that actions bring consequences. It is a cruel end, but it must be done. Guards—take her."

"You will do *no* such thing," Melissa yelled, approaching the crowd. She drew an elemental-detonator in one hand and a small blade in the other, stopping when she got to Serenna's side. "You *dare*?"

Forsythe grinned, not taking his eyes off Serenna. "This doesn't concern you, mechanist. Why don't you tend to your David? We both know you won't oppose me after all these years."

Melissa threw the detonator behind her; it erupted in a fire blast, knocking the guards stumbling in all directions. "Please, inform me more of what we both know."

Serenna's mouth dropped; she had never seen this side of Melissa. The woman could stop a war with a smile, but she apparently had a backup plan if that didn't work.

All the soldiers drew their swords, converging on them. "Halt!" Forsythe yelled, raising his hand in that way leaders did to feel important. "Consider your actions. There is no coming back from this."

"Melissa," Serenna whispered, "let me go. Death still waits

for his Harbinger; we can't risk losing two of us. I'll be fine…
I always find a way."

Melissa grabbed her, clutching her arms with an
unexpected strength. "I know what that means. Listen, I'm
willing to die by your side; this man will not intimidate us."

*She loves me far more than I ever realized, far more than I
deserve.* "You can't do that to David. Get the Guardians out of
Terrangus; I'll manage here. I won't…do *that*. You have my
word."

After a pause, Melissa let go, her eyes turning to Forsythe
with a fiery emerald wrath. "You are fortunate Vanessa is gone;
if she could see the husk of shame before me, her despair would
be endless."

Such terrible words brought no reaction. Forsythe nodded
and the guards took Serenna by the arms, handing her staff to
him—again. Melissa rushed towards the Guardian room as
Serenna followed Forsythe.

"Brave of you to stand down," he said, examining her staff,
"although Melissa surprised me. It's not often I misread people;
she hides a murderous *rage*."

"Melissa understands what's at stake. What's the endgame
here? The South will unite against you, and it's likely the
zephum will engage your central positions in the chaos. You
may even have riots at home. Is enforcing some century-old
rule really worth all that?

"Perhaps, perhaps not. Our war taught me much about
human nature. No one helped you in Mylor, and I wager no
one will avenge you either. I have found exceptional success by
threatening total collapse. It is a pity you haven't learned that
strategy for yourself. Even Wisdom fears what you're capable
of."

Oh, I wish Francis heard him say that. "As he should. As
should *you*."

Forsythe snickered, leading her to the familiar prison ward in the lowest part of the castle—lower than the filled prison below the east halls. Landon was still down there; he bowed, then unlocked her cell as his emperor approached. The other cells had no prisoners—this room must have been reserved for the most *vile* Terrangus scum. At least the smell didn't linger down here, which was surprising.

Serenna entered the dark cell, sighing as she sat on the bed that was chained to the wall. "Good morning, Landon, didn't expect I would run into you again."

"Silence, Pact Breaker," Landon said. "You speak when spoken to."

It was difficult not to laugh at his ridiculous scowl. He was similar to her father: an out-of-place older man trying to juggle stability while chaos surrounded him. Thinking of her father brought a cold despair; never in her wildest dreams could she have imagined the consequences of leaving that balcony. *He must be worried sick. I will not die here...*

Forsythe threw the Wings of Mylor on the ground like it was a worthless oak staff—such a petty attempt to mock her. "I would suggest rest, but you'll soon have forever," he said, leaving the ward with his guards behind him.

Landon watched them leave, then turned to her. "I do apologize for that. I have to...play a certain role here."

"You're a fool," she said with a chuckle. "I'm shocked he hasn't executed you yet."

Landon picked up her staff, then leaned it against the wall on the opposite side of the room with the proper respect. It would be unfair to ask him to risk his life handing it to her. "He thinks I'm a monster. It's both a relief and rather depressing to consider anyone could think so low of me."

She brushed her hair out of her eyes. "I can relate..."

He continued on about his daughters, responsibility, and

Guardian Everleigh from decades ago—who, apparently, had been a much greater Guardian than her—until his words faded out. He kept speaking, but all Serenna could hear was silence. True silence—the kind impossible in Terrangus, maybe anywhere. She took a deep breath, her heart racing as chilled air evaporated in front of her.

"Serenna…Serenna. Serenna. You thought you were free of me. I felt it in you…was that happiness? You dare feel such a thing? Beings like us never cross that threshold. All we can do is take it away, smother it for those who wield insignificance like it's my dagger. How long must you deny me? Burn them. Burn them all. Turn Terrangus into the next Boulom, a smoldering crater of ignorance and despair. I am nothing. I am forever. I am the end."

The vibration ran through her head far louder than usual. She slowed her breathing and clutched her legs, digging her nails into the holes in her armor to create enough pain for a distraction.

"Your link with the God of Death is remarkable. Honestly, I'm impressed."

Her eyes shot from the floor to General Nyfe, who stood next to Landon. The glow of his dagger radiated darker than it had in Mylor.

"Stand down," Landon said, drawing his blade and stepping back in surprise.

"Serenna, please ask your friend here to give us a moment alone. I actually like this one; I would rather not add another scar to his chest."

"I've been a proud husband, a proud father; you can never take that away from me. If I must die here, so be it." Landon turned to her, too proud to ever say it out loud, but his trembling hands begged her to say yes. Another one willing to die for her— in Terrangus, of all places. She had been wrong; some of them *did* thank her, just not in words.

"Landon," Serenna said, rising from her bed, "please be a nobleman and grab us some water. I can deal with this one."

He sheathed his sword, letting out a drawn-out sigh as he nodded and left the room.

Nyfe smiled. "So, how often does Death speak to you? I can't make out the words, but I get a...tingling feeling in my chest when it happens. Does the same apply to you? He speaks to me quite often; I imagine that would be tortuous."

What a strange man. He had wide eyes, genuinely awaiting her response, but the smile on his face forced the memory of his dagger crashing against her shield right before she'd turned to the void. "I have nothing to say to you."

"Oh, don't be like that. Aren't you at all interested? We're basically the same!"

Gods, he really believes that. One of us is delusional; I truly hope it isn't me. "The same? You're a violent murderer. How many innocent people did you take in Mylor?"

"I'd wager your body count is higher than mine. I used to be the same way; it gets easier when you stop caring. You'll wake up one day after a brutal war and simply...shrug it off. We're just toys for the gods; none of this matters. Make your own fire until some immortal cloud snuffs it out. Fuck it."

"Whatever you have to tell yourself. Can you leave me? I would rather spend my final days alone without listening to your nonsense."

Nyfe snickered, observing the black ceiling above them. "Well, that answers my question. You had no reaction when I heard his voice just now."

"If you're able to speak back, please tell him to go away. I will *never* touch that power again. You know, why doesn't he just make you his Harbinger?"

"Oh," Nyfe said, losing his grin, showing a flash of distress in his lost eyes, "I wouldn't want that. I've received the offer as well…but I've seen what it does to people. Sweet, gentle Vanessa became a *monster*. If you were smart, you would find someone else to pin it on—maybe Francis, or even Zeen is stupid enough if you can convince Death to give them the offer. Either of us could actually win; you don't seem to realize how terrifying that is. It's why we were chosen. The next Harbinger of Death is coming, and it won't be me."

Nyfe stepped up to the cell, then grabbed the bars above her hands. "I have suffered through this for over thirty fucking years. Whatever you think of me now, I wasn't always this way…" He stormed off, leaving her alone, until a faint gust of wind chilled her cheeks.

Not alone. Maybe never again.

CHAPTER II

WELCOME TO SERENITY

Francis Haide sighed, sitting in the Guardian room, pouring water on the brown and red stains of his once-white robes. Of all the textbooks that had been written about Terrangus, none accurately described the filth that lingered on the streets. So shameful. If only these people could see the ivory Alanammus Tower scaling into the perfect sky, they would riot with the fury of the first zephum warlord. Was it merciful or cruel to keep them ignorant? Ah, it was tactful. One consistent theme throughout the literature: Terrangus was often controlled by evil yet intelligent men. As long as your neighbor never saw all the gold in your pockets, the copper in his own would feel heavier. Light copper, heavy burdens. The legacy of western culture.

Focus. Today is the day. I'm going to speak to him, and apologize for the ignorance of my mother. I can finally fix everything.

I can finally be the hero.

He grimaced as water seeped through his robes and into his wound. *Outmaneuvered by a Terrangus mage. Is there no end to my shame?* Speaking of shame, David sat at the far end of the table—alone, as usual—drinking his *cheap* Terrangus wine. What dignified man drank this early in the day? Actually, what time was it? The wine must have been powerful—cheap wine usually was—since David was convinced Fear had spoken to him through the Harbinger. Utter nonsense.

Melissa stormed through the doors, panting as sweat poured down her face. "Grayson took Serenna; we have to act *now*. He's to have her executed."

Oh no, this may interfere with my plans...

David rose, stumbling a bit, grabbing the table to keep his balance. Impeccable leadership. "He wouldn't dare."

"I can't get involved," Pyith said, looking down. She favored her right side; it would be awhile before that wounded leg healed—especially with those amateurs working the healing ward. It was no wonder Zeen still slept.

Why are they looking at me? Oh, I should say something. "We'll all get our 'prized' audiences with the emperor later for saving this awful kingdom—again. Can't you just request her release then? Why is this difficult?" *Disaster. This is what happens when Terrangus and the Guardians have no leadership.*

Why are they still looking at me?

David let out a drawn-out sigh. "That's probably our best option. We're not in a position to storm the throne room." His gaze shot forward to Melissa. "How close is she to surrendering to the void?"

"Serenna swore to me that wouldn't happen," Melissa said, approaching the table and refilling her detonators. "I believe her intentions...but there is a limit to what she will tolerate. The threat will always remain; I do not agree with waiting."

"It's too dangerous to ask Francis and Pyith to risk all-out war. We need to play our cards in the throne room. Melissa, you'll need to make a hell of a spectacle to secure her release. This may all depend on you."

I was so awful to Serenna when she returned. Maybe I should focus on helping her? Hmm, Melissa can do it. You know, it really wasn't her fault with that whole Mylor thing. If anyone ever threatened Alanammus, I would show them the might of the elements.

Guardian sorcerer Francis Haide, defender of Alanammus...

They're looking at me again. "A fair strategy. The most logical order would be me, Melissa, then Pyith."

"No," Pyith said, gritting her teeth as she sat back down. "I go first. I'm on a mission from Sardonyx; don't make me say anything further."

She always got special treatment, as if being a large lizard-woman was more important than an elemental mage. Oh well, not worth arguing. As long as Francis went before David—*he* had a tendency to ruin everything.

The door opened and Zeen limped towards the table. "Morning, everyone. What did I miss? Where is Serenna?" His smile faded. Zeen didn't seem particularly bright, but the solemn expression on everyone's faces must have tipped him off.

Francis rose, nodding at Zeen. An imperfect Guardian, but his heart was in the right place. *Give it a few years.* "Pardon me, but I must prepare for later." He left as David began explaining the scenario. *Where can I get a bath here? Do I even dare bathe in their waters? Not worth it. Ugh, how can I see him when I'm utterly filthy?*

*

About two hours later, Francis took his reserved spot in the throne room up by the southern ambassadors, opposite the Terrangus senators. He sat next to Alanammus Representative Salvatore, an old friend of his mother. They never spoke much, mostly because of conflicting opinions on the divine entity next to the emperor.

The God of Wisdom.

Also, he was annoying. "Welcome, Francis. Surely you heard about Serenna? How odd that you're up here and not with the Guardians."

Wisdom's bronze sun mask and red and black cape floated eloquently in the air, casually wielding infinite power as he drifted by the throne, mostly ignored by the toads of men who likely forgot he was there. When Francis had been a child, Wisdom would bless Alanammus Tower, hovering around his archon mother, gifting them with wise sayings and stories. *Desperation is not a virtue.* Those words had burned into his memory, a final lesson before his mother had banished the god away. A *terrible* mistake: the kind only a genius could make. Archon Addison Haide had never told him why.

"Francis? Hello?"

Ugh, why is he talking to me? "Keep to yourself. For some of us, this will be a legendary day in our kingdom's history. I won't spoil the surprise."

Salvatore snickered. "Well, you're looking at Wisdom the way I looked at Sonia on my third wedding night, so I'll make a calculated guess. Subtlety isn't your strongest suite."

"There's no reason to be subtle if I don't value your opinion."

The throne room doors opened, revealing Pyith Claw, still in her tattered steel armor from last night. The room cheered, celebrating the future warlord's life-mate that would probably enslave them all one day. He grimaced as she hobbled forward. Gods, she tried to hide it, but that leg was a *mess.*

The speaker on the Terrangus end stood up straight. "Now introducing: Pyith Claw—zephum Guardian, hailing from our eastern allies in the Vaynex empire."

Allies? That's rich.

She kneeled at the head of the stairs.

Forsythe rose from his throne. "Ah, noble warrior Pyith. You will rise; we respect zephum royalty in Terrangus. I must ask, how fares Warlord Sardonyx? It has been quite some time since our paths last crossed. Is he still the calm, reasonable diplomat I remember?"

Pyith rose, using her sword as a crutch to avoid putting weight on the right leg. "Emperor Forsythe, it is an honor to be in your presence after defending Terrangus once again. I will send your regards to the warlord, but pardon me for altering the words. It's fortunate he's not in this room, for anyone accusing him of being a calm diplomat would be in a fight for their life."

Francis snickered. Pyith had always spoken like a Xavian pirate around her own, but she knew how to play the game of politics. Gods, she had been so...*refined* on her first visit to Alanammus. He'd assumed all zephum had Pyith's friendly demeanor until his first Harbinger in Vaynex.

That assumption had proven to be false.

"You see?" Forsyth asked with a laugh, his arms out wide. "This is the sort of banter I expect from Guardians. Nobles of Terrangus, forgive me, but I declare Pyith my favorite. One of these days, you must humor me with a duel—wooden swords, of course. I couldn't accept the guilt of injuring the future *warlord*."

Oh, he shouldn't call her warlord...but he knows that?

Pyith raised her sword and twirled it to entertain her mindless hosts, drawing cheers and more laughter from Forsythe. A grand spectacle for ungrand people.

"Perhaps one day, but don't waste my time with wooden swords. If we fight, it will be as warriors—though I warn you, only one human has ever bested me." She slammed her sword to the ground, to a reaction of gasps from the harsh thud.

"Emperor, I'm not a fan of subtlety; Vaynex knows of your plans to engage our forces in the north. The ruins of Boulom *do not* concern you. I won't have the audacity to demand your withdrawal, but I warn you—not as a Guardian, but as zephum royalty—you will be met with violence."

Forsythe crossed his arms and nodded at her. "Indeed, I share your dislike of subtlety. It is an art form used by the weak to pretend they have power. So be it, Pyith. I acknowledge your warning and meet you with one of my own. Tell the warlord to send his best, for he will battle Terrangus's elite. Oh, and ask Tempest to go too; perhaps we can speed up your ascension to the throne."

He's angering her on purpose. That doesn't seem wise...

"Enough! I let it go once, but openly insulting Warmaster Tempest Claw is unacceptable. When my life-mate takes the mantle of warlord, your tone will change, or he will embrace your home in shackles. I take my leave, Emperor. An icy grave awaits any human foolish enough to come north."

She stormed off, losing her hobble as she flung the doors open. The entire room cheered; war had no relevance for the ones that didn't participate.

Ah, one man didn't cheer. General Nyfe sulked in his post near the Terrangus speaker, his eyes lost on the moonlit stairways of the throne room. Proclaiming desire for the throne in a kingdom that didn't bother to vote on it had not been the wisest play.

I'm ready.

The speaker rose. "Now introducing: Francis Haide— sorcerer Guardian, hailing from our southern allies in Alanammus kingdom. Son of the late Archon Addison Haide."

My mother has been gone for five years; will I never escape her shadow? He began his descent from the ambassador section and made his way towards the throne stairs. The people clapped, but where were the cheers? Was it jealousy? Most Terrangus mages couldn't *spell* elements, let alone manipulate them.

Outrageous. At this rate, even David would get a better reception. Francis stood at the bottom of the stairs, waiting for Forsythe to do that silence thing with his hand. Francis didn't kneel.

He would *never* kneel to anyone.

Forsythe grinned, perhaps at the audacity. "Ah, Addy's son. You somehow look exactly the same after four years... How old are you at this point?"

Will I never escape? "Twenty-eight, Emperor. I remember the—"

"Ah yes," Forsythe said, stroking his beard, pacing around his throne. "You're close to that age where time takes away more than it gives." He stopped pacing and stared through Francis. "Are you here to ask about Serenna? You mages tend to stick together."

"No, actually I—"

"You will *not* like my answer."

Francis took a deep breath as heat rushed through his face. "I'm not here for her, and I'm not here for *you*!" His voice reverberated through the stunned halls. It would never be Alanammus Tower, but the throne room had a quaint beauty in the fading moment of silence. *Stop yelling. You aren't a child.*

To his relief, Forsythe chuckled at the outburst. "So, you *have* grown. What do you ask of me?"

This is it. Don't fail—you may never get another chance. This could be the most important moment of your life. "Emperor Forsythe, I formally request an audience with the God of Wisdom. It is imperative I correct the mishaps of my mother."

"That's it? Sure," Forsythe said, snickering as he shrugged, "he's all yours. If you could take him with you on the way out, that would be swell."

The room erupted in laughter as Wisdom floated down the stairs. He finally revealed spectral arms, clutching them together as he examined Francis with the bulging eyes on the mask. The platinum smile and black frown hid any hope of reading his intentions. Wisdom reached out his right hand, then a brilliant flash filled the normally dark room as the Herald of Wisdom staff appeared in his spectral grip.

They were done laughing.

Francis kneeled, begging himself to gaze at the deity, but kept his head down. He then shot up as another flash filled the room, this time converging into a bright white portal.

"My dear Francis, care to join me for some wine?" Wisdom chuckled as he floated through the portal.

Francis slowed his breathing to compose himself, then walked through.

*

Standard portals were always jarring when Francis arrived at the other side, but not here; it was like being cradled into a new world. His eyes opened, staring off into perfect skies and endless green fields from a high mountainous terrain. He had always thought Alanammus was the pinnacle of nature until this moment—was it cruel or merciful to shatter that belief? Was true enlightenment just a mixture of the two?

I have analyzed every kingdom, and this isn't one of them.

He navigated forward, no destination in mind, every step immersing him further into the dreamlike mural of perfection. The only sound was a waterfall flowing to his left; ethereal streams, rivaling the clarity of the azure skies.

Hmm. He reached the end of his path. An immaculate view but no way forward.

"*My dear Francis,*" Wisdom said through his thoughts. "*Welcome to Serenity.*"

Francis slowed his breathing. Whether from fear or excitement, something he couldn't control forced his heart to pound faster. "Thank... Thank you. I don't see a path. Where do you want me to go? Can you even hear me?"

A faint ringing filled the air as glasslike steps formed in front of him. Similar to crystal magic...but something *more*. Serenna had used to say deviating from the standard shapes took true mastery; her arsenal of spheres, barriers, and spikes had been widely accepted as the pinnacle of the crystal art. Apparently not. He wouldn't dare insult Wisdom by testing the strength of the steps, so he took a deep breath and began his ascension.

"My dear sorcerer, you are the first mortal to enter this realm in quite some time. Perhaps you heard of my last guest... She went by Addison Haide. Oh yes, I see physical similarities, but you seem to have avoided the closed-mindedness that clashed with her brilliance."

Ah, that was the voice from his childhood. The distinct Alanammus *thickness*...but it sounded almost like old Mylor? *Focus.* He climbed the steps, nearing the largest cloud in the sky. *How can I breathe this high up?* He hesitated before walking through. Would it be cold? Maybe fluffy? *Focus.* He continued his climb, stepping through the cloud and shivering from a gentle chill that forced a smile. That smile grew as he found a floating pillar of earth above the clouds: a flawless garden in the skies.

He stepped off into the garden, the ground so soft his sandals sank into the soil. "What a marvel this is..." The steps behind him vanished into birds, pearly white doves that scattered in all directions. Serenna would never believe him.

"Please, make your way to the center of the garden. We have much to discuss. Oh! How about some music?"

Cellos, violins, and a bass rose into the air, floating as they started a concerto: Thaddeus Emmanuel's fourth prelude in F minor, to be exact. Every note perfect, every harmonic emphasized with the proper technique of a master.

He approached Wisdom, who sat on a throne next to a small lake. The god had more physical features than normal, with a body, legs, and real arms instead of spectral ones. The face was still a sun mask, which looked slightly *off* atop the dark suit of his frame. "Lord Wisdom. This world—your home— it's beautiful. You honor me with this invitation."

Wisdom nudged his staff, creating a second throne. "Indeed. Please, have a seat." He nudged the staff again, creating a glass of wine in each of their hands as Francis sat. "Forgive me for assuming you prefer red wine, but as a fellow sorcerer of great taste, I take it you appreciate the superior flavor. It's aged, *oh,* is it aged. That drink in your hand is older than the unified Vaynex empire."

Up until that moment, Francis had preferred white wine. He took a sip, sighing in wonder as the sweet, berry-like taste touched his lips. His eyes lit up after he swallowed—no burn followed. The numbing hit faster than usual. Gods, did that feel good; the constant thoughts and tangents of his mind relaxed, allowing him to focus on one singular thing. That *thing* happened to be the most powerful entity in the realm.

So, he took another sip. "This wine is simply marvelous. The texture…the sweetness. I have so many questions; what is this place?"

Wisdom raised his chalice to his mask as some of the wine faded from the glass. "My dear Francis, you have arrived in my home: the grand paradise that is Serenity. All of us gods have a plane to call our own, shaped after our own persona and desires. I chose a paradise, as my ultimate goal is a perfect world, one rid of pain, war, and all the chaotic vices mortals desperately hail upon themselves."

"Your home," Francis said, leaning in, "this land, it's a treasure. I have never seen such beauty in person. Forgive me for asking, but you come across as a benevolent figure; what in the realm caused the rift between you and my mother?" He took another sip and leaned back, relaxing on the throne he'd always deserved. "Knowing her, it was likely something petty. Gods, she would stress over the most basic things."

Wisdom chuckled, vanishing more of his wine before refilling both their glasses. "Our unfortunate disagreement came down to a simple concept: my eventual plans to remove the burden of freewill."

Wait, what?

He didn't take another sip. "Lord Wisdom, I certainly misheard you. Are you proposing that freewill…is a bad thing?"

Wisdom rose from his throne, reverting to the bodiless form, then floated around him. "*Oh*, if you could only see the fear in your eyes now. A true scholar's fear: someone challenging the perception of something you already know *must* be true."

Francis stood and paced with his hands behind his back. "But, of course it's true. If we don't have freewill, what is the alternative?" He took a deep breath; the scholar in him already knew the answer. "Slavery…this is what you told my mother. Gods…everything makes sense now."

Mom, why didn't you tell me? We didn't have to part on such…agonizing terms.

"Are you not already a slave to your freewill? How many were lost in the recent war? In their dying moments, did any of them reach up to the heavens and thank us for the opportunity to suffer? Tragedies should never be acceptable, yet I watched children die in Mylor. *Children*, Francis! Everyone clings to freewill, but curses the results that come when they choose. The chaos, pain, all avoidable, all completely unnecessary. But to answer your question, no. I am not a tyrant. I would never suggest slavery."

Does he not understand? He's a god, of course he does. "What am I missing? I openly admit that freewill does not guarantee a perfect outcome, but—"

"*Yes*! You just admitted the flaw that no mind can ever debunk. If freewill isn't perfect, it can be improved upon. I suggest a divine alternative: that all life should be predetermined, all lives in all kingdoms, everything already planned out, while keeping the illusion of freewill intact. We could maximize progress, end suffering...*anything* is possible. My dear friend, believe this, it would be as beautiful as everything you see before you."

Francis stopped pacing, picking up his chalice and staring off into the infinite beauty below. The concerto reached the third movement, a piece that had made him weep the first time he'd heard it. He wanted to weep now, for more complex reasons. "What is the point of intelligence if it's not earned? It took lesson upon lesson, book upon book to get to this point. I deserve this. Others don't."

"Too often, the lesson isn't worth the pain. You have *no idea* what I have done...*no idea* what madness I have unleashed with my absurd choices. And you? If I wrote your life, there would never be a Guardian Francis. There would, however, be an Archon Francis. You threw that dream away. You *chose* to be unhappy."

Francis sighed, then took a sip of wine. *Archon Francis. Gods, it should've happened. I really did throw it away. For what? Pride? To be a Guardian? I abandoned Mom for no reason. I abandoned Serenna in Mylor...*

I abandon everyone. It's what I do. "You know, my mother was terrified of you. She would say you were more dangerous than Fear or even Death. While I find the thesis of your argument flawed, perhaps we can find common ground. My new goal is to prove you wrong. Perhaps it's arrogance, but I truly believe people can make their own path without sacrificing freewill."

Wisdom chuckled. "*Arrogance*...now that is a flaw I can

approve of. Do you remember my lesson from all those years ago?"

"Desperation is not a virtue. Wait, is that your mantra? Yours is the only one not on record besides Fear's. That... would be a remarkable find."

"Oh, no. You're not ready for *those* words. I prefer to hold my cards closer to the robes; it's in everyone's best interest if I keep a few...*secrets*. But in honor of our new friendship, here is Fear's mantra: *Where reality fails, dreams are eternal.*"

Francis nearly choked on his wine. "Gods, David was telling the truth?" *I'm failing him; I'm failing everyone.* "Lord Wisdom, I should return to Terrangus. David will need my aid...we are having *issues* with Forsythe."

"Forget about Grayson," Wisdom said with a laugh. "If a man is already on fire, it's not worth the effort to stab him. His constant aggression against the Guardians has made him an enemy of the Goddess of Fear, a dense but dear friend of mine. Once...a *very* dear friend. Let her deal with this one. While the gods and I are forbidden from directly taking life or giving it back, the deed will be done in the shadows, as all worthwhile deeds are."

"Hmm," Francis said, sitting back on his throne. "Then I would prefer to go home. There is much to ponder." *Do it. He's not evil, just wrong. He probably feels the same about you. Use your intellect. You have nothing else.* "Would you prefer to join me? I would...rather not introduce you to Archon Gabriel yet, but perhaps the two of us can learn and grow from each other? You're the God of Wisdom, the true god of Alanammus. I will *not* give up on you."

Wisdom chucked. "Oh, but of course, and here I thought you would never ask!" He nudged his staff and created a new portal, gesturing for Francis to go first.

The concerto ended. Something seemed...*off* about the now silent paradise as Francis entered the portal.

CHAPTER 12

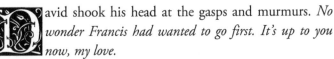

IS THIS CONSIDERED BEAUTIFUL?

David shook his head at the gasps and murmurs. *No wonder Francis had wanted to go first. It's up to you now, my love.*

"Now introducing: Melissa Euhno—mechanist Guardian, hailing from none other than our supreme western kingdom of Terrangus."

David kept his stare on Grayson as the crowd roared for their Guardian. Where Grayson's eyes went and the shape of his smile would speak volumes. Despite the most beloved woman in Terrangus approaching his throne, Grayson's eyes were locked on him. *So be it.*

He took another sip of wine to prolong the numbness, accepting the various frowns that had followed from the morning. Victory was supposed to be the temporary high that filled the void. Instead, Serenna's fate and Fear's words tore through him. *Where reality fails, dreams are eternal.* What did that even mean? Everyone had just assumed he'd been drunk, which, to be fair, was true.

"Get out of here," he said to Zeen. "If anything happens to us, meet Pyith in Vaynex. The zephum will protect you while she regroups. This…may not go well."

"No. I'm not leaving until Serenna is safe. Guardians don't abandon their own."

David grabbed him, pulling him close. "Do not *ever* make me repeat myself again." *Gods, I love him for saying that,* he thought, letting go. Young Guardians tended to fall for each other. It had made them bold and, more often, very stupid. David had found the constant threat of dying to be a better aphrodisiac than any arrangement of flowers or poems. It was difficult to blame Zeen after he'd walked the same path twenty years ago. For all his regrets, that wasn't one of them. That was the best thing he had ever done.

Melissa waved to both sides before kneeling at the head of the stairs in perfect form, letting the gray spotlight illuminate his favorite features. These events were normally mundane spectacles to restore faith in a recovering kingdom, but the very fate of the realm rested on her shoulders. Forsythe was either a fool or too far gone; Serenna would never accept a clean death by his hands.

She would destroy them all.

"Lady Euhno!" Grayson yelled, throwing his arms up and allowing the crowd to continue cheering. "The radiant pride of Terrangus will never kneel in my presence. Listen to these people, *your* people. Listen to them as they cheer you on, embracing you with love and affection. Arise, my champion."

She rose, brushing her hands through that curly hair before holding them behind her back. "Thank you, mighty Emperor. Your kind words are the highlight of my glory. To all the nobles and military leaders, thank you for always standing with the Guardians and fulfilling your own personal duties. Defeating Harbingers is but a small task in the greater being of hope. We are all Terrangus, and this empire only stands as we stand *together.*"

Her meaningless words were well crafted, filled with the vibrant fluff required to navigate political theater and draw cheers from mostly useless people. That life had never been for him.

They made a few more empty exchanges, dancing with words, never just conversing how they would in real circumstances. All the more absurd, considering they had nearly fought to the death that morning. David's eyes widened as Melissa took a deep breath and glanced down. She was about to ask. It would all come down to this.

"Lord Emperor, I hope not to insult your good graces, but I have a difficult request. While openly accepting her faults, I beg you to release Guardian Serenna Morgan into our care. She is vital to our team and, quite frankly, a woman I love as my sister."

The crowd murmured; this request was expected, but not from her. Ungrateful cowards. Terrangus had invaded Serenna's home, and she'd saved them anyway. Could these people even consider the discipline that took?

"Hmm. It was wise to make this request yourself, Lady Euhno; I wouldn't entertain such audacity from any other Guardian. Out of my fading respect, I won't have you strung up for treason. What an insult that you would use your clout to aid a Pact Breaker and a war criminal. Do you have any idea how many of *our* people Serenna murdered? She even accepted aid from the God of Death..." Grayson paced back and forth. "Serenna dies a week from today."

The crowd cheered in agreement, except for General Nyfe who flashed a quick grin while heading towards the exit. Was he smiling out of spite? He was too practical to make an enemy out of Melissa—no man seeking the throne would dare. "It's been a while, David," Nyfe said, as he passed by. "Looks like you and I just became allies. Good luck in there; try not to die."

What the hell is he talking about? Dammit, I hope he doesn't run into Zeen. Everything is falling apart...

Melissa yielded a deep frown; it *crushed* him to see her that way. "But Emperor, if you only—"

Forsythe drew his blade; the blade David hadn't seen since Vanessa's last night. "*Enough!* Do not test the limits of my kindness. If you continue to defy me, I'll have the two of you executed together."

The cheering stopped, replaced by concerned glances and murmurs. The people of Terrangus were fools, but even they recognized the absurdity of Grayson's threats against Melissa. David finished his wine, threw the chalice to the ground, then drew his blade and approached the throne. Grayson had threatened his love.

It was time for him to die.

The guards studied him as David drifted closer to the stairs; he couldn't count them with the wine blurring his vision. It didn't matter—the fear in their eyes was still as clear as a single drop of rain drifting off Melissa's cheek on a solemn winter morning. No amount of soldiers could defeat him in that moment, even if they were all gods.

Melissa grabbed him as he arrived at the center of the throne room. "Stop," she whispered. "Please stop. We accomplish nothing if we die here. Fall back and regroup; we haven't lost yet."

I'll stand down for you, but I swear I'll be the one to end this man. His right hand shook as he clutched his sword and pointed it at Grayson. "Vile tyrant. There was a point where I would've died for you. Your reign is on borrowed time."

Grayson just smirked. "Empty words from an empty man, drowning in his own flaws."

David sheathed his sword and stormed out of the room with Melissa following from behind. She spoke, but the frantic yells from all sides made it impossible to focus on anything except the ringing in his head.

I told Serenna not to break the pact. Everything is fucked now. Everything is completely fucked. I don't know how to fix this…

Nyfe stood outside the Guardian room entrance…with Zeen? "Welcome, Guardians," he said, with that advantageous grin. "Care to talk? I have an interesting proposal for everyone."

I don't have time for this, David thought, drifting his hand to his sword in plain sight.

Nyfe stepped back. "Now hold on, sir. I'm not here for that. Not today, at least. What chance would I have against the three of you?"

"Let's hear him out," Zeen said, moving next to Melissa. "He claims he can protect Serenna."

"You have thirty seconds…"

"Tomorrow, I'll be sent to command a small strike team against zephum forces up north in the ruins of Boulom. Our spies claim they're close to uncovering a new artifact… something related to the Goddess of Fear."

David's eyes lit up at the mention of Fear, revealing more interest than he had intended. "What do you mean by artifact?"

"Like this," Nyfe said, raising his glowing blade and tapping against the edge. "I wield the Herald of Death, but the other artifacts have avoided mortal hands. Wisdom keeps his staff close, and we know next to nothing about Strength and Fear. The possibilities are *endless!*"

An interesting lie, but an easy refusal. Zephum were *terrible* adversaries in battle. "Fuck off."

Nyfe sheathed the dagger and walked up to David. "Fine, but before you go—where reality fails, dreams are eternal. Sound familiar?"

It was more disturbing to find the possibility it could be real. They had to save Serenna…but at what cost? The same man wielding two of the Herald artifacts would hold unfathomable power. *What if I took the artifact? Could I save Serenna and deny Nyfe? I have to be careful…*

We might be playing into Fear's hands.

Melissa sighed. "How exactly is this helping Serenna?"

"Oh, it's simple. David and Zeen will join me up north to retrieve the artifact. I have strong support here, and assuming we succeed, it should fill the missing numbers to finalize my insurrection of the throne. Melissa, you can remain in Terrangus and stay with Serenna to ensure there's no funny business. I'll command my loyalists to protect her until our return. Deal?"

"I don't have a better plan," Zeen said, staring down, "but the idea of Emperor Nyfe is…troublesome. What do you guys think?"

Melissa snickered. "Not a chance. Let's get out of here."

It's not like we can do worse than Grayson, and I need to learn more about Fear. This can't be a coincidence. After that last Harbinger, I'm done with coincidences.

There was an uncomfortable silence as he searched for words. How to side with Zeen without insulting Melissa? David picked Nyfe up by his leather armor and held him against the wall. "If you even dream of betraying us, I will harm you in ways that would make your deity blush."

Nyfe just smirked. Another one who had dismissed his threats. Could they see through the mirage and into the empty man? Grayson always could. Nyfe didn't look too great himself; it must be a gift for broken men to identify their own.

"Listen, I really don't care about any of you, but with mutual cooperation, we can protect Serenna *and* get me on the throne. Unless the three of you want to storm the throne room and face an entire army. Let me know how that works out. Now…could you please let me down? After having Death scream through my head for a lifetime, I'm a bit numb to mortal threats."

"You guys are serious?" Melissa asked as David let him down. "We have a week to think of something better, and we're helping *Nyfe*?"

"Funny," Nyfe said, adjusting his armor. "I expected Zeen would be the holdout. Spend more time with Serenna; she's making that brain work harder. Probably other things, too."

"Whatever," Zeen said, blushing a dark crimson. "I'm stepping outside for some air. When do we meet tomorrow?"

"Meet me at sunrise in the trade district," David said before Nyfe could respond. "We'll stick together."

Nyfe's grin returned. "Excellent. Well, I would recommend hugging your loved ones tonight if you managed to acquire any. For all this arguing, we're still likely to die a horrible death in the bitter cold." He nodded and walked off.

That grin...he didn't expect this to work. Am I losing it? He rubbed the sweat from his face, then turned to Melissa. "We should—"

She stormed off, letting him begin his sentence first to get the full effect. She'd grown better at that over the years. Her radiant figure was a haze through his wine-kissed eyes, a glowing shadow that held his heart to keep it from evaporating alongside the vapors of fading Terrangus rain. Maybe it was the wine, but closing his eyes to stop the world from spinning gave him a wonderful idea. One he'd always considered, but had always yielded to the "what ifs" and "maybe laters."

I may not come back from this one. It's time. It's always been time.

*

David was up well before sunrise, unable to sleep most of the night before. Those nights were growing more common, but at least the hangovers had decayed over the past year. His mother used to say that was the point of no return. Drinking, not to celebrate or mourn, but because the sober world had lost its meaning. Reality had seemed to agree, sending her to the void not long after. It would kill her all over again to see him now.

He jingled his leather pockets as he navigated the trade district, ensuring all the gold was still there. Terrangus had plenty of thieves, but it was a clever man's craft, and clever men stayed away.

There was the tiny cart, right next to Jerry's Inn where it had remained open all his forty-four years: Francesco's Alanammus Treasures. He never learned Francesco's real name, or where he'd come from, but the short, skinny man certainly wasn't from Alanammus.

His love deserved a mountain of pure diamonds…but his gold was a bit tight. Kingdom leaders had gotten stingy over the years; Alanammus and…somehow Vaynex were the most charitable.

"Morning, big fella," Francesco said, eyeing David's filled pockets. "Come to celebrate another victory over the gods?"

David poured his gold on the table. He had counted it the night before, but that number was long gone. "Fuck the gods. Give me the largest diamond this gold can buy. I need something breathtaking."

"Ah…it's *that* sort of victory." He wouldn't dare count it in front of David; a skilled merchant could make a fair estimation. "I may have just the thing." Francesco pulled out a heavy box from behind his cart. He opened it to reveal a ring with a tiny diamond. The gem shimmered…but *gods,* it was small. "This diamond goes all the way back to Archon Consaga…your wife will be Terrangus royalty."

"Is there nothing larger?" David asked with a sigh.

"No, no. Women don't care about such things. Once you slip the ring on her finger, it's the largest, most beautiful diamond in all the realm… Plus, if you start small, you can buy larger gems for anniversaries and such. As a gold cloak once told my father: start large—end broke."

David snickered, picking up the ring and studying it. *Is this considered beautiful? Why does it mean nothing to me? To hell with it.* "I'll take it. If she's not pleased, I *will* be back."

"Ah, I expect your return, but in a few years, to upgrade. Enjoy your love and happiness, my friend."

David nodded, unable to restrain his excitement. He rushed over towards the noble district—an area he'd normally avoided—until he arrived at her tiny brown cottage on the far west end. It always looked out of place compared to the mansions and villas all over the ward, but it was by far the most grand, solely because of who resided within. He knocked on the door, his left hand trembling as he clutched the ring in his pocket.

She immediately answered. Gods, when did she find the time to sleep? "David? What are you doing here this early?"

"May I please come in?"

"Sure…" she said, eyeing him carefully. "Is everything okay?"

His heart pounded. Not in the normal, rapid way it did in tense moments, but in steady, profound pumps. "I need to speak to you about the future."

"The future? If this is about yesterday, I'm over it."

He walked over and held her hands. "The Harbinger's words stuck with me. I know I can never give you the life you truly deserve, but that doesn't mean we are destined to be miserable forever."

Melissa frowned, judging him with her gentle eyes. "David, we have been through this; I'm not going to quit being a Guardian. While this isn't my dream life, the fact that I can share it with you makes it worthwhile. The people still need us."

"No," David said, stammering for a moment. "That's not what I'm proposing. Melissa, to hell with it. Let's get married and show the entire realm we are one. Let's be a family. I...don't know if we can have children, that probably would've happened by now, but I'm asking you to become my Melissa Williams."

She laughed, letting go of his hands and stepping back. "Wow, you really have lost your mind today. We can't get married. Is that even allowed for Guardians?"

Of course she would ask that. Technically, the answer was no, based on classic rules, but leaders could make adjustments—particularly when they were convenient. "Who cares? Think of everything we do for these people. All the sacrifices... If they can't accept it, they don't deserve us."

"Oh gods," she said, wiping her eyes and staring into his. "You're serious about this? I don't know what to say; I...we couldn't get married here, not after you threatened Grayson. David... Do you truly want this? I mean truly?"

"Yes!" David said, taking her hands again. "Yes, more than anything. We'll do it in Alanammus or Xavian; it doesn't matter. Melissa, don't make me beg, you know I will."

She paused. "I love you, David—I always have—but I don't know if this is the right thing to do. Especially now. Terrangus has never been in worse shape."

"I see it too," David said, voice cracking, "and that solidifies my decision. When I considered two nights ago could've been the end, I had to look back on my life and wonder if it was all worth it. When I did, I couldn't say yes. There is a deeper meaning missing, a void inside me that never fills. It's not pain or fear, but some...sort of emptiness. Melissa, you are that missing piece of me. It has to be you; there is nothing else. *Nothing* else."

It was cruel to pause for as long as she did after letting go.

"Listen, we'll talk about this when you get back. If we were ordinary people living ordinary lives, I would throw myself at you and scream 'yes' as tears ran down my eyes. It's never been that simple; I need to ensure everyone's safe before making it official. We have too many enemies now, and somehow in a realm of gods, I'm far more afraid of the flawed mortals that rule our kingdoms. Please don't misread my hesitation; I have always loved you…"

I'm losing her. It's time.

David stepped back, rustling his hand in his pocket. He pulled out the small ring with a diamond on it, taking Melissa's hand and placing it inside. His eyes drifted to hers, the only ones who could ever see him cry. The only ones allowed to see the reality of whatever fragments remained of the young, hopeful boy who had courted her decades ago.

"I love you too. For now, please take this. You don't have to consider it a wedding ring, but at the very least, let it be a bond of friendship between two people that have lived a wonderful life together."

Melissa held the ring and smiled, handing it back to David, then holding her hand out. "The ring is beautiful, but this time do it properly." David slowly slipped it on her finger while his hand shook from the anxiety. When it was fully on, Melissa smiled at him. "And there it is, my love. I will wear this ring for the rest of my life; I wish I had one for you too."

He embraced her, likely too hard judging by the groan she let out. She didn't speak, and that was perfect. Emptiness was no match for the woman who gave him forever. A new fear rose inside him, the idea he was finally happy and could lose it all in Boulom. He actually *wanted* to come back alive, and clutching that feeling nearly rivaled the warmth of holding her in his arms.

You're the only one that ever loved me.

CHAPTER 13

INTREPID

Zeen groaned, wiped his eyes, then finished his jug of water. His muscles were still sore after a mostly unsuccessful night of rest, but at least it was easy to move again. He picked up his sword, studying the nameless blade with the familiarity of a new friend. The unlucky sword had been thrown at him—cast into a life of chaos—with no preparation to face the horrors of gods and now…

Zephum. It would be the Koulva mines all over again. Likely worse, with Nyfe there. At least if this went poorly, and they all died, Pyith would get a good laugh at their expense. *Damn, I didn't consider I'm actively working against her. I jumped at any chance to protect Serenna without thinking this through.*

He swung the sword down, smiling at the quick whistle from the practice strike. Rinso the Blue had always named his swords. What a plot twist it had been in Volume II, finding out Fortune was the same blade that had killed his mother. What to name this one? Zeen's last blade had deserved the honor; he wouldn't make that mistake again. *The name should have something to do with Serenna. No, stop it, that would be silly.*

It slayed a Harbinger of Fear. What beats fear? Hmm…
Intrepid.

Yes, that worked. He smiled, sheathing Intrepid and exiting out of his tiny room in one of the few undamaged barracks in the military ward. He stepped outside, sighing in relief at the temperate breeze of the fresh morning air. A bit warmer than he preferred, but this would be paradise compared to the ruins of Boulom. If he went south, he could meet with David and get going on their suicide mission. West would lead to the castle, where Serenna was held. Not the plan, but…

As he navigated west, soldiers pointed at him and whispered to each other. He'd been used to having enemies among his own with Nyfe, but these didn't seem spiteful. More…intrigued? *Come stare at the doomed man.* Two castle guards paused when he approached the entrance.

"State your business!" the larger one yelled.

"Guardian business." *I always wanted to say that.*

They shrugged and opened the doors. It worked! He walked through, finding several more soldiers rushing around the castle than on any other day. Many of them glared at him. These glares *were* spiteful; it would be best to say farewell and exit in a reasonable manner.

The stairs far left of the throne room entrance would lead to the prison cells, but he needed the stairs under the stairs to reach the room for the very worst of Terrangus; the room holding the woman with platinum hair who had taken over his thoughts.

He trekked downwards to the dank chamber, finding a familiar friend, then *many* unfamiliar, scowling faces. Nyfe had said he had people to keep guard, were these them? Most were huddled around the Wings of Mylor staff that leaned against an empty cell across from Serenna's. The eyes of the pale owl stared him down, reminding him of how hard it had crashed against his face in Mylor. Fortunately—despite the glares—no one approached him other than Landon.

"Zeen? What are you doing down here? Things are a bit…tense right now." Landon must have noticed him glancing at Serenna. "Ah. That shouldn't surprise me."

"Well," Zeen said, "a lot has happened since Mylor. Believe it or not, we are allies now."

Landon snickered, patting Zeen on the shoulder. "Your 'ally' is easy on the eyes, that's for sure. My first impressions were wrong. She's not evil—far from it, I dare say—but there is still a darkness inside her."

"Really?" Serenna asked. "You *do* know I can hear you guys?"

Zeen blushed, nodding at the grinning Landon before walking over to her cell. An enormous relief flowed through him as she sipped a jug of water. No signs of mistreatment; Landon had kept his word. Older years were kind to the once-vicious man. The things he'd done in Koulva…

The things they'd all done.

"Good morning, Serenna. While the circumstances are not ideal, it is wonderful to see you again." *Was wonderful too strong a word? Don't embarrass yourself; this is your teammate now.*

She smiled back for a brief moment, but dark circles dragged under her eyes. "Nice to see you, too. I wasn't sure we would have the chance to speak before I went back to Mylor, but it seems I'll be here longer than expected. Who am I kidding? I'm never going back home."

"Yes, well…I wanted to…I'm sorry."

"Let's avoid the awkward apologies. You have been kind to me in our short time together. I never would have imagined that random soldier from the bastion last year would end up being a Guardian."

"This may sound silly, but I always did dream of the day. I always thought you guys were mystical beings, infallible Guardians, who would stop at nothing to protect the realm from the horrors of Fear and Death. The first day when we finally met…you spared my life! No one believed me; Nyfe's side of the story said I was a coward that distracted him."

Serenna snickered. "Infallible Guardians? Oh, I do miss those early days of blind optimism. Now, I'm just…tired. Tired of being the villain. Tired of being tired. Tell me, Zeen, and be honest: if Terrangus was under attack, could you truly sit by and do nothing as your home burned? Forgive me for saying this, but I feel David and Melissa only stood aside because their kingdom was the aggressor."

It's not like I could make a difference in such a conflict. I guess being weak has its advantages. "Hmm," Zeen said, rubbing his chin. "It's difficult to imagine Terrangus under siege with such a military force. Honestly, I would…maybe? No. No, I wouldn't break the pact."

She sighed. "It must be easy to say such a thing when you haven't seen the dismembered bodies of people you grew up with. I…did the right thing. Even if I end up executed. Even if my actions start some long, arbitrary domino effect of Guardians influencing political theater. Do such views make me a terrible person? Is that how you see me?"

You're not the only one to suffer through dead friends. Damn, I guess it was silly of me to come down here and expect cheerful banter. There is such a sadness in those blue eyes. "Of course not, Serenna. Actually, if you read the second Rinso the Blue novel, this exact scenario comes up! Rinso raises his blade to the rainy Terrangus skies, then screams out, 'I abdicate the pact!' Rinso then trains with the zephum resistance force to overthrow the Warlord Vehemence. He is treated as an outsider, since he's a human—"

"What the hell are you talking about?" she asked, head cocked to the side.

"You're blowing it, kid!" some random guard behind him yelled. The guards all erupted in laughter as Zeen's face blushed.

"Um," Zeen said, stuttering. "Let me put it this way. I saw some terrible things in war, but nothing was more disturbing than the soldiers who committed atrocities without a moment's hesitation, only to laugh about it later. People like you, the ones that struggle with their morality, I often find those end up being the good ones."

Serenna took another sip of water, then gave him a curious glance. "Oh? Have *you* ever struggled with your morality?"

"Every single day," Zeen said, glancing away. "After spending so much time with Nyfe and the Terrangus military, I strived to be something...different. Better is difficult to define, but different is a reasonable goal. Anything that wasn't them. Guardians had always seemed like true heroes. Neutral defenders of all kingdoms, facing demons and evil gods. War is never that simple. A common theme in the Rinso novels is that each side always views the other as barbaric. But after seeing the God of Death and facing Fear's Harbinger, I know without a shadow of a doubt this is the side of good."

"A comforting thought, but it's difficult to accept your conclusion while I sit here in a prison cell like a common murderer."

Hmm. This conversation had gone much better in his head when he had rehearsed in the bath last night. "You're a good person, Serenna. It may take the realm some time to figure that out, but we'll have you out of here by tonight or tomorrow at the latest. Nyfe is a lot of things, but the man is efficient."

"Listen Zeen, while I am thankful we managed to avoid killing each other in our year-long war, the most likely scenario right now is that I get executed while you and David die up north in Boulom. If that ends up being the case, thank you for believing in me. Kindness is not a trait I often find with your people."

"Of course I believed. You are Serenna Morgan, Guardian of Mylor," Zeen said, trying to meet her eyes. "The Crystal Guardian…a hero. I believed in you years before we ever met." A tingling feeling crept through his chest as his hands gripped her prison bars. Serenna's cut up face and tattered cape and armor did nothing to hide the true beauty of the woman underneath. Long platinum hair; perfect, blue eyes—

Okay, relax.

That proved to be difficult as she met his gaze and didn't shy away. "Well, as of yesterday, you are Zeen Parson, Guardian of Terrangus. Assuming we both make it out of this alive, I would enjoy the chance to continue our strange journey together. Now go, don't leave David waiting—he *really* doesn't like that. Be well, my friend."

Friend! Zeen couldn't imagine how red his face must have turned as the soldiers snickered at her words. He quickly nodded to her, then to Landon before Zeen left towards the trade district.

*

Even with the countless people swarming around, he could spot David a *long* way ahead. Their leader had a unique presence, empowered by the lack of people in the otherwise-crowded kingdom. David wore a large dark coat, and as Zeen approached, he threw him one too. It was too warm to wear something so heavy, but this didn't seem like the day to argue.

Zeen put it on, and almost immediately felt drips of sweat form on his upper back. Where was the rain? It figured Terrangus would have a rare, beautiful day when it was time to leave.

David unexpectedly shook his hand. Well, off to a good start. "Listen, we need to have each other's backs today. Follow Nyfe's lead for as long as it remains convenient, but if this gets ugly, we won't be the ones to die."

That was about as blatant a threat as one can give in soldier talk. Despite the miserable years of serving under Nyfe, Zeen didn't wish the man harm. "Of course, understood. What sort of team are we looking at? I can't imagine it's just the three of us."

"Honestly," David said, "I know next to nothing about our entire mission. What I *do* know is that two things must happen. We prevent Nyfe from getting the Fear artifact and, more importantly, we survive."

David headed towards the outskirts and nodded for Zeen to follow. "Tell me, I've never actually fought with or against Nyfe. Is he as good as the rumors say?"

Zeen smiled. "Well, he wasn't very useful in Mylor, that's for sure." He waited for David to smile back, but nothing happened. "Right. Well, Nyfe is a bit of a wild card. Sometimes, the man is the best fighter I've ever seen. Other days, it's shocking he's still alive; his arrogance makes him far too careless."

"A fair assessment. There is an increasingly large chance this ends with him dead." David stopped. "I need your confirmation that won't be an issue."

Ah, there it is. Guess we're not using subtlety today. "I…would rather not, but I'll follow your command. You know, Nyfe blatantly threatened to kill me in Mylor if I stood between him and Serenna. All things considered, I'm happy she turned to the void. That brief influx of power was the only thing that kept her alive. Is that terrible to say? I'm rambling…"

David *finally* smirked. "I get it. This won't make sense to you now, but I was you once. Enjoy these days, for they are fleeting." He gazed up at the skies, staring intently—at nothing. "Never let her go. Even if she falls to the void, take her by the hand and bring her back. Guardian life is too painful to go it alone."

"Well," Zeen said, rubbing the back of his neck, "after our war in Mylor, I doubt she will ever see me that way. I went down there this morning to clear the air between us, and it got a bit awkward. In front of all Nyfe's soldiers, too. Definitely made a fool of myself."

David let out a heavy laugh, drawing stares from the concerned people in their vicinity. "Ah, Zeen, you really are me... Thank you for not turning down a role in the Guardians. We need you—*I* need you."

Zeen had to remind himself to breathe. *He needs me? The legendary David?* "I... I actually figured you disliked me. I'm nowhere near as powerful as the rest of the team. After meeting everyone else...it's difficult to justify why I'm here."

David embraced him, clutching him with a desperation Zeen had never received from his father. From anyone. "I know dealing with me is difficult, but please be patient. I've lost too many good people. No matter how cold or hard, or whatever empty description people want to use to describe me, that part never gets easier."

Zeen paused, then eased his hands to embrace him back. Today was looking to be an odd day.

"This morning, I asked Melissa to marry me. We're coming back alive. By *any* means necessary. Do you understand? Tell me you understand." David spoke calmly, but with a stern tone that was somehow more intimidating than anytime he had yelled.

Ah, that's why he's such a wreck this morning. "I understand," Zeen said, even though he didn't. "By any means necessary." They let go, then headed towards the outskirts portal together.

*

Maybe it was the coat, but Zeen's sweat spread from his back to his forehead. Terrangus outskirts were usually calm—compared to the city, at least—but the massive crowd around the portal was overwhelming. *How did Nyfe get so many followers? What do people see in this guy?*

David scoffed. "Clever bastard, he's protecting himself. If this crowd sees us go in together, it will be *very* difficult to explain if we come back without him. We don't need this mess with the pact still a sensitive issue."

"Does this change the plan?"

"No. He gets his chance, but if I give the word—Nyfe dies today."

They moved through the mass of people, nudging ecstatic city folk to make a path towards their strike team, which was…nine people?

Well, we're dead.

They all had wrinkly Terrangus uniforms, save for one bald mage with an oak staff and a familiar woman…

Gods, is that Mary? Mary Walker? She was far more…*built* than their time together in the Koulva mines. Her long red hair still flowed down her tanned face while she stood tall—nearly David's height—with her long-sword in one hand and a shield in the other. She wore the standard Terrangus black, but favored chain mail instead of leather. Zeen waved at her, but she turned away. Odd, but still an enormous relief to find another person who had experience against zephum.

And there was Nyfe, grinning at them. "Welcome, Guardians. As you can see, I've put together an elite force; there are no zephum in their entire empire that can stand against us." Zeen couldn't tell if he was joking, but either way, there was no reason to crush the team's confidence.

That would happen the moment they saw their opponents.

David and Nyfe stepped away in private, giving Zeen a

chance to catch up with an old friend. "It's been a while, Mary. How have you been? Who would've thought the two of us would face zephum again."

"Guardians shouldn't be here," Mary said in an icy tone. She'd never spoken that way before. "We finally have a chance to slay some zephum, and the only thing people are wondering is when the Pact Breakers will betray Nyfe. It's an insult to the Terrangus military, the military you swore your life to."

"What? Don't tell me about loyalty," Zeen said, frowning. "I was there in Mylor, fighting a losing battle, even standing against the God of Death. And where were you the past year, Mary?" To his surprise, she grabbed him, pulling him close. Her lean arms revealed through exposed spots in her upper armor. Whatever she'd done since the Koulva mines had made her powerful.

And empty.

"My battle is with the zephum," Mary said, gripping tighter. "The warlord murdered my father in Koulva; this is my only chance for revenge. I know all about your nonsense with Nyfe, so here is your first and final warning. Do not test me, Zeen; I need this. I *need this!*" She let go, then walked over to Nyfe.

It was a dreadful task to meet a lifelong friend for the first time.

David came back to Zeen's side, then cocked his head. "What the hell was that?"

"It doesn't matter," he said, keeping his head down. "The Mary I knew no longer exists."

Nyfe stared at them, that grin still engraved on his face. He drew his dagger, holding it high for the crowd to see. The Herald of Death radiated dark energy, to gasps and awe from the crowd.

"Fellow people of Terrangus!" Nyfe yelled. "I go now into

battle, but take this opportunity to gaze upon my blade. I am fiercer than any god, any Harbinger and, dare I say, any emperor. The Guardians and I will make quick work of our enemies, then return here with the artifact. All glory to Terrangus! All glory to *Nyfe!*"

Zeen grimaced at Nyfe's arrogance as the crowd erupted, and the idea that any reasonable person could find that inspiring. He glanced at the cheering Mary; his final confirmation the woman he'd once known was long gone.

Nyfe went into the portal first, then, one by one, his soldiers followed. David turned to Zeen, who shrugged, then stepped in. He'd arrived here with Serenna in his arms; it was more painful than he had expected to leave without her.

CHAPTER 14

HEAVY SNOW, HEAVY SILENCE

David opened his eyes, sighing in relief despite the unfamiliar terrain as the portal went dim. He would never admit to anyone—particularly Zeen—that portals still made him uneasy. What a fitting end it would have been to have finally given Melissa a ring, just to die in a portal accident the same day. Only one Guardian—Jasmine of Nuum—had ever gone out that way. That had been her reward after a lifetime of service.

A bitter cold replaced the warm breeze from Terrangus; the trees and grass surprisingly vibrant despite the light snow floating from the dead skies. There was a certain...*feeling* here. Not particularly of death, but a lack of life. A *loss* of life. He gripped his coat to make it tighter, accepting a thankful grin from Zeen as he did the same. David had never seen these lands before, but it could only be one place.

The outskirts of Boulom. The fallen kingdom.

"You two," Nyfe said, approaching them. "Let me make this perfectly clear. If for any reason I fall today, my men are instructed to strike you down. Understood?" Nyfe didn't shiver as snow clung to his leather armor. In an odd way, the ominous skies complemented his pale skin.

David put his hand on his sword underneath his coat. Just in case. "We're here for Serenna's safety. Protect her, and you have our loyalty. It's that simple." *This will get ugly once we find the artifact. Zeen and I are likely the only ones coming back. Actually… How can we return without a mage?*

Shit. We'll have to keep this one alive. Hopefully, he can work portals.

Mary scoffed. "You spit on the Guardian Pact as if you were a mercenary, with no regard for honor at all."

Zeen grabbed her and started whispering frantically before she pushed him away. How did such a cheerful boy constantly find himself befriending damaged people?

"And what of you?" David asked, keeping his hand hidden on the sword.

"I'm here to avenge my father. Those zephum beasts murdered him in cold blood."

"Then do not speak to me about honor. By pledging your purpose to vengeance, you have already surrendered to the past."

Mary froze, then drew her sword and pointed it towards David. That single moment of hesitation told him everything. She'd already lost. "This is your only warning, Guardian. If you question my honor again, you will die well before we face our first zephum."

David drew his blade and swung near her face, knocking the sword out of her hand, then held his weapon against her neck. Foolish girl had all the rage in the world, but no awareness. *Same weakness as Pyith. Hmm.*

"If I were a zephum, you would already join your father in the void. Stop grandstanding and be the warrior that I see in your eyes." He sheathed his sword, holding back a smirk at the "I told you so" grin on Zeen's face.

Nyfe snickered. "Well, I don't know about you guys, but I enjoyed being alive. Seems like that's going to end today."

Mary nodded at him, sheathing her sword. That was enough. Pyith had pushed him to strike that fat snout of hers when they had first met, but today, it was a relief to offer guidance without any true violence. *Gods, I'm getting old.*

An uncomfortable silence led the way as they navigated forward. The kingdom was at least ten minutes or so walking distance. Nyfe kept a good formation, leaving the weakest of his team in the back, Mary up front, and the Guardians next to the mage. Basic Terrangus unit strategy. Like the old days. A hint of nostalgia crept through David; gods, that had been so long ago.

Heavier snow swirled down as they progressed. "Ugh," Mary said. "Fucking snow. Is the North always this cold?"

Nyfe chuckled. "That's difficult to answer, considering most people wait until they're dead before going to graveyards."

"Here," Zeen said, taking off his coat, then holding it out for her. "I've always been resistant to the cold. You can have mine."

Mary slapped his arm away. "Fuck your coat."

"Oh!" the mage said, grabbing the coat. "I'll take it!" He threw it on, not giving a second glance—or thank you—at Zeen.

"Great," Mary said, smiling for the first time. "Now you can freeze too." Zeen *would* freeze, but knowing him, it would be worth it to get his old friend to smile—

David's eyes darted to the closest tree. *Something* had moved out of the corner of his eye. He drew his blade and prepared to rush forward, but Nyfe was already sprinting in that direction—towards a lone zephum.

The zephum ran, but Nyfe was *much* faster, tackling the zephum to the ground, then jabbing his blade in its left leg, followed by a non-fatal slash against half its throat. It was odd to see a zephum in leather—most favored heavy chain mail to complement their larger size. This was certainly a scout, and judging by the smaller tail, a young scout. A sudden dread entered David's gut at the zephum's wail; it had been so long since he'd heard that sound…not counting Pyith. *Gods, forgive me for hoping that injury is bad enough to keep her away from here.*

Nyfe grinned as he leaned on the scout. "Zephum scum, how unfortunate that you scouted me. How unfortunate that I cut your throat, watching you suffocate as you cling to your dying life. I can end the pain whenever I choose. Now, where is your squad?"

So, the rumors had been true. Both the one about Nyfe's power *and* lunacy. Zeen had underplayed his cruelty—likely on purpose—to ensure they saved Serenna. Foolish boy…*I would have done the same thing.*

The scout struggled to speak as blood gushed out of his throat. He made sounds but, gods, they were terrible. Even Mary looked squeamish, for all that talk about "vengeance"; she turned away, gazing intently at the pure white snow just a few feet over. The snow became her Melissa, a beautiful distraction amid a violent reality.

"Answer me… I am skilled enough to ensure you live forever. You will lie here in agony as all your dreams crumble, replaced by the illusion of a life where you could have died in peace."

Ugh, I said by any means necessary, but I just cannot condone this.

Enough.

David thrust his sword through the scout's heart, killing him instantly. Whatever came from this decision, so be it. Zeen nodded, drifting his hand towards his blade. The boy had learned quickly.

"*No!*" Nyfe yelled, slamming his fist on the dead scout's chest. "You damned fool; he would have told me everything. We do whatever it takes, no matter the cost. I will *not* warn you again."

David shook his head. "Every cost has its limits. When the debt becomes too high, you lose yourself forever."

As Nyfe grabbed his blade and approached, Zeen drew his sword and stepped back. He glanced over at David, well trained in waiting for his leader's signal. That signal wasn't coming. They could beat Nyfe. They could *probably* beat Mary and Nyfe.

In no scenario could they ever beat them all.

"Everyone…" David said, searching for a calm tone that never came naturally. "Stand down. Nyfe, no torture tactics. Otherwise, we're still on the same page. Let's relax and keep our composure; it doesn't have to be this way."

"I suppose I can't blame you for being ignorant," Nyfe said, still clutching his blade. "Wait until our first skirmish. When you see what those beasts do to our people, then we can revisit your morality of war."

Heavy snow. Heavy silence.

After a long pause, with everyone's eyes darting around to each other as they took their hands off their weapons, the team restarted their march to Boulom. To break the awkward tension, David approached Nyfe.

"Nyfe, I'm curious, what is your weapon and how did you manage to get a hold of it? I have never seen such a thing in all my days."

"This old thing?" Nyfe smiled, twirling his dagger. "It's just the Herald of Death. No big deal, I suppose."

David scoffed. "Yes, but…why you?"

"Long story short, I hail from a long line of Death priests from Nuum," Nyfe said, his gaze lost in the blade. "Death crafted the weapon as a gift several generations ago, mostly as a joke that anyone would waste their time worshipping him when all he wants to do is destroy us. My parents fled the kingdom after our second Harbinger in the same year; by that point, it became apparent nothing was ever going to change. Terrangus...wasn't exactly welcoming. I'm the only one left."

David had never seen such a pale man from the sun-kissed kingdom of Nuum. Was it a lie? If not, that dagger had taken a *harsh* toll on the man's features. *Maybe I shouldn't be seeking this artifact...*

"Ah, I've heard of that; it was the only time Fear ever hit a kingdom twice in the same year. I never understood why Nuum has so many Harbingers. Francis's theory claims that the heat makes people desperate."

Nyfe snickered. "The truth is more interesting. The people of Nuum are insufferable; many of them relentlessly dabble in time magic, even though the results are always the same. At least Death is an entity that will reveal himself. The Time God...no one knows anything about it. I bet even Francis doesn't know this, but Death fears it too. Successfully casting time magic creates alternate parallels...or something, causing Time great pain. Death stopped caring, so Fear is specifically charged with preventing any time magic in our realm."

Interesting, is that why she usually targets mages? What does she want from me?

"Remarkable. In all my years as a Guardian, I have never even heard the Time God get mentioned. The idea of anything intimidating Death is...difficult to comprehend. I only saw it once, and I cannot fathom how we have survived for this long."

There was no point in hiding the distress in his voice. It actually had been at Xavian, right near the end of his first Harbinger. Death had come down, blackening the entire sea with its presence. It had just laughed. Even though it had lost, all it did was laugh.

David had learned that day the purpose of the Guardians was only to delay the inevitable.

"Death isn't so bad once you get over the fact it's a deranged entity who has completely lost touch with mortal life. My dagger gives me a connection, though it's very rare that we have an actual conversation. I normally just hear laughs and screams. Honestly, I wasn't able to sleep much in the first few years; you have to teach yourself to grow numb to the violence or it all becomes too much."

David nodded. "I understand the necessity to grow numb; it's a path I've traveled myself. There is an obvious strategical use for torture, but at what cost?"

"Hmm. Decades of Guardian life have made you forget the horrors of facing fellow mortals. As bad as the gods are, we believe we're better. It's the ultimate delusion; it's what my parents and their parents understood about this realm and our role in it. Nothing we do matters; we are free to seek glory, power, or even nothing. Our choices have no consequences in the long term; we are playthings to the gods. Once you realize that, you are truly free."

Odd, how broken men found different ways of coping with their flaws. David had his wine, and Nyfe had his grand delusions. Considering the constant grin on Nyfe's face, David was nearly envious of how well Nyfe lied to himself.

"It's too bad you have such a violent outlook," David said as he smirked. "Your skill suggests you could have been an excellent Guardian in a different life."

"Sorry, but Guardian life is a hard pass for me. I'll leave that nonsense to those of you worried about honor and obscure labels of morality—"

"*To arms!*" Mary yelled out.

Everyone froze. There was a small group of six zephum in

the distance, all covered in blood, moving sluggishly towards them.

"They appear injured; what happened?" Zeen asked.

Nyfe laughed. "Well, you won't let me interrogate them, so hopefully we can find out from observing their corpses. Come, let's not waste this advantage." He moved to the front, standing next to Mary, pausing before he nodded ahead. "Go," he whispered.

Mary held her sword and shield out in front of her, charging at the zephum while the rest of Nyfe's team followed closely behind. The zephum drew their massive weapons and roared, with one falling to one knee. They were already completely out of breath.

If we're the only humans here…

They faced demons.

Mary slammed her shield into the lead zephum's face, then thrust her sword through its neck as it flinched back from the crash. Zeen put his hand to his sword, then looked over for confirmation.

"Hold," David said. "They're already defeated; I won't involve us in a slaughter. Let these bloodthirsty soldiers get some 'honor.'"

Zeen did a quick glance at the violence before gazing into the snow. "Thank you. I saw too much of this in the mines and Mylor. The things we did… I hate this side of war."

"Is there a side of war you don't hate?"

"I suppose…when it's over. Even though it's always temporary, I enjoy the illusion it won't happen again. I did some terrible things in those days. Serenna would never speak to me if she saw a glimpse of my past."

David put his hand on Zeen's shoulder. It had been a while since he had to console someone; a guilty part of him was relieved the boy had a violent side. *If he could change, so could I...*

"I wouldn't worry about that, Zeen. Serenna knows the reality of war better than either of us."

"Yeah, but she's so...honest about it, like it's an acceptable part of herself. At what point do future good deeds fix past mistakes? I still haven't gotten over the Harbinger telling me I 'will die alone, hated and miserable.' Is that fate inevitable? Am I doomed?"

"Do not despair, my friend," David said, patting him before letting go. "That will be my fate—not yours." He planned on waiting for later, but heart-to-heart talks should never be done sober. He grabbed his first flask tucked away in his right pocket, then took a swig of the zephum ale, only then realizing the irony. Oh, what a burn to his throat; it lacked anything that resembled sweetness. Zephum ale had one purpose: to kill your feelings. "Here," he said, handing the flask to Zeen, who took a larger swig than expected. It wasn't his first time. Interesting.

Nyfe's team made quick work of the remaining zephum. Zeen wouldn't watch, so David did. Leadership meant accepting the violence. Leadership meant accepting happiness wasn't for everyone. Nyfe drifted towards the last one alive.

"Terrangus warriors, we accept this death with honor," the zephum said as it looked up towards Nyfe. "Heed this warning: do not enter the ruins. Demons run rampant, and the warlord himself—"

Nyfe interrupted him, slamming his blade right through the side of the zephum's neck.

"Such meaningless cruelty," David said, sighing.

"Hey, you said no torture tactics," Nyfe said as he laughed. "The poor zephum was clearly in pain. I need some consistency with your demands; I'm trying to be diplomatic."

Waste of life. No one will mourn you after you're gone.

Mary glared at Nyfe. "I wish you would've let him finish; he was saying something about the warlord. Regardless, we are off to an impressive start, but why exactly are there demons here?"

"This is where it all began," David said, gazing into the ruins. "Boulom was the first empire, a peaceful paradise. Powerful, but with no knowledge of Harbingers. When the first one appeared...there was nothing to stop it; the massive size of Boulom's army only made the monster stronger. They couldn't defeat the Harbinger until much later, when the kingdoms we know today stood together and made the very first Guardian team."

David smiled. "That team was the first six. The current zephum God of Strength was their leader; a monumental warlord that stood against oblivion and won. He was made a god after he died, and guides the current warlord to this day."

Mary paused, gazing up into the ruins. "I'm sorry we got off to a poor start. Being here must be of great significance to you."

"Perhaps, if circumstances were different, but Guardians have no reason to come here. You can't save that which is already lost. These ruins...are a painful reminder of what is to come if we ever fail."

CHAPTER 15

FALLING, FALLING, ALWAYS FALLING

Melissa Euhno stood alone in the Terrangus Guardian room, studying the diamond on her engagement ring. It had only been a few hours since David had left for Boulom, but gods, it could have been years. Who proposes like that? Seriously? She sighed. That's just how it was with her David. If her parents could speak from the void...*oh,* would she get a scolding. *Never love a man who doesn't love himself,* her mother's voice rang through her thoughts.

It was too late. She did. She always did.

If she could accomplish anything, it would be to convince David of that, too. The drained look in his eyes after they'd embraced...it hurt her in ways he couldn't understand. Falling. Always falling. She'd defeated demons, Harbingers, all sorts of things in her forty-two years. She'd never managed to defeat his despair.

But she would *never* stop trying.

Too much to do. It always felt like there was more; that it was never over. Falling. Always falling. Everyone needed help. Everyone suffered. She would comfort Serenna later when the halls were less busy, then wait until David and Zeen returned. *If* they returned.

Stop it. You aren't allowed to think that way.

Grayson deserved a visit as well, but she wasn't ready for that. He'd blatantly threatened her life. Grayson! After everything! Everyone pointed his downfall at Vanessa's death, but they were missing the big picture. Once Empress Madelyn Forsythe had succumbed to despair after losing their daughter, that had been the man's true end. When the heart dies, the mind and body have no choice but to follow. Too much loss had broken the man; that had terrified her in ways she could only hide inside. Serenna was falling. David was falling. The rest seemed okay…but Melissa? Falling. Always falling.

And they would never see her that way.

The Guardian portal flickered. *Francis? Who else could it be? Gods, please don't be Pyith…* The shape forming couldn't be human…but it wasn't zephum, either. *What in the realm?* It materialized into a floating sun mask, with the red and black cape draped behind it.

By instinct, her hand moved to a fire-detonator on her belt, but she stopped herself. Wisdom wasn't her enemy. Hopefully. "Wisdom? What are you doing here?"

"I must say, it troubles me that I'm never greeted with a hello. No one other than Francis seems to appreciate all the good I do for the realm."

"In all my years, you never saw fit to say hello to me either."

"My dear Melissa, I *do* say hello, it's just not always in words."

She sighed unintentionally. Francis had always found the cryptic nonsense from the floating deity enthralling…but there was something *terrible* about this one. What were his intentions? Why did every kingdom he advise suffer chaos? All the signs were there. All the signs were ignored.

"I'll keep that in mind for the future. Wisdom, do you have news for me? Has something happened up north already?"

Wisdom chuckled. "Oh yes, it's been quite intriguing to watch, but I'll quell your greatest fear since you hold my respect. Your David is alive and well. The underwhelming one too; it's difficult to remember his name."

"Thank you...all things considered, that is comforting news."

"I wouldn't thank me just yet." It took a master of lies to appear smug with a mask. A fake visibility—the idea that if you saw something, it was enough. But there was nothing *truly* there.

"So be it. Whatever burdens you choose to lay at my feet...I'm ready."

"*Choose?* What an interesting word that one is. I am here regarding your Serenna. The husk of Grayson lied to you; he is preparing to kill her today."

No... Dammit all, why today? Heat rushed to her face. A kingdom ruler executing a Guardian would be *madness.* "I don't understand; we were supposed to have a week."

"Consider this," Wisdom said, floating around her. "With Pyith injured and David and Zeen stuck up north, he can kill her with minimal resistance. *Very* minimal."

"Francis. I need to contact Francis."

"My dear Melissa, Francis isn't coming, so it seems you must make a choice. Grayson has already chosen a mistake. Will you meet his mistake with a mistake of your own? Can you even tell the difference? Oh! Perhaps I should've been more specific. When I said, 'preparing to kill her,' I meant preparing to kill her *now.*"

She took a handful of elemental-detonators off the table and placed them on her belt. "We'll see about that."

"Oh yes, we will indeed. Ah, freewill. The chaos it spawns…" Wisdom went invisible, but she could still feel his presence. It was all just a joke to him.

A deep pain—like a cut—filled her chest. That happened more frequently now; she wouldn't dare tell David. Or anyone. Falling. Always falling. The girl she loved as a daughter needed her, and consequences be damned, Serenna wouldn't be the one to die today. She rushed out the door, and Forsythe was right outside, accompanied by his usual pack of guards in red mail. Wisdom's words had been true. She wished they weren't.

"*Grayson!*" she yelled out. Everyone in the grand halls before the throne room turned to her in shock. Just as she hoped. The larger the spectacle, the lesser the chance of violence. This scenario in the hallways was *perfect*. Perhaps Wisdom was a true ally? *Let's not go too far…*

Grayson smiled. A fake, political smile. The way his left eye twitched screamed alarm. "Ah, Lady Euhno. A pleasure to see you this afternoon. Why are you yelling?"

"Is it true?" she asked, not expecting any sort of actual answer. If he lied his way out and backed off, that would still be a victory.

"Indeed," he said, losing his smile and staring into her with cold, dead eyes. "Remind me to thank Wisdom for again plotting against me."

"Grayson, there must be a better way; I cannot allow you to kill Serenna."

"*Allow?*" he yelled, his voice echoing through the open halls. "You cannot allow me? Have you completely forgotten who I am?"

"I remember who you *were*. It's not too late to be that man again."

Grayson made a motion to his guard unit, who drew their swords.

She fought the instinct of reaching for any of her several weapons. Not yet. That would be the point of no return.

The six guards approached.

Gods, it was happening. "You would truly do this? I *will* defend myself."

"And I would expect no less. Guards, apprehend her. Use violence if necessary, but keep her alive."

Swords on her side, daggers by her legs, detonators sorted in elemental order on her belt. The key to combat was simple: have more ways to kill your opponent than they had ways to defend themselves. She grabbed a fire-detonator off her belt and stepped back. The first and only warning. Anyone from Terrangus should know better. They had all feared David, but *she* was the mechanist. Not born with enough magical amplitude to be an elemental mage, but *just* enough to trigger elemental-detonators with her mind. It took a rare balance; eager mages who had tried blew themselves up using too much energy.

Her detonator glowed red in her hands, yet they kept approaching. Out of duty? Fear of Grayson? *So be it. As David likes to say, show me your violence.* She threw the detonator in the middle of the guard cluster, then closed her eyes.

Fire.

The detonator erupted, knocking two less fortunate guards flying back. Surely, that would be enough? She chose fire on purpose; the spectacle of violence had normally sent even the most arrogant of men to their knees. And yet... They *kept* approaching.

I'm sorry, Melissa thought, drawing a smaller sword in each hand, then slaying the closest guard with a quick slice to the throat. No joy came from his death, but six against one was not the sort of fight to use mercy. That offer was long gone.

Falling. Always falling.

The second guard swung at her neck, seemingly unconcerned with the emperor's order to take her alive. She ducked and took another fire-detonator from her belt, then pulled the guard close and shoved the detonator into the lower gap in his mail armor. She dodged a quick thrust towards her center from another guard, then kicked that one straight in the chest with her right boot. The stumbling guard fell into the loaded one, who screamed for him to get away. He wouldn't. *I'm so sorry...*

Fire.

Blood and...parts scattered in all directions. Despite the brutal nightmare, onlookers cheered. What a sad thing, to worship violence. Ironic, considering they hated Serenna for the same reason. The two remaining guards clutched their swords and took a step back. They knew their fate, and she would give it to them.

She drifted towards them, holding a blade in one hand and a glowing blue ice-detonator in the other. Melissa dashed forward with a quick spin, then slammed her sword into the first guard's neck. Without looking, she threw her ice-detonator where the second—now final—guard would be.

Ice.

The detonator erupted on his sword, freezing it as he prepared to swing down. She drew her second sword, parrying the guard's iced blade as it shattered on contact. She took the blunt end of her sword handle and jabbed the guard in his head, knocking him unconscious. Never go all the way if avoidable. It was the vague—but ever important—line between murderers like Nyfe and Guardians like Melissa.

She glared at Grayson. "Emperor, it's not too late. We can go back to the throne room and work this out."

"No...it's *far* too late now. None may threaten the

emperor and live." Grayson drew his two-handed sword with the golden hilt and began his approach.

"Foolishness," she said, shaking her head. Madness. Ten, maybe fifteen years ago, she may have lost. The Grayson of old had been a tyrant of battle, one of the few men taller than her David. He'd been Terrangus personified: powerful, loud, reckless. Now, it would be merciful to give him an end.

Grayson raised his sword high in the air with both hands, then slammed it down. In that brief moment—with the blade held high—a shadow of the shadow he was now flickered in the cold castle halls.

She parried with both swords, shuffling her feet to keep balance. Despite the atrophy of his muscles, gods did the man have technique. She pushed his sword back, then hopped backwards and grabbed an ice-detonator. It glowed blue in her hand; if she could break his weapon, maybe that would force him to stand down.

"No!" he yelled, spiking his sword into the floor. "There will be no gadgets in this duel. We battle as warriors."

The crowd murmured, most nodding in agreement. *Dammit, I can't lose the crowd.* She hesitated before placing the detonator back on her belt. "Very well, I accept your terms." *End it quickly.* She rushed in with the same spin move that took out the earlier guard, aiming at his upper chest to ensure it wasn't fatal. He stepped back, dodging much faster than his fragile frame should've allowed, then swung at her head— barely missing as she flinched back.

She calmed her breathing, holding back tears. *He's aiming to kill me. Grayson would truly kill me... How did we get to this point?*

Falling. Always falling.

"The same move?" he asked with a smile, this time a real

one. "You will find I am far more observant than you give me credit for."

"Noted...*prepare yourself.*" Enough weakness. She had expected there was still a *faint* hint of kinship between them, but those decades together with David and the Forsythe family may as well never have happened. He'd made it clear he was prepared to kill her.

Now, she would do the same.

She rushed forward, then made a cross slash with both blades aimed at the emperor's neck. Dodge, parry, or die. His well-positioned sword saved a fatal strike, but he groaned as she pressed him back. The crooked angle was cruel; it forced him to rely on arm muscles he probably hadn't used in years. She disengaged the parry, then slashed towards his open shoulder, opening a significant gash that caused blood to shoot out as the crowd gasped.

The emperor placed his hand on the blow, observing the blood, then looked over to Melissa. Any reasonable man would have surrendered after such a wound. "Damn you," he whispered, charging back in and swinging his sword wildly with an embarrassing lack of finesse. A battle strategy she had taught David. Enrage them, dodge their reckless flurry...then kill them. Funny, most people had assumed it was David's strategy. He'd been...*slow* to correct anyone who praised him.

A two-handed strike with all his weight behind it took him off balance, then she used the opening to slice his other shoulder. He cried out in pain, falling to one knee before again rising.

"My offer of diplomacy still stands," she said. It would be absurd to continue; if any battle-savvy part of his mind remained, he would know she held back from finishing him.

Instead, he rushed back in, swinging with less finesse and more desperation. She dodged three strikes before deciding it was enough, then slashed his right leg, opening a wide laceration.

Letting out a wail, the emperor grabbed the leg and collapsed to the ground, to the gasps and moans of the onlookers. Melissa picked up his sword, then threw it far behind him. It was over. Ah, if only Serenna could have watched…

"I played right into Wisdom's hands," he whispered, struggling to speak. "Damn you, Melissa…you haven't lost a step in ten years. If only I could be so lucky."

After all the pain he'd caused in his later years as emperor, she took a deep breath and pushed down the urge to slice his throat. She still valued the Guardian Pact, despite Serenna, despite David and Zeen going north, despite…well, this. There was a better solution, one that didn't involve plunging the largest kingdom into a civil war for its next emperor. That day would come soon enough.

Damn you for everything. She reached her hand out to help him stand. He cocked his head, hesitated, then accepted. "Well fought, Emperor. Next time, don't be courteous enough to allow my victory."

The onlookers cheered as she raised his hand with hers. "All glory to Terrangus!" she yelled out to the crowd, offering them a smile. A fake, political smile—one she had learned from the best.

Hmm, Wisdom really helped us out today. Maybe his time with Francis is making him an ally? Maybe he always favored us? Maybe—

A sharp blade pierced her neck, numbing her entire body as she crumbled against her will. Grayson tore out the tiny dagger, with blood dripping down the hilt. She tried to scream, but nothing happened. All the problems of her Guardian family let go at once, leaving Melissa to wonder why there was no pain. There was no anything. In that fleeting moment of pure nothing, she saw the world through the eyes of her almost-husband. Falling. Falling. Always falling.

She'd never considered what would happen if she stopped.

CHAPTER 16

ONE ACT OF DEFIANCE

Zeen stepped into the fallen kingdom of Boulom, snow blowing into his uncovered face. He shivered and if anyone asked, it was because of the cold and not the sinking feeling in his lower stomach. Ruinous terrain of broken, unfamiliar buildings and whatever those gray rocks were laid out as far as his eyes could see, illuminated by the cloudless, white sky that burned his eyes if he stared too long. He'd always wondered what Terrangus would look like if a Harbinger won. Well, he got his answer.

Ruins. Dead history of a dead people.

Rinso had actually come this way in the second novel, meeting the mysterious Hyphermlo—however the hell that was pronounced—to train as a swordsman to battle the zephum forces of the usurper Warlord Vehemence. It had been revealed at the end that Hyphermlo and Vehemence were brothers! Younger Zeen had to put the book down and step outside, standing alone in the chilly Terrangus rain as he took a deep breath. Those had been simpler days...

"We shouldn't be here," he said, louder than intended.

David walked up beside him at the back of Nyfe's team.

After the standoff, they'd agreed that exposing their backs would not be wise. "I feel it too. We are the first Guardians to enter this land in quite some time. There is an emptiness here."

Nyfe turned to them from ahead. "The death of this place gives me such a *rush*. This is it, boys. Remember, we all live, or we all die. I don't need to tell you which outcome is better, so let's keep it tight and stop fucking around."

"Any idea where this artifact is?" Mary asked, drawing her sword and shield. "I imagine we just keep heading towards the center until we find it."

"Our spy unit claimed it should be in some priest's hall near the capitol," Nyfe said, caressing his dagger. "That information was stolen from the zephum empire, so there is a fair chance we won't get there first."

What? That doesn't make any sense. Something is off about this…am I being paranoid?

Mary grinned. "Good. Hopefully, they already found it, and we can just kill them and take it back."

"It's never that easy," Nyfe said, matching her grin, "but I appreciate your mindless optimism. Maybe you can teach these two to smile; Zeen's been a mess since he got here. Do you miss your Serenna? She's in good hands; I'm offended you still don't trust me after all these years. Is it because of the scar?"

Zeen's face grew warm. "Nyfe, I swear—"

Everyone froze as hissing filled the air. Zeen shivered again; these poor soldiers had no idea what awaited them. He had spent so long worrying about facing zephum that he hadn't considered the more dangerous opponents. The opponents that had nearly killed him two days ago.

"What the hell is that sound?" the mage asked, shaking, despite Zeen's heavy coat. Zeen still waited for a thank you.

"Stay close, my friend. David and I will protect you. What is your name?" In his experience, asking simple questions like name or age was an efficient way to calm soldiers in battle.

"Jeffrey," he said, grasping his staff and covering himself—and only himself—in a crystal shield.

Did Mylor's tactic of shaving all the men's heads to hide their magic class spread to Terrangus? Maybe he was just naturally bald... "Welcome, Jeff. You're a crystal mage? Don't see too many of those from Terrangus."

"Um...yes. Nyfe promised to cover my gambling debts if I aided him, but I think I'm way out of my league here."

Great...

Before Zeen could respond, he drew Intrepid as a crawler made its way behind Jeff. This crawler was pure white; it was only by luck—and maybe paranoia—that he noticed the slithering movement that blended into their surroundings. Crawlers could change? That would have been good to know earlier...

The crawler jumped in the air and screamed, startling most of the team while Zeen charged in and slashed at its neck. The demon stumbled back screeching, then launched a counterstrike that mirrored the patterns of the several he had faced in Terrangus. At least their behavior didn't shift with their appearance. He dodged the crawler's bladed arm, then lunged his sword through its chest while it was vulnerable. Even though its eyes remained wide open, silence was the best indicator it was dead. *Whew, I'm getting better at this.*

"Is everyone alright?" he asked, making sure all twelve were still there. The hissing dimmed, but didn't fade entirely.

"What the *hell* was that?" Jeff yelled, taking quick breaths on his knees within his crystal shield.

"That was a crawler," Zeen said, channeling the calm tone from his Mylor days. "Leave them to us; we will protect you against any of the demons in these ruins. You handled yourself well. I was just as scared as you the first time I saw one. Everything will be okay."

"No… I need to get out of here!"

Nyfe drew his blade and approached. "Shut up, you damned fool. Your whining will alert every hostile force in the area."

Mary took a deep breath. "Too late."

Oh no…

Ahead was a far more formidable zephum unit than the injured team from the outskirts. Zeen counted seven, fully armored, covered in blood, with no visible injuries. The largest zephum made his way forward, drawing a two-handed axe nearly the size of Zeen.

"Human, your assault on the crawler was impressive. You have my word, I will speak honorably of you when I tell the story of today. Prepare yourselves and may the stronger of our teams find glory."

Nyfe smiled. "I haven't killed one of these things in *years*."

"Jeff," David said, then took a *large* swig of his flask. "Cast crystal shields on Mary; we will handle the rest. Keep her alive long enough for us to flank their commander."

Jeff froze before casting a shield *only* on himself, then ran to the back of the team.

"Useless," Mary said, sighing. "Don't worry, Zeen. I'm a lot stronger than you remember. I bet I kill more of them than you do."

Zeen didn't respond, alarmed at Mary's lack of fear in what could be a losing battle. He nodded at David; they both agreed without words that their best strategy would be to split, hopefully preventing either side from being overwhelmed. David—bless him—stayed on Nyfe's side.

The zephum commander roared, causing his full unit to roar, then they charged the Terrangus squad.

Mary grabbed her shield with both hands then rushed *directly* at the zephum commander. The commander slammed his axe down, crashing against the center of her steel shield. Back straight, legs spaced wide, her technique was still as perfect as their Koulva days. One rather large issue, though—she had no way of countering. Trying to block with one hand would likely crack her arm in two.

Zeen couldn't focus on aiding Mary; she was far more skilled than the random soldiers Nyfe had hired to fill his unit. He drew Intrepid and engaged the closest zephum, a brutish warrior with a long polearm and tattered mail armor. At seventeen, Zeen had cried the first time he saw one up close in the Koulva mines. How could anyone stand against such…giant lizard men? Their snouts and long, green tails had made him feel so tiny. Not today; that couldn't happen while Serenna depended on him. Younger Zeen had only survived.

Guardian Zeen would be a hero of Terrangus.

The zephum lunged towards him before Zeen parried and stepped back, *carefully* treading his steps in the slippery snow. They still wore the same bizarre armor design from seven years ago: tan colored chained steel, with *so* many exposed spots on the arms and even neck area. Zeen flinched as blood splattered onto his armor; the poor man to his left took an axe *straight* through his head. He preferred to use speed and counters against larger opponents, but there wasn't enough time to fight on his terms. His team would all be dead in minutes.

Here we go.

Zeen charged in, his attention not on the polearm, but the warrior's arms to gauge his next move. The arms extended forward—the attack was coming towards his chest. The warrior lunged, then Zeen swung Intrepid down on the polearm, breaking it in half as he closed the gap. He made a swift strike for the zephum's neck, but the zephum flung his arm up, taking the brunt of the blade on his now heavily-bleeding arm as Zeen stumbled back.

The zephum wiped his torn arm across his reptilian face, roaring as the blood trickled down. He grabbed the sharp half of the broken polearm, making his way towards Zeen.

You can't intimidate me. Not while I hold Intrepid.

The zephum held the broken polearm with one hand, swinging it at Zeen as if it were a sword. Zeen dodged them all, zoning in on how to target the neck. No matter how large—or loud—an opponent, slicing the neck would end anything mortal. Even zephum were no exception.

The arms…watch the arms…

There. With both hands on his half-spear, the zephum lunged forward, stumbling off balance as his front leg slipped forward on the snow. Zeen spun, taking a slight graze against his side before executing a perfect slash across the zephum's neck. His adrenaline blocked the pain; *oh* would that hurt tomorrow.

"No!" the commander yelled, his eyes burning through Zeen as his ally collapsed. He flailed his axe at Mary's shield with a frightening strength that knocked her off balance and tumbling into the snow. Instead of finishing her, he marched straight for Zeen. Chest out, legs back, Zeen entered his battle stance, clutched Intrepid—

A thunderous roar went off and everyone stepped back and froze. That sound did *not* come from a zephum. A chill filled Zeen as he met David's wide eyes, the ruins shaking as thuds closed in on them. A colossal crashed through the rubble, launching one of the fallen buildings behind the few still alive on Nyfe's team. Maybe he couldn't remember correctly, but this one appeared *much* larger than the one in Terrangus.

"By the gods…" Mary said, stumbling as she rose.

Both units separated and regrouped by their allies, willing

to let the skirmish wait while the demons closed in on them. Aside from the monstrous roar, hissing again filled the air, nearly as loud as before the Harbinger in Terrangus. Even Nyfe lost his grin, which was somehow one of the most unsettling things Zeen had ever seen.

"Well, Guardians," Nyfe said, clutching his dagger. "You can kill that…right?"

A new zephum unit approached from the north, led by a monstrous figure in full metallic armor with a long black cape. The face was hidden under a steel guard that covered the entire snout. It was difficult to tell from a distance, but it could have been *two* feet taller than David. The zephum drew a two-handed sword that made the commander's axe look like a wooden toy.

"What a pity!" the zephum said. "I was observing the battle until these miserable demons appeared. These…*things* have no honor. Terrangus warriors, our skirmish is on hold until the battlefield is once again pure."

All the zephum soldiers behind him kneeled as the large one approached, followed by the commander's unit as he got closer. *What the hell is going on?* Zeen turned to meet David's eyes, instead finding his leader frozen with his mouth wide open. Mary had the same expression. Nyfe…grinned at the godlike being with that murderous gaze Zeen knew all too well.

Whoever it was charged the demon by himself. The colossal came down with a crushing blow, but the zephum blocked it with his right arm, letting out a roar as he fixed his footing. He then swung his sword across, instantly removing the colossal's right leg as it fell to one knee. After a pause, the zephum jumped high in the air, then slammed his sword with both hands through the demon's head, splitting it in two.

The taps of crawlers scuttering away replaced the hissing. For a moment, there was pure silence, other than the howling winds. Gods, it was cold. That damn mage had taken his coat and done *nothing* to help.

The zephum leader gazed directly at David, then removed his steel plated face guard. "David? Why are you here? My precious Pyith returns home injured, and now I find you slaying my people? What lunacy has befallen you?"

"Warlord Sardonyx," David said, kneeling before him. "You have my sincere apologies. Terrangus has fallen to dark times; we are here under protest to protect Crystal Guardian Serenna."

Wow, David kneeling? I can't wait to tell Melissa. Warlords were always written as villains in the Rinso Saga. Warmongers towering above humans and other zephum alike, speaking with a rather...undignified dialogue. He had assumed whoever wrote the books had a deep hatred for zephum culture. Gazing upon the warlord, maybe the author had a deep fear instead.

"Indeed! When my Pyith informed me of your human lord's disrespect, I came here personally to slay every human that dared come. To insult my useless son is one matter, but I will rip the spine out of any living being that refuses Pyith the proper honor."

Mary broke rank, marching towards Sardonyx with shield and sword drawn. "You murdered my father, Warlord. Now, I demand you face me; I will make these ruins your grave." She tilted her neck to stare up at him with cold, unyielding eyes. Zeen's old friend had clearly gone insane.

"Child, I have slain countless fathers," Sardonyx said with a laugh. "Impressive! Most of your kind flee in my presence. To challenge me is a bold choice! May the God of Strength smile upon you in the Great Plains in the Sky."

She took a few steps back, then placed her legs wide in a defensive stance, with her shield in one hand and sword in the other. If she could barely block the commander with both hands, this was lunacy.

"Mary—"

David ripped Zeen back mid-sentence. "Do not speak. Do not do anything. We're getting out of here at the first opportunity. Any mistake could lead to open war with Vaynex."

"She's going to die…"

"Right now, we're probably all going to die. That *thing* could kill our entire unit by himself. Let me do the speaking. Please, Zeen. I want to go home. I finally have something to go back to…"

There was nothing to say to that. Zeen nodded and kept his distance.

Sardonyx approached Mary, each step of his giant frame sinking into the soft snow. He drew his blade, then swung across, as if he were aiming for her shield.

Technically, she blocked, but the force sent her flying several feet backwards as a clang of steel striking steel filled the air.

Mary let out a pained groan, stood up, then threw her sword to the ground. Blood trailed down her face, dripping red on the stained snow. She rushed forward with both hands on the shield. Sardonyx swung again, likely expecting the same result. Instead of flying backwards, she got pushed back, but remained standing. She charged again, and as the warlord swung down, she dodged, then rammed her shield into his exposed face. Everyone—Nyfe included—gasped at the hit. Even Mary stood there stunned, not making any attempt to follow through. Maybe that one act of defiance was all she had wanted.

The warlord ripped the shield out of her hand, then pounded it into her face. A tooth came out, but Zeen lost track of it in the bright white surroundings. Sardonyx picked her up with one hand, then *smiled*. "Well fought, human! I apologize for the death of your father. He raised you into an honorable young woman. You remind me of my son's life-mate, and that is the greatest compliment I have ever given your kind." He pulled her close, now with both hands. "*Strength without honor—is chaos.*"

The zephum soldiers rose after those words, then cheered for their warlord. Sardonyx threw Mary to the snow by David as if she were weightless, then studied them. "Any other humans care to try? I am invigorated after facing...oh, I never caught her name!" He leaned back and let out a grand laugh.

David shot Nyfe a murderous stare. "Are the zephum after the Fear artifact too? Is it even here?"

Nyfe's smile grew, never taking his eyes off the warlord. "The hell if I know, but I couldn't think of a better way to ensure your cooperation. I hope all that drinking numbs the pain, because it's certainly numbing your senses. I'm close...so *close* to taking control."

"How did you know the mantra?"

"Death speaks to me... I know them all. I could be the only man alive that knows Wisdom's mantra. Oh, is it *vile*." Nyfe clutched his dagger and approached the warlord, who hadn't acknowledged him yet.

"It's alright," Zeen said. "Last time I watched Nyfe pull something like this, he got thrown out a window."

David grabbed the flask from his coat pocket. "Fuck him; he's a dead man. Whatever happens next, do not intervene. We're on our own from here on out."

CHAPTER 17

DON'T RESPOND

Serenna rose from her hard bed to lean back and stretch. Landon would arrive with her lunch soon; he had been gone far longer than usual. Meals were the only way to gauge time and break the boredom. A rather…odd turn of events after a year at war. Oh well, David would have her out soon enough, and then she could finally grasp the Wings of Mylor again. The pale owl's gaze stalked her impatiently from across her cell…

A gentle, yet frigid, breeze caressed her face.

"Serenna…Serenna, Serenna."

She shivered, and damn Nyfe's soldiers if they watched. That voice hadn't assaulted her thoughts since yesterday; the morning in her cell had nearly been tolerable because of the silence.

"Where is your pain? You must not know."

Know what? She wouldn't dare respond, but trying to remain calm made her heart pound faster. Something terrible must have happened to Zeen. Or her father? *Don't respond. Don't respond. Don't respond.*

"Ah… I love your defiance. So much more fun when they

think they can resist. The only answer you need are my words. I am nothing. I am forever. I am the end. Say it...

"*SAY IT!*"

She fell to her knees, feeling the weight of the room collapse on her. "No," she whispered, her eyes watering. She had been foolish enough to believe maybe she was free after just one morning. That was a fool's hope. She would never be free.

"Serenna?" Landon's voice. Thank the gods. "I'm so sorry...who told you?"

A pounding migraine pressed the upper right side of her skull until tears trickled down her cheek. Zeen was dead. She didn't need the words to know. There had been so much to tell him before he left...

"I'm so sorry," Landon said gently, sounding like her father. "I know what she meant to you."

She? The pressure in her head tightened, but Serenna rose and clutched the bars. "What did you just say?"

Landon stared straight down. "Um, forgive me; I assumed you were crying for Melissa. The emperor murdered her less than an hour ago. It's a *mess* up there."

The world went mute as her legs lost their strength. She fell into a sitting position on her bed, smacking the back of her head against the wall. There was no pain—even the migraine went away. Everything went away. Serenna sat alone, tears flowing in remembrance of the woman who had become a second mother.

Terrangus had killed their greatest Guardian. For *nothing.* Serenna was the only one that could properly avenge her; all it would take were a few words...

"*Serenna...Serenna, Serenna. Melissa died a terrible death. Butchered in the Terrangus halls by Grayson. Kill him. Kill them all. Everything you love crumbles...You have nothing left to lose.*"

I could kill them all, she thought. *And I would be right.*

"Just…a taste?" Determination faded to numbness. The words came out so easily.

"*No. Time binds me to speak the truth. If you accept my offer…you are mine forever.*"

She closed her eyes, welcoming the darkness as she took a deep breath. Breaking the Guardian Pact all that time ago had killed her Guardian mother. In trying to save everyone, she had doomed them all.

I'm next. I'll be dead before David and Zeen ever get back. How naive had it been to have hoped that David's plan would work? There *was* an alternative. One that prevented Forsythe from harming her again. One that prevented Terrangus from meaningless wars. One that would avenge…

No. Stop thinking that. You swore to Melissa you wouldn't yield.

She could kill them all. It would be so easy. Zeen wouldn't be here this time. No one would. Burn them. Burn them all. Maybe Melissa would smile at her from the void? *No, no, no. What is happening to me?*

"Serenna?"

"Help me, Landon. Please help me." Tears flowed down her face; in losing Melissa, she'd nearly lost herself. That part of her would never fully go away. If Zeen could see the chaos of her mind, he would stab her dead in this cell. And she would deserve it.

Landon opened the prison doors, closing them behind him as he entered her cell, then sat next to her. He held her like her father used to. For all her critical thoughts of Dad, she would do anything to see him again. Anything, other than *that*.

"Did I ever tell you the story of Guardian Everleigh?"

"Landon, I swear—"

"Shh. Relax and listen, child. Just listen."

CHAPTER 18

IF LIFE IS MEANINGLESS, WHY ARE YOU AFRAID TO DIE?

yfe clutched his dagger as he approached Sardonyx. What a fitting end it would be for the warlord to die in the snowy graveyard of Boulom.

"Warlord Sardonyx! I accept your challenge. You face the future emperor of Terrangus." He raised his blade high, letting it radiate void energy to mesmerize the crowd. Spectacles were important. People could be manipulated by words or fancy distractions; Nyfe had learned to use both.

"Worthless Nyfe… I will take great pleasure in watching you die. Serenna is nearly mine. Your usefulness is at its end.

"Unless, of course, you finally decide to say the words."

Even after thirty years of wielding the blade, that voice still haunted him. Every day. Once he finally became emperor and created his own purpose in an empty realm, he would throw away the Herald of Death. It was just a tool, a means to an end. A weapon that had cost him everything. But not yet. Just a bit more power. It was all he needed.

The warlord gazed at him. "What…are you? It matters

not, I suppose. While I assure you there will be honor, there will be *no* mercy."

That drawn out response was "I accept" in zephum talk. Nyfe dashed in, going for the quick kill by slashing at Sardonyx's neck. It would be hilarious to see the horror on the zephum unit's faces as their leader dropped in one blow. Instead, Sardonyx parried with his sword, then pushed Nyfe back with an *absurd* amount of power. How did such a large beast move so quickly? Maybe this would be more difficult than he had anticipated...

"Hurry and lose, so I can get back to Serenna. If life is meaningless, why are you afraid to die?"

Sardonyx roared, rushing in and flailing his oversized sword. There was *zero* finesse, and there didn't have to be. The sword was so large and overwhelming, it would tear through anything, replacing the need for skill, practice, or a lifetime of experience.

Nyfe dodged all the strikes until a particularly novice swing came down. Hmm, the lizard beast seemed to have issues with his down strikes. Nyfe dodged with ease, then stabbed his dagger into the warlord's upper body, causing several of the onlookers on both sides to gasp as he twisted it in. His arm burned from the strain of forcing it through the steel, but a small price to pay for another victory. A small price to pay to become Emperor Nyfe...

Or not. Sardonyx *laughed*, ripped the dagger from his chest, then threw it behind Nyfe. "The pain makes me invincible, Child of Death. You cannot perceive how powerful I truly am. You are just a human...*A HUMAN*!"

Nyfe flinched and stumbled back as the warlord let out a terrible roar. Such an extraordinary lack of intelligence to make a commotion in a land ravaged by demons, but Sardonyx didn't care. Why would he? He had been born a warlord's son, who then fathered his own warlord's son. Some people had won long before they drew their first breath.

Nyfe's hand shook as he picked his dagger off the ground. It was Mylor all over again. An opportunity for greatness, shattered by forces beyond his control. No. It wouldn't be that way. Not again. Nyfe rushed in, eyeing the throat, then slashed across.

Sardonyx grabbed his hand mid-swipe, then picked him up. They met eyes and, up close, Nyfe finally understood why the God of Strength had defeated Death's first Harbinger all those years ago in the same kingdom. "Death may be the end, human. But strength is the *now*."

"*Oh… I cannot wait to see you in the void. Serenna would have won. You will never be Serenna. You are nothing.*"

Nyfe held back tears as the warlord held him several feet in the air. It just wasn't fair. As hard as he tried, he couldn't *really* believe life was meaningless, but it was the only way to cope with the fear he had wasted his life. He had thrown away Emily all those years ago to hold the blade. This is where it led him, to a snowy grave in the ruins—

A steel gauntlet pounded into his face, blurring the world and pulsing his head with a throbbing pain. At least the voices stopped. Actually, this wasn't all that bad. He would likely lose consciousness soon and enter a deep sleep. A permanent sleep. Finally.

Sardonyx threw his fragile body into the soft snow, which cradled him into the cold death he had always known waited for him. Nyfe's hands never let go of the blade. That weapon was the only thing that had ever loved him. Other than her.

"Death!" Sardonyx yelled. "I know you can hear my words! Look upon the victor! Strength's children defy you once more!" He slammed his sword into the snow. "Strength without honor—is chaos."

Gasping for air, Nyfe crawled towards his team, ignoring the distorted chorus of zephum cheers. Zeen and David grinned at him; if he survived, he would *never* forget that. The throbbing pain spread from his head to his entire body.

"No. You are not allowed to die yet. This BEAST mocks my power; I could erase his entire bloodline if Time did not limit me. Find an alternative. Find it now."

Anytime Death rambled about the Time God, things were dire. The plan changed. If Nyfe couldn't defeat Sardonyx, there had to be a way to escape. He did *not* want to find himself in the void today. No one had ever come back to tell him if the threats of torture were real, but there was *much* to atone for if even the slightest of rumors held true. The Guardians were useless. His own men were useless, except for maybe…

You.

Nyfe rose with a surge of adrenaline, rushing towards Jeffrey: the realm's most useless crystal mage. The old bastard had been less helpful than the guy guiding the cart, and even that guy had somehow died. Imagine that: pushing a cart for thirty or forty years just to get mauled by lizard people. Jeffrey must have known something was wrong as he backed away. Too late.

Nyfe grabbed him. "Do you hear his voice?"

"Uh…what voice? Please let go of me."

Sardonyx stopped staring into the sky and back at Nyfe, then began his approach. "Make your peace, Child of Death. Your time has come."

I need to hurry. He jabbed his blade high into Jeffrey's shoulder. "Did you receive the offer? Say yes. Take it. Turn to the void…turn to the void *now!*"

Jeffrey wailed, trying to cast a crystal shield but never finishing the spell. "Please…no."

Nyfe could hear the thud of the warlord's steps, but he

wouldn't dare look back. Not enough pain. He slowly dragged his dagger down the wound, passing the point of no return. Jeffrey would die. Whether as a coward or a monster, that was up to him.

"I'm not ready to die…"

Nyfe ripped his dagger out, then jabbed it over and over in his other shoulder to maximize the pain without killing him. Only when the warmth of blood splashed on his face did he realize how cold it was. The screams went on *forever*. Zeen tried to rush over, but David held him back. Death was silent. Was he speaking to Jeffrey?

"A taste? Just…a taste? I accept!"

Nyfe lunged his dagger through and twisted it. "Say the words, you damned coward!"

"I… I am nothing. I am forever. I am the end."

Jeffrey stopped screaming, staring at the blade as if it intrigued him. All the horror left his eyes as he guided his hands down the sharp sides of the dagger, cocking his head as blood flowed down the grip.

Nyfe tried to back away before Jeffrey grabbed him. His grip was tighter than the warlord's. "I trusted you, Nyfe. Why would you do this to me?"

Even though it was mid-afternoon, the ruins descended to darkness, with a familiar black cloud filling the sky. His god laughed from the cold black, then spoke in his true voice, shaking the ruins surrounding them.

"Mage…you are the most pitiful mortal to ever summon my wrath. I am not wasting my gift on you. Five minutes. You have five minutes before I take it back. Kill as many as you can. Kill them all, and I will bless you as my next Harbinger."

Jeffrey let go, letting out a shriek as he fell to his knees. Spectral wings of darkness sprung from his shoulders, and his once-plain oak staff morphed into a misshapen version of the

Wings of Mylor. The crimson eyes of the abomination of an owl stared through Nyfe.

Yep. It was time to leave.

CHAPTER 19

GLORIOUS!

David took a swig of his flask, closing his eyes before the zephum ale burned his throat. It was impossible to explain how something so awful could taste so...*perfect*. He held back a grin as the zephum soldiers stumbled back, looking to him as if he had the answers.

He did. "Warlord," David said, grabbing his massive steel shoulder for a brief moment. Alright, no more ale, that was unwise. "Get your soldiers out of here. The demon's power will increase with the size of our forces. The three of us will be sufficient if we strike early."

Sardonyx paused, never taking his eyes off the empowered mage ascending to the dark, snowy skies. "You are certain? I have honorable warriors willing to battle this demon. What a pity."

"I am always certain."

The warlord's red reptilian eyes turned to him. It had been so long since David had seen him up close; he swore the giant zephum somehow grew larger. "Ah, what a rare privilege to slay one of Death's monsters *here*. The God of Strength watches from the Great Plains in the Sky; let us give him an honorable display."

Zeen nodded, but noticeably kept his distance.

Mary trekked over, cracking her neck and bashing her sword into her shield. The entire left side of her face was completely swollen. "I lost sight of Nyfe; it seems he grabbed whoever was left and fled when the skies went dark. We'll kill him later. For now, tell me when to rush in."

Fair enough. A zephum would be better, but David didn't trust them to follow his directions. Gods, if zephum forces ever learned the discipline of an Alanammus unit, all the realm would be in chains. He would never, *ever* tell the warlord, but his people's dependence on raw power was their greatest weakness.

Sardonyx smirked. "You would battle by my side? You surprise me, child."

"I…" she said, gritting her teeth. "My vengeance awaits, but this demon comes first."

Zeen eased closer to the group. "I'm proud of you for saying that. Welcome back, my friend."

"Fuck you, Zeen." Everyone—except Zeen—snickered at her words.

David didn't know Guardian history as well as Francis, but this was certainly one of the strangest groups to defend the realm. Fighting alongside kingdom rulers had been a disaster in the past. Oh, what a mistake it had been to bring Grayson against Vanessa all those years ago…

He froze at the thought.

He had never faced a demon without Melissa. She had been there for every single one by his side, throwing detonators and wielding dual blades like a goddess. Decades ago, this abomination would have chilled his core, but that man was gone. *Nothing*—god, demon or otherwise—would keep him from his future wife.

Sardonyx signaled both his units to leave the immediate area as the darkness in the sky continued to spread. David caught a glimpse of eyes from the center of the maelstrom, familiar crimson shadows that had gazed through him in Xavian after his first Harbinger.

Unlike that day, the entity *spoke*. "Do you feel the hopelessness course through you, tearing you apart? I see the warlord is here; what a fitting sacrifice to my wrath."

Sardonyx didn't even look up as he kept directing his soldiers away. What a legend. David had been declared a leader, but *that* was true leadership. Sardonyx came back to the huddle as the last zephum left. "David, what is our move here? This is your expertise; I will follow your guidance to ensure we defeat this *miserable* fiend."

"I'm ready. Let me engage," Mary said, her hands shaking as she clutched her shield. Bless her for keeping her composure. Perhaps she could…no, not yet.

David nodded. "Listen, without a mage, we are in a difficult position. Warlord, Zeen, our role is to kill this demon as soon as possible while Mary draws its attention. We cannot win a long running battle. Our assault will be a cross formation: Mary charges forward as each of us takes a side. The expectation is, at best, only one of us will get through. Whoever gets that chance needs to kill it, or all is lost. There are *no* exceptions."

"Glorious!" Sardonyx yelled, brushing his long black cape to his right side.

Mary sheathed her sword, holding both hands on her shield as she approached the demon. It still floated above the ruins, emanating void energy, but not yet taking action. David went to the rear, then nodded at Zeen and Sardonyx to take their respective sides in the east and west sections. It was surreal to have the warlord accept his commands. He had always assumed—unfairly, perhaps—the warlord was a simple-minded beast.

A loud crack filled the air as the demon roared, letting out a black nova that flew above their heads. Was that... Yes, it held some demonic version of the Wings of Mylor. "Mortals," the demon said in a distorted, deep voice. "I have ascended to my zenith. All life will die before me, starting with you. Tears of the Time God will flood the ruins of his dead children."

So be it. Show me your violence. He nodded at Mary; hopefully she would take that as a signal to rush forward.

She did.

Grasping her shield with both hands, Mary charged in, immediately gaining the demon's full attention. The mage raised his glowing staff at Mary, then unleashed a continuous stream of void energy. She closed her eyes and screamed, clutching her shield to protect herself from the glowing flare of darkness.

"Go!" David yelled.

As the void energy crashed against her shield, it did not pierce, but the constant force pushed her backwards, threatening her balance. Her defense was not sustainable, but it was her only option for now to allow the other three to get in range.

Zeen was the fastest out of the three by far, getting to the demon first, then jumping up from a shattered rock structure with both hands on his blade, yelling like a complete amateur. *You fool, why would you jump? Don't you dare die on me.* The mage turned his gaze on Zeen, then launched several void bolts in his direction. Zeen parried midair, causing him to lose his composure as he crashed headfirst to the ground. He desperately flailed his arm to find his sword, then clutched it with both hands as he lay there, dazed.

With the warlord slowly stomping forward, David arrived next. He dashed towards the demon, looking to thrust his blade straight through. No fancy tactics—most battles were won with simple swipes and stabs. Technically, Zeen had done his job, creating a distraction for David to get close. David yelled—like an amateur—as his sword pierced its chest. It was difficult to contain the rush of victory, particularly with Melissa waiting at home. The demon screeched in pain, grabbing David with an unexpected strength.

"USELESS MAGE!" Death screamed from the skies, with Boulom trembling as if there were an earthquake. "YOU NEED MORE POWER! TAKE MY POWER NOW!"

Letting out a roar, the demon ripped David's sword out of him, then threw it far into the darkness. He cast a crystal prison on David, lifting him high, giving him an incredible view of the broken ruins. Vast nothingness, memories of people who no longer existed. After a lifetime of emptiness, it would be fitting to die here and join them. Honestly, it was almost freeing. David was one of them. He always had been.

Tiny white specs of snow drifted in front of the distorted view from his prison until a void-imbued scythe appeared in the air. David closed his eyes and awaited the end. *Goodbye, my love. My only regret is not giving myself to you sooner. Don't forget me.*

Please, you're the only one who ever cared.

He flinched as a *true* roar filled the air. The warlord flailed his blade with a violent force so powerful, it slashed the demon's face completely *off*. The faceless mage gazed back at Sardonyx, screaming indistinguishably while blood poured out. Sardonyx would not yield, slamming his enormous sword into the demon over and over, ignoring the loud screams of rage and torment emanating from the entity of Death.

Jeffrey was gone. Both literally and figuratively, reduced to a near nothingness after the relentless blows Sardonyx continued to rain on him. The darkness in the ruins began to fade, with the god haunting them once more.

"Worthless mage…next time it will be Serenna. Warlord

of loss, Guardians of despair; I am nothing. I am forever. I am the end. I AM THE END!"

David gasped as his crystal prison faded, sending his body plummeting. The view had not been worth the price of the collapse, despite the snow saving him from a debilitating crash. He clutched his chest for air as the world spun. As much as this hurt now, it would be *torture* tomorrow.

Sardonyx kept his gaze to the now-clear skies where Death had been, then sheathed his blade. "Foolish deity. I am stronger than death. The void will not have me." He walked over to Mary, reaching out his hand to help her stand.

She gave him a bewildered look, pausing before accepting his aid. "I can't believe this is happening…"

"Believe it, child, our battle was GLORIOUS! You boldly fought with honor! It was as if I were watching my beloved Pyith again on the battlefield." He hugged Mary dearly, likely causing her great pain with his monstrous embrace.

Zeen approached Sardonyx, holding out his hand. "Warlord, it was an honor to fight by your side. My name is Zeen Parson. I am the newest member of the Guardian team and a friend to the mighty Pyith."

"Ah, so you are Zeen," Sardonyx said, ignoring his handshake and instead hugging him with the same devastating embrace. "She spoke highly of you, and from what I hear, you got the killing blow on your first adventure, an honor we now *both* share."

"Yes, I suppose I did," Zeen said with a smile.

"And you, David?" the warlord asked. "How did *you* fare your first time?"

David groaned. "I need a healing mage. Now." He forced himself to stand, refusing to look weak in front of the warlord.

"By Strength's name, you look ten years older every time I see you. How long do humans tend to last?"

"At this rate, not much longer." David laughed, slowly regaining the wind that had been knocked out of him.

"We should probably head back to Terrangus then," Zeen said. "Even if we supposedly have a week, Serenna and Melissa could be in grave danger if Nyfe gets there first."

"*Nonsense*! You will accompany me back to Vaynex. We must celebrate today's victory against that vile fiend."

"Thank you, but I must decline for now," Zeen said.

"Human...you are not following... This is not a request. Would you prefer to follow in shackles?"

David walked over to Zeen, placing his hand on his shoulder. "We accept, Warlord," he said. "Thank you for this honor. If you lead the way, we will follow."

"Indeed. Follow me; we are certain to run into my units if we continue south. We will join them and take the portal to my empire together. It will be *glorious*!"

CHAPTER 20

KILL THEM ALL

Why do I continue to fail? Nyfe thought as he trekked back to the Boulom portal in the mid-afternoon snow. Still dazed from the warlord's strike, fresh blood trickled down the side of his swollen face. The pain didn't bother him. The real pain was the mental anguish which lingered after yet *another* defeat. Why couldn't he best Sardonyx with the Herald of Death? How many more advantages did he need? Every failure exposed the man wielding the blade, the truth concealed behind the shadows of the void.

"Lord Nyfe," one of his soldiers said, "are we close to the portal?"

Nyfe gazed at him...what was his name? There were two left after the skirmish against the zephum; this one was a taller man who favored his right side. His armor dangled off with rips and shreds, open cuts all over his body. He would be a useful diversion if demons came their way.

"Stay sharp. We will be back in Terrangus shortly. Our people will hail us as heroes for what we did today."

"What exactly did we do?" the second soldier asked.

Nyfe shot him a glare. He was short and chubby, with his gut hanging out the front of his armor. Wait, wasn't this the man with the cart? Who had the other guy been then? Nyfe didn't have the time or care to remember their names, or whatever grand promises he had made earlier. So many long, tiresome stories: the solution was always gold. Childhood dreams didn't work out? Gold. Wife left for a Xavian pirate? Gold. Family member with a rare disease? Gold.

The portly soldier sighed. "Not all of us…Jeffrey was a close friend of mine. We came together to clear his debts, but it was all a waste…"

Friends with a volatile mage with a gambling addiction? Gold. "It's only a waste if we don't make it back. He will not have died in vain."

"We should have seen it through. It was dishonorable to abandon them."

Nyfe placed his right hand on his dagger as he approached the complainer and stared through him. "Honor is the most useless concept since hope. I *dare* you to question my command again."

"We stand with you," the taller soldier said, moving in between them. "Alan means no disrespect. We are not used to seeing demons or warlords; today has been a dreadful day." He gave a weak laugh. "I assumed Mylor would be the worst place I ever saw, but Boulom is far worse."

Nyfe took his hand off the blade and backed off. "Very well. Follow me and keep your ignorance to yourselves; we're almost there."

Both soldiers glanced at each other with a lack of certainty before they nodded and followed through the outskirts.

Nyfe looked ahead and paused, finding the unmanned Boulom portal gate ahead. *Dammit all, there are no mages. How am I going to get back?* He marched up with his dagger in hand, letting out a yell as he slammed his blade into the inactive portal. "Forsythe never intended for us to return from here. There must be a way…"

The shorter guard walked behind Nyfe with a melancholy stare. "You know, if Jeffrey were still here, he could've opened it for us."

Enough of that. Nyfe's eyes lit up as he slammed his blade into the side of…Alan's head. The annoying man's eyes and mouth remained open, but his life was gone. It was an instant death, or so Nyfe assumed. He didn't care either way.

The portal flickered as the man fell dead to the ground. Before Nyfe could consider what that meant, Death's voice returned to his mind as he shivered from an icy chill. Apparently, Jeffrey's taste of power hadn't lasted too long. He closed his eyes and braced himself; the silence had been nice while it lasted.

"YES! I WANT THEM TO DIE! I WANT THEM TO DIE NOW!" Death's voice was always loud, but this was far worse than normal. Nyfe's head throbbed as he fell to the ground and groaned.

The remaining soldier drew his sword and drifted towards him with caution. "May the gods damn you. Alan was a good man." The soldier looked down, clenching his sword. "You murdered him…we came here for your glory and you murdered him…"

It was impossible to focus on the rambling while Death assaulted his thoughts.

"Useless Child of Death…if you ever insult me with such an unworthy host again, I will grant you an infinite mass of pure torment. TORMENT! PURE TORMENT!"

"No…" Nyfe pleaded, shaking as he lay hunched over the cold, rigid grounds of Boulom. "Please, have mercy. I will do better; I will do anything…"

"You beg for mercy?" the soldier asked in disbelief. He

clenched his sword and moved forward, now within striking distance. "I give you a chance to yield, sir. You do not deserve it, but honor binds me to accept your surrender."

"Look at this mortal. He believes life has meaning, or that any of his actions have significance. Take that away and send him to me… I want to gaze upon his essence one last time before I forget he ever existed at all. End him, and I will open the portal… END HIM, NOW!"

The suffering ended as Nyfe stood with total clarity. The absence of pain and dread was enrapturing; it was a simple choice to heed his god's demand. He stared at his former ally, unimpressed as his sword stayed drawn upon him. "I never caught your name…"

"My name is—" Nyfe slashed his throat mid-sentence before the nameless soldier fell to both knees.

Nyfe kneeled to the dying man and smiled. "Thank you, whoever you are."

He pushed the man aside as his dagger and the portal lit up simultaneously. A piercing wind chilled him to the bone. The price wasn't too high, as long as someone else had to pay. He kept his blade drawn as he walked through; it was safe to assume whoever was on the other side would be his enemy.

*

Nyfe appeared in the Terrangus outskirts and immediately surveyed his surroundings, counting only five guards at the post. They paused and kept their swords sheathed before the lead guard stepped forward. Why was he smiling? Had all the sober guards taken off to enjoy the rare, sunny day?

"You're back," the guard said. "Our orders are to kill you on sight."

His dagger dripped with blood as Nyfe held it out in front of him. "I expected as much. You don't appear eager to face me; you must know how powerful I am."

The guard kneeled as the rest of his team followed. "Lord Nyfe, we await our new orders…"

Nyfe glanced at all five guards with a puzzled look, clutching his dagger. "Did…I miss something?"

"The emperor murdered Melissa with a cheap shot after losing a fair duel. His support has been wavering for a while; today was finally the breaking point for most of us." The guard stood and walked towards Nyfe. "You are the only worthy replacement. If you will have us, we will follow. The military's reign has been long overdue."

It took every ounce of restraint not to smile or laugh as Nyfe looked down and bit his lip. *It's almost too perfect to be true. Forsythe has done more for my reign today than I've managed in a lifetime…*

"Impossible…Melissa is dead?" Nyfe asked as his eyes watered. "A Guardian killed by an emperor…what madness."

"Did David and Zeen fall in battle? Serenna still lives, but it would put the realm in a terrible position to lose three Guardians in one day."

"Worse. David and Zeen colluded with the zephum and decimated my forces. It is only by a miracle that I stand here now."

The guard looked at him in sudden shock. "What? How can that be?"

A sharp pain shot down Nyfe's neck before he could answer.

"THEY SEE THROUGH YOUR LIES! KILL THEM! KILL THEM NOW!"

Nyfe closed his eyes and accepted the agony, refusing to drop his bluff as Death barraged his thoughts. "It's true. Zeen made an allegiance with the zephum to save the Pact Breaker; he would burn this entire kingdom to the ground to satisfy his lust. Warriors, rebuilding Terrangus will be a monumental undertaking. I will need you all if we are to succeed." He reached out his hand to the lead guard and stared through him.

The guard accepted his handshake. "Then you will have us."

Nyfe motioned for the other four guards to rise. "A wise choice. Let's get moving; if there's chaos in the streets we must act now."

"The castle is too heavily defended, but if you can secure more support from the military ward, a full strike would be possible by morning."

Nyfe could no longer contain his smile and let out a small laugh. "And so it begins…"

He marched into Terrangus, never more delighted to be back in his wretched kingdom. There was an ominous foreboding in the trade district as the sun descended and the merchants and common folk gazed upon him in awe. Nyfe arrived and dusk followed.

Adrenaline came over him as he stood in the center of the city and observed all the townsfolk and guards whisper about and point in his direction. So much attention. All of it on him. Most of the merchants locked their shops and rushed their carts off the streets. Several guards trickled in, bowing and showing their support to their next potential emperor, while others backed away and made a discreet exit.

A small group of nobles made their way towards him and his growing forces. While some townsfolk gasped at their presence, he didn't know who they were. Nobles meant nothing to him, a bunch of tired gray snobs who wouldn't wield a sword if you threw it at them. The old men wore gold senators' tabards, unaccompanied by guards and completely unarmed. Their purpose was clear: the rich were on their way to join the powerful.

"A pleasant surprise to see you, General," the first senator said. The others nodded in agreement. "May I safely assume you are informed of Melissa's death?"

Feeling the weight of his soldier's eyes on him, Nyfe paused before responding. While noble support would be beneficial in the long run; his immediate concern was military power. Kingdoms ran on blood, not gold. "You may assume *nothing*, Senator."

The senators stepped back as the soldiers laughed. "Pardon me for any offense; we come to offer our support…"

"Oh, your support?"

Nyfe circled them, holding his chin as he surveyed the senators. Aside from their golden tabards, they were all covered head to toe with illustrious jewelry. Nyfe came to a stop as a necklace caught his eye, gold all around except for a dark onyx gemstone at the end. He ripped the necklace off and held it in his hand.

"Even to me, this gem is beautiful." He studied the necklace and snickered. "I'd wager this is worth more gold than I've made in an entire lifetime as a soldier. Now tell me, does that make sense to you?"

The senators glanced at each other without speaking. While Nyfe was genuinely curious to hear their answers, there would be no wordplay that could save them.

The man with his necklace removed stepped forward. "When you become emperor, your wealth will have no limits. A lifetime of injustice will be resolved in the blink of an eye."

"A fair point," Nyfe said, before looking back at his soldiers. "Leave this one and kill the rest."

He turned around to take in the adoration of his followers before a loud rumble began. Large pillars of earth suddenly shot up around the senators, protecting them from the advancing soldiers with tall, mountainous terrain. Nyfe couldn't recall a single Terrangus mage with the ability to manipulate the earth with such potency until he looked ahead to a familiar face: Alanammus Guardian Francis Haide.

Damn, I should've expected this with Melissa dead. Hopefully Pyith isn't here too...

Francis clenched his staff with his eyes closed, developing an intense blue aura that radiated frost energy. He opened his eyes and stared directly into Nyfe. "Heed my words, General. While we share a common enemy, I will not allow you to murder all these innocent people. Stand down..."

"Stand down?" Nyfe asked with a fake smile. Stupid mage. Why were mages always so stupid? They could've just gone their separate ways, but with a crowd watching, now one of them had to die. "Sorry, but now that your mother's dead, no one cares about you, Francis. You're the *Invisible Guardian.*"

"I will not ask again."

Nyfe signaled his soldiers to surround Francis from a safe distance. "Your loss. The only solace I can offer is that I haven't decided if I'm going to kill you yet." That wasn't true. Francis wouldn't leave here alive, but keeping the option of surrender available in his busy head should make him less fierce.

Francis did an awful job hiding his fear. Nyfe could always find the sweat and quick breaths; he watched as Francis's wide eyes searched all around for a winning strategy, but to no avail. Being backed into a corner, he expected the Guardian to act in desperation.

And of course, he did.

His blue aura erupted, launching an ice blast in Nyfe's direction. Nyfe prepared to dodge before one of his soldiers jumped in front and took the full brunt of the spell, having most of his icy body shatter as he fell to the ground.

The soldiers surrounding Francis rushed in, but Nyfe couldn't take his focus off the dead one lying there. He kneeled down to check, pained to find a young boy, appearing no older than sixteen with remnants of dirty blonde hair. Whatever the true color of his eyes a moment ago, they were now deep blue, gazing forever into the void.

I have done nothing for this child, and yet he died for me without hesitation. That's all life is, isn't it? We spend our days desperately looking up, hoping the flawed beings or ideals we choose to follow have the answers. There are no answers, everything is just random and meaningless...

Nyfe snapped back to reality as a soldier flew above him, screaming from a lightning blast. Even after a lifetime of battling mages, the stench of burned flesh was always difficult to bear. Francis was making quick work of his soldiers, with an impressive array of frost and lightning spells raining down all over the streets of Terrangus. It was merciful not to use fire; Francis appeared to share the same weakness for mercy that had plagued David and Zeen. Serenna would have burned them all.

With Francis's attention on the mob of soldiers, Nyfe saw an opportunity to close the gap. He moseyed towards him to avoid attention, his grin growing with every step. Francis finally met his eyes, unable to hide his fear as he continued to shift attention between the soldiers and Nyfe. Francis launched a swift ice spell towards him that was so far off target, Nyfe didn't have to dodge as it flew past him. That was all Nyfe needed to see before he rushed in.

Goodbye, Invisible Guardian—

An unseen force knocked Nyfe back, floating him gently to the ground to prevent his body from crashing into the jagged terrain. The God of Wisdom floated above him; it was the first time he had ever seen the mysterious deity up close. Everyone had always said the sun mask had a black frown *and* platinum smile, but he never saw the smile.

"GET AWAY FROM THIS ONE! GET AWAY FROM

THIS ONE NOW! ARROGANCE! LIES! NOW! NOW! NOW!"

Nyfe fought back every urge to scream as Death tore through his head. Too loud. No one should ever have to hear such torture. He assumed the screams deafened the battle, but glancing back up, all his soldiers kept a *large* distance from the Herald of Wisdom staff pulsating in the middle of the trade district.

"Careful, Nyfe," Wisdom said, "tis a thin veil between service and slavery. You gaze up to your skies of death, enraptured by the shadowy aura of freedom, while the chains behind you grow farther than your dim eyes could ever hope to perceive. Our paths will cross again…quite soon, based on how things are going today." He created a portal and chuckled, then Francis and Wisdom went through it to leave the city streets of Terrangus.

I've never seen a god openly interfere like that. Death would never do that for me…

The silence lingered as the soldiers looked over at Nyfe for answers. The streets of the trade district were decimated. Several dead soldiers scattered about, with shops and carts blown to pieces or frozen. While it didn't feel like a victory, he remained while Francis was gone. That was good enough for today. Nyfe got up as the forces of earth crumbled, revealing the senators once more.

"I changed my mind. Kill them all."

CHAPTER 21

A DISHONORABLE LIFE IS MET WITH A DISHONORABLE DEATH

Zeen took a sip of his water, welcoming the late-day sun that beat down on his throbbing head after they had arrived in the Vaynex outskirts through the zephum's Boulom portal. Everyone had kept offering him ale throughout the journey south, but he figured venturing into the infamous kingdom of Vaynex would best be done sober. David didn't seem to agree; he had pounded ale since the battle, refusing to speak of the Fear artifact and leaving Zeen to answer the warlord's constant questions.

"Tell me, Zeen," Sardonyx said, "have you ever been this close to our lands?"

"No, Warlord. Anytime I ever had to battle your people, it was in our own terrain near the Koulva mines."

"Indeed; no human would dare get this close to Vaynex without my protection." Sardonyx glared straight through him with his face guard off. Gods, that was terrifying. "Are you *excited*?" Maybe it wasn't a glare? Sardonyx always *appeared* furious, but spoke with a gruff, cheerful voice.

"Yes," Zeen said with a cautious smile, "it's my

understanding that Guardians don't get to come here too often; your people have very few Harbingers."

"Not for six years! I am sure you have heard the tales; we govern our mages with a *strict* code of honor."

"That's one way to put it," Mary interrupted. "I prefer to call it *murder*."

The caravan came to a stop, with several zephum staring at her. Angry eyes. Zephum were difficult to read, but that expression was *definitely* anger.

The commander that had fought against Mary in Boulom drew his axe and pointed it at her. "Shield human, that is the last time I will allow you to openly disrespect the warlord without consequence."

"Stand down, Vim," Sardonyx said. "I enjoy this feisty human; her fierce hatred towards me is refreshing. She wears it like a golden plate of armor!"

"Yes, Warlord," Vim said. He sheathed his axe, then bowed.

David walked up to Mary, then pulled her aside, away from the zephum and closer to Zeen. Finally. Mary had been making snide comments the entire trip; it was only a matter of time before she struck the wrong nerve and got them all killed. "This isn't Terrangus; we have no protection here. If you step too far out of line, I cannot save you."

"And what of my father? I joined this mission to slay zephum, not join them!"

"That mission is *over*. You just saw the God of Death. Is the only thing on your mind revenge?"

"What else can I do? Honing in on vengeance overcomes my fears and doubts. I don't even know what to believe anymore."

"Believe this: you stood against Death and prevailed. Let hatred guide your shield, but not your mind. You have enormous potential; I wager one day you could make a fine Guardian."

"Thank you," she said as David walked over to the warlord. It was nice to see her smile. Under all that hatred was still the friendly young woman that had fought by Zeen's side. For the most part.

"At ease, David," Sardonyx said. "I acknowledge your fears, but rest assured she will remain safe in my lands. I admire rage; there is nothing more pure than to see a woman *murder* you with her eyes."

The caravan continued its path south, entering a green, vivid forest surrounded by swampy waters. Zeen normally hated the buzzing of flies and…whatever sounds those large insects were making, but finally trading the cold for the harsh humid air was a small victory as they trekked forward. Actually, it was very similar to the last Mylor summer, but with no mountains—

The warlord slammed his hand down on Zeen's shoulder, startling him as he jumped. "Zeen! Vaynex is straight ahead. Prepare yourself for a *glorious* sight. Take the lead. I want you to look upon it first."

Zeen moved forward, parting the giant tree leaves and branches as he looked ahead. Within the vast green plains stood the zephum kingdom of Vaynex. There were no castles, but enormous structures of tan blocks, with constant smoke flowing out to the sky, giving the appearance of the entire city being on fire. It was all surrounded by large, spiked towers, with the open gates drenched in blood to welcome them.

"Isn't it *glorious*?"

Glorious was one way to describe it, but Zeen could do better. "This is everything I expected and more. Thank you, Warlord, your kingdom is *beautiful*."

David sighed as everyone gave Zeen an odd look. Anger?

Those looks were definitely anger. Why? Rinso had always described Vaynex as a kingdom of harsh beauty. That seemed fair.

The warlord drew his blade, then held it at Zeen's neck. If either of them flinched, his head would likely roll right off. "Beautiful…is not the word to describe my empire. You are in a land of honor-bound warriors. We value strength, courage, and power. If you want beauty, go dally with the human mages in Alanammus. This is a kingdom…of GLORY!" The zephum cheered as the warlord sheathed his sword. "For your own sake, think before you speak again."

"Forgive me, Warlord. In the Rinso novels—"

"Human, if you ever mention that name in my presence again, I will slay you *and* David."

David pulled him to the side as Mary laughed.

"What did I do wrong?"

"Do I really need to explain this? They are giant lizard warriors who murder each other and yell about honor. Don't call them beautiful, don't call them handsome or pretty, just…don't speak at all."

"I don't understand…"

"Please just shut up before you get us all killed. I didn't come this far to die because you can't hold your tongue."

Whatever. He could follow and say nothing.

They entered through the gates, passing a dead zephum lying abandoned in the streets. Flies hounded the corpse, but everyone just went along as if this were normal. It probably was. He made it a point not to stare and averted his eyes, but sweat formed on his brow after he saw two more on the opposite side. *This place is miserable. Don't say anything—*

"What's the deal with all these dead zephum?" Mary asked, as Zeen shot her a shocked glance. Why was she allowed to say anything that popped into her head?

185

"It is not a human concern," Vim said. "A dishonorable life is met with a dishonorable death."

"Well, what did they do?"

"Maybe they asked too many questions, shield human," Vim said as the warlord laughed.

To Zeen's surprise, the Vaynex city layout seemed eerily similar to Terrangus. What were likely civilians and traders were immediately after the bloody gates, with the military wards up ahead. While there was no castle, Vaynex had a large stronghold in its place, an awkward-looking fortress that made no attempt to be anything other than a massive structure and an eyesore.

A decorated zephum with two guards made his way down to greet them. All the zephum other than Sardonyx kneeled on one knee as he got close. David kneeled and signaled for Zeen and Mary to follow.

"Greetings, Father. I am pleased to see you are well. May we speak in private?"

"Do not refer to me as 'Father' in front of the humans, Tempest. I am your *warlord*."

"Um, of course, Warlord," Tempest said, escorting Sardonyx further ahead. David signaled for everyone to rise after the zephum were up.

Zeen got a better look at Tempest Claw as they spoke. Tempest was barely Zeen's height, wearing a miniature version of his father's black cape, with loose, light armor. His sheathed two-handed sword could be mistaken for a Terrangus blade; it nearly mimicked the length and slim shape of Intrepid—

"NO!" Sardonyx yelled. "THAT CANNOT BE!"

"Father, stop. It's Strength's command not to tell them here. Not even Pyith knows yet…"

"There is no honor in this! We must tell them!"

Zeen kept his eyes down to avoid getting murdered.

Whatever zephum nonsense they were yelling about surely wasn't his concern. Hopefully, Mary knew better than to ask. She had been bold, but this was the first time they'd heard the warlord yell.

He would prefer to *never* hear that again.

Tempest came back to the group, rubbing the back of his head and looking down. "Right then...follow me to the citadel."

Zeen studied the warlord's face as the caravan moved through Vaynex. He had always found Forsythe an intimidating ruler—particularly when he was angry—but the empty rage in Sardonyx's eyes held no equal.

"Commander Vim," Tempest said, breaking the awkward silence. "I don't see your brother. I hesitate to ask if he's okay?"

Vim glared at Zeen. "No. Valore was slain in Boulom by the human Guardian Zeen."

"The polearm warrior was your brother?" Zeen asked. *Oh, I'm not supposed to talk...*

"Yes. If the demons did not appear, I would have killed you and left your body next to his."

"I'm sorry. For whatever it's worth, he was an excellent warrior. He nearly had me at the end."

"Do not apologize. You gave Valore an honorable death in combat. I will award you the same when I claim my vengeance."

Ah, I shouldn't have said anything. Now I'm stuck. "I'm not here as your enemy; I have no desire to face you."

"Tell him the rules, Tempest," Sardonyx interrupted. The cheerful gruff from his voice was long gone.

Tempest cleared his throat. "Zeen, Vim may challenge you as long as you remain anywhere in Vaynex. Regardless of your personal feelings on the matter, you must oblige. I apologize if our obscure methods appear unorthodox, but we revere tradition above all else."

Something resonated with the structure of his words, some sort of strange familiarity, as if they had been friends for years. There was no way this short, well-spoken zephum was the future warlord...or Pyith's life-mate. *How do I respond? Am I allowed to say his name? David didn't prepare me for this at all...* "Very well, Tempest Claw. I accept your judgement." He waited for sighs, threats, anything, but apparently he had spoken correctly.

The uncomfortable silence escorted the group to the fortress entrance. For as much as the warlord's yell had startled him, his silence was somehow worse. There was nothing particularly special about the fortress. It just happened to be the largest structure in the kingdom, and he swore the tan blocks of the left side tilted awkwardly. Sardonyx and his son entered first, then the rest followed from behind. Zeen held back a sigh, tired and unimpressed, missing Serenna. *I wonder how she's doing over there. Would it be unfair to think I have it worse—*

Zeen's mouth dropped as he entered. All the walls had masterful paintings of old zephum warriors lit by torchlight, and the grandest sight was the enormous statue of a zephum holding a sword behind the stone throne, overseeing the entire fortress.

It stood proud, with the presence of a god.

"Wow," Zeen said. "I've never seen anything like this. It's very...glorious."

"*Glorious indeed,*" Sardonyx said, back to his cheerful tone. "Humans, gaze upon our avatar: the God of Strength. The first warlord who unified the zephum now oversees us to ensure that we live honorably and carry out his legacy. The one true god."

The room rumbled as the statue began to glow. A blinding

light filled the room, burning Zeen's eyes far worse than the cold death of the Boulom skies. He gazed up as it subsided, to a giant glowing zephum radiating an incredible warmth of orange energy that may as well have come straight from the sun. The Rinso novels had mentioned Strength rather often—as the most honorable god—but never had they explained the radiant figure before them. Maybe it was impossible to do so? Zeen couldn't get a good look past the burning aura, no matter how badly he wanted to.

Oh, did he want to. This was the first Guardian, the savior of the realm, who had rallied his small team to defeat Death when no one else would. Sardonyx be damned, it was beautiful. It was possibly the most beautiful thing he had ever seen. If only Serenna were here. She could lean against his shoulder with that soft platinum hair and smile at the very avatar of hope itself.

We'll get through this. I swear to you.

"Greetings, humans!" his voice boomed, loud, but somehow gentle. "I am the God of Strength. Very few of your kind are worthy enough to enter Vaynex, but you arrive here as champions of the realm. David Williams, you continue to lead the Guardians with honor! Looking upon the man you are today makes me proud...even if you *do* enjoy our ale a bit much. Your path will not be easy. The pain inflicted upon you in the coming days will be *harsh*. Never turn back. Never let go. I may hold the honor as the first Guardian, but you stand before me as the best of us all. I will carry you in my heart, tiny human, no matter how dark the clouds form in the sky."

"Thank you, immortal God of Strength," David said, looking down, but keeping his smile. He looked genuinely happy, as if the compliments far outweighed the ominous tone from the god's message. "Strength without honor—is chaos."

"Indeed, my friend. Mary Walker! When the day comes,

you have my blessing to become a Guardian. You are worthy; that worn shield is a sign of a battle-tested warrior. Hand it to me *now*."

Mary was frozen, staring at the massive deity, likely not realizing how awkwardly long her pause was. She drew her worn, dented shield with both hands, then slowly walked over and held it out for the zephum god. Strength took the shield from her, then roared as a new blinding light struck down, creating a terrible clang of unknown forces clashing with steel. When the light and sound dissipated, he held the empowered shield out for Mary to reclaim.

"Behold, human! If you are ever to fall in combat, it will not be because of your shield. Wield this and continue to uphold your father's legacy. Never calm your rage—it will keep you invincible. Hate me. *Despise* me. Remember my people in your weakest moments. Draw our shame to bolster your shield. Draw your pain to bolster your resolve."

"This is an incredible power," she said, studying her glowing, flawless shield. "Thank you, God of Strength. I swear to make you proud. I…will speak the words in your honor. Words that have haunted my heart. Strength without honor— is chaos." Mary's conflicted gaze made it look like she was about to cry. Zeen had never seen her so happy. Never. Not even close.

Zeen's heart pounded—he was next.

"And *YOU*! Zeen Parson! I have been watching you for some time."

This is it. What will he say? Gods, I'm so excited—

"Stop!" Vim yelled, to gasps from everyone in the room. "God of Strength, I wish to claim my vengeance now in your presence. Will you bless the combat?"

Oh, come on. Seriously? How is this allowed? Maybe it wasn't—Sardonyx's expression was *seething*. Something terrible had just happened, and Zeen thanked anyone watching from above that it finally wasn't his fault.

"How *dare* you interrupt me," Strength said in a booming tone. "So be it. You are a fool to challenge this human. Zeen, draw your glorious blade and prepare for combat."

"Hold on," a familiar voice yelled. "I want to see Zeen kill Vim." Pyith entered the room, limping over to the crowd, favoring her right leg.

"Pyith!"

"Welcome Zeen," she said as she smiled. "Kill him quickly so we can catch up."

Zeen nodded, drawing Intrepid and entering his battle stance. "Commander Vim, I accept your challenge."

"God of Strength," Vim said as he walked right up to Zeen. "I dedicate this battle to you. I will avenge my brother and bring glory to the zephum—"

Vim was cut off—quite literally—by Sardonyx, who slammed his massive blade down through Vim diagonally, slicing him in half as his upper body flopped to the ground. The splat of blood drenched Zeen in warm red. Too much red. He had never wondered what zephum blood tasted like, but he could now describe the thick, bitter horror to anyone.

"*WHAT THE FUCK?*" Zeen screamed, trying to wipe the blood off his face. There was so much. He wiped off more and more, every quick rub down his face finding more.

"A dishonorable life is met with a dishonorable death," Sardonyx said, then laughed. Pyith joined in, along with all the zephum, other than Tempest and Strength. The chorus of pure joy at his expense made Zeen want to cry. He had never felt more alone.

Sardonyx sheathed his blade, not bothering to wipe any of the blood off. "A lesson for today: do not, under any circumstance, interrupt or dishonor the God of Strength. It is an *unforgivable* sin. Guards, throw his body into the streets."

"Well congratulations, Zeen," Pyith said, still laughing. "You are currently undefeated in zephum honor duels. What a champion; I am humbled to be in your presence."

"Enough nonsense for one day," Sardonyx said. "I am going to sleep. Guardians, stay as long as you like, but do not be here tomorrow." He left towards his chambers as the God of Strength reverted to his statue form.

"Please follow me," Tempest said. "I'll get us some wine and a cloth to clean your face."

They followed Tempest to an adjacent room, an exquisite-looking chamber with a fireplace and bottles of wine, surrounded by shelves filled with books.

Tempest walked over, handed Zeen a cloth, then poured wine for his guests. "On behalf of my people, please allow me to apologize. I cannot fathom how barbarous we must appear to outsiders."

"No apologies necessary," Zeen said. "I find Vaynex to be…very glorious."

"*Glorious indeed*," Pyith said, mocking Sardonyx's voice. "It's alright Zeen, the warlord isn't here. You can say whatever the fuck you want."

Zeen glanced over to David, who nodded in confirmation.

"Forgive my memory," Tempest said, handing Mary her wine. "Strength referred to you as Mary Walker; is that correct?"

"Yes. What room is this? It looks like something right out of Alanammus."

"Ah! You have a trained eye. Alanammus was the inspiration; you will notice the wine is from there as well. Father leaves me to deal with any of the foreign dignitaries since he has no patience for trade negotiations or subtlety. I created this room to host our guests; most zephum don't bother to comprehend the other kingdoms' cultures or values."

"You are unique," Mary said curiously. "Forgive me for saying this, but until today I thought all zephum were monsters."

"A reasonable conclusion," Tempest said as he smiled. "Fortunately, my beautiful life-mate here keeps me tethered to reality. Otherwise, I may succumb to my ferocious nature as well." Tempest sat next to Pyith, handing her a glass, then held her hand.

"Enjoy it while you can," Pyith said. "When you eventually become warlord, you cannot live this way. Our people will never allow it."

"We shall see. I may surprise you yet," he said, then turned his attention to the Guardians.

"David, I apologize that we do not have the means to aid your wounds in Vaynex."

"I understand," David said. "When we are finished here, we will head to Alanammus. The three of us desperately need some healing magic."

Zeen silently thanked David for saying that. The stress of…zephum honor duels strained his throbbing skull. *To hell with it,* Zeen thought, taking a large swig of his wine. *Oh,* that was a sweet taste. Maybe the rumors were true. Maybe Terrangus *did* have the worst wine.

"I wish you could take me too," Pyith said. "This leg is too slow to heal; it's such a waste to keep me off the battlefield."

"Why can't you come?" Zeen asked.

She sighed. "Most zephum are too fucking stupid to understand the benefits of magic. The few mages we have are forced into military life as soon as their talent is discovered. Any zephum warmaker can demand an execution for Harbinger suspicion with almost no evidence. You can thank honor and tradition for all this nonsense."

"We will move forward, my dear. You have my word; our

people will rise out of the darkness and into enlightenment."

Okay, who is this guy? I KNOW him. From where? Have we ever met?

"Time will tell," she said, kissing him gently.

"Pyith, you are adorable," David said with a snicker. Pyith finished her wine in one gulp, then threw the glass at him.

"Get me a fresh glass," she said to Tempest, who immediately rose.

David finished his wine and leaned in. "Pyith, on a more serious matter, I would like to nominate Mary Walker to Guardian status. Her valor in Boulom was a significant factor in our victory."

"Ugh, Strength told us of the battle. That should've been me out there. IT SHOULD HAVE BEEN ME!" She threw her second glass against the wall, shattering it to pieces. Tempest rushed to get a third glass ready while Pyith walked over to Mary and examined her. "A human engager. Now I have seen everything."

Mary stood up straight, in perfect posture to impress her superior. It reminded Zeen of their first day in the Koulva mines. "It is an honor to meet you, Pyith Claw."

"You are just so tiny," Pyith said. "Like a baby zephum. Alright, I only have one request before deciding. Punch me in the face. Punch me as hard as you fucking can."

Mary didn't hesitate, slamming her fist straight into Pyith's face, apparently with all the force she could muster. Pyith took a few steps back to regain her balance, then walked over with a ferocious glare in her eyes.

After a pause, Pyith raised her glass and clinked it with Mary's. "Welcome to the Guardians." Everyone cheered as Zeen rushed over to give her a hug.

Welcome back, my friend. He wouldn't say it—not here—but they had always dreamed of this moment in their harshest days at war. They *never* would have imagined the moment would come in Vaynex, of all places. He sat down, then finished the rest of his wine. Staring at the empty glass, his smile faded as he thought of Serenna. She was alone, surrounded by enemies in a hostile kingdom, while Zeen drank wine and celebrated.

"Thank you. This has been a dream of mine that I never expected to come true…"

Zeen sat next to David as the rest congratulated Mary. "Is it okay that we didn't run it by the others?"

"They will trust my judgement. We don't know how long Pyith will be injured, and it would be an enormous insult to get another zephum in her place. We are incredibly lucky to have found Mary; she can engage while Pyith is out and even when she returns, a warrior of her skill will be an invaluable asset."

"That makes sense, thank you. I hope you know how much we appreciate you."

"You did good, Zeen; the feeling is mutual. As soon as we heal in Alanammus, we will return to Terrangus and deal with…*everything*. I fear the worst. Melissa and Serenna probably believe we are dead, especially if Nyfe is already back." David rose.

"Must you leave so soon?" Tempest asked.

"Forgive me, but yes," David said. "I put on a strong front for your father, but I need to lie down and recover before tomorrow."

"Well, don't be a stranger," Pyith said. "I have a feeling Zeen will never come back here after today. Maybe Mary can be my new human friend."

Zeen smiled. "I think next time, you can come visit me in Terrangus."

CHAPTER 22

TEAR THE BANDAGE OFF

"My dear Francis, they have nearly arrived…"

Francis sighed, checking the Guardian room in Alanammus Tower over and over. Perfection was a two-part story. The diamond chalices, stained glass table, and vast chandelier hanging from the high ceiling—illuminating a wide array of colors—were the first half. Fragrance was the conclusion; he'd had the servants clean the room three times since morning to ensure the fresh lavender scent still lingered in the air. It was just as important—if not more so—to augment the limitations of the eyes. Non-scholars weren't intelligent enough to understand the perception created by their own minds. Alanammus was a kingdom of perfection, but perfection could only exist if created—a lesson his dear mother had never learned.

David will kill me when I tell him. He will bash my skull into the diamond walls…

Keep cleaning. Francis wiped a speck of dust off the table. Everything must be perfect. "I just don't understand… Why didn't Strength tell them? Why do I have to do it? Why do I have to do everything?"

Wisdom chuckled. "Oh, I wouldn't say everything. You didn't *have* to engage Nyfe in Terrangus now, did you?"

Invisible Guardian… I'll never forget those words. "Ugh, out of all the Guardians, Forsythe had to kill *her*. I would have been the hero if Nyfe didn't have so many men. He is *nothing* compared to me. How can people follow such fools? Where are my followers?"

"Focus, my dear Francis," Wisdom said, floating around him. "I need you to focus. The reality is that if Nyfe had called my bluff, you would be dead. Heed my words: my wisdom may be infinite, but my ability to interfere is not. As for my zephum colleague, I assume he feared David's reaction upon hearing the news. It would be quite the tragedy if he threw a tantrum in Vaynex and got himself killed. Oh, what a tragedy indeed…"

Keep cleaning. Francis took a small cloth and polished one of the diamond chalices. How did a smudge get there? Who had dared enter this room without his permission…

David is going to kill me. This is my last night alive—

He let out an unintended shriek as the Guardian portal flickered. The figure materializing…had hair. Zeen formed, *drenched* in blood. Unbelievable. The lavender scent Francis had worked so hard for immediately surrendered to the pungent wrath emitting from Zeen's sweaty body. A perfect representative of Terrangus—

The portal flickered again. The figure materializing…was a woman? *Now who is this?* A tall, stocky beauty appeared in Terrangus armor, waving her scarlet hair to the side as she cracked her neck. They met eyes—and she *smiled*. Maybe this could end up being a splendid night after all.

The portal flickered again.

And…there was David, with his cold stare and empty demeanor. Some people felt the need to wear their emotions like jewelry. He utterly reeked of alcohol, an unholy blend of wine and some other harsh scent—hints of ale? Francis couldn't place the origins; ale wasn't a scholar's drink…

They're all looking at me. Say something. "Uh, welcome! It's, um, been a while. How are things?"

"Now Francis," Wisdom said through his thoughts. No one glanced at the god, so it was safe to assume he was visible only to him. *"I find the best remedy to a tragedy is to tear the bandage off. Do not make this more awful than it needs to be."*

"It's been a journey, to say the least," Zeen said, offering a weak smile. His face would eventually grow tired of feigning happiness.

"I can only imagine…who is this?" Francis asked, pointing at the red-haired woman. *Dammit, don't point at people. You always do this around girls…*

"My name is Mary Walker. David invited me to the Guardians with Pyith's blessing after we defeated one of Death's mages in Boulom."

"Remarkable," Francis said as his eyes momentarily lit up. "Wisdom didn't mention you." *Why didn't he mention you? I hate that he keeps secrets. I should know everything.*

Everything.

"The battle was difficult, but we had the warlord on our side," she said. "Part of me will always hate Sardonyx…but wow, the legends of his power speak true."

"Fascinating… Oh! My name is Francis, by the way. Francis Haide, elemental sorcerer, Guardian of Alanammus."

She smiled. "I think everyone knows who you are. My mother used to take my sister and me to Alanammus once a year and sometimes I saw you by the tower. It's an honor to finally meet you."

A cultured, alluring woman…from Terrangus? Surely, this was a mistake. Surely, David had meant to recruit one of the loud, homeless men off the streets. "The honor is all mine."

"When did Wisdom inform you we were coming?" David asked. Of course he would ask that.

I need to get him out of here. "Call it a hunch, dear leader. You don't look well…perhaps you should rest up and we can speak in the morning?"

David stared through him. Damn him for that. "I do not approve of your deity's growing influence on you. We will speak of this in the morning. For now… I will show myself to the healing ward."

They *would* speak tomorrow. But it wouldn't be about Wisdom.

"It was a pleasure to meet you, Francis," Mary said, stretching back with a yawn. "I think I'll do the same for tonight."

Oh, I was hoping she would stay.

"Rest does sound good," Zeen said. "Hopefully, I won't sleep all day again."

"No!" Francis blurted out. *Speak with more finesse. They're all looking at me again.* "Zeen, take a seat and remain a moment. I must speak with you."

"Why?" David asked, sharpening his stare. "Is there something I should know?"

"No. No…no, it's not that. Get some sleep; the four of us will have a meeting in the morning. It can wait."

Wisdom sighed. *"Oh, dear…"*

"Come on," Mary said, patting David's shoulder. "Let's deal with it tomorrow. If he only wants to speak with Zeen, there's no way it's important."

Bless her confidence despite being so wrong. They exited the room, leaving Francis and Zeen to sit at opposite ends of the table.

Zeen's face grew exceptionally pale. "It's Serenna, isn't it? Please tell me she's okay."

Why does he care? "As of this moment, yes. Forsythe attempted her execution, but Melissa was tipped off by Wisdom and intervened. She defeated him in a duel in the castle, buying Serenna some more time. Oh, and Nyfe is currently leading an insurrection of Terrangus in an attempt to make himself emperor. I tried to save your noblemen… but…ugh, your kingdom is a swamp."

"Whew… That's a lot to take in, but as long as Melissa and Serenna are okay, this isn't a terrible outcome."

There was a long pause after Zeen spoke. Ah, if only he were more intelligent; silence was screaming out the answer.

"Zeen… I'm not particularly skilled at these things, so I'm just going to come out and say it. Melissa was murdered by *your* emperor."

"*What? No!*" Zeen yelled in a pained voice, as he shot up to walk around. "No, no, that just can't be. Francis, you said she won the duel; what happened?"

"According to Wisdom," he said as he stood, "Melissa offered peace after his defeat, only to find a dagger in her neck. A coward's tactic. I would expect no less from Terrangus."

Tears filled Zeen's eyes. "That's not fair… She dedicated her entire life to the realm just for it to end like this. I always imagined this would eventually be my family. Fuck…"

Sorry, Zeen, this is no one's family. "Melissa's warm personality always kept the team together when things got dire. I cannot fathom how David is going to take the news."

"Oh, no…" Zeen said, full on sobbing. "David…this will destroy him. He…they were going to get married…"

Poor David? How about poor me? I have to be the one to tell him. How is that fair? Unless… "I have endured the man's chaotic tendencies most of my life. Zeen, it humbles me to make this request, but I will need your help to break the news. I cannot do this alone."

"Then I will stand with you," Zeen said, wiping his eyes. "He deserves to hear it from both of us. We must prepare for his reaction; it's a near certainty he will rush off to Terrangus for revenge."

Hmm, he's a good man; I regret my judgement from earlier. I need to stop doing that... "Yes, a wise observation indeed. I pity Mary as well. This is a troublesome time to be a new Guardian."

"Is there ever a good time?" Zeen asked as he forced a smile. Why was he so desperate to convey happiness? What did that accomplish?

"No, I suppose not. Get some rest; my instincts are telling me tomorrow will be a nightmare. I'll be the first to wake, then I'll come get you. David can't hear the news from anyone else first."

"Could you show me the way? This is actually my first time in Alanammus. I wish the circumstances were different; I always wanted to see your kingdom, especially the unicorns."

"Oh, of course. I forget you are so fresh to the team. With everything happening, it feels like you have been one of us for a while now—" Francis flinched as Zeen hugged him.

I didn't shed a single tear after I learned of her death. She tried to be a mother after I lost Mom, never judging my...who I am. I wish it hurt more. I wish I could conjure tears...

How much can a person be damaged before they are considered broken?

"That means the world to me, Francis. Thank you."

This is terribly uncomfortable. Please let go. Please let go... Zeen released him, not bothering to apologize for tainting his pure white robes with blood. Francis could now smell himself. It was not perfection.

He guided Zeen to the healing ward and left him in

sorceress Brianna's care. David was already relaxing in one of the baths, while Mary's soft humming rang from the adjacent room. Outrageously off-pitch, but a gifted face always pardons an ungifted voice.

Francis would bathe in his own chambers, where he could relax with a glass of wine and enjoy solitude. Solitude had a familiarity he could always appreciate, but he had never considered until tonight if it was a choice or a consequence of personality. No time for such thoughts. He leaned back in his warm waters, then took a sip of wine.

Hmm. It was rather disappointing. Oh well.

*

Sunlight crept through his window the following morning. The advantage of being too scared to sleep was not having to wake. He threw on fresh robes and grabbed his oak staff. Just in case.

"Good morning, my dear sorcerer! You may want to move with haste. The underwhelming one decided to improvise. For the record, let it be known that I advised you to tear the bandage off. Well, good luck..." Wisdom chuckled, then went invisible.

Oh, no... A terrible mistake. Unintelligent people could never be trusted. He rushed out towards the healing ward—

"*Why* didn't you tell me?" David yelled, his furious voice ringing throughout the tower halls.

No...no, no, no. He followed the voice to the ambassador's balcony, a grand room on the highest level of the tower with perhaps the best view of all Alanammus. David held Zeen off the ground, pressing him against the diamond encrusted walls.

"David," Zeen said, "I am sorry. From the bottom of my heart—I am so sorry."

"You..." David said, turning to Francis. He dropped Zeen

to the ground, then approached. "You knew? And didn't tell me? How could you do this to me? *WHY?*"

Francis was too ashamed—and terrified—to look him in the eyes. "It's…it's not my fault. I didn't…it's not my fault—"

"While we sat there, drinking wine with the zephum," David interrupted, his eyes bloodshot as tears streamed down his face, "my Melissa died *meaninglessly?*"

Zeen reached his hand out to comfort David, but David retracted and struck him in the face with a wild swing, knocking Zeen to the ground.

"No!" Francis yelled, still struggling to regain his breath. "Taking your pain out on us will not save her! Be a leader for once! Just *once!*"

"*Coward.* I swear on your mother's grave I'll kill you if you keep speaking. The two of you have failed her."

It should have been you who died. And you know it…

"We all failed her," Zeen said, struggling to stand after shaking off the blow. "We were fools to go to Boulom. I supported the plan when Melissa said no. Direct your anger on me; this is my fault."

"I regret making you a Guardian," David said, staring directly in Zeen's eyes. "Your fate should have been a forgotten corpse in a forgotten war."

Zeen didn't feign a smile; the words must have cut him *deep.* "Be that as it may, I am here for you. If the day ever came, I would die for you without a second thought, as Mynuth did for Rinso. You are my Guardian brother."

"I have no brother," David said, turning his back to them both. "Leave me. Leave me, *now.*" Zeen kept his head down as Francis walked over.

"The most valuable thing we can offer right now is time and space," Francis said in a hushed tone. He placed his hand on Zeen's shoulder and motioned for them to leave. "I'll be your brother, Zeen. We'll get through this together."

CHAPTER 23

A SHATTERED PERSPECTIVE

With the room clear, David was finally alone. A familiar feeling, but this was different. Worse. Much worse. He would never hear that laugh again. Never kiss those lips. Never cry in her arms while she lied to him and said everything would be okay. Alone would last forever, with isolation's grip the only thing left to embrace him. Nothing could ever truly fill the emptiness, but gods, did she try. Some days, some nights, she had succeeded. It was all for nothing.

David screamed, tearing open his dry throat from the wail, then threw a chalice into a mirror beside him. A familiarity followed the glass plummeting to the ground. No matter how grand the mirror once was, all it could do now was show a reflection of nothing, a perfect portrayal of the man staring back. A shattered perspective. The way a bright white fades to a pale death. The way a vibrant black descends into a shadow of a shadow. Life ended, but the man living still remained. Maybe not for much longer.

He walked out to the edge of the balcony, gazing out into the lands of Alanammus from his high vantage point in the tower. The scenery of decades past hadn't changed. Doves flew by, winds blew green tree leaves softly through the air, even a family of unicorns galloped through the fields of the outskirts. The first time David had seen it, he thought it was perfect enough to be a dream. Now, it could be someone else's dream.

David wiped his eyes and stepped over the balcony, holding the railing behind him as he leaned forward to perceive how far the fall would be. More than enough. He slowly loosened his grip, closing his eyes to reminisce a last time.

Wait for me in the void, Melissa. We will fade together into the dark infinity. I love you…

David let go, keeping his eyes closed, welcoming the one thing that could bring peace.

As his feet left the balcony, he was weightless…

Free…

An icy hand grabbed him, keeping him suspended in the air. He opened his eyes to the fall that would have been his end. *Is this a dream? Am I already gone?*

"Look upon me, David," the entity said. The voice was distorted, a bizarre mix of a young woman and a demon, strangely familiar, but he couldn't place it. He finally looked behind him to the staggering angelic figure, radiating darkness with two ethereal wings and a golden crown. She had long shadowy hair, with her left eye replaced by a beaming onyx gem that sucked in light like a vortex.

The Goddess of Fear? Now? "No…let go. Please, let go. Leave me to my end…"

"No, my sweet David. This is not your end. This is only your beginning."

Francis and Zeen reentered the room from his peripheral vision, gaping at the celestial being with dumbfounded expressions as it turned to them. The angelic figure created a portal underneath David, letting him go as he collapsed into the darkness.

*

"Open your eyes, David…"

He awoke, already standing in an unfamiliar metropolis, rich with life and filled with foreign colossal structures. Snow fell from the skies, collecting on the busy carts drifting through the city streets. He shielded his eyes from the brightness. They used a more advanced version of the light towers in Alanammus, with groups of mages channeling bright yellow auras that illuminated *everything*. The pale sky suggested a numbing cold, but David felt nothing. *Am I dreaming? Maybe this is the afterlife?*

"She is waiting for you," the voice said again. David turned to his left at the messenger: a young man in a black cloak with half his face missing, replaced by the same dark energy the goddess had.

"What is this?" David asked. "Who are you?"

"She has the answers. You will find her, and then you will leave here as a *god*." The cloak fell to the ground as the man faded to dust.

David paused—something flashed in the corner of his eye. He turned to his right and got a glimpse of an enormous crawler that scurried behind a building once David noticed it.

There are demons here… Why? None of the city-folk had any reaction. How could they not see it? Now, finding several crawlers all over the structures, David drew his blade and entered his battle stance, stepping backwards until he inadvertently bumped into a merchant.

"It's okay, David," the merchant said, as wings unfurled from the man's back. "I'm surprised you haven't already figured it out."

"Figured out *what*?" David asked, clutching his sword.

"*Where reality fails, dreams are eternal,*" the man said in a demonic voice, spreading wings as he flew out into the white sky. A crawler turned its gaze on David, then jumped directly in front of him.

David held his sword out to defend himself, his heart pounding as the creature morphed into the shape of a young girl who gazed at him with a smile. *I'm afraid,* he thought, his hands shaking. They *never* shook. *That must mean I'm alive?*

"On behalf of the empress, allow me to welcome you to Boulom."

Impossible. I saw the fallen kingdom with my own eyes. "Boulom? How can that be?"

"Never forget our mantra: Where reality fails, dreams are eternal. You will follow me now." The girl walked through the immaculate city streets as David followed from behind. The city-folk turned in and out of demon form, while the clouds constantly changed from white to red to black to white and so on.

"Who are you?" he asked, wiping snow from his face. Why wasn't it cold?

"You are the first mortal to enter this plane of existence. I will fulfill my purpose, and then I will fade away forever."

"I don't understand…"

"The empress has been watching you, Guardian. Life has been cruel to you both. You will find that death can be far more accommodating."

"Does that mean I'm dead?"

"Maybe, isn't that what you wanted?"

"I…yes. The demon saved me against my will."

"*Demon?*" she yelled in a booming voice. "Is that what you think we are? You aren't paying attention. I get *very* angry when you don't pay attention."

Everything froze in place as the girl reverted to the angelic form of the entity from Alanammus tower. Even the snow stopped dead in the air. "Stop being a fool, David," she said in her distorted tone. "Suffering is no excuse for ignorance."

Fear picked him up by his neck and held him in the air; the city descending into total darkness as he struggled to breathe. Did he have to breathe until now? It was impossible to remember. "I can read your fear. Every failure you have ever experienced is as clear as the darkness surrounding us."

She threw him back into the nothingness. Pure numbness took over. Not a single one of his senses worked—other than fear. He was truly afraid, and he clutched his fear as the only hope any part of him still remained. The idea of the void had always seemed welcoming: a deep sleep that never ended, or something of that nature. Oh, what he would give to rest. Instead, he floated through oblivion, wishing he could feel his arms and legs to flail them in defiance. Hints of a soft voice. From where? Who else was here?

"And there it is, my love. I will wear this ring for the rest of my life; I wish I had one for you too…"

"NO!" David screamed.

He opened his eyes, finding himself in an odd mix of a gray throne room and a court, with David much lower to the ground than the throne and senators' seats towering above him in a circular formation. The chamber was prestigious, with a shimmering glass ceiling, completely uninhabited except for the young woman sitting back on her golden throne with her legs crossed. She was the fully human version of the angelic entity, with the same shadowy hair and light brown skin, with a plain sword sheathed on her back. No onyx gemstone: both hazel eyes judged him from above.

The royal figure rose. "Welcome to the world that lies beyond reality and dreams, between regret and desire. Perfection, in all its temporary glory. To the past, I am Empress Maya Noelami. To the present: the Goddess of Fear."

She was the goddess of fear? The second Guardian? The

last empress of the fallen kingdom? "*Fear...* Have you brought me here to mock me? To revel in my misery?"

"No, my sweet David, I brought you here for a meeting of past and present Guardians. You and I are one and the same."

He didn't bother to hold back a laugh. "One and the same? I wasted my entire life battling your Harbingers to protect a kingdom that discarded me. Go ahead and kick me while I'm down. It means nothing to me anymore. You win."

"Don't be so simpleminded. If not for my methods, there would never be a force ready to defeat Harbingers of Death. I didn't have a Guardian team when the first one arrived, and I had to watch my entire peaceful kingdom crumble before me. *Do not* even attempt to imagine what that's like."

David scoffed and shook his head. "What nonsense; you justify sacrificing some because it saves a few others? How dare you... *How dare you?*"

"I create fear, because fear is the root of all strength. When people become complacent, they grow weak, and lose any incentive to prepare against the unknown threats that always loom. Did you forget my message? The threat of destruction is the only way to ensure peace."

David paused, struggling to find words. Any words. He was in no emotional state to debate ethics with a deity, but every moment of silence surrendered to her logic. *What would I have done in her position? I controlled my Guardians with fear; it's impossible to deny that.* "I always assumed you despised us. It's difficult to reach any other conclusion when your demons murder fellow Guardians and innocents. No... Results be damned, I cannot condone this; there must be a better way."

"Starting today, there is." The empress raised her hand and teleported David from the floor to right in front of her throne. "I have a proposition for you. From one fallen Guardian to the next."

He checked his hands to make sure he really did teleport. "What... What do you want from me? Haven't I suffered enough?"

"As with any true sacrifice, it is *never* enough. I want you to become the first mortal to ever wield the Herald of Fear."

David took a step back; it was what he had sought in Boulom...but at what cost? How did life get to this point? "I saw what Death's blade did to Nyfe... I will not become a mindless demon that brings pain and misery."

"Not a mindless demon or Harbinger; you would be my champion. I offer untold potential while leaving your freewill intact. What you do with this gift is up to you, but my only demand is when I call upon you to slay a time mage, you *must* answer the call."

Hmm...

Stop it. What would Melissa say that I'm even considering this? "No... I am content with fading into the void. I have nothing to live for anymore."

"Revenge is a powerful motive," Noelami said, glaring at him. "You say life has lost its meaning. What greater purpose could there be than slaying the man who murdered half of you?" Noelami raised her hand and created a mirage of Grayson stabbing Melissa in the neck. "At the very least, kill him. If you choose to die after that, I will not stop you. You have more than earned the right to rest. But please, consider this opportunity...we could accomplish *anything*."

Tears ran from David's eyes as the vision played out. Those soft green eyes. Melissa screamed without words for someone, anyone, to help. No one did. If he couldn't save his love, avenging her would have to do. He could rest easy after that.

Rest forever. "Why are you helping me?"

She turned her back, then tilted her head down. "I threw

myself off the ledge of this very room after we finally won. The Harbinger was defeated...but it didn't bring anyone back. I know the emptiness all too well, the permanent numbness that comes from a loss that cannot heal. I will never have my revenge on the God of Death, but orchestrating Forsythe's end would please me. He has your Guardian team that I never had, and yet he throws it all away. I will *no longer* suffer this fool."

Noelami drew her sword and approached David, holding it in the air. "This blade is the Herald of Fear. Wield it, and you will gain the ability to absorb fear and thoughts from anyone who specifically fears *you*. The sword is pure void energy; you could even kill a god. Do you accept this burden? As much as I desire your cooperation, choose wisely. No one will ever accept you again. You will only have me..."

Melissa always loved Terrangus. I can't save her, but I can honor her memory by protecting the realm. By any means necessary. The threat of destruction is the only way to ensure peace...

He paused for what could have been forever. "Where reality fails, dreams are eternal." David took a deep breath, then reached out. The blade erupted with void energy at his touch, as the dream of Boulom was replaced by the reality of a dead kingdom. Corpses and shattered buildings were all that remained. A graveyard as far as his eyes could see. The failure of reality. "Noelami, Goddess of Fear... I am your champion."

The empress morphed into her goddess form, then created a portal to Terrangus. "Go forth, my champion. I will smile upon you as the emperor dies screaming."

CHAPTER 24

THAT DOESN'T MEAN I HAVE TO LOSE

"I'm ready," Zeen said, nodding to Francis from the Alanammus Guardian room portal. His face still throbbed from David's strike, but the adrenaline of preparing to see Serenna again swept away the pain.

"I'll trigger it now. Be quick. We will need you and Serenna to defend Alanammus from whatever that demon was. I'll alert Archon Gabriel and ask Wisdom what's going on once he reveals himself again. Failure is not an option. Retrieve her, then return here *immediately*."

A swirl of black energy surrounded Zeen before he could respond. *Gods, I hate portals,* he thought, closing his eyes and taking a deep breath.

He materialized in the Terrangus Guardian room, to a chorus of gasps from the four men already there. Terrangus bells rang relentlessly. The bells were normally reserved for Harbingers, but maybe someone had finally realized Terrangus was the greatest threat to Terrangus. His hand eased to Intrepid as one of the guards approached.

"Oh shit, a Guardian finally showed up. Are we supposed to kill this one? Which side are you on?"

"I side with the realm."

The soldier snickered, then drew his sword. "Sorry, Zeen. Need a real answer and not wordplay. Pledge your allegiance to Nyfe, or we have orders to kill you." His one-handed grip on the sword was embarrassing. Apparently, civil war had made unskilled soldiers *bold*.

"Can this wait? The conflict between Nyfe and Forsythe is not my concern. I just want to retrieve Serenna and head out. I still honor the Guardian Pact—"

The soldier attempted a cheap shot with a sudden thrust towards Zeen's neck. Zeen easily dodged, then countered with a fierce slash across his face, sending him to his knees with a pained cry. *Damn, I should've held back. These guys have no battle experience whatsoever.*

"Ha. He really thought he could kill *you*?" another man asked, who was sitting in Melissa's old seat, studying her elemental-detonators. "I swear, everyone has lost their minds since Nyfe returned. Fuck that. If anyone asks, we never saw you."

Zeen shook his head. "Why is this happening?"

"Eh, welcome to the party. The kingdom is divided between Forsythe and Nyfe. Melissa's murder plunged the military into chaos, and the three of us figured Nyfe would eventually win, so we joined his side. That guy over there is nuts, but I find the crazy ones are better as allies than enemies."

"Do you even believe in Nyfe's ability as a leader?"

"Who cares? What has the emperor ever done for us?"

That much was true. Zeen had seen the downsides of leaders commanding by fear. Soldiers had followed men they hated...until they didn't. "I understand, but you're just replacing one mad tyrant with another."

"Fuck it then. We have nothing to lose. The poor don't fear change."

"Well, good luck with that," Zeen said, not bothering to hide his disappointment. Before he could exit, the "crazy one" rushed over from the corner and grabbed him.

"Be on the alert for David. He has become a *monster*."

"David?" he asked, flinching back. "Surely you can't mean Guardian David?"

"That man is no Guardian. Not anymore. He killed…he killed so many of us. His blade tore the fear from our hearts; I could see it fade from us and join him. Zeen, I could do nothing to save my squad. *Nothing*."

What madness is this? I don't even know if David is alive anymore—

Is that why the bells are ringing? It can't be… "Please, speak clearly and tell me what you saw. Your monster cannot be David."

The soldier clutched Zeen, not in a threatening manner, but as a man terrified. "I *swear* to you, on whichever god you follow, David has gone mad. He wields some cursed blade of darkness; it has completely altered him into a demon."

Zeen's eyes grew wide. "Demon? That…cannot be true. Where did you last see him?"

"In the military ward, laying waste to soldiers on both sides. Rumors are that he arrived to kill Forsythe, but so far he has shown no loyalty to Nyfe."

The other soldiers shrugged, all their eyes to the floor. Hmm. "Damn," Zeen said in a hushed tone. Somehow, the monster from Alanammus had to be involved. Francis had been convinced it was a Harbinger, but there was a different sort of *terrible* about that winged creature. "What is your name, soldier?"

The soldier stepped back and stood straight. "James Matthews, Terrangus infantry!"

Zeen nodded. "Stay here with them. This room should remain safe."

"Could...I join you? It would be an honor to aid you in rescuing Serenna. She doesn't deserve to be jailed after protecting our kingdom."

At least some people still have their senses. Maybe I can recruit a few more. "Of course. Thank you, James. You are a true hero of Terrangus. Any of you three want to join us?"

"Na."

A wave of anxiety hit Zeen's gut as he left the Guardian room for the castle halls. Blood stains were all over the walls, all over the floors, with haunting screams and rings of steel clashing from every direction.

"When did this begin?" Zeen asked, gripping his blade with his eyes forward.

"Sometime last night. Nyfe must have overestimated his followers because he started to lose fairly quickly and barricaded himself in the prisons, probably figuring he could use Serenna as a bargaining chip. But once David appeared, chaos erupted everywhere. I have never seen Terrangus in such miserable shape."

"Neither have I," Zeen said, before reaching his arm out in front of James. Two soldiers stared him down as they approached. "Stay behind me."

Both soldiers drew their blades, then the taller one spoke. "Zeen? When did you get here? What side are you on?"

"The side of Terrangus." He gripped Intrepid, preparing to dodge another cheap strike.

"We are still loyal to the emperor," the shorter soldier said weakly, stepping forward. "I am truly sorry about Melissa, but Nyfe is not the answer. We fought with him in Mylor. The man is a *disgrace*."

Zeen slowly lowered his blade. "Agreed, but even if you

did support Nyfe, neither of you are my enemy. I have no wish for further violence; James and I are here to release Serenna."

The taller man sheathed his sword and motioned for his ally to do the same. "That will be difficult. Nyfe is by her cell to ensure the Guardians do not release her. Zeen, he is waiting for you...specifically *you*."

"I see," Zeen said, as he lowered his head and closed his eyes. "This has been a long time coming."

Both soldiers turned to each other and nodded after a brief pause. "If you would have us," the taller man said, "it would be an honor to fight by your side." They both dropped to one knee.

Zeen turned red, rushing to help them stand. "My friends, I will gladly accept your aid, but please, you are under no obligation to kneel. We are all equals in Terrangus. What are your names?"

"Desmond White."

"Alex White."

Zeen studied them both with a smile. "Ah, you are brothers. No matter how this turns out, it is an honor to have you."

The three soldiers nodded at Zeen and drew their swords, following him closely as they navigated through the castle. A few soldiers with hostile eyes gave Zeen a glare, and one even spat in his direction, but the threats kept their distance. A large force of men patrolled the doors to the throne room halls, which, unfortunately, was right next to the stairs to the cell.

"And look who it is. About time you showed up," one said... Oh! It was Captain Marcus. He looked so different with his goatee grown out. "We are trying to stabilize this portion of the castle, but Nyfe's men have barricaded the prisons. I won't stop you, but you would be a fool to go down there."

"Sorry Captain, you already know that's the plan."

"Yeah, of course. I appreciate that becoming a Guardian hasn't changed your outlook, crazy as it is. Zeen, there have been daunting rumors about David... I don't suppose you saw him?"

"Not yet. I won't believe anything until I see for myself, but you have my word I'll stay alert. Regardless, we won't be here for long. Once we rescue Serenna, I'll be out of your way."

Marcus shrugged. "Fair enough. Not for nothing, but everything went to shit once she arrived. Get her out of here, and this time, *keep* her away. Oh, if you get a chance, try to kill Nyfe or David, or both of them, while you're down there. Would make my life a lot easier."

Zeen saluted, then headed down the stairs. An ominous silence followed the small team as they descended to the very bottom and reached the door. "Listen, before we enter, anyone who wishes to leave may do so. This...may not go well." They all nodded with a fierce determination. It brought him back to his Mylor days...until he considered how his Mylor days had usually ended up.

He opened the doors to the vast prison chamber filled with soldiers and Nyfe himself sitting in a small chair beside Landon and Serenna's cell. Her staff still leaned against the wall on the opposite side of the room.

I didn't plan this very well, he thought, finding Nyfe's forces *massively* outnumbered his own. Several soldiers approached to disarm Zeen's allies, but left him alone. Zeen's team glanced at him; he motioned for them to stand down and not die needlessly.

"*You,*" Nyfe said, with an enormous grin.

Serenna rose from her cell and rushed to the bars. "Zeen!" she yelled. Her wide eyes shrank, likely after she saw three random soldiers and no other Guardians.

Zeen ignored Nyfe and smiled at her. "Hello again,

Serenna. I have some wonderful stories for you once we leave here together."

Nyfe stood from his chair and paced near the center of the room. He motioned for his soldiers to stand down and leave Zeen by himself. "Oh, Zeen. Despite all the terrible things you have done to me, I will still become emperor in a few hours." He drew his dagger and gazed into the void power emanating throughout the room. "Have you come to bow before me? The other options are far less favorable."

"I am here for Serenna," Zeen said, his sword still sheathed. "Return her to the Guardians, and none of us will interfere with your bid for the throne. Despite our differences, I have never been your enemy."

"Never been my enemy? You interfered with my glory in Mylor, then left me to die in Boulom. Enough is enough. Not even Francis could defeat me; what chance do you have?"

"One of these days, I hope you can find the good inside you. It's in there somewhere, Nyfe." Zeen drew Intrepid and kept a safe distance. "I did not come for violence, but I will *not* leave here without Serenna."

"You will not leave here...*at all!*" Nyfe rushed in and launched a quick swipe towards Zeen's throat.

The soldiers in the prison ward cheered as Zeen parried and kept a defensive position. He planned to feel his opponent out before attacking the quicker foe; there was too much risk to go on the offensive since they had never faced off before. Nyfe tended to wound or kill anyone who would challenge him to a "friendly" duel, and regardless, there was never a good reason to out-show a superior officer.

Nyfe slashed again, this time towards Zeen's mid-body, which would have been far more difficult to parry because of the angle. Zeen instead stepped back and dodged a flurry of strikes, then counterattacked, swinging at his chest to avoid a fatal blow. Nyfe ducked, then lunged forward, immediately closing the gap, and held his dagger to Zeen's neck.

The glowing blade was so cold, and yet, sweat poured down Zeen's face. A terrible mistake. *I failed you, Serenna. Please forgive me...*

He would die alone, hated and miserable.

"You are too slow!" Nyfe laughed as he backed off, holding his glowing dagger in the air as he stared into Zeen's eyes. "Count that as death number one—there will be many more. It will be my choice when it's finally over. I want the darkness from a blink to never end, life fading with no warning. Show me the terror in your eyes..."

Zeen ignored his monologue and the laughs, slowly inching towards Nyfe and studying him up and down to find a weakness. *I must do better; this is likely my last chance. How can I use his arrogance to force him into a mistake?* The distracted Nyfe rallied his troops, whipping them into a frenzy as they watched him out-duel the Terrangus Guardian.

What would Rinso do?

Something unpredictable. Zeen charged forward—he feigned an attack, then stopped to counter. Nyfe ignored the bait; he instead stepped back and waited for a better moment. Zeen followed through, slashed towards his leg and missed, then used the momentum to spin, targeting his head.

Hopefully, Nyfe expected a bit more finesse, and not the violent swing that would tear his head right off if it went unblocked. Nyfe parried, but the force of the desperate strike knocked them both backwards with their weapons flying. The Herald of Death and Intrepid skidded far across the room in opposite directions.

Both duelists froze before Nyfe rushed over to grab his blade.

This is my only chance. I can't win, but that doesn't mean I have to lose. Zeen dashed in the opposite direction, grabbed Serenna's staff, then sprinted to her cell. He threw the Wings of Mylor at the Crystal Guardian with all the strength he could muster.

It's up to you now.

CHAPTER 25

FEAR AND DESPERATION

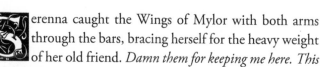erenna caught the Wings of Mylor with both arms through the bars, bracing herself for the heavy weight of her old friend. *Damn them for keeping me here. This will never happen again.*

Zeen smiled, before taking a slight graze across his face from Nyfe's blade. He fell to the ground, then Nyfe kicked his sword across the room.

"Drop the staff, Pact Breaker," Nyfe said, holding his dagger against Zeen's neck. His eyes wide and chest stiff, the words were empty. She would *never* drop her staff again. His soldiers likely already knew that; the terror in their eyes surrounded her like she was about to destroy them all.

Depending on Nyfe's next move, maybe she would.

Clutching her staff, she closed her eyes, then cast a crystal shield on Zeen. The vibrant platinum brought a wide grin to her face; at least all that rest had been good for something. She raised Zeen to the high ceiling not a second later, then met Nyfe's stare. "I see your threat and offer you one of my own. Leave this room if you value your lives."

"*No!*" Nyfe screamed, seemingly enraged at the murmurs

and hesitation of his men. The real duel was for the morale of his soldiers. Unless she did something terrible, she couldn't defeat the entire room. A man like Nyfe knew that. He would also know that she knew that.

Nyfe rushed over to the three unfortunate men Zeen had brought, then dragged his dagger across the shorter one's neck.

"Alex!" the closest man yelled, clutching his dying friend, attempting to close the wound with his bare hands. An awful sight. Enough.

Serenna drew more power from herself than was likely wise to form a large crystal spike. The crystal shimmered with the dark glow of his dagger, creating a beautiful display of shadows cascading on the prison ward walls.

"Stand down!" she yelled.

Nyfe snickered. "I'm tired of Guardians telling me to stand down." He jabbed his blade into the third man's neck, then tore the bloody dagger out as he collapsed.

"*Damn you!*" She launched the crystal spike towards the grinning Nyfe, a move she regretted immediately. A terrible mistake. Nyfe slashed his dagger through the crystal, shattering it the same way he had done in Mylor all that time ago. The fear in the eyes of his soldiers ascended to wonder as he defied their cursed Pact Breaker. *Damn it all.*

Not many options with Zeen held in the air. Entering her empowered form would drop him before she could recast the spell. Nyfe would break through a crystal prison that wasn't full energy. Barrier would just delay his approach. Hmm. There *was* another option.

No. Don't think that. I didn't come this far to submit now.

Nyfe approached Landon. He wouldn't dare. "Your key, sir."

"Never," Landon said, backing into the bars of her cell.

"I really hate to ask twice," Nyfe said, touching his dagger to Landon's neck. A tiny drop of blood flowed down.

He wouldn't dare.

Forsythe had told her the advantages of threatening a scenario where everyone lost. It had seemed so wild. Reckless.

Efficient. "Death...come to me now," she whispered.

As if on command, a cold chill gusted through the ward. Nyfe kept his blade on Landon's neck, but she caught the shiver. "This is my final warning," she said, with a trickle of blood flowing down her left eye from using too much energy. "Back down, or I burn this entire kingdom to fragments of dust. Your families will die *screaming*."

"Serenna, stop!" Landon yelled. Zeen pounded on his crystal shield; the barrier muffled whatever he was saying. She took a deep breath, staring into Nyfe's eyes.

"I am nothing..."

The faint gust became a howling wind. Men gasped in terror, but Nyfe stood there, meeting her stare with no reaction.

"I am forever..."

"Serenna...Serenna, Serenna. One more. Say it. Say it now. I need you. I will have you. I NEED YOU!"

She grasped every ounce of strength not to collapse from the pounding in her skull. *Please stand down. Please don't let this happen...*

I can't do it—

Nyfe sheathed his dagger. "Fine. Soldiers, we regroup at the west end of the castle. There is no reason to unleash a Harbinger of Death when victory is at hand." There was a collective sigh of relief after Nyfe gave the order.

He turned to her a last time as his final soldier left the ward. "I pity you for this. You have opened a gateway that will never close. In any time of grief, anger, or despair, Death will be your first choice. You're just like me, except somehow *worse*. Goodbye, Serenna."

There was no reason to respond. She floated Zeen to the ground as Landon unlocked her cell. Landon frowned at her, then left.

Forgive me. I will always treasure you, but I will never be your Guardian Everleigh. A happy life doesn't exist for me. Zeen would leave her too; he had no reason to—

Zeen rushed over and hugged her, his eyes filled with tears. "You're safe. You're finally safe. I'm so sorry for everything. I've been a terrible Guardian." She refused to cry as he wrapped his arms around her. "That was a wonderful bluff; I knew you would never turn to the void. You're too good a person."

"Zeen…please don't ever change." She wasn't sure how long they embraced, but she was sure that she didn't care. Zeen let go to check on his only surviving ally before a terrible agony tore through her.

"NO! I am not a tool to be used. I am the God of the Death, the one that defies Time and scours the realm with infinite nothing. You have made a terrible enemy this day. A terrible enemy. I will never heed your call again. Before the end, you will scream my words to the heavens, yet nothing will happen. I loved you, Serenna. We could have destroyed everything. The Time God would wake to an empty world…

"Nyfe will have to do. He will crumble everything you love into ash. Whether he wants to or not."

The pain ended. A burden left her shoulders, replaced by her pounding heart. She wanted to cry out in joy, but the ominous words of the deity kept her grounded. *I did what I had to do. Whatever comes from my bluff, so be it.* Zeen drifted to his remaining ally, who remained sobbing with the corpse in his arms. She had forgotten about them in the chaos.

"Desmond," Zeen said, "forgive me. Alex was a good man.

It won't heal the pain, but you will carry my thanks forever."

Desmond rose, then embraced Zeen. "Thank you, sir, and thank you too, Serenna. It was an honor to be on your side, but please, promise me you will kill Nyfe. Terrangus deserves better. We all do."

"His day will come," Zeen said. "I swear to you."

I hate to do this now... "Shall we head out? Pardon me for rushing, but I cannot stand to be in this room any longer. I want to go home. Please..."

"Not yet," Zeen said, with a particularly gloomy look in his eyes. "James mentioned earlier that he saw David as a demon. I...will not believe he spoke the truth until I see it for myself."

Wait, what? Demon? What the hell happened while I was down here?

Desmond drew his blade. "I'm with you until the end. For Alex."

Gods, I want to go home... "Lead the way. Sounds like nonsense, but we can investigate."

They climbed the stairs to the castle halls, finding corpses *everywhere*. Zeen sheathed his sword and surveyed the room; his shocked expression suggested it wasn't this way when he had come earlier. Misshapen bodies were scattered about, with black energy radiating off the fatal wounds. She would never tell them, but this could only be done with void energy. That narrowed it down to Nyfe...

Or her. "The wounds on these men are surreal. These didn't come from any normal battle. I have never seen anything like this before... Zeen, over here."

"What is that?" he asked, keeping a fair distance from the glowing corpse.

"Look at the size and depth of the cut. This was done with a sword, not a dagger. I...don't know what's going on, but this wasn't Nyfe's work. Someone else has void energy."

"This doesn't look good," Zeen said, keeping his head down. "Serenna, if it's David, I will not kill him."

"Don't be naive," she said, glaring at him. "If David succumbed to a demon or Harbinger, the most merciful thing we can do is end him." She hated herself for saying it, knowing the irony of her fate in Mylor, but it needed to be said. Since Zeen didn't respond, she walked over and held his hands. "Listen, if I ever fall again...I want it to be you that slays me."

He flinched back, grasping his hands away. "*Never.* After everything we have already been through, I would never give up on you. You could become the God of Death itself and I would find a way to bring you back."

Bless his kindness. His ignorant, woefully inexperienced kindness. May the horrors of the realm never change him. "Sometimes, it's too late. I hope you learn to understand that when the time comes."

Desmond cleared his throat at an exaggerated volume.

Oh, I forgot about him...

"Sorry," Zeen said, picking his sword off the ground. "Let's move forward."

She placed her hands on the hallway door that would eventually lead to the throne room. She hesitated as an ominous chill filled her chest. "Something terrible is behind this door..." Stepping back, she cast a crystal shield on herself, then the two of them. Any good crystal mage always shielded themselves first.

"I'll take the front," Zeen said. "Stay behind me. Desmond, stay close to Serenna. Keep her safe and everything will be okay."

As he opened the doors, the chill in Serenna's chest grew worse. A tall, imposing figure stood in the middle of the hall, holding a glowing dark sword, surrounded by fresh bodies.

What happened to you, David? she thought, before Zeen eased forward, sword drawn.

David turned around, staring at her team with cold, pained eyes. A yellow essence left Desmond and Zeen, flowing into David. *Essence of fear? But how?*

"Ah, Serenna is free. A welcome outcome," David said in a deep, distorted tone. "Turn back; I have no desire to face you. My vengeance lies beyond these doors."

An essence of fear left her body. *No, they can't see me this way,* she thought, stepping next to Zeen. "We can't do that, David. While I take no joy in this…you know what must be done."

"I do. It makes me proud to hear that; the Guardians are in good hands with your leadership. I love you both, so please believe me when I say you are no match for my new power now that I wield the Herald of Fear. No one is." He drifted forward, his glow radiating darker as he collected their essences. "The man you knew is gone. I now serve the Goddess of Fear as her champion. My vengeance will not be denied; it is too late for anything else."

"It's never too late," Zeen said. "We can save you."

"No…it's *far* too late. I can read your fear, Zeen: you actually care for me. From the bottom of my heart, I thank you for that."

Tears rolled down his face. "I will not lose you…"

"You already have. It was all in an instant. The moment I learned of her death, everything collapsed into nothingness. Every joyful memory I once held is now a painful reminder of all I have lost—"

Desmond charged in with a yell, clutching his sword before he swung at David's head. David effortlessly parried with the Herald of Fear, flinging Desmond's sword down, then driving the glowing blade through his chest, piercing his crystal shield as if it were air. Desmond collapsed to the ground in silence, with dark vapors drifting off the hole in his chest.

"*No!*" Zeen yelled, ignoring the essences of fear rapidly flowing off him.

Serenna stepped back. "My shield…did nothing?"

"A cruel, but necessary lesson," David said, stepping over Desmond to get closer to her and Zeen. "The weapons of the gods are incredible; I can only imagine what the Herald of Wisdom is capable of."

"Defend yourself," Zeen yelled, his sword shaking in his hands. "I will not kill you, but I must incapacitate you until we find a way to reverse this."

"You are not capable of either. So be it. Show me your violence…"

"Stop!" Serenna yelled, grabbing Zeen by the hand. "We are outmatched; let's regroup and figure out a plan. We didn't go through all of this just to die now."

He offered that warm smile, completely oblivious to the doom awaiting him. "I swear I can save him."

"Zeen, if you are my friend, comrade, or whatever the hell we are, you will back down. Please." Between tears and the bright essence leaving her body, most of the room was blurred, but he stood as clear as the most vivid crystal barrier she had ever cast. She felt so powerless, going from coercing an entire room of soldiers to begging Zeen to run away with her.

Pride be damned, she would do it for him.

"Oh Serenna, if you only knew." He gave her hands a light squeeze before letting go. Zeen drew his sword and approached David. The most foolish man in the realm stood against the most powerful.

She refreshed his shield—even if it was for nothing—before he slashed towards David's right arm. David parried, shook his head, then swung his blade across. Zeen's crystal shield crashed to fragments before he flung his sword up to block. The swords collided, then Zeen's blade shattered like a broken crystal.

Enough. He wouldn't die alone. She closed her eyes, drawing every hint of energy to enter her empowered form. Rays of platinum light meshed with David's void aura, creating a bright array of fear and desperation.

David sheathed his blade. "Hold. I will do no true damage. I would never inflict a loss that cannot heal on either of you. You have my word."

"And what value do I place on your word?"

"Hmm. I suppose that's up to you."

Zeen groaned, trying to salvage his broken blade off the floor. Tears rolled down his cheeks as he held the empty hilt in his hand. "You broke Intrepid... I...what happened to you, David?"

David slammed his fist into Zeen's face, knocking him out cold to the floor. "Take him and be gone. For whatever it's worth, I owe you an apology. I understand your struggles with the void far more clearly now."

She created a crystal shell around Zeen, hovering him to her side. "You understand *nothing*." She traveled to the Guardian room portal, carrying Zeen in his shell. It was time to go home.

CHAPTER 26

LONG LIVE THE EMPEROR

David kicked open the throne room doors. He had expected a final gauntlet of soldiers, a defiant charge to protect their fallen emperor. Instead, Grayson sat alone on his throne, covered in darkness, as no one had bothered to relight most of the candles. Clouds blocked any light from entering from the glass above. David approached, Herald of Fear in hand, blood dripping all over. It was the quietest he had ever heard the castle, even with the taps of rain above them. *Everyone has fled or died. There is nothing left but us.*

It ends how it began.

And yet, no essence drifted from Grayson. The emperor just sat there, staring, panting from his wounds, as if he were hours from death. No smile, no frown, just emptiness. David had thought he knew the feeling better than anyone, but the blank nothing on Grayson's face haunted him. *Him,* the champion of Fear. Each pain was unique, each loss wounding at a different level. Serenna had feared herself. She feared how easy it was to become desperate. How easy it could be to solve all her problems by destroying them. Zeen had feared the reality of not being powerful enough to protect everyone. Maybe the wisest fear of all.

"Impressive," David said, nearing the stairs before the throne. "You show no fear in the face of death. I was rather curious, but perhaps, like most fools, you fear nothing. May you find redemption in the void."

Forsythe eased himself off his throne, groaning with one hand still on the armrest. Bandages fell off various wounds on his leg and upper body. "I never had the time for fear. Honestly, it is a relief to be at the end. I won't insult you with an apology, but *oh* how I yearn for those golden days when the two of us were close. They are so far behind us. So far…"

Damn him. Damn him for everything. "You were supposed to be afraid," David said, grabbing Grayson. He shook him until the crown fell off his head. "Why would you deny me this? *Why?*"

Tears filled Grayson's eyes, partly covered by his pale, unkempt hair. He appeared ten years older than the day he had threatened David. "I am not well. I have not been well for ages. Please, remember me as that blond-haired boy you met at the summer festival all those years ago. Not like this…I…killed Melissa. I killed Melissa!"

It wasn't fair. His vengeance was supposed to be fulfilling, a final defeat of the evil tyrant who had taken his love. There was no joy in this. There was no joy in the massacre of nameless men in the halls before him. There was no joy in the way Zeen had cried over his sword.

Intrepid…he feared the sword would never forgive him. That stupid fucking boy…

I'm just as bad as Grayson. The two of them cried together as he eased his hands to the Herald of Fear. With one hand, he drove the blade through Grayson's chest, then hugged him for the last time. "Long from now, when our kingdoms are dust and our names forgotten, we will reunite in the void. Melissa, Madelyn…Vanessa. It will be how it was. How it was always supposed to be. I love you Grayson. As your brother from better days, I forgive you. If you see Melissa in the void, tell her I love her…

"*Please.*" David's voice cracked at the final word, then he removed his sword and turned away from the fallen emperor. Some men just lived too long; Grayson was no longer one of them. David wanted to cry, but he wasn't alone.

Nyfe and a large force of soldiers approached from the entrance. He motioned for his men to hold, then approached David. "So it's true…" he said, his eyes lost on the Herald of Fear. "I don't suppose we're going to have a problem? I've had a *long* day."

David grabbed the crown off the ground and threw it in front of Nyfe. "No. You are the perfect ruler for this miserable kingdom. Long live the emperor." Nyfe's men parted as he drifted to the exit. He could read all their fears.

Even if he didn't want to.

CHAPTER 27

THE ROGUE AND CRYSTAL GUARDIAN

'm home, Serenna thought, taking in her Mylor Guardian room from the dimming portal. The shimmer of the pale walls had lost their glow long before she had become a Guardian. Rock hard chairs were scattered in no particular order, with a red stain on the far side of the table; the side where no one ever sat to avoid the wobbly legs that cracked a bit more each year. So what if it was the least impressive Guardian room out of all the kingdoms...

It was home.

She gently hovered Zeen's crystal shell to the cold stone floors, then released him as he regained consciousness.

"Where...am I?" he asked, rubbing the side of his face. He rummaged for his sword before yielding a *deep* frown. David and Francis had always found it childish to cherish a particular weapon—let alone name one—but anything that keeps you alive becomes a part of you.

The Wings of Mylor had developed a legend of its own. In several ways, it had become more beloved than the woman wielding it. *I'll get him a new sword. Something special.*

Serenna chuckled. "I suppose you wouldn't recognize the

capitol from here. The only time you were ever in these lands was as an invader."

His eyes darted around the room. If he were wise, he would choose his next facial expression carefully. "Mylor?" he asked with a smile. Good man. "Shouldn't we head to Alanammus? Francis is already a bit of a grouch without making him wait."

"True, but after being locked in a prison cell, it's time for a hot bath and some fresh food. Your kingdom isn't exactly hospitable to their captors." That wasn't *entirely* true. *Thank you, Landon. I swear someday to make you proud.*

"Fair enough; I could use some rest myself. My face feels like it's on fire."

She shot him a glare. "The next time I tell you to stand down, heed my advice. Your good fortune will not last forever. I...thought I would lose you. You can't do that anymore. People depend on you."

"I'm sorry," Zeen said, his eyes dodging her glare with the floor. "My emotions tend to get the best of me. Well, at least you're okay. I have missed you dearly."

"I missed you too, Zeen. Now, allow me to formally welcome you to the kingdom of Mylor. It is a pleasant change to have you as my guest and not my enemy."

They met smiles before he stood with a groan. "Thank you, Serenna. Your kingdom is very...*glorious.*"

She cocked her head slightly. "What?"

"Sorry, force of habit after Vaynex. I'll tell you the full story later."

Serenna handed him a cloth to wipe his face, then poured them both a cup of water from a small barrel. "I haven't seen any of my people since...the Death incident. My father will always support me, but I fear my reputation has already shattered among Alanammus and the rest of the south after breaking the pact."

"Is there anything I can do to help?"

"Well, as the last Terrangus Guardian, your words hold significant value. I may need your aid to speak on my behalf when we arrive in Alanammus." She drank the full cup in one gulp to quench her thirst. That feeling would always haunt her. Especially here.

"Oh! You wouldn't know. We recruited a new Guardian from Terrangus after Boulom. She is an engager named Mary Walker. The two of us are actually military friends from years past; David said you would support his decision to make her a Guardian."

Seriously? "You recruited a new member without consulting me? Am I *nothing* to this team?" She took a deep breath. "Damn it all… I understand why he did it. David was an excellent leader; it will be some time before I can accept his fall."

"Melissa's death crushed him. I cannot fathom the sadness he must've felt before turning himself over to Fear."

"Pain is no excuse. As Guardians, we must always do better. Forgive me, I know it sounds cold, but David would say the same thing to any of us. But enough of this. I owe my father a visit."

Serenna took the lead as Zeen followed through the Mylor capitol building. Far less grand than any other castle or stronghold, it was a simple structure for a simple land. The corridors were cold and dark, with no real ornaments outside of some paintings of past senators and archons on the walls.

Zeen paused, staring at a portrait that caught his eye. It happened to be her least favorite piece of art ever created. "It's you!" he said with a laugh, gazing at the epic portrait of Serenna in some inexplicably tighter and less protective armor, wielding the Wings of Mylor as lightning crashed on the storming waters behind her.

This is all I am to them. My eye color isn't even correct...

She sighed. "Yes, it's quite the portrait. It's titled *Guardian of Mylor*; the young man who painted it took several...liberties with some of my attributes."

"I don't suppose I have any portraits here?" Zeen asked with a chuckle.

"Absolutely not. Don't take this the wrong way, but you are not loved in Mylor. It's not directly your fault, but my people have suffered considerably from Terrangus."

"Not directly my fault?" He gave her a disappointed glance, as if this were shocking information. Seriously?

"Don't be naive. No one in war is innocent. You have slain many of my people, and I, countless of yours."

"True...but here we are, and I am grateful to finally be here as your friend." He turned away and towards the portrait, still enthralled at the superhero in front of him. She wasn't thrilled with where his eyes lingered. Maybe he liked that version better. Maybe everyone preferred the sultry woman that wasn't so quick to anger. "Your people truly love you. After what I saw in Terrangus earlier...I envy that. Everyone who follows my lead just ends up dead. I am not the hero you are...it's unlikely I ever will be."

I'm too hard on him, she thought, noticing a familiar handmaiden approaching from the end of the halls. The young girl squinted her eyes as she got close, then let out a gasp as she dropped a chalice of wine to the ground.

"Lady Serenna?"

"Hello Sophia," she said with a smile. "I am home."

Sophia ran over to hug her. "It's too good to see you! Your father has been a wreck since you disappeared. Does he know you are here? Does anyone?"

"No, not yet. Honestly, I fear the worst."

"Don't be silly; you are his daughter. You can do no wrong in that man's eyes." Sophia's smile turned to curiosity as she noticed the Terrangus crest on Zeen's arm. "Hmm, Terrangus... you must be Zeen?"

"Yes, madam," he said in an uplifting tone.

"You wouldn't know this, but you are sort of a legend here after your battle with Serenna. They deemed it the Duel of the Rogue and Crystal Sorceress!"

"What?" Serenna asked, her mouth stuck open.

Zeen had a great laugh. "No one has ever referred to me as a rogue, but I'll take it. Serenna, from here on out, I am the Rogue Guardian, or the Guardian Rogue, whichever one gets me a portrait in these halls sooner."

"The Fool Guardian is most fitting," she said, meeting his smile. *I'm glad to see him happy again after what happened to David. If such nonsense brightens the day, so be it.* "Sophia, we have much to catch up on, but the time has come to see my father."

It was a quick walk to the senator's chambers. Serenna paused, then turned to Zeen before she would open the door. "I am more nervous than I care to show. Thank you for coming with me; it was unfair to bring you here without asking."

Zeen gave her a warm smile. "I would do anything for you. How do I address your father? Does Senator Morgan work?"

She nodded, then opened the door, stepping through quietly. She took a deep breath, unnoticed by her father, who was preoccupied with some sort of ledger.

"Hello Father..."

Senator Charles Morgan rose without saying a word, almost losing his balance. "Serenna?" He rushed over to embrace her, letting out a massive gasp as tears filled his eyes. "I was near certain I would never see you again after the rumors.

What… What actually happened? Tell me everything!"

He mostly appeared the same—with his bald head and scruffy white beard—but his senator's robes now had an embarrassing amount of wine stains on them.

"Long story short, I was a prisoner in Terrangus. Forsythe sentenced me to die for my role in the war, but…" She turned and gestured towards Zeen. "This man aided my escape. I would not be here without him."

He approached Zeen, then offered a handshake. "Young man, you have my eternal thanks for aiding my daughter. I am the senator here in Mylor. Ask any favor of me and consider it done."

Zeen accepted his noticeably weak handshake. She would critique Dad for that later. "I appreciate your kind words, but there is no debt. Guardians always look after each other. Serenna has saved my life on more than one occasion."

Charles studied him inquisitively. "*You* are a Guardian? I have never seen you before."

"Yes, Senator, my name is Zeen Parson. I joined right before the Harbinger of Fear in Terrangus."

"Ha! Forgive me, but I tend not to follow such events. I haven't been too efficient at my job lately with my daughter missing."

Lately? "Dad, Zeen is the one I fought in Mylor."

"Oh! You are the rogue?"

She shook her head, ignoring Zeen's laughter. "Why exactly is this a thing now?"

"Well, keep in mind, most of us believed you would die in Terrangus. We needed something to lift our spirits. I don't need to tell you there isn't much good news in Mylor these days…or any days, really. Romanticizing your duel led to a grand story. It was a welcome distraction from the barren reality we faced without you."

"So you did this?" she asked, not bothering to hide her amusement.

"Oh no, I am not wise enough for such things. But be assured, I did take credit. I will exhaust every advantage being a senator offers."

Serenna gave him a loving grin, pushing down the disappointed gaze Landon had given her before he had walked off. Her bluff had been worth it, but the price was *harsh*. "You never cease to amaze me, Father."

He returned her smile. "Good. That is my most important job. You must be famished…poor Zeen here looks like he's about to collapse."

Zeen corrected his posture and stood straight, likely unaware of how it highlighted the dark circles under his eyes. "I do not wish to burden you, but I could definitely eat."

"Then it's settled!" Charles said, clapping his hands together. "We feast tonight in honor of Serenna's return. Let me get some servants in here to help freshen you up; we have a great time ahead of us…"

*

Later that night—after a hot bath—Serenna approached Zeen's chambers, the guest room by her father's office meant for visiting leaders from the Southern Alliance.

She knocked on the door. "Zeen, are you ready?" She heard rustles of clothes being shifted in haste. *What the hell is he trying to wear? Ah, I have my Guardian armor on. It's been so long since I wore normal clothes…*

I must be the avatar they expect of me. The woman from the portrait. The Guardian of Mylor.

"Just a moment… I have never worn anything like this before." The rustles grew louder before coming to a stop. Zeen opened the door, revealing himself in a Mylor nobleman's dark vest, with matching black pants, sporting a curved hat with a white feather sticking out.

She laughed as Zeen's face grew red. "Wow…they really committed to this rogue idea. You look good, Zeen, consider me impressed." He was always handsome, but it was almost surreal to see him in normal clothes. It was too easy to forget that life outside of battle existed, that beneath this lifelong soldier was a regular boy with hobbies, friends, and family. Actually, she knew nothing other than his smile and warm demeanor. Why was that enough? How could she possibly grow attached to someone she barely knew? Her wondering eyes and mind were interrupted as the Mylor insignia on his shoulder—the pale owl with ebony eyes—caught her attention.

Maybe one day, he would wear it forever.

"There is no way I could ever battle in this," he said with a snicker, "but I'm ready if you are."

Serenna entered the banquet hall with Zeen by her side. The room was already filled with her father, Sophia, and several more familiar faces. Two seats were reserved next to the senator, and everyone in the room cheered as they made their way to sit down. *I have missed this. We haven't feasted since the war began,* she thought, eyeing the display of meat, apples, and wine.

She sat next to her father and motioned for Zeen to take the seat next to her. A boy she didn't recognize poured wine and stared at her, his hands shaking as he poured her glass. She nodded in thanks, steadying his hands. They had feared her in Terrangus for her violence; Mylor feared her in awe. She then realized how much she hated both. *Why can't they just love me? Why do I intimidate them? No one hates Zeen…not here even. It's remarkable.*

It's unfair.

Speaking of Zeen, he got a head start on his wine, drinking

half his chalice before she finished her second sip. His eyes darted around the room and his breathing grew heavy. Why was he nervous?

Charles rose, then raised his hand to silence the small crowd. There was a large red stain on the front of his robes; he had somehow seen it fitting to change into something worse. "My fellow people of Mylor, thank you for joining us this evening to celebrate my daughter. In a land of constant darkness, she alone is the light that guides us forward. *All glory to Mylor!*"

"*All glory to Mylor!*" most of the room yelled back. It filled her with pride to see her father inspire his people for once. This was not the man who had floundered in Alanammus against his senator peers. *Maybe if he was this good before the war...no, that's not fair.*

About an hour into the feast, Charles glanced at Zeen. "You look well, young man. The Mylor crest on your arm is a welcome change of pace."

"Thank you, Senator. It is an honor to wear this crest in your kingdom."

"Hmm. Perhaps you would consider wearing it in every kingdom?"

Zeen took a heavy sip of wine. His face was already red. "While I hold great respect for this kingdom...and particularly its Guardian, I am forever Terrangus." The servant refilled his chalice—again.

Serenna glared at her father to convey the message to stop this line of questioning.

He accepted her glare before taking a large bite out of his pork chop. "Indeed. How are you enjoying your regalia? You may not realize it, but you are dressed the part of an influential Mylor nobleman. Normally, I would hound you for your vote, although thanks to being Serenna's father, I always seem to win!"

"I appreciate your kindness in lending me this suit. It's been…years since I wore anything outside of my military uniform or plain townspeople clothes."

"Truly?" he asked, rubbing his chin.

"Yes. Unless you're born into noble life, most of us in Terrangus are quite poor. The military doesn't pay much, but it's the best option to survive. That or barter in the streets."

"What a barbarous kingdom," Charles said before he took another angry glare. "I welcome you, Zeen, but forgive me if I do not speak kindly about your home. Terrangus…has been a brutal enemy."

"I understand that better than most." He took a sip of wine and gazed ahead into nothingness. His lost eyes reminded her of David. "Senator, I'm glad Serenna helped your kingdom win the war. The realm is better off with our defeat."

Serenna gave him a puzzled look. "Oh? I figured you felt the opposite after our last talk. What changed your mind?"

Zeen took another large sip of wine and avoided her stare. "Look at Forsythe; look at Nyfe. If you have to bend the rules to defend yourself from such monsters, who am I to say you're wrong?"

Charles cleared his throat. "Well, funny you mention those two. We received official confirmation about four hours ago: Forsythe is no more. I would celebrate, but Nyfe is the new emperor of Terrangus."

Zeen slammed his chalice on the table, drawing a considerable amount of attention. "Good. I'm glad he's dead. That man was an insult to everything Terrangus was supposed to be. Tell me…was it David?"

"Yes, which leads me to my next bit of news. Warlord Sardonyx Claw has called a meeting between the Southern

Alliance and all remaining Guardians. His son—the weird one—got them to agree on Alanammus for the meeting spot. We're all heading there tomorrow…"

"*What?* Why are we accepting demands from *him?*" Serenna asked, with no effort to hide her disapproval. The Vaynex Harbinger six years ago had been her first one. Sardonyx had threatened to kill her afterwards for questioning why they treated their mages with such disdain. No one had defended her. Not David, not Francis…not even Melissa. *I never want to see him again. Just a large tyrant beast…gods, no.*

"The warlord is apparently furious with current events. Between Nyfe's insurrection and whatever the hell happened to David, he wants all of us to deal with it together before it endangers his empire. 'Chaotic humans,' I believe were his exact words…"

She finished her wine, then held the chalice high to get a refill. "The warlord in Alanammus? Now I have seen everything…" She closed her eyes, trying to block out the surge of terrible memories coming up at once.

This is Vaynex, child. Hold your ignorant tongue in Strength's presence. You saw firsthand what happens to mages that seek what they cannot control. I see it in you too…perhaps I would do the realm a favor by beheading you and throwing your tiny corpse into the streets? I do not approve of this one, David. Get a better human after she dies.

Zeen rattled his chalice, then intercepted the servant heading towards Serenna to get his refill first. "The warlord…is very GLORIOUS!" he yelled, words slurring.

"What the hell are you doing?" she whispered in his ear.

"I…wasted my life for an evil kingdom. Terrangus murdered Melissa, abandoned David, drove my father to an early death… I don't know what I'm fighting for anymore. I'm envious of you…your purpose seems so clear. They all love their Guardian of Mylor."

"Don't be a fool, Zeen. They all need their Guardian of Mylor when the time comes, but no one loves her. Not anymore."

Charles glanced at both Guardians with a weak laugh. "Are you two always like this? You should go into politics; I swear it's easier." He paused for a moment before his eyes lit up. "Stay right there."

Charles rushed up to the musicians, waving his arms for their attention. She couldn't make out his words from afar, but the annoyed sighs likely meant he was making demands. The current song ended abruptly as he made his way to the middle of the banquet hall. Which song—

No…don't do it Father…

"This next song goes out to the Rogue and Crystal Guardian. Come up here and give these people a show!"

She brushed her hair out of her face nervously as the room cheered. To her surprise, Zeen didn't hesitate to stand and reach out his hand. The wine had clearly liberated him from his anxiety.

"May I have this dance?" he asked.

With no other options, she took his hand and guided him to the middle of the hall, avoiding the smug smirk on her father's face behind them. The musicians nodded at each other before beginning their song. A slower song, one dear to Serenna's heart: "The Bevy of Doves." Her mother had used to play it on violin to help her fall asleep when she was a child, lying awake, trying to grasp what crystal magic was and why people gasped at her platinum hair. Better days, back when there had been no one to protect and nothing to fear.

"Do you know how to slow dance?" she asked, already knowing the answer.

"No, but I hope you can save me from being the Fool Guardian tonight."

"It may be too late for that," she said with a warm smile. She then cradled his hands to ease them to the correct positions. "Follow my lead and everything will be okay."

"That has been the plan since I met you."

She gently guided him with a cautious precision around the center of the room to the slower tempo of the ballad. He caught on faster than she had expected, meeting her movements and keeping a somewhat dignified rhythm. *He follows better than he leads,* she thought, meeting his eyes and allowing them to stay there, surrendering the safety of subtlety for the peril of honesty.

He leaned in close, gently placing his head on her shoulders. "Forgive me; I always lose myself when you are close."

She froze, no longer caring about the mountain of eyes surrounding them. *How much of this is the wine?* "Zeen... I don't know what to say..."

"You don't have to say a word. Just keep holding me; may this song never end."

"But it does. The song always ends. No matter how beautiful the first note, the end result is always silence."

"The way I see it, silence is an acceptable price for the fleeting joy of the music."

Serenna had no more words for him, accepting his tender embrace and laying her face by his own. Her hands caressed him with a gentle motion from his shoulders to his back, and she was startled by how satisfying it felt to be held in his warm arms. For a split second, she was a normal woman, and not the Guardian of Mylor, and in that second, she was happy. She nearly trembled at the thought that, for most people, life could always be this way.

I wish my mother had chosen a longer song...

The song met its end—as it always did—to cheers from the crowd and her father clapping with approval. "Bow to them," she whispered, then they went down in unison. Charles nodded to the musicians, who went back to their forgettable music from earlier. She grabbed him on the way back. "That was an unfair tactic. Thank you, Father…"

Zeen was content to go back to his wine, unable to wipe the goofy smile off his face since their dance. He glanced at her, his eyes asking without words what would happen next. She ignored his glance. Not out of spite, but because she truly did not know.

Another hour passed as the mood of the hall remained lighthearted and cheerful. Serenna sighed, nudging her father. "I imagine we will end this soon?"

He let out a giant yawn. "Yes…we probably should not have stayed up this late with our meeting tomorrow."

Oh right. "I still can't believe the warlord is coming to Alanammus. This is just the worst…"

"Believe it, my dear," he said, grinning. "Get some rest soon. For all I know we may die tomorrow." She hugged him, then approached Zeen as he told a story in drunken gibberish to a trio of handmaidens.

"So…this zephum…Vim. He's just looking at me, making all these threats, then…BAM!" Zeen slammed the table with a violent force as the maidens gasped. "The warlord slices this guy in half. Right in front of me. Blood EVERYWHERE!" He leaned in, horrendously attempting to mimic Sardonyx's voice. "'An honorable death…is met with a dishonorable life'…something like that."

They giggled as Serenna pulled him up from his chair. "It's time for bed, Zeen. We have a long day tomorrow."

He did not resist; his eyes widened with alarm as he struggled to maintain his balance. "Rest sounds good…" She let him lean on her as they traveled at a relaxed pace to his chambers. Entering the room, she led him to his bed, then searched for a blanket and a flask of water.

"Ugh," he said, groaning, "and to think I was nervous to be here. What a wonderful night this was!"

She filled a large glass with water. "Drink this, you will thank me tomorrow."

Zeen chugged the water, then let out a relieved sigh. "Thank you... Serenna, I have to tell you something."

"Yes?" She sat on the bed next to him, then he took both her hands and held them.

"I cannot fault David for what he has become."

"What? How could you say that?"

"If it were you that died instead of Melissa, I would've given myself to Fear too."

She threw his hands away, then rose. "Then you are a drunken fool, Zeen. The fact you could even consider such nonsense tells me you have no idea what we stand for. One life can never be more important than the entire realm. No matter who it is, or how much you may care for them...there is no excuse to increase the amount of suffering in our realm."

She stormed out of his chambers, then slammed the door behind her. Onlookers scurried away as if they were damned crawlers. She sighed, leaning on his door to catch her breath.

Why must he be such a fool? No, I won't let tonight end like this... Serenna re-entered the room after a brief pause, then approached Zeen's bed to stand over him. He lay there under his blanket, staring at her with his adorable, apologetic eyes.

She leaned down, placed her hands on his face, then closed her eyes as she went in to kiss him. His sweet lips still tasted of wine; she had to shift her right leg to keep her bearing as his hands caressed her sides. His soft touch guided down her armor with a gentle desperation, finding the few spots where her skin wasn't protected. He could touch anywhere he wanted, if he dared to be so bold. Such a *rush* to feel his desire; how long had he wanted this? *How long have I wanted this?*

Stop...

Stop it...not like this. She slowly released him, stepping away and accepting his immense frown. "Not tonight, Zeen; you are a drunken mess. Sleep it off...if this...*us* is to happen...it will be proper. We must use caution; our enemies will use it against us."

"Let them try. For you, I would tear this world in two with my blade."

"Bold of you to say, but you don't even have a sword!" She laughed, until thinking back to Nyfe's dagger against his throat, then David's sword shattering his own. "I am heading back to my chambers. Thank you for tonight; this was the most fun I've had in a while. Good night, Zeen..."

He rustled his blanket to get comfortable. "Good night, Serenna...I...you are very dear to me."

She froze, his door halfway closed. *Say it, you stupid girl. You have cared for him since the very beginning. Don't let this go. Don't be afraid to be happy. You are more than the Guardian of Mylor.*

"Good night, Zeen."

CHAPTER 28

FEAR IS THE BALANCE

David walked the rainy streets of the Terrangus trade district with a dark cloak covering his face and the Herald of Fear behind his back. Since the blade only drew power from those specifically afraid of him, keeping a low profile had been wise. Only two days had passed since Nyfe's ascension, but there were already subtle adjustments from his influence. The soldiers grew bold, with fresh bravado in their eyes and arrogance in their steps. A certain...*pride*, as if choosing the winning side had made them better people.

They weren't—and neither was he.

Most of the shops and inns remained closed, with far fewer carts in the streets, not counting the busted ones from Francis that no one had bothered to clean up. He had stayed his nights in Melissa's empty home in the noble district, unopposed, and...unnoticed. Almost no nobles had remained. That would be a problem later on as the gold ran dry.

David considered Fear's promise that if he still preferred the void's embrace after his vengeance, she would not stop him. He didn't particularly want to live...but the moment of self-harm had long faded. He found a neutral emptiness; the way time drifts differently once noticed.

Grayson's end had brought him no joy. Avenging his love didn't bring her back; it didn't really accomplish anything, other than make the realm worse off. Nyfe would certainly be a terrible ruler, and all those men David had killed... *Melissa would curse my name if she still lived. If only I died instead of her; I am not strong enough to be alone...*

His breathing accelerated, and all he wanted to do was scream. While Zeen would be naive enough to still love him, the rest of the Guardians would kill him on sight. And they would be *right*. A lifetime of friendship squandered forever. He leaned back against a closed inn and sighed before a woman cried out for help nearby.

David drew his sword.

Three soldiers were harassing some sort of necklace vendor. Her familiar voice was that of a young woman, but long white robes covered her face.

"Am I being unreasonable?" the lead soldier asked. He was a scrawny young man with dark hair and a flimsy blade. David could see through those rookie blue eyes and well-kept beard; the man had never seen a true battle in his life. Likely a cutthroat who had rolled the dice and got lucky when he'd backed Nyfe.

"Please, my lord," the woman said. "I...I will give you a discount, but I cannot give this necklace away for free. It will ruin me; I have nothing else..."

The boy struck her in the face, then signaled his men to wreck her tiny shop. "Serves you right," he said, looking at his throbbing hand in surprise.

The woman lay on the ground sobbing as the soldiers stomped on her fallen shop and rustled through her wares. One laughed as he grabbed the golden necklace and placed it in his pocket, with the lead guard taking anything he could and handing it off to the lookout.

A fiery rage filled David's eyes as he surveyed Terrangus. Whether from fear or apathy, not a single person in the city streets came to her aid. His goddess had only been half right. A lack of fear didn't always make men weak; it could regress them into monsters.

Fear is the balance. This girl has too much, and they have none. I may never be a Guardian again, but I can remind these men what it means to be afraid.

The lookout was too busy stuffing his pockets to notice David approaching from behind. David stood directly behind the fool, who was still too infatuated with his greed to turn around. He pulled his hood back, then slashed across the man's left ankle. The soldier collapsed, screaming as blood gushed out from the wound. The other two turned to him, their bravado vanished, replaced by shaking hands and silence.

David's eyes grew wide, with a sudden rush of power from the essences flowing through him. It was like a cool breeze underneath his skin. "I can read your fear…" he whispered.

"Gods, no! We have no quarrel with you, David," the lead guard said, flinching back.

His essence hit first. "Ah, Willis Green. From what I see today, your fear is accurate. You will never live up to your brother's achievements. He died in Mylor, a hero's honor, while the last remnant of the Green name hounds defenseless women on the streets. The better brother is dead. It would be a mercy to send you to him."

Willis stumbled back. "How? How do you know of my brother?"

"With this," he said, waving the Herald of Fear by Willis's face, "I am nearly a god." He could feel the vibrations of Willis's heart beating as he pulled him up by the collar. "Fear is your new reality. Give this woman back her jewelry before I send you to the void, screaming." He threw Willis into the last guard standing, far harder than intended. *Hmm. I must get used to this new strength. Their fear just…gives me so much.*

The woman stood up and groaned before she stared at him; her face still concealed by the robe. "Thank you, sir, but I have one request." She turned her head towards the lookout who had taken her necklace. "I want this one to die."

Dammit, I wanted to let them off with a warning. I…can protect without becoming a monster. "You are certain? Death is forever; not even I can alter that fate."

"Yes," she said, batting her eyes. "I know more about death than you could ever imagine."

Considering he couldn't read her fear, perhaps that was true. "So be it."

"No!" the guard yelled, his sword drawn against David. "No, please…"

David drifted forward, taking a deep breath as the essences continued to flow through him. Lian feared spiders; he'd thought they were the most terrifying thing in the realm until now. Tall spiders, red spiders…loud spiders? "If it's any consolation, you are now free from fear forever. Some men would die for this gift. May you find redemption in the void."

He tore across Lian's face with a swift slash of his sword. Void energy radiated out of the spot where his face once was, with trinkets spilling out of his pockets as he crashed to the ground. No one dared approach the empty husk as the woman casually collected her jewelry.

The chatter behind him broke his focus from the essences. He glanced backwards to a large gathering of people, all wide eyed and…smiling? *I can't read most of their fears.* The crowd roared as the two injured guards limped away at a desperate pace, leaning on each other and trembling. David strained to hold back tears as he took in their adoration. Since becoming Fear's champion, he had accepted that no one would ever love him again.

The woman placed the last of her goods by the rubble of her shop, then glanced at him. "I was right about you."

"Who…are you?"

"My sweet David, I am insulted that you still don't recognize my voice." Noelami pulled back her hood. He had been a fool for not seeing it, but gods, she just looked so…*normal* without her empress regalia.

"Noelami? What is the meaning of this?"

"Not here," she said before creating a door-sized black portal. "Your heroism has drawn quite the crowd. Now get in. There is much to discuss."

He gazed at the crowd a final time before he entered. Even if he could never return to Terrangus, leaving as a hero was a better fate than he deserved.

*

After a bright flash, he appeared in Fear's kingdom of Boulom. The illusion returned, with the busy metropolis filled with townsfolk and demons. Tension filled his chest as he let out a drawn-out sigh: something was different. The white sky remained, and he shivered as a frigid wind blew against his exposed face. All the inhabitants stared at him. *This is something more than an illusion…or a dream.*

Empress Maya Noelami materialized in front of him in her human form, her regalia and crown back in place. All the townsfolk and even the demons kneeled in reverence.

"No goddess form today, Noelami?"

She snapped her fingers as a ripple went out, then all the entities in her kingdom rose to continue their normal movements. "The form is irrelevant once you understand it's all the same woman. I am pleased, David; you grow comfortable in your new home."

He shivered again; how much from the cold or the idea of this being home, he couldn't say. Noelami raised her hand and a dark coat covered him. "Thank you, Empress. It wasn't this cold the last time I was here."

"You didn't believe it was real," she said with a grin, "but you catch on quick. Do you remember the words?"

He would not *dare* forget. "Where reality fails, dreams are eternal."

Smiling, she drifted towards him. "Ah, you were a wonderful choice. Do you understand my mantra now?"

"I assume it's relevant to why you deceived me in Terrangus?"

"No. Consider *that* a favor. I don't give many of those."

"What? How was that a favor? I killed a man for you…" It had always been easier when he didn't know their names. Lian—a man of twenty-seven—had died after one fatal mistake. His sister Maria would never see him again…

Noelami placed her hands on David's face, then gave him a gentle slap. "Let's try to avoid ignorance," she said, then stepped back. "I had to remind you of the man you were before Melissa died."

How dare she, he thought, before taking a deep breath. David wasn't sure if she could kill him, but it didn't seem wise to tempt fate. "While circumstances are obviously different, I am still the same man. Not even *you* can take that away from me."

"Hmm. I cannot decide if you are a liar or delusional. You must be delusional, because I know you would not lie to me." The frigid winds picked up as her voice distorted. His coat did nothing to help. "You would not *dare* lie to me…"

He closed his eyes, bracing against the cold, refusing to

shiver. "I stand by my words. Pain does not change us; it just shows who we truly are."

Fear nodded as the winds stopped. "Weak theory, but I accept the basis of your answer. Tell me, David, you had no desire to slay that guard; why did you follow the request of a random woman?" She stepped back; her eyes locked on him.

"It had to be done. For fear to be effective, it must be real." He paused and smirked. "Ah, that's the point, isn't it?"

"Well said. I apply that to everything. Words mean nothing to archons and emperors; it is only when their lives are at risk does anything get done. Know this: when I accept a Harbinger, I do not hold back. A weak kingdom doesn't deserve to exist. If life must end, I would rather it be from me than Death. Anyone but *him*."

What a vicious, yet logical woman. I fear it speaks volumes about myself that she views me as a friend, or at least a tool to be used. "Empress... What is my role in all this? I am best suited to being a Guardian, but they will never accept me in my new form."

"Do whatever is necessary. I do not know what Death has planned, but it will be devastating. It always is. I know he targets the crystal girl, but Nyfe is gaining his favor. You must be ready. Let fear be your beacon of hope, an unyielding strength, a nightmare keeping order in the name of balance. Fear is the true Guardian of this realm. Everything else is just a means to an end."

Even in his most obscure nightmares, David could never imagine his former nemesis would end up his muse. "I...will not fail you."

"We shall see. For today, I have a different task in mind. The second part of your bargain."

"What do you ask of me?"

She raised her hand, then created a portal. "You will head

to Nuum, where another time mage dabbles with the forbidden craft. I warned him once, and he ignored me. *No one* gets two. It would please me if you made his end brutal, but you don't seem to work that way. However it gets done, take this portal and kill him."

Interesting. So Nyfe spoke the truth about her role with the Time God? "I don't suppose I have a choice?"

"There is always a choice, but this one is easy…" She morphed into her goddess form, as blinding snow fell from the Boulom skies. "Do not make me ask twice. Remain my ally, or find yourself on the other side of a nightmare."

Even if it was for nothing, he stared directly into her eyes. If she could read his fear, maybe she could read his disdain. "The mage will die as promised, but I will not accept your threats again."

Fear raised her hand, and the Herald of Fear flew into it. She let out a yell before dark energies from all the inhabitants of Boulom flowed into the blade. His vision was blinded as the maelstrom of white snow and dark energies collided. It all stopped at once, then she floated the Herald of Fear back at him.

He grabbed the sword from the air. "What did you do?"

"Consider it a truce. From here on out, the blade will allow you to return to Boulom whenever you choose."

David examined the blade. All the marks and blood stains had vanished from the now-flawless steel. "Interesting. Let's get this over with."

"Then go. I will be watching. I will *always* be watching."

Images of the former Guardian Thomas Byen falling to Fear's Harbinger reemerged as he entered the portal. He had hoped to never see Nuum again, but any veteran Guardian would know that was a fool's hope.

*

The oppressive heat from the withering air immediately smothered him as he appeared, drenched in sweat as his boots sank into the sand. If there was a Goddess of Fire, she would live here. He threw his coat onto the tangerine sands and stripped down to just his pants and boots. Still, it wasn't enough. A jug of water rolled out of his large coat as it hit the sand: a welcome gift. It was impossible to trust Fear, but at least she wasn't callous enough to let him suffer through dehydration.

There was nothing for miles other than a small apricot cottage in front of him. This shack was far from the kingdom streets, which was standard procedure for Nuum missions. Most Harbingers had found their way to the isolated sections in the outskirts, easy targets for Fear and Death to find desperate souls. After two decades, he had lost count of all the Harbingers he had slayed in Nuum, but after losing Thomas two years ago, that battle would always haunt him.

David took his shirt and wrapped it around his hand before he clutched his blade. Studying the cottage, he paused before taking a large swig of water. *I have never faced a time mage before. What nightmare awaits me in this room? Enough. The champion of Fear can never have doubts...*

He kicked the door open and rushed inside. The more startling his entrance, the more fear he could absorb from his target. Strangely enough, there was no person, but various torn up books and pages all over the compact room. Obscure mathematical formulas were scribbled all over the papers; the room seemed more fitting for an eccentric alchemist rather than a deadly sorcerer.

"Who's there?" a man yelled from the adjacent room. David didn't need an essence of fear to realize the terror in the man's voice.

An elderly mage burst into the room, wielding an old, woeful sword. With the dull edge and dark marks all over, the weapon would more likely slay him by infection before it managed a fatal wound. Where was his staff? David stepped back as an unholy odor followed, the foulness amplified by the merciless heat.

This…is who threatens the gods?

David studied the man, unable to find any hint of danger in his feeble, pale body. His gray beard and tattered clothes likely hadn't been washed in weeks. The clouds in his eyes guarded him from seeing his own essence flow towards David.

David could read his fear, but he didn't want to.

"Be gone!" the man yelled. "I am on the precipice of fixing everything…"

"Do you know why I am here?"

"You are a slave to Fear! The demoness is a whore, and you are her butcher!"

David closed his eyes and accepted the essence of fear. His target was Jove White, a disgraced Nuum senator whose son had become a Harbinger. Jove's obsession with trying to change the past had driven him on a descent to madness.

Ah, the senator's son. I remember that one. At the time, I never considered what sort of toll that takes on a man. When his fiery staff came crashing down, that should've been the end, but Melissa saved me at the last second. After forty-four years, all my memories collapse onto her. I will never be free again…

David approached, then placed his hand on the mage's shoulder. "It's okay, Jove."

"No… I can fix everything… I just need more time."

Gods, I'm no good at this. What would Zeen say? "Caleb lives. The price was your own life, but you didn't hesitate in the face of death. You are a good man."

"Ah… I would suffer it all again to see his face one last

time. Take your toll, demon. My soul will gaze upon Caleb from the golden clouds of Nuum."

David thrust his blade through Jove's heart, then held him one last time as he laid him to rest. His blind eyes stared through David and into the infinite darkness he had likely known for so long.

The deed was done. Closing his eyes to focus, David held the Herald of Fear in the air before it glowed and created a portal back to Boulom. David gazed at the corpse a final time before he entered.

Some men just live too long. You are no longer among them. Rest well, my friend.

CHAPTER 29

TRANQUILITY

Zeen awoke, staring at the white ceiling above him in his Mylor chambers as if it were the Great Plains in the Sky from the Rinso novels. His heart thumped in his chest as he played that kiss in his head over and over. Her lips had tasted like the sweet, Mylor wine he had drank *far* too much of; her skin softer than the blanket across his chest. He couldn't remember everything from last night...

But he would *never* forget that.

It was finally real; nothing could bring the proclaimed Rogue Guardian down, not even the throbbing force in the back of his head, or the vast shriveled pain in his eyes as he struggled to focus on the surrounding room. *Oh, gods... I need water,* he thought, then leaned up until a powerful nausea crept through his stomach. He lay back down, letting out a rough, dry cough that ripped at the insides of his throat.

Alright, let's take it slow...

Forcing himself up, he searched the room for something to wear. Sardonyx would throw him off Alanammus Tower if he dared show up in a sporty vest and pointy hat. He let out a sigh of relief when he saw fresh armor lying on a chair close to the chamber door. A mirror was on the wall to the left, but he wasn't prepared to gaze upon the disheveled Guardian of Wine that would judge back in shame.

After putting on his armor, the Terrangus crest of the Ebony Blade caught his eye. With Melissa gone, Nyfe as emperor, and…well, David, it was difficult to find any kinship with the kingdom that had raised him.

Could Mylor be my new kingdom? They appreciate me here, and I doubt Serenna would ever live with me in Terrangus…

It was a simple choice. Zeen ripped the Terrangus crest off his arm, then traded the Ebony Blade for the White Owl. The owl's eyes were normally too foreboding for him, but today he met the bird's gaze as a brother. He could only get half of it to stick on his leather as the rest flapped off—which was kind of fitting for a bird, to be fair. He pounded an entire jug of water that had been placed by his bed, then left his chambers.

Serenna stood outside the door waiting for him, gasping when she saw his face. "Oh, gods…your eyes!"

"This will pass," he said with a smirk. "All things considered, life has never been better."

There was a long pause as his bloodshot gaze met her inviting blue eyes. Chaos stared into tranquility, and tranquility had never appeared so beautiful.

Do I hug her? Lean in for a kiss? Is it business as usual until she signals otherwise? I think I'll stick with that one…

Serenna placed her hand on his shoulder to shift his armor around to make it more presentable. "I'm glad you are in good spirits. Honestly, I am…less than excited to see the warlord again. His intolerance of mages is vile, and yet…I was too fearful to stand up for myself. I am no longer that girl. Today, Sardonyx will meet the *true* Guardian of Mylor."

Hopefully, she couldn't hear his heart pound while her hands were near his face. He welcomed the anxiety for the first time in his life as pain and nausea yielded to the dominance of fear. "Sardonyx threatened me too when I first met him. I called his kingdom beautiful...and then he held his sword against my neck."

Her eyes lit up. "No! Beautiful? You didn't!"

"I certainly did. Looking back, I dodged death more times on that journey than against my first Harbinger."

They laughed together before Serenna stopped and stared down. "Zeen, about last night... There is too much on the line to tell anyone. Please be patient with me; this has to be eased in."

"I understand," Zeen said with an unintentional frown. "You have my word; I'll remain silent for as long as you need." This sort of thing never happened in the Rinso novels. They would "mate," as the author had preferred to write, then his new girl would end up dying in the next chapter or betraying him near the end. Actually, this wasn't too bad.

"Thank you. Follow me; I'll show you to the Mylor Guardian portal. Francis must be distraught; we've kept him waiting for far too long."

*

He took a deep breath as he materialized in Alanammus; nausea and post-portal dizziness were a brutal combo. Hopefully, Francis wouldn't be too upset about the whole Mylor thing. It had been entirely against the plan, but how could he have refused? Zeen followed Francis's voice from the next room over, who was speaking in an unusually...*cheerful* tone.

"And remember, what is most important about Archon Jude was her influence on taxation rates based on magical aptitude. The 'Sorcerer's Tax,' as historians now call it, was wildly unpopular among her peers. Really, it was no surprise that she met her end by poison. Now, there are several suspects on who actually poisoned her chalice. I'll begin with…"

Mary met Zeen's eyes and mouthed, "Help me…"

He grinned, but held back a laugh. "Hello Francis!"

Francis stopped mid-sentence and turned to him, gasping when he saw Serenna, who materialized in the portal, then approached. "You're here," he said, giving Serenna a quick, awkward embrace. "I…missed you. Forgive my words from Terrangus; I spoke unfairly."

"All is forgiven," she said. "It is nothing short of a miracle we are all here."

Mary came up to Serenna and held out her hand. "Good morning, Lady Morgan. My name is Mary Walker; it is an honor to finally meet you."

Zeen's smile grew as Serenna accepted her handshake and kind words. She would meet the true, foul-mouthed Mary soon enough. "Welcome, Mary. The honor is all mine; I will accept any friend of Zeen as one of our own. Unfortunately, you have joined us at a difficult time. There is…much to discuss."

"Oh, about David?" Mary asked casually. "We heard some awful rumors. Francis, I suppose your Wisdom god was correct."

"Wisdom is *always* correct. He is our only ally among the gods; I advise you to follow his council as I have."

Strength seemed like an ally, Zeen thought, keeping the words to himself. Mary glanced at Zeen, who shrugged. While he had no trust for the deity, it didn't seem proper to openly attack Francis's beliefs.

"Hmm. Do we have to kill him now?" Mary asked.

Zeen smiled at the audacity. No one would truly consider ending their old leader—

"Yes," Serenna said, then let out a sigh.

"Absolutely not," Zeen blurted out immediately after. "We must save our friend. He needs us now more than ever."

I probably shouldn't raise my voice to her...but seriously? How can she even consider this?

Francis shook his head. "You aren't thinking logically. I know you aren't particularly...never mind, but we have no capability of saving David. The most merciful thing we can do is end his pain. Listen to your intellectual superiors."

Serenna stood next to Francis, giving Zeen a stern glare. "I am not saying this to be cruel, but the man we knew is gone. It's too late, and he knows it. Deep down, you know it too."

"Well, I stand with Zeen. Can we vote on it?"

Ah, there is the Mary I know. It's been a while, my old friend...

"There are only four of us here, so that won't do us much good," Serenna said.

Francis let out an exaggerated sigh. "Enough of this foolishness. Serenna, please join me; I have much to tell you about the wonders of Serenity. Our new ally is...*incredible.*"

"Fine. Zeen, Mary, we meet back here in an hour for the meeting. Take this time to consider my words. We need to be united on this. Please..."

Mary smirked at Zeen after Serenna left with Francis. "So, why do you look like shit, and why the hell is the crest of Mylor on your arm?"

A strained cough interrupted his laugh. "You were never one for subtlety. Is it really that bad?"

"I leave subtlety to the rogues. Listen, you know I don't care if you have your jollies, but we're Guardians now. Don't let your new crush make a mess of things. If you get a crystal shield before me and I die, I will spit on you from the void."

Zeen smiled as he glanced at the overly-shiny floor. "I missed you, Mary. It's been a long journey since the Koulva mines. Who could have thought we would both turn out to be Guardians?"

She poured two chalices of water. "I figured we would turn out dead. Koulva still feels so fresh. I'll never forget the fury in their zephum eyes when our blades pierced them. It was more than hatred; they *begged* their Strength god for one final act of defiance that never came. I didn't even think Strength was real back then…those days are long gone. Now, by some cruel joke, I'm allied with the warlord. Dammit Zeen, you and I must stick together for Terrangus's sake. The sorcerer worries me."

"Serenna is stern, but behind that is a wonderful woman who would give anything for her people."

"No, you fool. Not her. Francis is the dangerous one. I like the guy…he's cute, kind-hearted, but Wisdom is manipulating him. After what happened to David, I can't trust anyone but you. You are too stupid to succumb to manipulation."

"You can't be that way, Mary. If we can't trust each other, this team will fall."

"Spoken like a true leader?"

Zeen didn't appreciate the grin on her face. "I'm not here for politics. I'll follow whoever is chosen; it will almost certainly be Francis or Serenna."

She stepped forward, then placed her hand on his shoulder. "Or *you*. You are the only acceptable choice. I know your skills firsthand; if you take the reins, I will follow."

He eased her hand away from his shoulder. "Don't be so quick to promote me. I may enact a Sorcerer's Tax, and then someone could poison my chalice."

"Gods, you are a fool," she said, heading towards the exit. She stopped right before she closed the door. "Just think about it. Glory to Terrangus."

"Glory to Terrangus…" The owl crest stared at him after he spoke, its dim eyes proclaiming judgment for the false Mylor Guardian.

CHAPTER 30

ENEMIES, BEWARE

arlord Sardonyx Claw—son of Fentum Claw—emerged from the Alanammus outskirts portal with his son Tempest, both staring into the clear, sapphire sky.

Today would be a *glorious* day.

The smile on his son's face infuriated him. There was no glory in these lands. All the unnaturally green fields and grand silver structures were worse than the rumors, a shameless ode to the horrors of sorcery. The platinum Alanammus Tower scaling into the sky of lies was the worst offense. Where was the scent of blood? The misty violence in the air…where were the *bodies*?

Sardonyx wore his steel face guard which covered his entire green head. It was always an advantage if others couldn't follow his eyes and, either way, politicians didn't deserve to meet his gaze: an honor only reserved for warriors.

A large force of humans greeted them, led by the infamous gold cloaks Tempest had kept gushing over like a child on the way to the portal. Mages remained in the back of the unit, wearing nothing more than their loose cloth armor and wielding wobbly wooden staffs. They all bore that ludicrous Alanammus crest: the sun mask of the Arrogant One. Despite casting him out, they still wore his face in celebration of the paragon of their deceit. How fitting.

Enough. "Where is the archon?"

A gold cloak stepped forward—a brutish man by human standards, but still more than an arm shorter than the warlord. An odd skin tone, darker than Zeen, lighter than David. Hmm, human features were always so frustrating; so many colors and facial variations that had no real influence on any of their traits. What was the point? Everyone should just be *green*.

"Warlord Sardonyx Claw, we have been assigned to escort you and Warmaster Tempest to the tower. As the first warlord of Vaynex since the God of Strength to honor us with your presence, we welcome you." Sweat trickled down his black beard despite the cool breeze.

Sardonyx stood like a statue. "You will die screaming if I am forced to repeat myself."

Tempest rushed forward. "Thank you, kind sir. You must mind my father; while tradition dictates an archon's greeting, we are willing to put this insult behind us in the name of cooperation."

"Forgive me, my lords," he said, accepting Tempest's handshake with his trembling hand. "The insult is not intentional. Please allow us the honor to regain your respect."

The statue did not budge. "You cannot regain that which you have never lost."

Tempest whispered in the man's ear. While Sardonyx couldn't hear the words, knowing his son, it was likely, "Oh glorious human lord, please hush your mighty tone," or some other dishonorable nonsense.

Ah, the shame… What will happen to my people after I am

gone? Hopefully, my dear Pyith can just make him a puppet warlord and rule Vaynex with her iron will. I thank Strength for her every waking day...

"Apparently, my son now speaks for me. Gold cloak, what is your name and rank? Speak *now*."

"Gold Captain Julius Cavare, my lord. I command the entire gold cloak unit. The archon deemed it more fitting to greet you with our warrior force."

"Hmm! A warrior force that avoids *war* from what I hear... Tell me, is this your first-time face-to-face with a zephum? Your terror intrigues me."

"I have met Warmaster Tempest and Guardian Pyith...but never seen anyone like you. Honestly, I always assumed Tempest's stories were exaggerated out of respect."

Sardonyx stepped in front of the man to stare him down. "Well, were the stories exaggerated?" The face guard hid his smile. It was a delight to make the large human stare up and sweat; he likely believed he was the tallest thing alive until today.

"No, Warlord," he said as he wiped his brow.

Sardonyx took off his face guard, then slammed his hand on Julius's shoulder with a mighty laugh. "Well met, Captain. Escort me to your grand tower of shame."

With a grimace of pain, Julius looked away to hide his reaction, but such things never escaped Sardonyx's gaze. "Right away. Please, follow me."

They followed the path towards Alanammus Tower, stopping outside the city gates before a great white horse approached from the plains. To the warlord's shock, the beast had a large ivory horn coming out the top of its head. The horse galloped up to Tempest, then sniffed at him.

"What...in the glorious hell is that?" Sardonyx asked.

"A unicorn!" Julius said, blissfully unaware of the

abomination in their presence. "You will only find them here in Alanammus!"

Sardonyx no longer liked this human.

Tempest stroked the monster's hazel mane as it neighed in approval. "Several decades ago, Archon Consaga's daughter asked him for a unicorn from the storybooks, so he simply infused platinum horns on their heads with powerful magic. The change ended up being permanent because all the altered horses gave birth to natural unicorns. They are a miracle of magic and nature."

Julius nodded. "Ah Tempest, your knowledge of our people never ceases to amaze me."

Sardonyx held back a scream. He wanted to kill them both. He wanted to kill them *all*. To see nature so permanently scarred by arrogance was...staggering. "You *dare* call this a miracle?" He approached the beast and rubbed its neck. "You come from a glorious chain of majestic beasts. I will never fault you for the abomination you are today; may you frolic for all eternity in the Great Plains in the Sky."

With a sudden force of his wrist, he snapped the beast's neck. The unicorn made no cry, collapsing to the ground with a loud thud. An honorable death.

Tempest fell to his knees and let out a horrible shriek filled with an agony Sardonyx had not heard since he used to beat him as a child. The vision of his tiny son screaming while blood trickled down his blackened eye made him shudder. Honor could take a heavy toll, but the future warlord had needed to learn strength by any means necessary. No matter the cost.

No matter the cost. "My son, when you are warlord, you will understand."

Julius placed his hand over his mouth and shot him a loathing gaze. "Why? Why would you do that?"

Tempest rose, his eyes lost in the endless emerald plains. For all his flaws, the boy always accepted pain with *honor*. "It has always been this way with my father. This is why when humans think of zephum, their first thought is brutality."

"No, they think of strength! The humans took this once-proud beast and turned it into a mockery for their entertainment. This would be us if we weren't more powerful than them. They would turn us into dogs, pets to waddle about and beg for food from our human lords. Maybe *you* would enjoy that, but a true zephum would rather *die*."

"Our people could be so much more…and yet we cling to our barbarous traditions like it's holy doctrine."

"Honoring tradition is the only reason we are free. Have I taught you *nothing*?"

"You taught me lessons of pain and fear. Lessons that will haunt me forever." Tempest took a deep breath, then turned to Julius. "Please pardon this terrible affront to your people. If you would be so kind, we are nearly at the tower."

"Yes…of course," Julius said before approaching the city gates. He nodded at the guards at the top, who pushed their iron mechanisms to open the gates.

Sardonyx would never admit it, but the massive steel barricade impressed him. It was refreshing to finally find something honest in Alanammus. Despite the veil of radiance, the platinum gates offered the same signal as the barriers of Vaynex: *Enemies, beware.* He placed his face guard back on and followed Julius through the entrance.

Walking through the tar-paved streets of Alanammus city, his mighty heart pounded through his chest. Large castle-like structures surrounded them, making shops and barracks indistinguishable, with all sorts of bright color patterns that made his eyes sting. Towers of light emanated from various posts, using what could only be magic to give off a yellowish hue that illuminated every corner of the busy streets.

The mire of humans was deafening compared to anything back home. His son's expression of a "sea of humans" finally made sense. *They all yell! By Strength's name, why must they yell?* Sardonyx's giant figure stood out like a zephum with no tail, as all the townsfolk gawked at him, a dishonorable mix of fear and resentment in their eyes. He had to accept the murmurs and head shakes. In the capital of the Southern Alliance, he was a foreigner, and more importantly: an enemy. The reality of being alone set in, and for the first time in his life, his individual strength could do nothing to help.

Madness! Utter madness—

He flinched as a young mage to his left tested out a vendor's staff by launching a fire blast into the air. No one in the vicinity gave it any notice. Back home, such an offense would lead to another corpse in the streets. The flames accelerated his sweat, and the smile of wonder on Tempest's face filled him with rage.

By Strength's name, I have failed as a father. Part of me is envious; if he realized the horrors of Alanammus and what a threat this is to our future, he would scream in boundless terror. My son is wrong: Terrangus needs stability, not chaos. If the South has no threats to the west, we will be their sole enemy. We are not strong enough—

Something grabbed his armored tail. An unforgivable offense. Whoever it was would suffer a death these humans could yell about for *ages—*

It tugged again.

Glancing behind him, he found a tiny human girl with small orange dots on her face and some sort of red hair shape that resembled a plant. The child didn't even reach his knees.

Aged humans were usually disgusting creatures, but this girl was *adorable*!

"Get away from him!" Julius screamed, drawing his polearm.

She did not oblige. "Mister, why do you have a tail?"

Sardonyx removed his face guard, then kneeled to the girl's height. "I am a zephum, dear child. Do you know who we are?"

"Lizard people!" she yelled back with a giant smile.

He had a great laugh before he stood. "A fair response! Where are your parents?"

The girl pointed to a young woman with the same dots and red hair. A bright paleness overtook her entire face as she stood frozen. The child may not know who he was, but her mother certainly did.

With extreme caution, Sardonyx held the girl's hand and led her to her mother. "Enjoy it, human. Our children grow too fast."

Julius sheathed his polearm, then let out a sigh, his face drenched with sweat. Perhaps he was ill?

They approached the tower and stopped at the entrance. Before Sardonyx would enter, his eyes grew lost in a large pool of water surrounding a golden replica of the Arrogant One east of the tower. The water was completely transparent, revealing several lavender fish with glowing platinum eyes and scales of *pure* gold. More abominations. He squinted his eyes to read the plaque at the foot of the statue.

We become so intimate with imperfection that the thought of any alternative becomes too precarious to comprehend. Flailing against paradise—we yearn to sleep—but beg not to dream. Yield your incomprehension and let Wisdom cradle you into the Serenity you swore could never be real.

Wisdom

"The Arrogant One speaks of slavery," Sardonyx said, shaking his head.

Tempest rushed over. "Father, please tread with caution. This deity is still their god for many of them."

"It's okay, Tempest, your father speaks the truth; Wisdom holds no love from my gold cloaks. We follow the one true god." Julius pounded his right upper chest. "Strength without honor—is chaos."

Adrenaline coursed through Sardonyx's blood; he had never once heard a human speak the words with such honor. "You…are a *glorious* man. If the day comes when our kingdoms do battle, I will ensure to seek you out and grant you the most glorious death any human has ever known."

"An honorable end," Julius said with a smile.

With his arms crossed, Tempest chuckled. "And to think you didn't want to come. I told you, we are more similar to humans than you acknowledge."

"Hmm. Today—and only today—I will yield to that point. Lord Captain, escort us to our meeting. I have a fresh new vigor to deal with your kind."

Julius laughed, then snapped his fingers towards a decorated mage. "Those people are not my kind. Alexis, come with me to open the gateway."

They entered the tower as Alexis channeled some sort of sorcery to open the illuminated portal in the center of the room. Portraits of old archons and the Arrogant One were all over the silver walls, with a small band of men playing human music that was just *awful*. Humans had always preferred stringy instruments instead of drums. There was no soul…just drawn-out screeches that made his ears sore.

He approached a portrait of an archon who appeared to be an older version of Francis, with identical dark skin and brown eyes. Unlike her son, she had long silver hair that matched the tower walls, posed sitting with a gentle—yet powerful—grace that most humans failed to match. Archon Addison Haide—the woman responsible for casting out Wisdom—had always held his respect. "Now *this* is an archon. How unfortunate that we never met."

"She was brilliant," Tempest said, "and just between us, I prefer her to Archon Gabriel. Father, would you like me to point out Archon Consaga?"

"No."

The center portal erupted with energy before Julius nodded them over. *Ugh…more human magic. I suppose it beats the stairs. What an inefficient design. It needs more width than height. Such is the consequence of arrogance.*

They entered together, then instantly appeared at the top of the tower. Silence replaced the maelstrom of strings as Sardonyx gazed down the seemingly endless hallway to the imposing platinum doors of Gabriel's room. The fake radiance of diamond chalices and flawless silver coating on the walls was one final illusion offering the same warning as the city gates: *Enemies, beware.*

Tempest glanced at Julius. "Will you be joining us, sir?"

"No, only Guardians and kingdom leaders are welcome. I will be outside the door to escort you back home when the meeting is concluded. Be well, my friends."

Sardonyx put his face guard back on. "Tempest, you will do the majority of the speaking. I will not interfere unless necessary. Do *not* fail me…"

Julius opened the doors as the zephum entered the room; he then bowed and closed the doors behind him. Diamond chalices were all over, with some human abomination of multicolored glass hanging from the high ceiling. Did such a structure suggest a threat? Where was the throne? *Damn you,*

Tempest, stop smiling. Show honor. HONOR!

They were late: by design, of course. The most important people in the room should always enter last. Two empty seats remained at the enormous shimmering table opposite of who was likely Archon Gabriel, based on Tempest's description of a gray-haired, bearded man who relied on a cane. Such weakness would never be tolerated in Vaynex. Sardonyx had kept Pyith home despite Tempest's begging to ensure they would never see her with a limp. The zephum sat, pleased by the holes in the back of their chairs for their tails.

Archon Faelen Gabriel rose, aided by his platinum cane. By Strength's name, he was short. "Warlord Sardonyx Claw, Warmaster Tempest Claw...welcome to Alanammus."

Tempest rose, then bowed. "Thank you, Archon; it is an honor to return to your kingdom. Please, pardon my life-mate Pyith Claw for her absence; she is still resting her wounds from the Terrangus Harbinger. We appreciate this opportunity to discuss the unfortunate events in the West threatening both our great empires. Simply put, we have a common enemy. The Child of Death must *die*."

Sardonyx studied the eyes of all the people in the room after his son spoke. Other than Zeen, whose bloodshot gaze stuck to the floor, all eyes were on him, as it should be. Ah, the girl was here...a pity she hadn't died since their first meeting. The Pact Breaker's hate-filled stare went straight through his steel. Her fury was *glorious*.

"Great empires indeed," Gabriel said with a smile. "Sardonyx, I am told you are the first warlord to visit Alanammus since the God of Strength was a mortal. I hope we meet your glorious standards."

Sardonyx sat motionless. *Is he mocking me? I will not hesitate to kill him. I will kill them all.*

Tempest cleared his throat. "On behalf of my father,

please allow me to state that your kingdom is far more glorious than we could ever hope to expect. Before we proceed, may I ask who now speaks for the Guardians?"

More silence.

"We are undecided on a leader," Serenna said.

His son smiled. "Well, you spoke first. In zephum culture, your actions would reflect a desire for the role. Am I mistaken?"

No, you fool. Not her. I will NOT allow it…

She finally took her eyes off the warlord and onto Tempest. "That is not for me to decide."

The older man next to her stood. "My daughter would make a fine leader of the Guardians. I am certain no one objects?"

Ah, so that is Charles Morgan. I expected…something more. The golden-skinned man must be Jason Wraith of Nuum, and the older woman Alice Reilly of Xavian. Too many humans!

"Nuum will always support Serenna," Wraith said.

"Xavian stands with—"

The archon raised his hand to interrupt Reilly. "No. After what happened in Mylor, Serenna cannot lead the Guardians. No Pact Breaker or anyone with a connection to the God of Death can be in a position of such power. That is the entire basis of our meeting, is it not?"

By Strength's name…the archon and I stand united?

"How *dare* you?" Serenna yelled, rising as her father sat. Sardonyx swore the old man shrank in his chair.

"I nominate Francis," Gabriel said, ignoring her glare. A fair choice, all things considered. Perhaps he had misjudged this crippled human.

Francis kept glancing and nodding behind him at nothing, then rose. Mages were always so odd. "I have no desire to lead the Guardians. Serenna is the optimal choice; I ask that my support be given to her."

The archon sighed, tapping his cane onto the floor. "You would turn down another opportunity at greatness? What lies does your shadow offer you? Haides are always so disappointing."

"Spare me. I have seen greatness; it is nothing a mortal can offer. My 'shadow,' as you deemed fit to describe him, has advised me not to pursue the role. I follow his counsel, and thus conclude: Serenna is the best choice."

By Strength's name, Francis is insufferable. My son was right; we should have brought Pyith. It is long past that a zephum leads the Guardians.

With her blessed shield strapped to her back, Mary rose. "I nominate Zeen Parson. We should follow tradition and anoint a Terrangus Guardian as leader."

If Zeen receives a single vote, I will kill them all.

Zeen's stare shot from the floor to Mary's face. The wider his eyes got, the redder and more drained they appeared.

Wraith snickered. "The last Terrangus Guardian leader is now a monster murdering people in the streets, while your emperor openly serves the God of Death. As far as I'm concerned, no one from Terrangus is qualified to run a trade cart. Anoint Serenna and be done with it."

"For the first time," Reilly said, "in a very long time, I agree wholeheartedly with Senator Wraith. No offense, Zeen."

Zeen simply shrugged. "None taken. I too stand with Serenna. Sorry, Mary."

Mary shook her head before taking her seat.

No, not her. Not the Pact Breaker. I CANNOT allow this...

Tempest paced around his chair. Was that a human thing? Leaders should hold a position and let the realm move around them. "Archon, I do not wish to impose, but a majority has revealed itself. Do you truly wish to obstruct—"

"ENOUGH!" Sardonyx yelled, slamming his fist into the table. Everyone gasped as he rose and drew his sword. He slammed it through his end of the table, shattering the edge, launching the other side flying, filling the air with splinters, chalices and wine. "Serenna is an abomination! She has no right to lead the Guardians! I would kill her in cold blood if she *ever* stepped foot in Vaynex again. You...all of you...have lost control. Now, *I* am in control."

Serenna signaled for everyone to stay back as she stepped forward, but Zeen did not leave her side. She grasped her bird staff, then pulsated with a platinum glow. "This isn't Vaynex, Warlord. You will find my power has grown a great deal since six years ago."

Sardonyx drifted forward, gripping his blade with both hands. Serenna's death would be *glorious*. "You know nothing of true power. This is why I despise magic. A tiny human girl stands before me as the second most powerful being in this room."

Her platinum aura erupted and she cast a dense, vibrant crystal shield in his path. Sardonyx snarled before he held the blade behind him. Leaning in with his full body weight, he slammed his sword into her shield with a ferocious strength that would make his god proud.

The shield cracked—but did not break—and the blowback sent him stumbling backward until he lost balance and fell on his back. Upon his collapse, his face guard came off and rolled down the floor. All the senators and Guardians glanced at each other, but none dared speak.

Forgive me, God of Strength. I have given everything to our people, but the supremacy of magic is inevitable. Chains... pets...slavery. We will be their dogs...no...

No...

Unlike the shield, his reality shattered. All sound vanished, replaced by a tonal ringing. His sight became drenched in crimson rage as his eyes twitched, and the burning sensation in his forehead swelled.

No…

No. It was time for honor to yield to the madness of chaos.

Sardonyx rose with a roar. He picked up his sword with one hand, stepped forward, then flung the blade directly into the barrier. The sword broke through as the barrier shattered into a rain of dishonorable glass.

Zeen tackled Serenna to the ground before the blade flew past her head. All the leaders and even Francis drew their staffs and stepped forward. Serenna had been correct; this was not Vaynex.

Zeen rose and grabbed Mary's sword from her sheath and rushed in front of the warlord. He grasped the tiny blade with both hands as if it were a glorious zephum artifact, entering his battle stance without saying a word.

Sardonyx took a deep breath as his rage subsided. There was no point in murdering the boy. "You would die for her… Why?"

"Guardians protect their own. No matter what."

The Mylor crest on Zeen's arm caught his eye. "Ah, you have the *flying rat* on your arm. Are you mating with the sorceress?"

Zeen's bravado faded as he froze with his mouth wide open. By glancing over to Serenna, he may as well have screamed out the answer. Several people snickered, but Serenna's face grew redder than any of the bloodstains on his massive sword.

"You are indeed, how interesting. I withdraw my objection. Tempest…finish up this nonsense." Sardonyx sat in his chair, ignoring the decimated table. He couldn't blame Zeen; the fury of love drove males to pure madness. Ah, his dear Vatala; he would kill every person in the room for a chance to hold her one last time. The only remnant of their ferocious love was a diplomat trying to play warlord.

Oh, how I yearn for you. Strength without honor is chaos, but life without you is despair. Strength save me…did I just quote my son's book?

Tempest paused for a soft moment to survey the wreckage in the once prestigious meeting room. "Right… Well, let's get back to Nyfe. That was the whole point of this meeting… While we would normally never interfere with human politics, Nyfe is unacceptable. It is far too dangerous to allow him the unlimited power the position of emperor will grant him."

"How convenient. And I suppose you have a plan?" Gabriel asked.

"We do not expect you to allow our armies to portal through any of your kingdoms, so we offer my father and I instead, and encourage the Guardians to strike with us too since the God of Death is involved. The Terrangus military is weakened after the insurrection. Attack through Mylor, then once Nyfe is slain, Senator Reilly will be the interim empress until a more stable long-term choice is available."

"What? Why me?" Reilly asked, shocked as everyone else in the room. Tempest's schemes were always so…annoying. True honor would just be to kill them all. All this nonsense about creating instability in the South by worsening the situation in the West with their own incompatible leader had too much risk.

Tempest snickered, always pleased with himself when he drew gasps. "Wraith is unacceptable, and Morgan's ties to Serenna are a liability. It's either you or me…and I doubt Terrangus is ready for a zephum emperor."

"Never," Mary said.

Gabriel walked over to the balcony and gazed out onto Alanammus City. The empty gaze of a true leader. "And when does our interference end? Is it our destiny to spend the rest of days creating problems, only to solve them with more problems? For a zephum of such intelligence, you never bothered to comprehend the true meaning of the Guardian Pact. Nyfe only managed to secure the throne with Guardian interference. How long will Reilly struggle to maintain order before she requests their aid? Tradition is never shattered in a single blow. It comes crack by crack. Chisel by chisel. This can only end in blood, but I will stand with you to ensure said blood is not mine. Tempest, Serenna: may you avoid the consequences of your actions, and live short, boring lives."

Serenna finally rose, brushing the debris off her armor. She shot Zeen a glare with such spite, it would knock the mightiest of zephum to their knees. She then turned to Archon Gabriel. "You could have avoided all of this by aiding Mylor. When you choose to do nothing, you choose to accept the desperate responses of those forced to suffer. I accept this plan. As the new Guardian leader, it is official: Nyfe must die."

CHAPTER 31

HOPE

A week after the meeting, Zeen leaned forward against the balcony in his guest chambers high in Alanammus tower. It wasn't often he awoke in time to see the sun rise, but today the ascending amber blessed the sleeping city of magic, illuminating the green plains with a golden hue. The silence was a temporary miracle, and the vivid sky filled him with more warmth than any god or magic. More warmth than anything but *her*.

If only we could watch it together. It's almost cruel to view something this beautiful alone...

After making a fool of himself in the meeting, it would be some time before she forgave him. She had spent most of her days and nights accessing the Mylor Guardian portal with Francis to speed up the arrival of their southern allies. Wine and dehydration had long passed, but shame had refused Zeen sleep, a luxury that had faded the longer his Guardian life went on.

Zeen shivered as a frigid chill pierced his skin. With the plains stagnant and the air a mellow warm, the foreign breeze was well out of place. He instinctively reached for his missing sword as a loud *snap* emitted from a portal forming in his room.

What the hell is going on?

The outline of a broad, taller man emerged from the spectral gateway, and the cold air howled in fury before coming to a complete stop. David appeared in front of him with his glowing weapon sheathed behind his back. *Large* dark circles weighed under his eyes.

Don't panic. This is still your friend. Still, he took a step back. "David? What are you doing here?"

"Are you not pleased to see me?"

"Well," he said with a faint grin, "you *do* have a tendency to strike me in the face."

It filled Zeen with such a warmth to see David snicker again. "Fair point, but if you still trust my words, I am here as an ally."

Zeen crept forward, shocked that an essence of fear didn't leave his body. "More importantly, are you okay? I won't pretend to understand what you're going through, but please know that I'm here for you."

David hugged him with a desperate embrace. Any hint of fear faded from Zeen as he held him. "I know. After everything, you are far more than I deserve."

"Never think of it that way," Zeen said before letting go. "You will find happiness again."

"Perhaps, but it seems unlikely." David stepped forward to gaze out into the sunrise. He flinched back after his hands touched the balcony. "This scenery still doesn't hit me the same way as it did before. It never will, and I have to accept that."

Zeen walked up next to him and smiled as a trio of unicorns galloped through the plains. *YES! FINALLY!* he screamed internally, keeping his excitement in check for his somber friend. They were so...majestic. If Rinso the Blue could ride one off into the Terrangus sky-break in all three of his novels, maybe Zeen could too? "Give it some more time. Pain blocks the beauty from your eyes, but I swear to you it's there."

David sighed, staring into the fields, then turned back to Zeen. "When are you heading back to Mylor?"

"Soon, I think, the majority of the southern armies finished arriving last night. How... Do you know about Mylor?"

Zeen flinched as David drew the Herald of Fear and pointed it at the left corner of the room. The blade lit with a dark glow before it launched a void blast that erupted on contact with the wall. After a dark flash, a floating, lucid window appeared, revealing the Guardians in Mylor conversing by a fire.

Zeen *carefully* approached the window. "This...this is happening now? How is that possible?"

"My power grows with each passing day. The longer I wield the Herald of Fear, the more I understand it. The more I understand *her*." David spoke with pride, but up close, the color had faded from his skin, and the wrinkles creasing his face were far deeper than the man who had recruited Zeen in Terrangus.

"There is more to life than power, my friend."

David closed his fist, then the window vanished. "I pray you never understand just how true that is. What would you do...if you couldn't save Serenna? Pyith? Even Francis? What about when you realize I'm already lost?"

"An unfair question. I won't judge, but the blade is taking a heavy toll."

"The only path open is always the best one," David said before he sheathed the blade. "But enough about me. Are you prepared to face Nyfe? Death has been unlocking the true potential of his dagger ever since Serenna insulted him. Now, Nyfe is nearly a *god*."

"He can't beat all of us...especially with you on our team."

"No, that isn't possible. Your forces would kill me on sight, and they would be right to do so. I will offer my aid when a Harbinger of Death reveals itself, but this is not my battle."

Damn. "I understand. I'm doing my best to convince them you are not our enemy in the meantime. Mary agrees, but that's about it."

"Such is my fate." David drew his old sword out of its sheath and examined it. "Zeen... I fought with this sword for over twenty years. It has never failed me and, now, may it never fail you." He held the sword out.

After a pause, Zeen accepted, then swung it up and down with one hand. David *did* owe him a weapon after breaking Intrepid, but Zeen had expected that debt long forgotten. "Ha, I assumed this was the heaviest damn thing in the world. Your strikes were nearly unblockable."

David grinned. "I used to fight like you. Give it ten years; speed fades, but the strength remains. When we're forced to strike slower, we learn to strike *harder.*"

Zeen held the blade behind him, then slashed downwards, filling the air with a sharp whistle. He still missed Intrepid, but this was a worthy substitute. "Does it have a name?"

"Adults don't name their weapons."

"Well, you have the Herald of Fear and now I have... Hope," Zeen said with a smile. He had considered naming it in reverence of Melissa, but he would not dare speak her name.

David sighed, letting out a hint of a smile. "An awful title, but you have earned the right to do as you wish. Fight boldly, my friend—I will be watching." He created a new portal, turning to Zeen before he walked through. "I will *always* be watching."

Ironically enough, Fear's champion quelled Zeen's doubts. No matter how much David's physical appearance deteriorated, or outlook dimmed, the man he respected still remained. Hope would find a way.

*

Zeen appeared in the Mylor Guardian room after a mage helped portal him from Alanammus. Tempest and the Guardians greeted him with a nod, while Serenna stayed focused on the fire adjacent to her. The heat from the flames matched the fury in her eyes. Hmm. His apology would come, but not today. Maybe not tomorrow, either.

Tempest Claw approached and shook his hand. "Good morning, sir. I never had a chance to properly greet you since the meeting. I admit, I am quite excited to battle by your side. My father speaks highly of you, and he doesn't speak highly of anyone."

Zeen grinned, holding back a much larger smile. Holding the warlord's respect was an unexpected honor. "The feeling is mutual, Lord Tempest. How exactly is this going to work? I am more than happy to face Nyfe, but I want no part in slaying my own people."

"Indeed," Tempest said, "we would never ask you of such a thing. The Guardian team will be split in two. You, Serenna, and Mary will be on a strike team to take out Nyfe, while Francis, myself, and the warlord aid the southern kingdom's forces in the front."

Zeen gave Francis a concerned glare. "Is that really a good idea?" The plan was efficient enough, but his teammates could barely keep up with the less experienced mages in Mylor, let alone the Alanammus Guardian. They would get decimated...

Which was likely the point.

"*Your* people didn't hesitate to attack me," Francis said, "and now, let them burn by the fire of their consequences. That subject is closed, but we are in disagreement on a key issue…Nyfe's fate after his defeat. Serenna and I prefer him alive for a trial. He needs to answer for his crimes in front of everyone. Never waste a good execution."

Mary pounded her fist on the table. "Like I said, there is no point to this shit if we just take him prisoner. Kill him and be done with it. I swear, you damn mages and your trials."

Tempest stood with both arms behind his back. "While I concede we risk making Nyfe a martyr, he is too dangerous to be left alive. Securing Senator Reilly's power will not be possible as long as Nyfe lives. *However…* I will yield to the Guardian consensus. This is not a zephum decision."

This whole plan is nuts; Terrangus will never accept a foreign ruler. Tempest should know that…right?

For the first time since Zeen arrived, Serenna turned away from the fire and towards her team. "We take him alive and that's *final.* It would be outrageous for a Guardian team to slay a leader, no matter the circumstances. With a trial, we can get the same outcome minus the controversy." Her eyes finally met Zeen's. Odd, how her fire offered no warmth. "Do you have any issue with that?"

By reflex, he turned away for a brief moment to his old friend: the floor. "No, I happen to want him alive as well. Maybe there is even a chance for redemption?" A bold ask, but if he strived to save David, maybe Nyfe was not lost either. Redeeming his nemesis would be an incredible victory for the realm, proof that no one was too far gone.

"Do not mistake my intentions as mercy," she said. "Once anyone binds themselves to the God of Death, their life is over." She approached, his heart pounding with each passing step. "I'll tell you again. You can't save everyone…"

"No, but it's unforgivable not to try." It was a rush to defy her; he could only hope she felt it too.

Instead, she sighed. "You have your orders," she said, then

rushed out of the room. A familiar dread crept through his gut as she left. Only now did he consider the complications her new leadership role would cast on their relationship. *Was Mary right? Am I making a mess of things?*

Francis watched Serenna leave, then nodded at Zeen. "Look, I understand your perspective, but simple people are easily fooled by flashy ideas gilded in good intentions. It's not that we can't save everyone. The reality is that some simply do not deserve it." He took Serenna's old position by the fire. "I have a fiery urge to exact revenge on your people. Nyfe told them to attack me, then they rushed right in, no questions asked. After a lifetime of service, I was nearly slain by the people I wasted my life protecting."

Mary laughed, patting Francis on the shoulder. "Come on, Francis. After knowing Zeen, you should know most people from Terrangus are fools." She walked up to Zeen, whispered in his ear, "Stop fucking this up," then smiled back at Francis. "Let's get this over with, and then maybe you can take me to Serenity to drink cheap wine with your Wisdom buddy. Tell him to work on his subtlety; he remains invisible, but I see him all the time."

"Ah…" Francis said, watching her leave the room with wide eyes.

Tempest shook his head. "To be fair, you *do* need to work on your subtlety. I recognized Wisdom was behind you the entire time during the meeting; it is a miracle my father didn't grasp his presence. They would still be cleaning up our blood…"

Zeen stumbled back as Wisdom revealed himself by Francis's side. "My dear lizard lord, perhaps you didn't pay attention, but your father would be the one slain. Did you catch the failure in his eyes after Serenna exposed him as an outdated brute? Oh my, it was *glorious*…"

Tempest glared into the lifeless husk of the floating sun mask. "Strength guides us…not your arrogance. My father and I may have our differences, but we stand united against you."

"A fitting title for that one. Strength is a limited concept. Magic, however, is *infinite*. Do not despair; when I untether this realm to the paradise of Serenity, your people will know a new future. They will no longer shield their eyes to the wonders of intellect, but instead, embrace enlightenment, gazing back on centuries of ignorance in shallow remorse. My dear zephum, know this: the farther out you can see forward, the more difficult it is to turn back and smile." Wisdom chuckled and vanished.

Zeen flinched as Tempest roared and slammed his fist through the table. The future warlord became his father's son and snarled at Francis. "Your deity is pure evil. It bewilders me that a sorcerer of your intellect falls for his lies. Your mother would be ashamed. *Ashamed*!" He flipped his cape behind him as he stormed out of the room.

After a moment of standing frozen, Francis sighed. "Between the two of us, we aren't very good at this."

"More reason to stick together," Zeen said with a forced grin. "Dare I ask what Wisdom thinks of me?"

"Let's…revisit that question another day. For now, follow me outside. Our forces should nearly be ready."

*

Francis triggered the Guardian portal to send them to the Mylor outskirts. It was odd to arrive at the same portal where Zeen had spent the past year fighting against his new allies. Actually, it was more terrifying than odd. He had never seen all four southern kingdoms' armies at once; his old Terrangus forces never would have made it into the bastion against such power.

His eyes searched for Serenna by the Mylor armies, with

their pearly white armor and owl banners fluttering in the sky from the swift wind. The owl's eyes called to him. Terrangus would always hold a special place in his heart, but Serenna's grip held him now. He would answer the owl's call, if only for her.

The sapphire armies of Xavian and beige-clothed mages from Nuum gathered on their own, but the true wonder was the massive infantry from Alanammus. Gold cloaks stayed in the front, forming a triangle formation around a protected force of mages. To his shock, Warlord Sardonyx mingled by the gold cloaks, laughing with a large, bearded man who patted him on his spiked shoulders, either too brave or foolish to fear a terrible death. Out of all the banners, the platinum crest of Wisdom stood tallest of them all. Even after casting him out, the deity still held them in his grasp.

Francis smiled in wonder. "Look at it...*this* is the glory of the combined southern kingdoms. Think of all the good we could do with such power!"

Zeen tried to smile back, but he was gazing out to Terrangus's doom. Maybe the Terrangus of old could have prevailed, but the shattered kingdom of Nyfe would crumble. "Your forces are overwhelming. I can hardly believe what I see."

"Don't worry," Francis said, remaining giddy. "This is all to save Terrangus. Your kingdom will know a prosperity completely foreign to you once we win. Pardon me for now; I must greet Julius." Francis darted off towards the gold cloaks, leaving Zeen surrounded by people, yet completely alone.

He found a friend as Mary rushed over, out of breath, with her hands shaking. "Zeen...look at this. What are we doing?" She grabbed him, holding on with a desperate strength. "What the *fuck* are we doing?"

"Listen," he said, easing her hands off, "everything will be okay. We can fix this. The sooner we defeat Nyfe, the sooner this all goes away."

"Stop *lying* to me! This has nothing to do with Nyfe. They see an opportunity to destroy our kingdom…and we're helping them!"

"As long as you and I remain, Terrangus will never fall. Kingdoms are people, not places."

She glanced at the Mylor crest on his arm and shook her head. "You're a fucking traitor. And now, I am too. I should've just died in Boulom." She pushed him away, then stormed off. He had been much better at talking her down in their Koulva days…which felt like a lifetime ago at this point.

Zeen drifted through the Mylor armies to find Serenna. Despite their crest on his arm, Mylor did not welcome him. Soldiers parted from his path as he approached, but the cold glares in their eyes made it clear it wasn't out of respect. After a year of combat, many of their friends and family likely died by his sword. No matter how fanciful the tales of the Rogue Guardian, many would never see him as anything other than an invader.

And a murderer. *There you are…*

Serenna stood atop a hill, gazing out into the mountainous outskirts with somber eyes. Both hands grasped the Wings of Mylor while the wind flapped her white cape and long platinum hair. With the most powerful army in the realm behind her, she became a mortal goddess. He approached with caution, then stopped by her side.

She broke her gaze to glance at Zeen. "Ah, welcome, Zeen. Forgive me for being distant lately; there is a lot on my mind."

Expecting far worse, her words filled him with a warm calm, matching the tranquil winds that covered him like a blanket. It was an *enormous* relief she didn't seem to share Francis's newfound lust for violence. "I think I understand."

"No…you don't. You *can't*. Mylor's suffering was all for nothing. Look at these forces; I can never forgive the archon for using my people as pawns to solidify his power. I wanted to respect him, to believe he was different, but it's just another corrupt leader. They're all corrupt; by some joke, Sardonyx is the only one with any integrity."

"Well, after this, I can't see Terrangus threatening your people for a very long time. Even if we deserve it, this will be a difficult moment."

She sighed. "Forgive me, I did not consider that. For whatever it's worth, I'll be by your side. We will see this through together."

"It's worth more than you know," he said, smiling. "I, too, apologize for my actions during the meeting. For being the Rogue Guardian, subtlety doesn't appear to be my strong point."

She returned his smile, but shook her head. "I had a feeling you would crack, but I hoped you could at least manage one day." Her smile ascended to a laugh. "Zeen, you didn't get through *one* single day!"

"Well, you can be assured I'll remain faithful and honest, since I obviously can't keep a secret to save my life."

"No...and it's a good trait to have. My empathy is already slipping. Please, always keep me grounded with your kindness. If I grow cold...it's up to you to make me warm again."

Her openness startled him. Trying to prevent his face from turning red made it far worse. "You can count on me. As a fellow Guardian—and so much more—I am yours, forever." He held out his hand.

As her gentle fingers closed on his own, their hands joined to become one. "Forever..." she said.

They gazed up together at the sun, now set in the flawless blue sky. Even if the sun couldn't match the former glory of its initial rise, he watched it with her, and nothing could be more beautiful.

CHAPTER 32

THE ECSTASY OF DESTRUCTION

After a grueling eight days' journey northwest, Serenna finally stepped forward and surveyed her rival kingdom of Terrangus from their own outskirts. The prisoner returned as the conqueror, and she could only wish Forsythe was still alive to see her now. They were greeted by the night's veil of darkness and typical torrential rain. The skies wept for their kingdom, pouring out frigid tears to wash away the blood of Terrangus's soon to be fallen. There would be *many*.

Bells rang from Terrangus as soldiers lit torches undercover to shield their flames from heavy rain. The banners of the Ebony Blade flailed hopelessly in the stormy winds as dancing fires scattered light at random, illuminating innumerable soldiers all over the gates. Most of them were young men, like her Zeen. Most of them would die, but she would protect him forever.

She turned her head for a final reassurance. The most powerful force in the realm awaited her command, and even the warlord stood in front of the gold cloaks, anticipating her words. "Guardians…to me!"

It was rare to see a grin on Francis's face as he approached. "Let us show Terrangus the supremacy of southern magic."

His confidence had grown considerably since meeting the God of Wisdom. *Is he still with you? I can only wonder how this plays into his plans…*

Mary trekked forward; the rain splashing against her chain mail armor and her drenched red hair hanging down. A battle was the perfect time to *really* meet a new Guardian; she must have been impressive to gain David's respect in such a short time. Serenna smiled at her, but Mary did not return the gesture. "I'll say this once. If you prioritize that fucking idiot Zeen over me with your shields, I'll step aside and watch them beat your face in."

Gods, it's like having a human Pyith, Serenna thought. "I would have it no other way."

Her dear Zeen stood across the field with his sword leaning on his shoulder. His eyes were lost on the banners of the Ebony Blade. Zeen had likely heard her call, but it was only fair to give him a moment to take it all in. For her, he would burn the past, and lay waste to the kingdom that had raised him from child, to soldier, to Guardian. She wouldn't do the same for him. She wouldn't do it for *anyone.* He met her eyes with a smile, then walked over. Whatever conflict burned within was buried by the soldier's resolve.

Sardonyx and Tempest approached. She did a double take as Tempest got close; his massive golden armor likely weighed more than he did as he waddled towards her. Sharp spikes curved off his shoulder guards, with bent goat-like horns attached to his shimmering face guard. Flickers of light flashed off the diamonds on his cape as it flew in the wind.

"Oh, shit," Mary said with a chuckle. "Look at this guy."

"Shh," Serenna whispered.

The warlord took the opposite approach, with plain steel

armor covering his entire body, and his rusty face guard hiding the monster underneath. Standing at least a foot taller than anyone else on the battlefield, he was pure, simple terror. And he knew it. "I have not visited these lands in nearly a decade. It will be *glorious* to slay these humans again."

"Father...not now," Tempest said.

Serenna thanked the gods for Tempest. A guilty part of her wished Sardonyx would drop dead and finally allow the zephum a reasonable leader.

"Stop your nonsense," Sardonyx said. "You did your talking, now let the true warriors prepare for combat. Mary, your first use of Strength's shield will be to slay your own people. The irony is *glorious!*"

"There's still time; I could kill you first," Mary said.

Serenna slammed her staff down. "*Stop!*"

Sardonyx snickered. "Hush, mage. *Your* kind cannot understand the mentality of true warriors. Mary happens to be my favorite human!"

Zeen crossed his arms with a frown. "What about me? I thought we had something special."

"Hmm," Sardonyx said, rubbing his face guard. "You are third."

"Fair enough; you rank three out of my favorite zephum as well. I have Pyith, Tempest...then you."

"TEMPEST OVER ME?"

Zeen laughed. "Tempest is a lot nicer to me than you are, but Pyith is still my favorite. I really can't wait to see her again." He looked over at Serenna—likely for a response—but she kept her eyes on Terrangus and stepped away.

She could never imagine such nonsense happening before a siege of Mylor. Back then, young mages had sat on the floor crying while soldiers gazed with dead eyes into nothing as they waited for the end. It had been impossible to shield everyone, so she'd shielded them with lies.

The warlord approached her alone and placed his hand on her shoulder. "Never underestimate the power of fear—it is inevitable before battle. Your job is to ensure it is the *other* side who is afraid, and you managed that with your mere presence. Let your people be eager and your enemies *tremble*! Oh…and pardon my dishonorable lie. *You* are number one." He took his giant hand off her shoulder…gently?

After a pause, she turned to him, regretting her harsh judgment. "Thank you, Warlord. I was under the impression you despised me."

"Ha! I only despise weakness! While you have several faults, a lack of power is not one of them." He paused as he walked away. "But know this: if you ever again turn to the void, I will personally hunt you down and destroy you. Zeen will not…but I *will*."

She nodded, accepting his threat as a compliment. Did he finally see her as an equal?

Walking back to her Guardians and Tempest, they locked eyes as she approached. "It's time. Zeen, Mary, stay by me. Warlord, tell Julius to commence."

Sardonyx clapped his armored hands, and Francis and Tempest followed him over to the gold cloaks.

She opened her mouth to wish Francis good luck, but couldn't find the words before he faded away into an ocean of platinum mages. David had never wished them luck. If he did, it was "don't die," or some other hollow statement. She could only wonder if that had been by design, or if he'd struggled as she did now.

An enormous silver tinted crystal shield formed over the armies of Alanammus to ward against projectiles. The rest of the kingdoms followed suit, as one by one the armies were engulfed in protective crystal spheres. To her shock, the gold cloaks of Alanammus led the charge. It was finally happening. Marching towards the gates, the bells rang louder as horns blew furiously into the night.

She glanced at Mary and Zeen. "Stick with me; we can't risk trying the Guardian portal in the middle of a battle. We will need to find another way to the castle; the night should cover us."

Mary sighed. "Fucking hell, there will be a lot of blood on our hands tonight."

"Let me lead," Zeen said. "I know these streets better than anyone, and I wager many of the men on the other side of those gates are not fully loyal to Nyfe. Any violence we can avoid with words will be a blessing." He was too emotionally invested to lead, but his dim, pleading eyes won her over.

"Granted, but be realistic. *Do not* risk the mission. If the three of us fail, this was all for nothing. We'll join up with the Xavian Army. Once they breach the gates, we can break away through side streets towards the castle. We must be swift; Nyfe will likely flee once he realizes his defeat is imminent."

Zeen grasped his sword with both hands. "No. He cannot walk away from this. The entire war is his fault."

Mary scoffed. "Whatever you have to tell yourself, Zeen. Right now, we are just as guilty as he is."

"Enough," Serenna said, attempting a gentle tone that did not come naturally.

They followed Serenna through the pale Mylor crystal shield. Soldiers lauded her with smiles and bows as she made her way towards the Xavian army. *Never* could she imagine Mylor in such high spirits before a battle. *It's much easier to lead when you're expected to win...*

Entering the blue-tinted crystal barrier, they made their way to the front. Xavian followed behind Alanammus as ladders dropped all over the Terrangus barricades. It was an expected strategy. Terrangus had a larger quantity of soldiers, but lacked the magical amplitude to battle in tightly packed gates once they opened. Terrangus would hope to fight inside the trade district, then flank from behind. It would be up to Mylor and Nuum to prevent the flank outside the gates.

She held her staff with both hands, closed her eyes, and cast lucid crystal shields on the three of them—her own first, as always. "Zeen, take the lead, but stay close. We go together, or not at all. The gate is coming down any second." He nodded in appreciation, but Mary solemnly gazed ahead.

As if on command, a scorching blast of fire from within the Alanammus mages exploded onto the steel gates. The gates held, but weakened parts came tumbling down, filling the air with an awful aroma of burnt wood and steel. From that moment on, the cold faded. Anyone who shivered did so purely out of fear.

The frantic yells of men from both sides of the gates were deafening as sweat dripped down her face. She searched for the source of the heat, finding Francis with the gold cloaks, radiating a brilliant orange glow that rivaled the Mylor sun. She had never seen him so powerful. He yelled, then a second fire blast crashed into the gates. A loud screech rang through her ears as more pieces of gate crumbled off. It would not survive a third.

All the yelling stopped. Every drop of rain made a unique tap as it splashed. Francis glowed again, and the sphere of flame above him grew massive. He launched his arms forward. The inferno exploded on contact, launching scattered layers of steel in every direction.

Roaring commenced as the forces of Alanammus and Xavian charged through, led by the bulky gold cloaks in the front. Men poured down the ladders to meet Mylor and

Nuum. She begged herself to aid the people of Mylor, but that wasn't the plan.

Zeen glanced at Serenna before he ran through the wreckage. The three of them paused when they entered the chaotic trade district. An endless wave of Terrangus soldiers rushed forward, with mages strategically placed in the windows of buildings all over the city, launching fire spells at the gate's chokepoint. Soldiers clashed, rain reddening as it hit the ground. The familiar stench of death already filled the air as combatants on both sides fell.

A small group of Alanammus mages stood behind the warlord, casting crystal shields over and over as he advanced. Sardonyx slashed his sword across, sending two soldiers to the ground from one staggering swipe. The rest backed away from the blood-stained demigod. Sardonyx picked up an entire trade cart, held it above his head, then launched it towards them. The screams only lasted a second before the cart took them.

A blast of fire erupted right on top of him, a perfect spell by an unknown mage. The warlord's mages were knocked backwards as they gazed in terror into the flames, but Serenna knew better than to fear for his safety. Sardonyx walked out of the inferno completely unphased, his cape still burning as he continued his advance.

Her Zeen stood frozen, his hands whiter than a Mylor uniform as he clenched his sword. Mary put her hand on his shoulder and whispered into his ear, but he had no reaction. She turned to Serenna, shaking her head with gritted teeth.

Serenna rushed over, then slapped his face with all the strength she could muster. A single drop of blood rolled down his lip as he snapped back. "I'm sorry," he said, avoiding her eyes. "I wasn't ready to see this…follow me."

He ran behind an abandoned inn to their left. The back road was narrow, but she couldn't find any immediate threats.

A lone soldier sitting with his hand on his stomach leaned against the building. The soldier looked up with a groan before he gazed back to the ground. Zeen kneeled next to the man. "No... Henry, are you okay?"

"There is no time for this!" Mary yelled. She picked Zeen up by his armor with one hand, then pushed him forward. They ran behind the next building; some sort of shop Serenna had never seen before. Two younger men with long hair froze when they met her eyes.

"Oh, shit!" one yelled, before he threw his flask to the ground, bolting towards the castle.

Sorry Zeen. She clutched her staff, then created a crystal barrier to block their path. Maybe they wouldn't alert Nyfe, but it wasn't worth the risk. Mary—apparently thinking the same way—rushed forward, but Zeen didn't move. Leaning back, Mary kicked the first soldier several feet in front of her, then turned to slam her shield sideways into the other man's face.

The man fell to the ground with wide open dead eyes as his blood stained red on her steel shield. Mary rushed over to the other one, who groaned from the ground, then thrust her sword through his neck. She glared at Zeen. "If you're not going to help, get the fuck out of here. Serenna and I will just do everything."

Zeen closed his eyes, taking a deep breath as he approached the barrier. He slashed downwards with such speed, Serenna could barely follow his sword shattering through. "I understand. I'll be the monster you need me to be."

The broken fragments and his innocence flowed towards Serenna as the rain carried them both away. As he stared straight through her, she wished to bring him back home and hold him in her arms like their night in Mylor. Standing in the burning kingdom of Terrangus, that night may as well have been years ago.

Zeen drifted through the back streets, always keeping both hands on his sword while his eyes darted all over. He paused, then yelled, "Take cover!" A mage on a balcony above them launched a fire blast towards him. Zeen dashed away as the blast crashed down and shot his eyes at Serenna. "Get that guy down *now!*"

Serenna trapped the mage in a crystal prison, hovered him off the balcony, then dropped him from the air. Zeen slashed his sword through before the body hit the ground, ensuring he was slain. Zeen continued forward, not taking a moment to check the body. The man she adored was gone, replaced by the man she needed. *Forgive me, David. I understand why you were so hard on us. There really isn't a better way, is there? Zeen will hate me before this is done. I accept that.*

After a few more buildings, they reached the gates of the military ward and regrouped behind cover. Soldiers poured out into the trade district, but the entrance to the adjacent noble district was a ghost town. The once-grand colorful buildings stood dead while relentless rain pounded the empty structures.

Zeen nodded them over. "Wait until this unit leaves; it will give us an opportunity to sneak through. We'll go through the noble district, then we can jump the back gates to enter the castle through the kitchen entrance. I don't see any other way."

Mary smiled. "Welcome back, my friend."

As the last of the Terrangus unit marched towards the battle, Zeen clutched his sword. "Go," he whispered, before rushing forward.

Serenna followed him into the noble district, then sighed. Even after saving the kingdom twice, David had specifically commanded her never to step foot into the rich, prestigious section of Terrangus—the only section that didn't reek of rotting garbage and wasn't plagued with endless noise. The nobles had wanted Nyfe, not the rebellious pact breaker from Mylor, who dared to frighten them. *How did that work out for you?*

"Something's wrong," Zeen said. "There is…no one here. I expected a lack of people, but this? Stay close. We are in danger."

Serenna didn't want to alarm Mary, but she had the same instinct. The night hid the streets in pure darkness as thunder rumbled in the sky.

They weren't alone.

Something skittered out of the corner of her view. She grabbed Zeen and pulled him towards her. "Did you see it?" she whispered.

"No," he whispered back. "I can't see them, but I *hear* them." They met eyes and shared silence. Thunder rumbled again.

Mary stomped forward. "Hello? What the *fuck* is going on?" She then drew her weapons as a faint hissing entered the air.

Serenna refreshed their crystal shields. Sharp lightning lit up the sky for a brief moment, revealing crawlers on the villas that scattered away.

The hissing grew louder.

Zeen stood directly in front of her with his sword drawn. "Careful, everyone. It will be difficult to defend ourselves in the darkness."

Dammit, we really need to recruit another mechanist. She took a deep breath, clutched the Wings of Mylor with both hands and let out a yell as she erupted with platinum energy. Radiant streams of light flowing off her aura illuminated a limited space in front of them. "Move quickly, I cannot hold this for long…"

They drifted forward, trading blindness for an open

invitation to attack. A crawler finally screeched as it rushed towards the light. It dove at Zeen, who dodged to his left and into the darkness out of Serenna's view.

No! Where is he? I'll use more… I'll use everything for him.

She tensed *far* harder than normal to amplify the aura, but a sharp stabbing pain in the back of her neck forced her to one knee. Too much energy. The aura faded entirely, leaving her to the mercy of darkness once more. She'd failed them and David's disappointment smothered her as she pictured his passionless headshake. Zeen deserved better. They all did.

No…please no…

A loud thud startled her as the crawler's corpse crumbled to the ground, splashing rain from a red puddle into her face. She spat out the crawler's blood and would die a gratified woman if she never had to taste the thick, bitter fluid again. *Focus. The next thud could be Zeen.*

The hissing continued.

"We need light!" Mary yelled.

Zeen turned to Serenna, his face concealed by the darkness. "We'll make do. Mary, use your ears. These things tend to screech right before they launch forward."

"What if it doesn't—"

A screech interrupted Mary, who instinctively held her shield to the noise. The hidden crawler crashed through her crystal and slashed into her steel. Her left foot shifted back, but she stood in place, then grabbed the monstrous creature with her free hand to force it to the ground. Ignoring her sword, Mary clenched her shield desperately while she stomped on the creature's neck over and over. It shrieked in defiance before going silent.

Zeen took Serenna by the hand to help her rise. Mary needed the help more…but it was appreciated. "Can you move? I'll protect you until you can regain enough energy." He froze as a booming roar went off. Only one monster could make that sound.

Damn it all, I can't lean on him like this. This is my team now; everything depends on me. It always did.

Serenna wiped the blood off her face and rubbed it off on her armor. Torn fragments of cloth dangled off, but that didn't matter right now. Enough. She smiled at Zeen before turning towards the roar approaching in the darkness. Desperation had always been her muse, but today, she would turn to something more intimate.

I don't need the void… I have you. "Stand aside, my dear. I will *never* fail you again."

She closed her eyes, clutching her staff, hearing her mother's song ringing through the banquet halls as he'd embraced her and said, *I always lose myself when you are close.* If she failed, she would never again feel his gentle hands caress her body, or the soft kiss of his lips. Zeen would end up as her Melissa. She hated herself for the thought, but it filled her with a vicious endearment.

I am falling for him.

Opening her eyes, the aura radiated a dazzling light that lit up the entire vicinity. She didn't have to strain; the platinum form came naturally as she surveyed all the crawlers surrounding them and the demon colossal stomping forward.

She raised her staff with minimal effort to capture the colossal in a crystal prison. The vivid multicolored fragments were *far* thicker than normal. The raging beast pounded against its prison as the hissing grew louder. Several crawlers screeched and attacked at once, then she created a tremendous platinum crystal barrier to hold them all at bay. They could jab at the shield all night and never break through.

No one she loved would ever feel pain again.

Her muscles tensed as she raised the demon high into the

air. She motioned her staff in a circular formation to turn the prison upside down, then plummeted the prison to slam the beast neck first into the ground. The crystal exploded, launching fragments everywhere, obscuring the vision of the limp demon slain before them. Fleeting skitters filled the air.

The hissing stopped.

As her aura faded, a staggering soreness grew in her arms and shoulders. She groaned with a grimace of pain before a grin filled her face. She didn't need Death. She never did.

"Damn," Mary said, eyes wide. "You're a goddess. What the hell are you doing with this scrawny bum?"

Zeen smiled. "Please don't answer that."

"Of course not," Serenna said with a fading laugh. "I...don't understand why demons are here. I can't sense Death, but something truly terrible is ahead. It...must be Nyfe."

"Last time I spoke to David, he warned me the god was unlocking his dagger. I guess this is what he meant."

David? When did he see David? No use worrying about it now.

They traveled to the end of the noble district and approached the gate. Zeen climbed up first to scout the area. "Looks clear," he said from the top. Mary went up next.

Neither of them watched as Serenna struggled to climb. The deep soreness in her arms spread to her back, robbing her of all upper body strength. She wanted to scream as she pulled herself up the flimsy steel, but they could never see her like that. *Never.*

Mary likely noticed the desperation in her eyes and helped her up. "Sorry," she whispered.

Serenna tried to thank her, but nearly lost balance as the stinging pain blurred her vision. Mary's mouth kept moving, but no sound pierced the high ringing in her ears. Serenna glanced at Zeen, who blurred into three Zeens, all three of them rushing over to help. That was nice. He was always so nice… She rested her eyes, welcoming a deep sleep, along with an unwelcome voice she hadn't heard in what could have been forever.

"Serenna…Serenna, Serenna. Pitiful girl. You confuse the desire to protect with the ecstasy of destruction. Desperate for power, yet you ignore the only being that offers such wrath it would drive the lesser gods to their knees. Call on me tonight…I may just answer."

CHAPTER 33

TRUE APATHY IS A SILENT STRUGGLE

"I am nothing. I am forever. I am the end. I AM THE END!"

Serenna's eyes shot open as she rose, startling Zeen, who nearly slipped and fell into the Terrangus rain. "Where...am I? What happened?" She held her soaked hands to her face and blinked to regain focus.

Zeen took a deep breath. "Oh, thank the gods." He nodded to his left, where the castle of Terrangus stood valiantly, backlit by its burning kingdom. "It's been about an hour. Are you okay? Mary and I can finish this ourselves."

"Yeah, listen," Mary said, "you've done enough. We got this; Zeen and I owe this bastard for Boulom."

Serenna groaned as she stood. The soreness spread to her legs, but the pain kept her alert. No more rest. No more...*him*. "We're in this together. Death is already here...this will get ugly."

Zeen's face faded to an empty white. "Ah, that explains the demons. Mary, stay by Serenna, I'll take the front."

Mary nodded at Zeen, then turned to her. "I got you, stay by me."

I must do better…they will never follow my lead if I'm not the most powerful. They have no other reason to listen. She grasped her staff and covered them with lucid crystal shields that were dim and fading in color. None of them would be well defended against the Herald of Death. Even if they knew, she was thankful neither of them pointed it out.

Zeen opened a wooden door at the side of the castle and nodded at them. They followed from a short distance as he made his way through the castle kitchen.

It's far too quiet…

Zeen held one hand on the door, then looked back. With his sword drawn, he drifted towards the next room. Eyes darted all over for enemies that didn't exist. "If this goes poorly… run."

Zeen pushed the door open and walked inside, seemingly unphased by the handful of heavily armed Terrangus soldiers standing in the halls before the throne room. She moved forward to close the gap, but he motioned for her to stop.

The largest soldier approached him. "About time you showed up, kid. Nyfe is ahead; we won't stop you. We…saw the demons outside. If Terrangus must burn, it should be you that wields the torch. Forgive me, Zeen. After Forsythe, I really thought we were on the right side. I'm sorry…"

Zeen sheathed his sword and embraced the bearded man with a deep hug. He whispered in his ear, and the only words she could make out were, "You will always be my captain." With a tear in his eye, the man signaled his soldiers to follow, then they lined up on both sides of the hallway to kneel. Zeen nodded at the Guardians to follow down the open path. "This is it. We only get one chance at this."

They stood before the ebony throne room doors. For the first time in her life, she wished it was Forsythe waiting on the other side. She refreshed their weak shields and turned to them.

"No matter how this goes, thank you for everything." She pushed the doors open, then approached the center of the throne room.

Nyfe sat on his throne, completely alone, holding his cursed blade which radiated the darkest void energy she had ever seen. Shadowy rays filled the empty seats with a pulsating glow. "Took you long enough. Welcome, Lady Serenna, Zeen, and…who the hell is this one? You're not Melissa are you? Isn't she dead?"

Mary scoffed. "Fuck you. I actually believed in you. All those people out there dying for our kingdom believed in you."

"Ah, you believed. My journey to the throne has been carved from the bodies of those who believed. Why don't you relax a bit? We are all just items to be used. Serenna uses you two, and Death uses me. Once you let go…life becomes a wonder."

Zeen drew his sword. "Will you stand down? I still believe there is a hint of good in you. It doesn't have to be this way. Even *you* can't beat the three of us."

"Oh?" Nyfe finally stopped gazing into his blade and at Zeen. "Death favors me. My endeavors entertain him, so he continues to grant me power. I suppose I should thank *you* for that, Serenna. Didn't you see the demons? You have no idea what I'm capable of now."

She clutched her staff with both hands, standing tall, ensuring not to reveal any of the pain already ripping through her entire body. "Enough talk. Surrender, and you have my word safe passage will be granted for your trial in Alanammus."

Nyfe stood from his throne, then approached, stopping before the stairs. "If you had even the slightest chance of defeating me, we wouldn't be having this conversation." He examined his blade with an empty grin. "I see the pain in your eyes. I see *everything*."

Dark wings of void energy emitted from his shoulders as he drifted down the stairs. "Death spoke to you... I can feel it...his voice lingers on your skin. Cherish this moment, Serenna. You will never feel hope again." He pointed his blade forward—it shook violently before launching a void blast at them.

They jumped out of the way in three different directions, with Serenna crashing to the ground and yelling out in pain. The void energy erupted when it hit the floor where they once stood, creating a large, black portal. Winds blew from the open gateway, howling with a frigid cold. A colossal entered from the hazy portal into their realm, letting out a roar as it stomped across the throne room.

Mary rushed in with both hands on her shield. The monster's arm came crashing down as she positioned herself to block only what was necessary. It was a relief the woman hadn't learned to rely on crystal shields yet. Mary deflected its arm to the ground, drew her sword with her free hand, then jabbed it through the wrist. While she lacked Pyith's brute power, she had far more finesse.

Zeen sprinted towards Nyfe with his sword drawn, but got tackled to the ground by a hidden crawler. Nyfe laughed as the crawler slammed his fangs through Zeen's crystal shield, shattering it in one blow, cutting his face.

The crawler attacked again and Zeen rolled to his left to dodge and grab his sword. With a swift—yet awkwardly positioned—swipe of his sword, he cut the crawler's arm off before it fell to the ground. He finished it through the head and immediately swung to his right to face another shrieking crawler that was mid-strike.

A new roar interrupted Nyfe's laughter. A second colossal entered the room and turned its attention to Serenna. She grabbed her staff and forced herself to stand, despite the agony in her wobbly legs. It gazed her up and down—the charge would come any second.

Nyfe walked to her side with a smile, gazing at the new colossal. "You didn't even consider you could lose tonight, did you? I bet Zeen dies first. Crawlers are vicious things. Once they get his legs, well, I wouldn't want to be him. What an awful death that will be. What an awful death you unleashed on the man you supposedly care for."

He's right...we should've regrouped after finding demons. They're all going to die because of me. I can't lead, I can't do anything other than destroy...

The first colossal knocked Mary across the room. She shrieked in pain, but shot back up and clenched her shield. Zeen stood his ground against the crawlers, but the small wounds were adding up—he wouldn't last much longer. Tears rolled down Serenna's cheeks...there was one more option. *Call my name tonight...and I may just answer.*

I was finally happy. It wasn't supposed to end this way. I...

Time slowed as she took a deep breath and examined the battlefield. Mary blocked the colossal again, but blood poured down her exposed arm. Zeen backed himself into a pillar, swinging at random, all his finesse replaced by terror. A crawler got through and slashed down his leg. He screamed but didn't fall. If he hit the ground, the demons would tear him to pieces. At this rate, Serenna would watch them both die before Nyfe finished her himself. An unacceptable fate. Even worse than *that*.

She clutched the Wings of Mylor, the only one that would understand.

Forgive me, Zeen. We should've lived happily forever, but that life was never meant for us. Remember me as that girl in Mylor, the one that still believed. Not this. Not the demon about to be unleashed.

"I am nothing...

"I am forever...

"I am—"

A new portal formed by her side. While still black, the distinct door-like shape clearly wasn't Nyfe's. Hopefully. As the spectral gateway shimmered, the outline of a familiar man materialized.

You...

David nodded at her, then looked ahead. The judgement in his pained eyes was more damning than any words he had ever spoken. Her staff fell to the ground with a *clang*. Tears poured from her eyes as she trembled, dropping to her knees. She could no longer shield herself with lies. When all was lost, Death would be her answer.

He drew the Herald of Fear and casually approached the rampaging colossal. The demon continued its charge, letting out a roar as it got close. Its fist crashed down before David slashed across to tear the arm right off its body. Blood splattered all over David and increased several-fold after he finished the demon through the skull. An essence of fear flowed towards him, seeping into his skin as his blade radiated dark energy.

He smothered Nyfe with his glare. "I can read your fear..."

The demons immediately ignored Zeen and Mary, all turning their attention to the champion of Fear. The crawlers jumped towards him together. He then let out a deep yell, unleashing a void nova that erupted from his body, launching the crawlers back to slam them against the high walls. The few crawlers and the colossal that still lived rushed back into Nyfe's portal to flee.

Zeen limped over to David, not bothering to check if Serenna was okay. She wasn't. "Nice of you to join us. I'm surprised you could absorb his fear."

"It's all a mask. Those who constantly state how much they don't care are always the most afraid. True apathy is a silent struggle."

Using her staff as a crutch, Serenna forced herself to stand. "David… Thank you."

He simply nodded back. From one monster to another, they shared a silent acceptance. Relief aided her wounds. Even if she could barely stand in the morning, tonight she would stand taller than Nyfe. "Mary," she said, "are you okay back there?"

Sitting with her back against a pillar, Mary's pained breaths were labored as she gave a thumbs up.

Nyfe's blade dimmed and his portal closed as he backtracked to the throne. "You couldn't just let me rule? The entire south, the Guardian team, and now *this*? I'm glad Forsythe killed Melissa…*none* of you deserve to be happy."

David drifted up the stairs, showing no emotion at the bitter words. "Farewell, Nyfe. May you find redemption in the void."

"No!" Serenna yelled. "We are taking him alive."

"That is a mistake—"

Nyfe lunged at David's neck mid-sentence, but David parried and pushed back. Nyfe's dagger tumbled down the stairs as he fell.

Rushing over, Zeen stepped on Nyfe's chest with his sword to his neck. "Why? Is there really no good in you? None at all?"

Nyfe laughed. "The boy burning Terrangus to the ground lectures me about good. I love you, Zeen; you're the embodiment of everything wrong with this realm."

With a groan, Mary forced herself up, then approached Nyfe. "Alright, that's enough." She pushed Zeen aside and leaned her knee on Nyfe's chest, then pulled her fist back before slamming it into his face. Blood rolled down Nyfe's mouth as he lay unconscious. "Can we kill him now? I'm all for mercy, but fuck this guy."

"No," Serenna said, panting. "My decision is final. Our southern forces will have the kingdom secured by the end of tonight, and then we can escort this one back to Alanammus for a trial. The plan went perfectly."

David sighed. "You have no reason to listen to me anymore, but this is a terrible mistake."

"So be it. I apologize if I let you down."

"Leadership takes defiance. I have never been more proud." David approached the Herald of Death with his sword drawn. "A parting gift." He pounded his seething weapon down, shattering the dagger to pieces. Without saying a word, he left through his own portal.

CHAPTER 34

INSPIRATION

Francis sighed, his white robes *soaked* from relentless rain. The fun part—his vengeance—was over. Now, a disorganized mesh of southern kingdom military leaders finalized Terrangus's surrender under covered torchlight, with soldiers lost in a daze nodding their heads "yes" to every question. For a grand battle, the ending was rather…uneventful. Terrangus soldiers had thrown down their arms upon accepting reality. Once men had seen their brethren kneeling and staying alive, the rest came down faster than a senator's career after getting caught with a mistress.

Defeated Terrangus soldiers lined up in the streets. It was rather barbaric to leave them so close to the dead bodies of their own, but why show mercy? These were the men that had killed Melissa. These were the men that had followed *him*. The invisible God of Wisdom floated by his side as Francis stood before an entire kneeling squad that had surrendered earlier.

"My dear Francis, look at them…they are bowing to you! Last time you were here, they wouldn't even look you in the eye. They still don't—but now it's because they can't. Take it all in. You will remember this moment forever."

"Forever," Francis whispered, his eyes lost on the crowd—
"FOR TERRANGUS!"

The startled Francis surveyed the crowd to find a crazed brute rushing towards him, wielding a small, bent sword. *Actually, the steel is a bit thin to classify as a sword. A dagger, perhaps? Yes, based on the classic Alanammus definition and not Terrangus or Vaynex, that is certainly a dagger—*

The man slashed wildly as he fell. He grazed Francis, tinting his white robes with a seeping red. Why hadn't anyone stopped him? Forever nearly came to a swift end.

In pure rage—or maybe fear—Francis charged his oak staff and glowed a harsh yellow. He pointed his staff at the fool, then a bolt of lightning launched him back-first into the closest building. The silence of the defeated soldiers amplified the echo of the thud.

With his adrenaline fading, the sharp pain in his chest made itself known. *By Wisdom's glory, I nearly died from a nobody. What a pitiful end that would've been.*

A small chuckle came from within the Terrangus squad.

They dare laugh at me? The Guardian of Alanammus, Wisdom's chosen one? Francis gripped his staff and erupted into a fiery orange glow, his new favorite. Terrangus soldiers, and perhaps his own, yelled out but he ignored them.

A blazing circle surrounded the wounded man, too injured from his crash to move away. Francis erupted his aura as the circle detonated into a seething inferno. His arms strained to keep the flames going.

Nothing ends the sound of laughter quite like the devastation of fire.

"My dear Francis, you can stop now. While I always appreciate a showing of magic's supremacy, the man's assault is finished—for he is quite dead."

Francis stopped and an empty dread ripped through his

stomach as he gazed upon the scorched remains of his attacker. Even with the rain pouring down, smoke drifted off the corpse. The burning stench was unfathomable; he thanked the raging winds for blowing it somewhere, anywhere away from his direction. *What is happening to me? What would Mom say?*

How much can a person be damaged before they are considered broken?

Tempest waddled over in his encumbering armor while Warlord Sardonyx burst out laughing from afar. "That *thing* is ruining you. Get it together. You are acting more barbaric than my father."

His father? The empty dread grew worse. For Tempest to compare Francis to *him* was a grievous insult. But Tempest was wrong—it would be childish to blame Wisdom, the god who guided him towards something greater. This scorched... nameless man had been a necessary steppingstone on the path to Serenity.

It will all be worth it in the end. It has to be.

Captain Julius yelled out with his hands waving, then Francis and Tempest drifted towards him. The gold cloak hunched down, struggling to breathe, but his smile grew as Tempest approached...very slowly. "Guardian Francis, Warmaster Tempest. I have official confirmation from Serenna: The Guardians have defeated Nyfe. He is in our custody."

Of course they did. I bet Nyfe dropped to his knees and begged for mercy like the coward he is.

Tempest removed his golden face guard and held it by his side. "Strength, damn this thing... Thank you, Captain Julius, those are comforting words. It would seem tonight was a massive success for human and zephum cooperation; may there be many more to come."

I wonder how Mary fared. Surely, Wisdom would have told

me if something happened? "I require details. Is everyone okay?"

"No casualties," Julius said, his eyes darting around, "but there is much to discuss."

Great. Just great. "Then we discuss it *now*." *Too direct, tone it down. Leaders speak with subtlety.*

Julius cleared his throat, shooting Tempest a quick glance that didn't escape Francis's notice. "Understood. We are still learning the details, but somehow, the Guardians faced demons. They all have some wounds. Nothing fatal, but they need rest."

"What? Demons?" Francis asked.

"I'm afraid so. Serenna said they would've died if David hadn't interfered. Apparently, he is now some…Fear champion thing. I don't really understand what the hell she was talking about, but they're alive so it doesn't matter."

Francis struggled not to shoot a glare at Wisdom and reveal his presence. How could he withhold such vital information? *Say something, it's taking too long to respond.* "I…could I please see the Guardians?" *Dammit! Speak more clearly!*

"Of course. Tempest, will you be joining us?"

"Pardon me, but I must get back to Vaynex and remove this armor. Father forces me to wear it for my protection, but how can I be safe if I cannot move? Regardless, my presence won't do any good for the tension. The warlord and I were the most hated people here until Francis took the mantle. Be well, my friends. There are tough times ahead for Terrangus."

"Tough times indeed," Julius said, before giving him a quick hug. "When will we meet again?"

Tempest smiled. "That, sir, is up to you. I officially declare you an honorable ally of the zephum. As of now, you may enter Vaynex any day with my blessing."

Julius's ignorant eyes lit up with joy. He must have been

the only human in Alanammus history to truly welcome an invitation to the wretched zephum empire. "Thank you... Strength without honor—is chaos."

The words grabbed Sardonyx's attention from afar, as if they were screamed from the top of Wisdom's sky garden. He rushed over. "What is going on here?"

"I'm heading home, Father," Tempest said. "I gave Julius the blessing to come visit. He may be the first human to do so voluntarily."

"Put your face guard back on; *you* are staying. *I* am leaving. This human kingdom is too wet and dishonorable... Francis! Well fought for a mage! You finally got some blood on you!" Sardonyx put his hand on Francis's wound and examined the blood. His cold, armored hands filled Francis with a burning pain. "Ah, that is how I wish to die. Rushing into certain death with nothing more than my blade against a treacherous sorcerer. You gave him a *glorious* death."

With no further words, the warlord simply walked away. Only he could say the words "treacherous sorcerer" as a compliment. "Your father is...unique," Francis said with a grin.

"My father is a...ugh." Tempest placed his face guard back on. His groan echoed through the gold. "Julius, please escort us to the Guardians. Seems I will be here for quite a while."

"Forgive me for being pleased."

They navigated towards the castle at a gradual pace. Bodies and kneeling soldiers littered the military ward, lit by the uncontrolled fires running rampant through the barracks. While Francis had never cared for Terrangus, this was...rather brutal.

"Take it all in. Maybe now you will reconsider my stance on freewill? Behind every painting, every concerto, is a massacre. Some...man-made catastrophe in the name of progress. Look at

that woman over there. She was a singer, and the last sound her gifted voice let out was a scream of agony. This would never happen in Serenity. With everything predetermined, everyone could be happy.

"Even you."

Francis shuddered, unsure if from the cold or his god's words filling his thoughts. He couldn't respond without revealing his presence to the others. Freewill *did* have its flaws, but to dismantle the entire concept in response to a handful of fools was clearly an overreaction. *Right?*

Tempest snickered when the distressed Francis caught his eye. "Perhaps the four of us are the most unlikely group ever assembled?"

"Four?" Julius asked.

"Francis knows what I'm referring to...yes?"

Why is he doing this? Is it worth lying at this point? No, he already knows. "Fine. Julius...have you ever met the God of Wisdom?"

"That one? No. I waved at his statue once, but he never waved back."

Remaining invisible, Wisdom's voice echoed through the air. "Now, my dear Julius, that simply isn't true. You *have* cursed my name, but never had the courtesy to wave at me. I tend to wave back. Not literally, of course, but I *always* wave back."

Julius froze, then drew his polearm. His friendly smile plummeted to a scowl. "What? You guys are serious?"

"Unfortunately," Tempest said. "Strength says he is the most dangerous of all the gods. While Death and Fear are out to destroy us, that one seeks a fate far more sinister."

Wisdom chuckled. "Only a *zephum* could refer to paradise as sinister. Ah, Tempest, you are your father's son. Another simpleminded beast, yearning for change, but flailing desperately to avoid it ever coming true. Strength is nothing more than a resistance to pain. Since pain is all you know, by instinct, you kneel down and worship it. How sad."

Don't smile; it's not worth it.

Tempest sighed. "Out of respect for Francis, I won't respond. I'm *done* with this conversation. You are a reasonable mage; can we agree to disagree?"

"Fair enough. Lord Wisdom, we can finish this discussion another day." Wisdom didn't respond. No one did. *I shouldn't speak to him that way...*

An uncomfortable silence cursed the remainder of the journey to the castle. As soldiers' screams plagued the air, Francis wished anyone would speak to drown out the mayhem. Arguing over Serenity had to be preferable to the aftermath of battle, but his stoic companions begged to differ. *They truly hate him, don't they? I suppose they hate me too. If only they could see it my way...*

But what if I'm wrong?

Staring at the castle before them, Tempest finally broke the silence. "I'll admit, it's quite unsettling to enter here without Forsythe. He has been the emperor my entire life. I...never cared for the man, but a small part of me misses him."

Francis cocked his head slightly. "He *did* kill Melissa. You are reminiscing because his replacement somehow managed to be worse. A brutal future does not excuse a brutal past."

Tempest leaned his head down. "Well said, my friend. Forgive my misguided words. To see a transition in leadership result in such ruin is difficult. When my father dies..." He took his face guard off and stared into the lifeless shell in his arms. "This could be me. I read, I study, but honestly, I don't have the slightest clue on how to lead. The zephum are a brutal people, and they favor a brutal leader. That will never be me."

Ah, I have been far too awful to him. "All the more reason why it *needs* to be you. I too apologize; you are a good friend, Tempest. I know your burdens all too well. My mother was one of the most revered archons in our history. She was impossible to follow, so I took the easy way out by becoming a Guardian…"

"Hmm. I would have done the same, but I'm far too weak to become one of your people. There is no escaping my fate. One day, I will rule Vaynex."

"Well, on the bright side," Julius said with a laugh, "your father will likely live forever. I've never seen anything like him. Took a flame blast to the face and it just *bored* him."

Tempest snickered. "Indeed. Perhaps I deceive myself; odds are, I will fall decades before him. Let's go. Francis, it would be most proper if you led the way."

Francis nodded and approached the already ripped off castle doors. It was surreal to trek towards the throne room as his own soldiers saluted him. Terrangus had suffered terrible defeats in their history—particularly against the zephum—but *never* had the entire city been occupied by an invading force. *Forsythe must be laughing from the void.*

They entered the throne room and stood frozen at the sight of demon corpses scattered throughout the once-radiant hall. He couldn't imagine how a dead crawler found its way high up on the east senator's section. *Two colossals? How did they manage this? Will I never surpass Serenna?*

The Guardians sat on the throne room stairs huddled next to each other. All three had blood trailing down their faces with dead, drained eyes.

There he is…

As Nyfe lay on his back unconscious, Francis couldn't tell if he was breathing through the dense crystal shield keeping him in place. His dagger had been shattered into several remnants, each still radiating a dark glow. "Invisible Guardian,

you say? Now that your eyes are closed, everyone is invisible."
With a rush of adrenaline, he rushed over to the Guardians.
They all smiled at him, but none had any strength left to match
his excitement. "Well done, everyone!"

Zeen struggled, but eventually rose. "Thank you. As you
most likely noticed, it was a hell of a battle."

"Indeed. David is gone, right? Right?"

"Yeah. It's…difficult to explain. His sword is growing in
power. At this point, he can create his own portals and jump
around the kingdoms. I have no idea when we'll see him again."

"Hmm. And Nyfe?"

"I didn't check, but I assume he's still alive. Your good
friend Mary over there probably took a few years off his life
with her fist. She just…BAM!" He did a punching motion
before letting out a strained laugh. "Francis, we need a healing
ward. I'm in the best shape out of the three of us and I can
barely keep my eyes open."

Francis turned to Serenna and Mary as Zeen struggled to
sit. Hmm. Of course! They needed inspiration. "My friends,
my allies. What you accomplished tonight was nothing short
of incredible. Serenna, I am honored to have you lead us. When
the next Harbinger arrives, you will command my staff as the
mage Guardians stand united against the wrath of Fear and
Death. Mary, you continue to impress me every time we meet.
You have been one of the most successful new recruits I have
ever met. Over time—"

"Oh, *please* stop talking," Mary groaned. "I can't take
another soulless thank you. I need SLEEP!"

Serenna stood, her eyes widening with shock as she bore
her full weight on her legs. "We all love you, Francis. Give us
a day; you have my word that I'll tell you everything. Now,
could you please escort us to the Guardian portal? I cannot
exaggerate how badly we need rest."

"My dear Serenna! All you have to do is ask," Wisdom said. All the Guardians other than Mary flinched back and stared straight through him. The southern forces in the room one by one grew silent and gaped in awe. About half the room kneeled, while the rest—Tempest and Julius included—backed away.

"What? They can see you?" Francis whispered.

"A fine theory, or perhaps everyone is suddenly fascinated with *you*!" Wisdom floated towards Nyfe as the Herald of Wisdom staff materialized in his spectral hands. "Ah, the Child of Death sleeps soundly. Look at his shattered toy...my staff would never crumble that way. Wisdom is *clearly* superior to Death! Perhaps I underestimated my colleague Fear. I'll have to invite her to Serenity for some wine. Mary, you are welcome to join us, of course. My dear Francis has grown *quite* fond of you."

Francis shot Wisdom a glare with such force it caused a sharp pain in the side of his neck. *Why is he doing this to me?*

"I'm aware," Mary said with a smile. "You're doing an awful job teaching him subtlety."

None of these people respect me. This was supposed to be my night, and instead it's all nonsense. Maybe I really am the Invisible Guardian...

With a small chuckle, Wisdom's staff radiated energy before it vibrated and created a dazzling white portal by the throne stairs. "Oh, I like you. You could be the only thing Strength and I agree upon."

Zeen sighed. "Another portal? No way am I going in there."

The Herald of Wisdom vibrated again, then Zeen yelled as he flew through the air into the portal.

"I do insist. Ladies, it's your decision, but I *strongly* suggest you enter this portal."

Serenna turned to Francis. "If you trust him, I will too." Mary followed her as they both entered.

Finally, some respect...

CHAPTER 35

INSIGNIFICANT MEN DOING INSIGNIFICANT THINGS

Fyfe lay on his cold cell floor, shivering and groaning from hunger. Steel chains bound to his hands and feet limited him to a small corner in his massive cell. All the space in the world, but nowhere to go. With his dagger destroyed, the voices had stopped. No more screaming. No more warnings. No more anything...

I have never heard pure silence. If it wasn't a nightmare, it would be a dream come true.

He didn't mind the irony of being in Serenna's old cell, but he *did* mind that they had taken out the bed and candles to make it less comfortable. Time passed since he had first been thrown into the corner and passed out. A few days at the least, maybe a week at most. He had lost track after the third sleep, never realizing how disorienting time could be without candlelight or any sort of company. His only interactions had been with men who came to torture him. The rusty door screeched open as he gazed into the familiar darkness, his body tensing from the anticipation of their horrors.

And there they are...

Light steps suggested it was only one individual approaching. Odd, his tormentors had always come in pairs. A candle was lit, revealing a face he had grown to despise.

Zeen examined him with a pained frown. He stumbled back—likely from the smell—before he regained himself and placed a plate of food down with a heavy jug of water. "Morning, Nyfe. I apologize for the way our people have treated you. Despite everything…no one deserves this. Hopefully, you can enjoy this meal. I would've brought wine, but I figured you're nearly dried out."

The aroma of fresh beef reminding him of his old life was more tortuous than any of the blades that had cut through his skin, but the water was pure gold. Nyfe grabbed the jug and downed it all like a wild animal. He would have cried in joy if Zeen wasn't there—murderers aren't supposed to have feelings. "The irony of my torture isn't lost on me, you know. In all my pain, all my failures, there is always one constant: *you…*"

"Nyfe, I didn't do this to you. Everyone would've left you alone if you let go of the dagger. What did you expect to happen? I'm not saying this to gloat, but there are consequences for allying yourself with the God of Death."

"And where are Serenna's consequences? She allied herself with Death and her life has never been better. How do I get that deal?"

"Deep down, she is a good person. I want to believe that for you too, but all I see is violence after violence. How does a person live your life?"

"With the conviction I am the only thing that matters. You do it too, but shroud it in some faint nonsense you believe to be empathy. I know the desperate man behind the smile. You are always one death away from becoming David. Don't even *try* to deny it."

"For all my faults, my feelings for her are not one of them.

Maybe if you bothered to let anyone in, you wouldn't be here today."

Nyfe thrust forward, stopped by his chains right in front of Zeen. "You think I want this? I'm envious of your Serenna, even of David's Melissa. I...just don't get those feelings anymore. None of it *matters* to me. Do you know what it's like to be handed the God of Death's artifact when you're only a child? I killed my first man when I was seven...what kind of life could I ever lead?"

Zeen sat against the wall next to him. "In all our years together, not once have I seen any hint of compassion or mercy. Are you even trying?"

Nyfe gazed back into the darkness and shook his head. "No. Not for a long time. I loved a girl once: some mage on my team way back when my rank was just captain and my hair still brown. I don't even remember her name anymore...or her hair...or *anything*. Not even her eyes. I *always* remember the eyes. I just see an outline when I think back, clear lines shifting to illuminate the shape of a beautiful woman. The only one."

That got his attention. Zeen hunched forward, staring at Nyfe with...pity? "What happened?"

"The blade. The *fucking* blade. As my happiness grew, I saw less need to follow the void. Most don't venture down that path until there is no other option. *He* didn't appreciate that. Death warned his gift would fade forever unless I killed her. I was afraid to be weak, fearing she only admired me for my power. I was young. Figured there would be others..."

Of course she only loved you for your power. There is nothing else; just a weak husk that clings to the shadows of the void.

"The stab came from behind. I would never—even now— have the courage to look her in the eyes as she died. That moment... It was just a *snap*. Nothing mattered after that. I made the wrong choice, Zeen, but I'm so far invested in this nightmare there is no turning back. Honestly, I died years ago, but it hasn't caught up with me yet."

To his shock, Zeen shifted over and placed his hand on his shoulder. "Ah… I wish we spoke sooner. I could've helped you. I don't know how, but we would have found something."

After an agonizing moment of silence, Nyfe stared at him. He had never learned how to use pleading eyes, but gods, did he try. "You can help me now…"

"How?"

"*Kill me.*"

Zeen flinched away. "No… No, I won't do that."

"I've had a good run, but it's over. Look at my life now, Zeen. Somehow, you are my only friend left in the realm. It is *impossible* to grasp how pitiful that is. Give me a quick swipe across the neck. Tell them we fought valiantly to the death or something and that I was defeated. They will brand you the Hero of Terrangus. You always wanted that."

Picking up the candle, Zeen stood and stepped back. "Forgive me, but I will not kill you. Not because Serenna gave the order, but because I'm not a murderer."

"Not a murderer," he said with a laugh. "Your pile of bodies grows each day. Either kill me…or get the *fuck* out of my cell."

The weak flame matched Zeen's frown. "Very well. I'll be back tomorrow with more food and water. We can get through this together." He stopped before the darkness engulfed him and turned to Nyfe a last time. "I won't give up on you yet," he said with a smile.

The creak of the closing door damned Nyfe back to solitude. *He's the only one that cares. Why did I let him leave? Why, why, why did I tell him about Emily?*

The aroma of burned beef interrupted his loathing; he had nearly forgotten about the small feast. Zeen apparently didn't trust him enough to leave a fork or a blade—which was surprisingly smart for him—but Nyfe was more than happy to just eat the damn thing with his hands. No one was watching. No one would ever watch again.

He finished the feast, then lay on his back. The icy touch of the hard floor soothed his wounds. *Zeen said good morning, I probably shouldn't sleep yet. To hell with it, not like I have anything else to do...*

Physical pain had never bothered him, but the mental exhaustion of reminiscing about *her* was enough. He closed his eyes—his surroundings not changing at all—then welcomed the gradual fade from consciousness.

Maybe I'll be lucky and never wake again...

He awoke again, however much later, opening his eyes and seeing nothing. Taking a deep breath, he swore his breath lingered in front of him despite the darkness. His hands remained invisible, but they trembled. They trembled like they had in Boulom.

The door creaked open. *How long was I out? Is it truly the next day already?* Louder steps, two men approaching out of rhythm. His tormentors had always come in pairs.

Ah, shit...

"Heard you had a visitor!" a man's voice yelled. He forced Nyfe up and slammed him against the wall. His second guest lit a candle, revealing himself in a pale Mylor uniform and the other in standard Terrangus black. The Owl and Ebony Blade united to tear down the Child of Death. Serenna would be proud.

Holding him against the wall, the Terrangus man drew a tiny dagger and held it to his face. "What's wrong, Nyfe? Nothing to say for once?"

Nyfe sighed. "Can you just get on with it? The last two men didn't waste my time."

"Arrogant fuck." He plunged the dagger slightly above Nyfe's knee. An unbearable sting flourished from the wound, but only a trickle of blood flowed down. It would take a man hours to murder anyone with such a blade, but that was likely the point.

"Why does everyone go low first? My face is still beautiful; why don't you aim there?" *If I can get them angry enough, maybe they'll finish the job. That's my only hope here... Not the way I expected to go.*

The man obliged, poking the dagger into his forehead just enough to draw blood, then slowly carving downwards. By the time it reached Nyfe's nose, blood trickled into his mouth, replacing the savory remnants of meat with the all too familiar taste of his own blood.

Nyfe spat blood on the man's face with a laugh. The candle illuminated the splatter and, more importantly, the eyes. The man trembled, pure rage coursing through him. Even the tiniest of blades would be fatal through the neck. *Do it... Do it NOW!*

Instead, the man took a deep breath before returning to his work, continuing at the curve of his nose where he had left off. It wasn't all that bad so far, but as the blade continued under the skin of his nose, Nyfe braced himself for suffering. Thirst had already torn the life from his lips; it would be unbearable to have a blade rip downwards. *Stop breathing so heavily...*

His torturer's eyes lit up. "I've waited too long for this. I lost everyone to you. We both did..."

The dagger leisurely pierced the top half of his lips. *Don't scream. Don't scream.* He gasped as it continued down. A stinging sensation started at his lips, then tore through his entire body. *Don't scream.* He kicked and squealed; the horror amplified by the man's crazed grin.

Finally, the man backed off and turned to his accomplice. "Fancy a go?"

"Sure. I'll be quick." The Mylor soldier—or whoever he was—took a blacksmith's hammer from a sheath by his leg. Unlike the dagger, this hammer was not tiny at all.

Nyfe breathed heavily and fell to lean against the wall. *That has a far greater chance of finishing me, at least. Still, I'm afraid to anger him. I'm so afraid...*

He glanced up to a boot soaring towards his face. For a brief moment, he could smell the leather before it crushed his nose inwards, launching him against his will to the cold floor where it had all started. He lay there dazed, gazing into the ceiling as it blurred in and out. *Yes...go unconscious. Fade away...*

"We're losing him," one of them yelled.

"One more before he goes. Something he'll *never* forget."

The ceiling continued to blur. Something grabbed his left arm, but Nyfe didn't bother to look. *They're just so underwhelming. Now that my dagger is gone, all these insignificant men are rushing out like roaches. I could kill them both with one—*

He screamed as a thunderous slam crashed against his left hand. A sobering wail vibrated through the empty halls as his dry throat tore from the strain. Any dreams of peace shattered like the bones in his wrist.

"That was for Melissa. A daughter for a hand. By no means a fair trade, but I'll sleep easier now that I can think back to the agony on your face. You are the lowest scum."

Nyfe rolled over, holding his broken hand in vain. "I didn't kill Melissa, you fucking idiot!"

"Not the Guardian, my daughter. There are countless lives ruined and you don't even know who they are. I wish everyone from Mylor could kill you over and over."

"Enough, no more words. I don't want him to identify us to Zeen."

"Bah, you're right. Fuck you, Child of Death. May you suffer forever..."

As they left, the creak of the closed door blessed him back to solitude. He let out a pained shriek and rolled over onto his back. With the candle gone, the ceiling was shrouded in darkness. Maybe it still blurred, but it was impossible to tell. Aside from his shattered hand, everything was as they had left it. The chains, the darkness...the cold. He shivered again before his mind went blank, allowing the pain to carry him to a deep sleep.

His eyes opened as a frigid chill pierced through him. *Wind?*

He struggled to move, his pain emerging as his senses returned. Leaning against the corner, he held his knees to his chest and trembled. The howling grew louder. *Am I finally losing it?* The cell doors rattled as a deep rumble filled the air. *I'm not alone.*

His eyes squinted at a dim red glow near the ceiling. The glow enhanced to a burning crimson, splitting and forming the shape of two eyes. The two eyes of Death. "You...is this a dream?"

"No. You will never dream again. Reality is far worse, but it is all that remains. I come with an offer. The last one you will ever receive." To Nyfe's surprise, Death spoke out loud and not through thoughts. Perhaps with the Herald of Death destroyed that link was no longer possible.

"What do you want from me?"

"*Everything*. No more Child of Death, no more ridiculous dreams of grandeur. Become my Harbinger, the vast encompassing nothing you were always destined to be. Answer me...*now*."

Nyfe's chains faded to dust as he looked down and struggled to breathe. *I knew this day would come. No. I am Nyfe, not some mindless, demonic husk. How did life end up this way?* "Is there any other choice?"

"Ah, the last one obsessed with choice burned Boulom to the ground. I do not care what your decision is. Pain is everywhere; lesser men are lined up for the opportunity to serve. It has been two years. Too long... TOO LONG!"

After a long pause, Death let out a rumble, and its red eyes dimmed. "So be it. We will never speak again. The next time we meet will be in the void. You will look upon me a last time as all men do and then the void will consume you forever. A boring choice. I *despise* boring choices."

"Wait!" *To hell with it. I'm going to die anyway, at least I can go out like a legend. If he gave me enough power, I could crumble entire kingdoms. Most of these things are just angry mages. Imagine what I could accomplish!*

I could kill them all.

His eyes left the floor and grew lost on his deity. "I want power. Real power. I don't want to end up as just another Harbinger that gets defeated by the Guardians. If we do this...I want to be a *god*."

"You will *never* become a god, but I can make you far worse. The only limits of your power will be set by the limits of your violence."

Zeen asked if there was any good left in me. I guess the answer is no. I guess the answer has always been no. "Show me."

A bright flash erupted in the dark cell, illuminating everything with pale spectral candles that finally granted him vision. Before him was a dagger, nearly the same design as his beloved Herald of Death, but the power radiating from it was completely foreign. As the darkness flowed through him, all his wounds and remnants of torment pulsated in agony.

He fell to his knees, leaning to his right and keeping his shattered left hand on his chest. The pain was unbearable, but all he could focus on was the power. It coursed through him, teasing him with a wrath that would bring the entire realm to their knees. Never again could Serenna, Sardonyx, or even David defeat him if he wielded such madness.

The cost was everything, and he would gladly pay it.

His hand reached for the blade before it rumbled and shot him back to the wall of his cell. "Not yet. The Time God binds me to make my terms clear: this is not a taste. If you accept, you are mine. The Child of Death will be no more, but the Harbinger of Death will reign. Make your decision…"

My father always warned me of this moment. All men of the blade get tempted at their lowest hour. But no hour is lower than mine. I wonder if all those waiting for my end are watching from the void. They will have to wait a bit longer.

Or maybe forever.

"I accept," he whispered, then cradled the grip as if it was the only thing left that still loved him. Void energy erupted and swirled all around him. Fragments little by little launched inside his body, filling him with a wrath he had never known possible. The pain vanished and his right hand was never more free. The darkness returned but lost its terror. There was nothing in the unknown that could ever threaten him again.

"I always loved you, Nyfe. As a final gift, I will keep your mind intact until you take your first victim. Thank you for this. The Time God will finally wake to a barren crater. Finally…after everything he did to me. Finally…"

Fair enough. With his dagger held behind his back, Nyfe sat in the corner, awaiting the next unfortunate pair of tormentors to send them to the void. He would make sure it was worth it before succumbing to madness. The door creaked open. Light steps filled the air. Only one man approached.

"Good morning," Zeen said. His cheerful voice echoed through the dank chamber as he lit a candle and placed his goods at Nyfe's feet.

Shit. "Back so soon? Has it truly been a whole day?"

Zeen snickered. "I suppose I can't fault you for losing track of time. Did you have any visitors? I was promised it would stop."

"It *never* stops. But soon it won't matter."

The dagger tensed in his hand as Zeen examined him and shook his head. "Oh no, look at you. They lied to me...who were they?"

Why am I hesitating? Kill him. Kill him, NOW! "Does it matter? Underwhelming men doing underwhelming things. Such is the story of Terrangus."

Zeen grabbed the jug of water and held it out. With his arm in the air, Nyfe had a clear shot at his upper ribs. It would kill him instantly. As would a blow to the neck, left upper chest, anywhere lower stomach. Too many options.

And he refused them all. Instead, Nyfe accepted the water, drinking it without the feral desperation of yesterday. That *was* yesterday, right? "Zeen, why are you doing this for me?"

"Despite everything, you deserve to have a friend before it's over."

Nyfe scoffed, loosening his grip on the blade behind him. "You sure know how to pick them. You have me, a champion of Fear, and a pact-breaking Guardian that tapped into Death's power. Why do you flock towards monsters?"

"Hmm. Maybe it's monsters that flock towards me. And, to be fair, you were right."

"About what? I forget most of the nonsense I rattle off."

"If Serenna ever died, I wouldn't be able to handle it. I told her that once and...well, let's just say she didn't appreciate it."

Nyfe snickered. "What a stupid thing to say to a girl you're trying to bed." The laughing ended with a deep breath. "Zeen, I lied to you. I remember everything about Emily. Greenest eyes I ever saw. *Pure emeralds.* I don't hate myself for choosing Death; I hate myself because it was easy. There is no hope for people like me. I'm not you. Hell, I'm not even David. Zeen...you were good to me in my final days and for that I am thankful. I want you to know that before it's over."

"It's not over yet."

"That is truer than you realize. Now, leave me. Leave me and get far away from Terrangus."

Zeen smiled. "I'll be back tomorrow."

Enjoy your final days with Serenna; the days I never had with Emily. Even if it's all meaningless, I hope you relish the temporary joy. This isn't ending the way you want it to...

Some time—hours maybe—passed before the doors rattled again. Giggling men stumbled into the room, and the herd of footsteps suggested there was at least four of them.

"Oh, Nyfe!" some man yelled in a drunken slur. They all laughed, prepared to finally face their monster, who had no hope of fighting back. The perfect enemy for the imperfect man.

"Kevin, light the damn candle. I can't see anything in here."

"Yeah, just give me a second." After a few scrapes, the man lit the candle and held it to the wall where Nyfe once sat.

"Huh? Did Reilly send him to Alanammus already?"

"Not a chance. I already paid the bribe; he's here until next week. Check the other corner—"

The door slammed shut behind them with such force it blew out the candle. As darkness engulfed them, their eagerness diminished to silence. Nyfe drifted forward, each step creating a vast rumble that shook the room. The words were finally his to speak.

"I am nothing. I am forever. I am the end."

CHAPTER 36

GOLDEN SCHOLARS

Here we go again, Francis thought. He stood solemnly in the middle of the Terrangus trade district, gripping his staff, keeping eye contact with a soldier that held a blade to a young girl's neck. Another frigid afternoon, but it was the first day in a week it hadn't rained. Small victories. *How long must I do this? Where are the rest of the Guardians? This is beneath me...*

"This *wench* has been charging us different prices! I asked that gold cloak what he paid, and my tab was double. Double!" The man's dagger shook around her neck, pricking tiny cuts from the random movements. It was far too early for any dignified man to be intoxicated, but dignified men were a great scarcity since the battle.

Francis broke eye contact and turned to Tempest and Julius—his fellow Terrangus peacekeepers during the miserable occupation. "Can you guys please do something? Anything? I would really prefer not to use magic again. We don't need any more riots."

The invisible Wisdom chuckled. "I, for one, would prefer

a fire spell. With the alcohol in his system, the man would likely *explode!*"

Julius shrugged. "Sorry, I handled the last guy. Tempest, this fool is yours."

"Fine. I always get the drunks," Tempest said with a sigh. He approached in his full golden armor, stopping right outside of striking distance. Despite his constant complaining about the weight, he had worn it every day after his father's departure. "Human Lord, my name is Tempest Claw. I am the diplomatic representative of Vaynex. I would be more than happy to discuss your troubles once you unhand the woman. Let us speak as gentlemen."

The man took the blade from her neck, pointing it at the future warlord. "Fuck you!"

"A fair rebuttal, sir. If I may, how about I just pay your tab?"

"You're a LIZARD! You don't have any gold."

"Sir, I do believe my *golden* armor is ample evidence to dispute that claim…"

"Hmm." He threw the girl to the ground, who scurried off before the man approached Tempest. "Five gold…no, make it seven—"

With a swift headbutt, Tempest's face guard crashed down against the man's skull, unleashing a week's worth of frustration from being designated a Terrangus peacekeeper. Blood flowed down the man's face as he crumbled to the ground. "You," Tempest said, pointing to a guard. "Get this one back to the military ward. Tell General…whoever the hell is in charge to get these guys under control. This is *embarrassing.*"

The guard shrugged and walked away, leaving the injured man to lie dormant in the streets. Uninterested murmurs filled the air as the crowd dissipated and went back to their routine as if nothing had happened. Chaos was the new normal.

"Just leave him," Julius said. "If no one else cares, neither should we. I'm done with this grunt work, let's grab some drinks."

He's right. I have no reason to care about this place. It's only Terrangus. "A fair idea. Tempest, will you join us?"

Tempest shrugged. "I could use a drink. Where shall we go?"

Francis surveyed the shattered kingdom. Most of the shops and inns remained closed, and—by a miracle of incompetence—the burned trade cart from his duel against Nyfe was still lying in the streets. Newly homeless people had flooded the trade district, clinging to wine and begging for gold. The fires were out, but the true wounds would take *years* to heal.

To his left was a rundown tavern, with one door missing and all the windows on the second floor shattered. A sign wobbled above the entrance, displaying an absurd caricature of a zephum smiling with giant, bubbly eyes, wielding an iron sword with both hands...and its tail? "The Three-Handed Sword," the sign read. "Hmm. How about that one?"

"YES!" Julius yelled with a laugh, slapping Tempest on the shoulder.

"But... Why is he holding the sword with his tail? We don't do that. Do you have any idea how impractical that is? Ah, whatever. I'm in."

Time to be bold. "Wisdom, would you care to join us?" Francis whispered.

"No...*he's* here. Too soon. I need to leave *now.*" The god vanished, leaving an ominous chill that was always there.

Who? He must mean Nyfe? I swear, if they let him escape, I'm quitting as a Guardian.

As he entered through the missing door, a variety of smiles and leers met him from the tavern's inhabitants. Mostly men and women in armor, but oddly enough, a fair mix of Terrangus and southern soldiers sat together with their drinks. A cheerful atmosphere, one he hadn't seen in far too long. *This tavern is a haven...*

A Serenity.

The barkeep nodded him over, twirling his red mustache. "Who you after? No trouble here. Not that sort of place."

Oh right. Francis placed his staff behind his back. "My companions and I are looking for a place to drink. In private, of course. Is the upstairs open?"

The barkeep gazed curiously at Tempest before turning back to Francis. "Hmm. I have the upstairs closed for...renovations, but maybe I could make it work."

Does this lowly man even know who I am? He should be paying me to drink here...

Julius grabbed what appeared to be at least ten gold and placed it on the counter. An outrageous price. "Done. If anyone asks, we aren't here. Terrangus deals with Terrangus today."

The barkeep raked in the gold, then nodded to a young girl. "Take them upstairs. Whatever they want."

They followed the girl—a redhead, his favorite—to the second level, a grimy, barren room with shattered glass still scattered by the windows. A small round table stood near the middle with two barrels of *questionable* wine stacked in the back. No hovel would ever exist in Alanammus, and the depravity made Francis eager for home.

The girl opened one of the barrels and poured drinks, filling the room with an intense aroma that only the cheapest of wines could make possible. Julius sat first, then the rest followed in a triangle formation. How fitting.

Taking a sip, Francis welcomed the strong, bitter taste. It was the right kind of terrible, *well* below his normal standards, but anything that numbed his senses would do. "Ah, that burn; I didn't realize how much I needed this."

Julius raised his mug in the air. "Cheers!" They clinked mugs and took a large gulp, then chatted among themselves for about an hour.

Tempest sighed after finishing his third refill. "Oh, how I miss my dear Pyith. I can't believe I'm saying this, but I want to go home."

"We all do," Julius said. "I haven't seen my husband since this whole thing started. Robert must think I'm having the time of my life."

"The time of our lives," Francis said with a snicker. "Well, as unfortunate as this week has been, there is solace in suffering together. You guys…are my best friends in a while." *I can't believe I just said that.*

Tempest slammed his empty mug on the table, shattering it and signaling for another. "Well spoken, Guardian."

Julius finished his drink, then leaned in. "All we're missing is someone from Terrangus. Francis, if you had to pick: Zeen or Mary?"

"Mary," Francis said immediately. *They're looking at me again…ah, to hell with it.* Wine had finally liberated him from his anxiety, and not having Wisdom constantly invading his thoughts with obscure philosophy was a luxury he had nearly forgotten.

Tempest shook his head. "To hell with Terrangus. The three of us are good enough to make our own Guardian group." He leaned against the table and stared at them both. "We need a name."

"A name?" Francis asked.

Julius rubbed his chin. "Hmm, I like it. How about…the Golden Guardians?"

After taking another large swig, Francis's eyes lit up. "No!

I have one; the title unifies all our cultures: Strength and Wisdom."

Tempest's head shook more vigorously than before. "No, no, no! Fuck the gods, this is our thing. Wisdom is a tyrant and Strength is irrelevant. Mortals stand on their own, together." He stood with pride, staring them down. For a brief moment, he was a true zephum. "The Golden Scholars."

Fuck the gods? Such blasphemy. Still, this is the most fun I've had in a while. These are good people.

These are my friends. "The Golden Scholars…"

With a snark grin, Julius finished his drink and threw the mug behind him. "The Golden Scholars!"

Their laughter was interrupted by a frazzled Terrangus guard rushing up the stairs. He staggered, out of breath, turning to the trio with pure terror in his wide eyes.

"The Golden Scholars are on break!" Julius yelled. "Be gone!"

"Lord Francis," the man said, stuttering at the words. "We need you at the castle immediately. Please…"

No one in Terrangus ever calls me Lord Francis, unless… "What happened?"

"It's Nyfe. He's a Harbinger. Reilly said he could be a Harbinger of Death…"

Unless it's a Harbinger. This is what Wisdom sensed. Why did he leave me?

"We're all going to die." Disappointed eyes assaulted him, but no words came his way. *Oh, I just said that out loud…focus, Francis, focus!* "We need to support the barricade and get assistance. Harbingers of Death are too powerful for three people alone." He rose, tapping his staff to the ground like Serenna had always done. "Everything depends on us. *Do not* engage Nyfe; now is the time to be practical."

Tempest nodded. "This is your area of expertise. We will follow your every word."

They rushed outside into the frigid cold as glimpses of dusk shadowed the kingdom into the gradual darkness of night. Screaming people darted all over, frantically rushing to the outskirts to flee.

A high-pitched screech entered the air. Not the screech of a crawler, and definitely not the deep roar of a colossal. Harbingers of Death could create their own demons, so Francis pushed through the crowd to find their unknown enemy. To his relief, Terrangus castle was surrounded by a radiant mix of crystal shields, which would limit the destruction to the already shattered kingdom. No one was there to let them through, so Francis created an opening with his staff for the three of them. *An odd thing, to be the first Guardian to enter.*

Nearing the castle entrance, a demon in the shape of a frail, young woman floated in the air with her back facing them. Both her arms had been replaced with long, jagged scythes. A rare mix of southern and Terrangus forces joined to face a swarm of crawlers, but no one engaged the banshee-like creature.

Francis grasped his staff, charging a blue aura. "While I cannot specify what that is, I'm certain we must—"

The banshee's body remained in place, but the head spun around, gazing into them with glowing white eyes as it let out a piercing shriek. With his focus shattered, Francis lost his aura and clutched his staff desperately.

"Golden Scholars!" Julius yelled out, then charged with Tempest lagging behind. The banshee came down with both scythes at once, but Julius blocked with his massive polearm and pushed her back. He lunged forward, but the demon bent in an impossible manner for a human, nearly mimicking a spider as it ignored Julius and charged Francis.

Francis stood frozen. He reminded himself to breathe and launched a sudden ice blast in the demon's path. The blast was so far off target, it didn't even have to dodge.

Just like last time.

No Wisdom. No Serenna. No David. *I'm alone. Francis, do something. Please, do something…*

He did nothing, but Tempest lunged forward and tackled the demon to the ground. It screeched and knocked his face guard off with its blades, but Tempest roared back and slammed his fist into the demon's face. After Tempest rained down several more blows, the banshee stopped screaming and went limp underneath his golden frame.

Tempest rose and nodded at Francis, before two more banshees rushed towards them, each contorted in a random matter. Julius ran by his side, then they drew their weapons together to defend Francis.

They each engaged a banshee as Francis closed his eyes to control his breathing. Thinking back to his mother, then David, then Mary, the chaos of his thoughts withheld any sort of calm. He opened his eyes to find Wisdom floating in front of him.

"My dear Francis, we are to leave. *Now.*"

Yes! Leave! This isn't your home. Terrangus doesn't matter. Zeen and Mary should be here, not you. The thought pierced him like a blade as he gasped. What would Mary say? "I can't leave yet. My friends need me."

"Friends? Oh, Francis, I'm the only friend you can trust. Are you incapable of learning? I advised you last time in this *very* kingdom not to engage Nyfe, and here we are again, not a month later. There are limitations to my interference. If you ignore me today, your dreams of Serenity will fade to the reality of the void."

"I understand. Thank you, Wisdom; our short time together was truly a pleasure."

Wisdom scoffed. "Another brilliant mind lost to the madness of freewill. I will mourn your death, just as I mourned your mother." He vanished, leaving Francis with a pristine clarity that had always been there.

"Golden Scholars," Francis whispered, grasping his staff and evoking a bright yellow aura. Fire and ice were too dangerous with allies in melee range, but lightning was swift and efficient.

And deadly.

The aura erupted, then he flung his arms down with his eyes on Tempest's banshee. A bolt of lightning crashed through its back, knocking Tempest a few feet backwards, but causing the banshee to spasm as it collapsed. *Sorry, my friend. More power than I expected.*

He eyed Julius's banshee and considered attempting a weaker blast, but Julius pierced it through the neck and flung it to the ground with his polearm. They regrouped, finding a large gathering of mages approaching, led by Xavian Senator Alice Reilly.

I hope she saw that. "Senator...or is it Empress now? We need to barricade the castle until the Guardians arrive."

Reilly nodded at them. "Well met. Our forces have most of the perimeter secure for now, but I'm afraid it may only be temporary. From what I saw...he is a *god*."

"Fuck the gods," Francis said. They all flinched at his words, but he stood with pride and soaked in their shock. *I was meant for this...I am a true leader!* "Empress, get your mages to safety. The four of us are a fair match for the Child of Death if you heed my words." Maybe it was true. While Reilly *did* have shades of platinum in her hair, she wasn't Serenna, but any crystal mage of skill would be a blessing.

Reilly sent her mages off in different directions, then grasped her staff, radiating a faint glow as she covered the four of them in crystal shields. The shields were far dimmer than Serenna's, but they didn't need to know that. They formed a square formation, with melee in front and the mages behind them.

Francis channeled his radiant, sapphire glow. *Freeze him, and his speed is useless.* "Stay strong, remain focused, and we can't lose. Let's make Mary proud." He regretted that last line, but the pending victory thrilled him.

Francis Haide, the Guardian of Alanammus, savior of the realm...

Silence smothered the barrier as a glowing entity stepped out of the castle. Harbinger Nyfe clutched his new dagger, filling the air with a vortex of dark prisms that reflected off the barrier surrounding them. He raised his blade in the air, then it erupted with a nova, launching void energies in all directions. It shattered their crystal shields and knocked all four of them to the ground.

Terrangus castle shook. Pieces shattered off, creating a domino effect as small fragments of stone led to larger pieces collapsing downwards. The neck of the tower cracked, followed by the whole top end crumbling down to rubble and taking the rest with it. Terrangus castle was no more. The ruins of the once-grand structure matched the ruins of his once-grand confidence. *I did it again. We're all going to die because of me...*

"Ah, I see you, Invisible Guardian..." Nyfe's distorted laugh echoed through the air, reverberating off the barrier and harassing him over and over.

Wisdom, please help me. I'm not ready to die. Someone, anyone...

Nyfe drifted towards them, revealing the arrogant smile Francis could never erase from his nightmares. Other than his pale white hair, nothing else was the same. Crimson eyes glowed and spectral void wings sprouted from his shoulders. The sheer force of his dagger made it difficult to stand. It commanded a vortex of dark energy, absorbing the white essences that flowed towards him.

Julius glanced at everyone before turning to Reilly. "Get them out of there. I'll hold on for as long as I can."

"An empress goes down with her kingdom," Reilly said, before giving them new crystal shields.

Tempest began walking towards them, but Reilly blocked his path with a crystal barrier. "No! Let me stand with you! This whole plan was my idea. I deserve to die. Please… I can't face my father after such a failure."

Julius only smiled. "The future warlord must survive. Make the realm a better place, my friend. Please, whenever time permits, tell Robert I love him dearly. Strength without honor—is chaos."

Francis finally rose, refusing to look any of them in the eyes, for fear of them asking him to stay by their side. Bless them for not asking. Bless them for not cursing his cowardly name. "I… I'm sorry," were the only words he could force out.

Reilly gave him a warm smile; the same one she had given him at his mother's memorial. "Watching Addy raise you into the man you are today is one of the highlights of my life. Guide our people to a beautiful future. I have never believed in Serenity, but I always believed in you."

Francis leaned against the barrier. He could easily shatter it, or go the long way around, but he wouldn't. Only a hero would do such a thing. Maybe if his destiny had been predetermined, he could have been a hero. "Golden Scholars," he whispered, likely not loud enough for them to hear.

Francis grabbed the frantic Tempest. "We run. Please… *please.*"

Tempest said nothing but dashed back towards the trade district with him. Between Francis's robes and Tempest's armor, they ran at an embarrassing pace, but it didn't matter. They just kept running towards the outskirts portal. So many eyes on them. So many screams, begging Francis to do his duty and save the day. He wouldn't.

For the first time in his life, he yearned to be the Invisible Guardian.

CHAPTER 37

DREAM OF THE FUTURE WE CREATE TOMORROW

h! Don't forget the water, Zeen thought. A brisk wind flew through the Alanammus Guardian room window, cooling Zeen as he wiped the sweat from his forehead. Nyfe's plate was prepared on the table, with a small fresh turkey and some burned rice. He took a whiff: passable, but not his best work. *Ah, I'm sure he won't mind. Even if my cooking is awful, it must be better than what they're serving him…which is probably nothing.*

Serenna shook her head. "I cannot understand why you're doing this. At the very least, can it wait until morning?"

"Well, I think I'm confusing him by bringing dinner for breakfast, and I have to speak to Reilly again after I arrive in Terrangus to drop this off. The torture needs to stop. I know he's a terrible person, but if we stoop to such a low, what does that say about us?"

"It says that we *won*," she said sharply.

Laughing, he abandoned the plate and gave her a warm embrace. As his arms wrapped around and pressed her gentle body against his own, everything was finally right in the world.

Almost everything.

She held him, but her eyes stared off into nothing, as if they were several kingdoms away. Some unspoken burden had occupied her since the battle. She had been warm, but distant. Physically close, but far from his embrace. Victory was hollow, if it meant losing her smile.

Still, it beat being dead. "You know you can talk to me, Serenna," he said, letting go.

She broke her gaze away from the nothing and met his eyes. "It's difficult to speak of it... I nearly lost everything that night."

"*Almost*, but not quite. We won because of you. You saved the realm."

"Stop it; we only won because of David. He had to rush in and clean up my failures before I finished speaking the words. The void called..."

"And you didn't answer. You have nothing to regret."

"That is not for you to decide. Sometimes, I need real words and not empty acceptance. Blindly following someone isn't support, it's giving up."

Giving up? How could she say that? "I... Whenever you want to really sit down and talk, I'm here." He stepped away and picked up the plate of food, welcoming the distraction as Serenna gazed solemnly into the Alanammus plains. He had always been better at facing demons than words.

I'm forgetting something—

The Guardian portal flickered, creating a high-pitched ring that filled the open room. The first figure was a zephum, then a shorter man wielding some sort of sword...or oak staff. *Francis and Tempest? What are they doing here?*

Panting, Francis gazed at Serenna, then honed in on Zeen. He threw his staff to the ground and rushed forward, his murderous eyes never turning away. *What did I do?*

"You!" Francis yelled, slapping the plate of food high into the air. "You're feeding him? A Harbinger of Death? While you sit around and leave me to deal with *your* kingdom, Reilly and Julius are dead!"

Zeen staggered back, struggling to find words. *How could Nyfe be a Harbinger? I just saw him in Terrangus yesterday...*

Serenna stepped in between them. "Reilly is dead? You are certain?"

"Certain? Of course I'm certain. If anyone else had bothered to help, you would have seen it yourself. Instead, I lost two friends. Two people...who actually cared for me. For *me*!"

"Dammit," she said, turning away. "I should have killed him. These deaths are on my hands. We will need David if it's a true Harbinger of Death. Would you be able to reach out to him through Wisdom?"

"Okay, first off, Wisdom isn't some petty messenger boy. Second, he abandoned me for trying to protect Terrangus. I'm all alone now. With you people, I always was." He stormed off, leaving a stinging silence in his wake.

Tempest rose with a groan, reaching for his face guard. "Now is not the time for blame. They both died as heroes and will be avenged. Serenna, would you be so kind as to portal me to Vaynex? I need to alert my father about Nyfe. I...am unsure what sort of aid we can offer, but at the very least, I swear to fight beside you. Guardian or not."

She nodded. "Of course. It will take some time, but I'll get everything else together. Spread the word: we meet in Mylor tomorrow morning at dawn. I can't believe I'm asking this...but please convince your father to join us. We need the warlord." The portal glowed a bright red as she raised her staff.

"And you will have him," Tempest said, before exiting through the portal.

The portal flickered again, adjusting to a paler shade of white. Without saying a word, Serenna rushed through.

Goodbye to you too, then. Zeen sat at the table, yielding a gentle frown as he took a sip from Nyfe's jug. The luxurious room was much larger than he had remembered, far too large for one to sit alone and contemplate failure. But there he was.

Steps approached from a distance. Hopefully, it wasn't anyone asking about the mess of rice on the floor, or even worse, Archon Gabriel demanding information about Harbinger Nyfe. He had no answers. *For all I know, this is my fault.*

His eyes lit up as David entered the room. He sat next to Zeen and checked his jug, nodding his head in approval. "Water? A wise choice. I pounded zephum ale the night before my first Harbinger of Death. That was twenty years ago, in Xavian of all places. I was hungover as shit the next morning," he said, laughing. "Ah. That faded once I looked up and saw Harbinger Richard's floating visage. His aura coated the Xavian sea with an ebony sparkle, an endless shimmer that spread as far as my eyes could see. I never told anyone this, not even Melissa, but that was the most beautiful thing I have ever seen. Fear and doubt faded, replaced by something I couldn't comprehend. Hope."

That's the closest to a thank you I'll get for naming his sword. Zeen grabbed two chalices, emptying the jug to fill them both. "Whew, twenty years ago? Time must fly. It still feels like I became a Guardian yesterday."

"It will always feel that way until it doesn't. Time speeds up after you watch people die. When that happens, all you can do is replace them one by one until everyone is gone. You'll look at the five or six hopeful eyes leaning on you for guidance, and then it hits like a blast from the void. The past is dead. You are the only one left. You are the leader."

That seemed unlikely. "I can't imagine I'll outlast Francis or Serenna. They are far more powerful than I am. Actually, everyone is…"

"You can't imagine it because you don't want to. We are not special, Zeen. For some reason, though, people like us persevere. I have always been afraid of falling in battle, but this is the first time I fear victory."

Perhaps wine would have been the better choice. He paused and glanced at David. "Not sure that I follow?"

"I am a monster. My only use to this realm is to defeat other monsters. Once there are no more enemies, I am the only horror remaining. My hero status is on borrowed time."

"You will *never* be a monster to me," Zeen said with a smile. "There are good days ahead, my friend. Even for you."

David finished his water, gazing forward with a stoic frown. "No. I am done looking ahead. Every day of my life, I create more memories that linger behind me, but the longer I go on, the ones I truly cherish drift farther away. Love her, Zeen and never let go. *Never* let go."

I'm not nearly afraid enough of this battle. All I can think about is her. And he knows. "I won't. You have my word."

David rose with a weak smile, drawing his sword and pointing it towards the portal. The portal lit up with the same pale light that had carried Serenna off to Mylor. "Thank you; I'll alert Francis and Mary. Now stop wasting your time with me and go to her."

"Is that really a good idea? She's mad at me again."

"Stop it. Don't forget, I was you once."

Zeen gave him a quick hug before letting go. As much as he appreciated David, Serenna held his immediate focus, and so much more. "I am thankful for that every day." They nodded, and then Zeen rushed through the portal.

*

Zeen entered the empty Mylor Guardian room. The simple room lacked the silver and diamonds of its Alanammus counterpart, but the warmth of being home filled him as he took in the plain white walls. They had shared their first kiss in Mylor. Their first dance. The first time he had confessed he was falling for her. She hadn't returned his words, but maybe tonight would be different. They could die tomorrow; he may as well try again.

He stepped outside, hoping to avoid attention, but his loose dark armor stood out like a beacon in the pale hallways. Random people greeted their Rogue Guardian, with a young girl even bowing. Being known outside of Terrangus was still odd—especially here—considering the cold reception their military had given him before the battle of Terrangus. *Hmm, I have no idea where her room is. Oh! I can ask her father.*

On second thought, let's not do that.

Wandering forward, he stopped at Serenna's grand portrait. The perfect woman painted on the canvas was an illusion, with none of the tiny scars prickled across her face. Her signature white armor was replaced by scantily tight leather, that all but exposed a large chest and bottom, neither of which existed on his Serenna's gentle frame. The eyes were a darker shade of blue. Actually, the only thing that matched was her hair. Exceptional effort had been spent detailing the long, wavy platinum blowing valiantly into the wind.

But when they fought together it always fell straight down, clumping on her shoulders or hanging in front of her eyes. Messy, unkempt, *pure*. Lies become boring in the light of the truth.

I love her. I have never been more scared.

"Zeen?"

A warm sensation filled his chest as her voice called to him, a maelstrom of excitement and pure terror that only she could create. "Serenna…"

"What are you doing here?"

"I'm checking to see if I have a portrait yet," he blurted out.

"What?" Her head cocked to the side as she approached.

Ah, she's not laughing. I'm blowing it. "I want the same artist you had. He will paint me as a seven-foot god with a massive frame and unstoppable muscles."

"How do you know it was a guy?"

"I have my suspicions," he said, nodding his head towards the large chest in the painting.

She finally giggled. "Yes, it's quite absurd. You didn't seem to understand the last time you were here. The hair and staff are perfect, though. It shows what I am to Mylor. The woman behind the Guardian is irrelevant."

Hmm, I didn't notice the staff. "You could *never* be irrelevant. Even if you didn't have magic, they would paint the same picture with a sword. I would be out of a job, that's for sure."

Her face lit up with a smile. Whether from his joke or the idea of never having magic, he couldn't know. "You have been kind to me our entire journey. Even that first day. I fear that I do not deserve you."

"No, that isn't your fear." Mylor always made him bold for some reason. This time, he couldn't blame the wine. "You fear turning to the void when things grow dire. I don't know if I can ever make that go away, but I want to struggle together. Share your pain with me. The only void I know is the one that grows when we are apart."

She stared at the painting in silence for what could have been forever. A rush of adrenaline shot through him as she finally approached and leaned in towards his ear. "Not here: too many people watching. Follow me."

Glancing behind him, several onlookers instantly turned away towards whatever fake task they were working on.

He followed her through the hallway, smiling at his old guest chamber before arriving at a room with a sturdy wooden door close to the senator's chambers. Holding his hand, she guided him inside before closing the door.

Is this really happening? I'm not ready...

She grabbed him, holding him tight with a gentle strength—and began sobbing. "I don't want to care for you. Back in Terrangus, I was moments away from becoming a Harbinger when you were about to die. I have fallen for you, and now I have a weakness."

He had been called many things, but never someone's weakness. Pressing his face against hers, his hands caressed her back as he stalled for words. *This is what you asked for. She's giving herself to you; this is the reality of love.*

"I saw you as a demon here, and as an angel in Terrangus. The true Serenna is in the middle, the woman that held my hand and watched the sunrise. Tomorrow, we beat Nyfe, and then we can go right back to that moment. We deserve this."

Wiping her eyes, her sobbing reduced to simple tears trailing down her cheeks. "I don't know what we deserve anymore. My poor judgement got Reilly and Julius killed. It was easier when David stood in the front and took the brunt of reality."

"You don't have to carry that burden alone. I am here for you. Today, tomorrow—*forever.*"

She took a deep breath, cradling both his hands. "Zeen...you really care for me, don't you? Despite everything."

"Not despite everything, but because of it. Serenna Morgan... I love you." As the words left his mouth, anxiety dispersed like Rinso riding off into the sunset. Even if she said no, or nothing at all, the words were spoken. He would stand proud in the face of defeat—

"I love you, too."

Time froze. The woman who had stood above him and offered mercy all that time ago now offered her heart. The void mage he had carried in his arms, the angel who had lit the darkness with radiant platinum. *How is this real? What could she possibly see in me?* A poor soldier from Terrangus—the weakest Guardian—now standing on the precipice of forever.

Silence engulfed the room as they embraced. His head rested on her shoulders, taking in the subtle lemon scent from her hair. She pulled back, gazing into his cautious eyes and studying him. *Please make the first move. I have no idea what I'm doing.*

Serenna closed her eyes and tilted her head, gently guiding his face to hers. He kept his eyes open, far too nervous to smash faces or kiss the wrong spot. Their lips met, and the sweet taste of the tip of her tongue sent a burning thrill down his chest. He pulled her close, brushing the other hand through her platinum hair. Her armor kept him off her skin, but he wouldn't *dare* be so bold. Darkness and euphoria arrived simultaneously as he finally closed his eyes.

I am forever yours.

Their lips parted after a final kiss, and they returned to a silent embrace. Time passed in her arms. For how long, he couldn't tell, and there was no reason to care. "Where do we go from here?" she asked.

"Anywhere we want."

Letting go, she went and lay on her bed. "Then I want to stay here. I want to fall asleep in your arms and never face a war or battle again."

While most of Mylor wasn't extravagant, someone must have spent a small fortune on the bed. Emerald curtains hung from the canopy, offering a near transparent veil of the woman lying there waiting for him. She patted the vacant spot to her left.

He joined her, breathing faster as she lifted his arm to nuzzle beside him. "We only have one more battle. Let's win this and then your father can throw another feast."

"Will you drink too much wine again?"

"Yes, that does seem likely," he said, smiling at the drapes above.

Her smile faded. "Zeen…will we win tomorrow? This is everything I wanted. The thought of it only being temporary is too much to bear. I…am not strong enough to lose you."

"I've never faced a Harbinger of Death, but I have fought Nyfe a few times now. He's better than me alone, but together, he doesn't stand a chance. We *can't* lose." Maybe it was true. She had asked him for real words and not blind acceptance, but with his lover's head resting on his chest, he would say any words imaginable to keep her there. Everything was so fragile. Either of them could die tomorrow, and a selfish guilt rose within hoping it would be him if that became their fate. What was the point of existing if only to be alone?

She adjusted her head to the left side of his chest. "Your heart is pounding. It's okay to be afraid. I'm afraid too. We can share it together."

Damn… "I'm trying to take the burden off you. It's no use if we're both afraid."

"No, it *is* useful. Be afraid. Let it drive you to stay alive, to keep all of us alive."

He held back tears. Fear was never the answer. *Hope. Stick with hope.* "Hmm. Do you know you sound like David sometimes?"

"Good. He's forty-four and still fighting, so he's doing something right. I want to live that long with you."

"Forty-four isn't nearly enough. I want forever."

"Forever," she whispered, taking back his arm and nudging herself against his side. "I love you, Zeen. Now, no more words. Hold me in your arms and close your eyes. Dream of the future we create tomorrow. A future together."

"I love you too. I always have." Lying with Serenna in his arms, he refused to close his eyes and gazed endlessly at the fragile world above him. Life would never be the same, and the sudden reality of their battle tomorrow tore through him like a knife.

I love her. I have never been more scared.

CHAPTER 38

~

I AM NOTHING. I AM FOREVER. I AM THE END.

have fallen for you, and now I have a weakness.

Serenna's eyes eased open, revealing her Zeen lying awake, staring into nothing with tired, bloodshot eyes. He likely hadn't slept at all. She'd never had that problem; rest always came easy when everything was on the line. An odd gift, an advantage she had never considered until seeing her lover's worn, fatigued face. "Zeen? Are you awake?"

Zeen sprung out of bed and grabbed his sword, apparently eager to get moving. "Yes, dear. I had all night to think about it and I'm not afraid anymore. I believe in this team. More importantly, I believe in *you.*"

She wouldn't fault him for lying; not today, at least. "Zeen, wait for me in the banquet hall and grab something to eat. Hopefully, the others are already there." It was unlikely. She had done a terrible job organizing their final battle. Other than the zephum, no one had been given any direction. *He's distracting me. I'm almost out of time...* No more nonsense. Most battles were lost long before the first spell was cast. This wouldn't be one of them.

Zeen nodded with a frown before turning away and exiting the room. She grabbed a white battle armor from her clothes rack, then swiftly swapped her worn suit for the new one. Maybe when it was over, she could buy a dress or two and attempt a normal life with Zeen until the next Harbinger. She had never considered such things, but the words were spoken. Love was a dark, confusing path. Demons were easier. They appeared, you killed them, people cheered for a few days, then forgot until the next danger arrived. That was the simple life of a Guardian, whether it be for two days or twenty years.

A trickle of sweat ran down her head. *Will we marry? I'm a Morgan; I can't take his last name. What will our kids look like? What will it feel like when we finally…*

Her face grew red. Nyfe. Think about Nyfe… *I don't even think we can marry. I'll have to break that rule too. I may end up the worst Guardian that ever—*

Think about Nyfe. Despite her best efforts, Nyfe didn't matter. He was a spoiled old fool, an accumulation of Terrangus's worst flaws. If he didn't have that dagger, no one would know who he was. Such a weak target for Death. *It was supposed to be me,* she thought, taking slow, controlled breaths to calm her pounding heart. *Stop it. The last time you were this overconfident, you nearly lost everything.*

She freshened up, grabbed her staff, then took a final glance at her room before exiting. It could be the last time. The capitol halls were always empty at dawn, but there was no time for small talk, anyway. The banquet doors were already open, filling her mouth with a spicy aroma of some freshly cooked meal. Delicious maybe, but she never ate before a battle.

To her surprise, Zeen, Francis, and Mary already sat at the senator's table in the back, with David leaning against a wall alone in the far corner. David had likely gathered them. A good start, but where was the zephum—

Steps approached the banquet entrance. Large steps. "What the hell happened?" a familiar voice asked. "I take a short break and everything goes to shit?"

Her eyes widened as Pyith approached. The zephum engager was armored head to toe with spiked steel armor. Tempest wasn't with her, but Warlord Sardonyx stood by her side, crossing his arms and nodding. They were late. They were *always* late.

Everyone rose, but David rushed over first, letting out a great laugh. It was the first time she'd seen him laugh in too long. "Well, look at you," he said. "They fixed everything except your face!"

Pyith didn't laugh or smile; she glared at him with her cold, zephum eyes. "Those days are over, David. After this battle, do not stand in our presence again. I hope vengeance was worth it."

"As long as the realm still stands, it will always be worth it," David said, before walking out of the room with a sigh.

Nothing was more awkward than a long, noticeable silence. Serenna tapped her staff to the ground, drawing everyone's gaze. "Enough. Warlord, thank you for aiding us in this battle, but where is Tempest?"

"Tempest is unworthy of such a battle! If we are to die gloriously, Vaynex will need a Claw on the throne. The worst one, unfortunately, but a Claw nonetheless."

Zeen approached Pyith with a smile. "Oh, I have missed you! How is your leg?"

She raised the once injured leg and tapped on the armor. "Never been better. I tested it out by running all the way from Vaynex."

"Wow," he said, as if he believed such a thing.

Never change, my love.

Sardonyx examined him. "Your eyes are bloodshot again.

Did you spend all night mating with the sorceress? Never mate the night before a battle. Save it for the victory. It is far more passionate, and all but *guarantees* children."

They all laughed, but she could have died right there. Zeen grew a bright smile, as if the prospect was appealing. The thought made her even more red. *They never treated David this way when he was leader. At least spirits are high. If mocking me raises morale, I'll allow it.*

For now.

Mary approached with Francis behind her. "Well met, Lady Pyith. It is an honor to finally go into battle together."

"Just *Pyith* will do," Sardonyx said with a grimace.

Pyith smirked. "I would slap Zeen if he said that, but you can call me anything you want. How have you been enjoying that blessed shield from Strength?"

Mary's eyes shot down. "Well," she said after a few moments, "maybe I'm doing something wrong, but it feels exactly the same."

"It *is* exactly the same," Pyith said with a snicker. "Strength finds it hilarious to 'bless' random objects. Something about finding true meaning within…or something."

Sardonyx nodded. "It all comes down to one thing. Strength without honor—"

"Is chaos," Francis interrupted. "They were Julius's last words. While we sit around and make small talk, a literal god is preparing to end all life. Wisdom and Strength have abandoned us, but at least we have Fear, I guess. Let's get this over with." Whatever he had seen in Terrangus haunted him. The Francis of old never would have spoken to the warlord, let alone interrupted him.

Serenna tapped her staff again to break the silence. "Francis is right, but before we face Nyfe, I dedicate this battle to Reilly, Julius…and Melissa. We will honor them by surviving. Now, raise your weapons." She raised her staff high in the air, then one by one, all the Guardians and Sardonyx raised their weapons in a circular formation. Francis was last, letting out a sigh, but eventually completing the salute. "When you're ready, meet me in the Guardian room. We head to Terrangus."

Before she could leave, Pyith tapped her on the shoulder. "Serenna, can we speak?"

"Of course—walk with me," she said, heading towards the south exit.

"What the hell happened while I was gone?"

Where to begin? "Well…Zeen and I have fallen for each other. I apologize if it makes things complicated. I never planned on it."

Pyith laughed. "Oh, I don't care about that. You fuck Zeen and I'll fuck Tempest. I mean the other two fools—David is a monster and now Francis worries us too. He wouldn't even look at the warlord in Vaynex, and now he interrupts him?"

Somehow, that question was more difficult to answer than her personal affairs. The zephum had a particular dislike for the God of Wisdom, and if Tempest hadn't told her already, it was probably for good reason. To hell with it. "Francis has been collaborating with the God of Wisdom. It has made him more bold and apparently…more *violent*."

Pyith shook her head. "We suspected as much. Tempest is an awful liar, but I admire the fact he at least had the courage to try. David's deity is a whole different story. Strength doesn't even allow us to mention *her*. These gods are getting too involved in our affairs. This can only end poorly."

She put her hand on Pyith's shoulder, carefully navigating the steel spikes. "We see the world through the same eyes; it has been very lonely without you." Her hand left her shoulder after a pause. "You're still injured, aren't you?"

"There was a point where I wasn't sure it would heal. Listen, I'm not in perfect condition, but I would *never* miss a Harbinger of Death. I'll have your back, Serenna, you're my human little sister."

She had suspected as much. To miss the battle of Terrangus and suddenly make a full recovery was... coincidental, at best. "Little sister? I'm older than you."

"In human years maybe, but humans have easy lives, so it doesn't count. My life-mate is a fool, and my Claw father is deranged. Serenna...if anyone dies today, I demand the next Guardian be a zephum. I will *not* back down on this. We need more influence before Tempest takes command."

"*No one* is going to die." There was a logic to her request, but a total lack of subtlety. *It's Pyith; I'm not talking to a senator or the archon. Brute strength, blunt words.* She took a hushed breath. "If it happens...I will strongly consider your request."

"Thanks, leader," Pyith said, smiling. "See you in the rain." Pyith turned away towards the Guardian room, leaving Serenna alone in the empty hallway.

Serenna took the long way to the Guardian room. They were probably anxiously waiting for her to lead the way, but it wasn't her own life she feared losing. Not anymore.

You didn't even consider you could lose tonight, did you? Each hollow step brought Nyfe's voice, a haunting reminder of the man she could have ended. Mercy was a complicated concept. It had given her Zeen, the potential love of her life, and now Nyfe, the potential end of her life. *What an awful death that will be. What an awful death you unleashed on the man you supposedly care for.*

Passing her father's chambers, she yearned to hear his blind optimism one more time, but she had never spoken to him before a Harbinger. Her hand leaned against his door as she stared into the ground. *Today will be Mylor's finest hour. I swear to you.* Pulling back, she took a deep breath and headed to the Guardian room.

Silence shrouded Serenna as she entered the room last. All eyes were on her, as it should be. She raised her staff, triggering the portal to glow a deep ebony. "This is it. Any words before we begin?"

No one spoke. No one said anything. With no more options to stall, she nodded and entered first.

*

She appeared at the Terrangus outskirts portal with David already there and, one by one, they followed, lining up behind her. Mylor's radiant dawn did not carry over to Terrangus. Torrential rain poured down, accompanied by frigid winds that howled as a warning. The storm blocked out all hints of life, engulfing them as if it were midnight's shadow.

Behind them could have been an entirely different kingdom. An endless sea of tents and carts spread out, filled with refugees. Terrangus had no disaster plan, clearly never intending to lose everything. But then again, who does? The storm was breaking, but far behind them, with joyous sunlight and tranquility hinting through the clouds. It was beautiful and familiar—as if the gods were mocking them.

They were going the other way.

She glanced over at Zeen to reassure him, but his eyes were lost in the darkness ahead. "I don't see the castle," he said. "Where is the castle?"

He's right. Where is the castle? More importantly, where is the barrier? "We likely can't see it in the storm. Our vision will be clearer as we head in."

Francis sighed. "No. It's gone. When Nyfe stepped outside, he unleashed a void nova and the whole thing just *collapsed.* I have seen my share of Harbingers, but there is something different about this one. We must win. Julius and Reilly cannot have died for nothing."

They all flinched as a faraway screech filled the air. Serenna grasped her staff and began shielding them. "Francis, did you happen to see his demon? Nothing I know makes that sound."

"Yes. Some girl-thing, with scythes in place of her arms. We called them banshees. They're quick and can bend to run on all fours or dodge strikes. Pure nightmares."

"Emily," Zeen said, looking around. "Don't ask me how I know that." She wouldn't—not now, at least.

The closer they came to the entrance, the less sound that followed from the encampment. The open gates of Terrangus stood in ominous silence, complemented only by the relentless hammering of rain. She swore it got louder as they entered. *Where is the barrier?* Dead soldiers from both sides littered the trade district. Their lifeless eyes and torn bodies screamed out the answer.

There is no barrier.

Nyfe's distorted laugh filled the air from afar, rumbling the ground and cutting through the rain. "Ah, and so you have come. Of course you did; what choice did you have? Ask the Invisible Guardian what comes next. Everything you love...everything you are...I will take it from you."

Screeches went off, this time much closer. She grasped her staff and radiated a faint platinum, illuminating their immediate vicinity, but not much else. It was too soon to use her full power. She nearly stumbled back as a barrage of demons surrounded them.

Guardians, attack!

The words screamed through her head, but nowhere else. It was impossible to hold the form, control her breathing, *and* scream out the orders. Fortunately, it would go without saying to attack the demons trying to kill them. The melee charged in, but Mary stayed close to her and Francis, drawing her weapons and darting her eyes between the two of them.

Formation good. No one vulnerable.

Francis glowed a deep…orange? *What are you doing? Don't use fire!* He launched several blasts, not in the direction of the demons, but towards abandoned trade carts scattered throughout the city streets. He seemed to know their locations despite the limited vision, giving them a clear view of the overwhelming amount of demons now closing in. His form morphed to a glowing yellow, allowing him to pick banshees off one by one, focusing on the closest ones that weren't already engaged with their melee.

Mary intercepted a banshee rushing towards him, then Serenna refreshed both their shields, just in case. *Stop focusing on him; Francis is nearly more powerful than I am. Zeen needs you.*

Zeen and David fought back-to-back, slashing through crawlers and never bothering to check behind them. Without any fear to absorb, David was the man from her memories, and not the demigod that had saved them in Terrangus. *Nyfe won't be afraid this time. He probably doesn't know what fear is anymore.*

A banshee appeared above Zeen, screaming and coming down with its right scythe. Zeen was mid-slash against a crawler's throat as the banshee crashed through his crystal shield, leaving him vulnerable.

"No!" Serenna screamed, tensing her aura to cover him with a thick, lucid shield. He glanced at her for the briefest of moments before turning towards his new foe and blocking the next strike aimed at his neck. His training and experience kept him grounded, but that wasn't enough to calm her rage.

Grasping her staff, the platinum burned as she trapped the banshee in a crystal prison. She raised it high in the air, let out a scream and tore the prison in half, tearing the shield and demon inside in two. She had never used—or considered—such a spell, but the creature had attacked her lover, and the only acceptable outcome was to die by her hands.

Her eyes honed in on Zeen, watching his every movement as he slashed with stunning precision. She observed each enemy's attack carefully, prepared to refresh his shield the exact moment he was in danger.

My love, you will never feel pain again—

A crawler lunged forward, tackling her to the ground as the Wings of Mylor flew out of her hands. Its fangs slammed against her crystal shield, causing a sharp crack after the second strike. Mary ripped the demon off her, slitting its throat with her one-handed blade, then tossed it aside. She picked up Serenna, held her, then slapped her face. "What the *fuck* are you doing? Focus!"

I love him, and it's going to kill us all. "Mary…I need my staff." She glanced at the staff, which had found its way under a colossal.

Mary sighed, letting her go, then rushing into the fray. Grasping her shield with both hands, she darted towards the demon, then held her ground as it crashed a wild fist down on her shield. Mary screamed out with an awful cry as her ankle cracked, twisting horribly to the right. While only a few feet away, the staff may as well have fallen into another kingdom.

"NO!" Francis yelled, his oak staff shaking in his hands. He glowed a dark green, covering Mary with an earthy terrain that stood taller than the colossal. The demon swung its arm, knocking the earth away to expose the injured Mary. "You will not harm her!" he yelled. His green glow darkened, then—to Serenna's shock—meshed with a blue and orange aura, surrounding the elemental sorcerer with a prism of vivid colors.

The colors settled on blue and yellow, whirling around

and beaming out in distinct tones. He pointed his staff forward and let out a blast of ice towards the colossal. The spell coated the beast in pristine ice, freezing it solid and leaving it at the mercy of the elemental mage. He took a deep breath, losing the blue glow in favor of pure *golden* yellow. Only one bolt came down, but it pierced through its frozen neck, decapitating the colossal.

Francis has grown so much. Not even Gabriel or his mother could multi-form…

David and Zeen finished the last on their side, while Pyith and Sardonyx stood before an entire pile of slain demons. *This…this is the best Guardian team that ever existed. And I nearly failed them.*

Francis approached Mary, apparently not interested in watching the colossal fall awkwardly under its own weight and shatter to icy pieces. "Can you stand?" he asked, reaching out his hand.

"Somewhat," Mary said, struggling to rise. "How did you do that? Are you feeling okay?"

"I feel incredible!" he said, resuming the multi-colored glow for a moment before returning to normal. "We can actually win this… We can win!" He hugged her dearly, and Serenna could see the grimace of pain in Mary's eyes as she returned the embrace, but stared off into nothing. Serenna knew that stare. It was the lost gaze of someone who had drifted too close to death. Not the god, in Mary's case, but death all the same.

Serenna grabbed her staff, then immediately refreshed everyone's crystal shields. David's eyes grew lost towards the darkness where the castle had been, but everyone else was laughing and cheerful. *Do I let them stay this way or demand focus? They have no reason to listen after that display. I nearly got Mary killed…*

Never again. Everything depends on me, it always did.

"Guardians!" she yelled. "Resume formation. We continue forward." Her words ended the laughter. Was it the right choice? David nodded at her at least; he clearly approved. Most leaders don't yearn to be feared, but it *is* useful.

Various roars and hissing noises stalked them as they entered the military ward. Terrangus's castle had brought her nothing but anger and grief, but ironically, its absence only inspired fear. Terrangus was naked—torn to shreds by war— now left for the void by the short-lived emperor. There were far more bodies the closer they came to the castle's remnants. The dead couldn't hold her attention; that was reserved for the entity radiating void energy in the middle of the castle rubble.

Nyfe…

All she could make out was the dagger. It glowed so harshly that it chilled her skin just to be anywhere near its presence. The tiny hairs on the back of her neck lifted. This is what Francis had seen. This is why he was so distraught. "Zeen, Warlord—Harbingers of Death grow more powerful from absorbing life essences. Basically, if any of us die…we *all* die." That wasn't entirely true. They had lost one or two people in past battles, but it would get *very* dangerous after that. Force the burden of life on them all. Make them believe that if they died, they were killing their loved ones. Leadership meant finding the balance between fear and love.

Sardonyx removed his face guard and laid it at his feet. "Indeed. I want him to look me in the eyes before I slay him. I want Death itself to cower from the Children of Strength and know defeat once more." He drifted forward, stopping after a few steps and turning his head. "Guardian Serenna, no matter how this goes, I declare you and your life-mate honorable allies of the zephum. You have my blessing to enter Vaynex…or if fate wills it, the Great Plains in the Sky."

For all his flaws and primal ignorance towards mages, Sardonyx had a warm soul. She *would* enter Vaynex, if not just to see the look on Tempest's face as she casually strolled through the citadel. "I love you all. It is an honor to defend the realm by your side." She glanced over at Zeen to find a smile, but his eyes were locked on the dagger—

"Shield us. Now!" Zeen yelled.

The glow of Nyfe's dagger diminished to a darker shade of night, shaking violently as it left his hand and floated slightly above him. "Guardians, shield yourselves if you must, but it would be a kindness to take this void and die without pain. You could all close your eyes and let it end. Think of how beautiful that would be." His eyes shot to Serenna. "Except *you*. Death wants you to suffer for turning down his gift. Serenna…you were supposed to be me."

I nearly was. Whether luck or determination, here we stand. Grasping her staff, she radiated platinum and covered them all with individual shields, then the entire party with a barrier.

Nyfe's blade erupted, launching a nova of darkness that expanded throughout the entire military ward and noble district. Their barrier shattered, but each individual shield stood strong.

"Mary, stay by Francis and I. Zeen, Pyith—" Serenna paused as a loud hissing filled the air. "Take care of that. David, Warlord…kill him."

"GLORIOUS!" Sardonyx yelled, charging in with David behind him.

As Nyfe approached, his Harbinger form became clearer. Despite the new appearance, his snarky grin was the exact same from their battle in Mylor. She would *never* forget the happiness in his eyes right before she'd turned to the void.

Her heart pounded. If they won, all her fears and doubts would end for at least a year. She could not only defy Death, but utterly defeat the deity that had tortured her by refusing his gift and defeating his Harbinger. The possibility of nearly being free brought her to tears. *Happiness is just one victory away.*

Nyfe dies now. Taking a deep breath, she clutched her staff and radiated a glowing platinum, this time allowing all her energy to flow through her. The quicker they won, the less chance of anything going wrong.

Francis closed his eyes and channeled his multi-form, then turned to Mary. "Stay by me. If anything comes close, I'll burn them to ashes." He approached Serenna, meeting her smile. Both mages stood side by side as beacons of hope, countering the darkness with shining prisms of light.

She created a large crystal prison, capturing three banshees and a handful of crawlers in one shell. Without her having to say anything, Francis favored his orange and incinerated the shell, increasing the intensity of his flames until the prison exploded. Their side was safe. She turned towards Sardonyx and David and refreshed their shields.

Sardonyx roared, swinging with a downward thrust towards Nyfe's head. Nyfe blocked with only one hand on his dagger, then laughed as a void blast erupted and launched the zephum several feet backwards. His armored body tumbled through the rubble, but he immediately rose, letting out another roar and charging back in.

David kept his blade drawn at striking distance, circling Nyfe and waiting for a strategic time to counter like he had always done. Sardonyx wasn't making it easy to attack as one, wildly rushing in and getting knocked back again. *Dammit, these two have no synergy. I should have used David and Zeen. No. I couldn't send him. I must keep him safe.*

Nyfe glided to his left, dodging another chaotic swing, then countered by slamming his dagger towards Sardonyx's chest. The dagger shattered his crystal shield in a single blow, which enticed Nyfe to strike again at the same location. Sardonyx cried out, flinging his sword up to block a fatal strike. It was the quickest she had ever seen him move, likely out of pure combat instinct.

Serenna immediately gave him a new shield, just for it to shatter from the next strike. Even in her empowered form, this was an unsustainable race to protect the warlord. Tensing her shoulders, she groaned and created a thick, vivid shell around Sardonyx, then pulled him several feet away to help him regroup. Nyfe's glowing red eyes shot towards her, losing his wretched smile for a scowl. *If he's angry, I must be doing something right.*

Nyfe dodged a quick thrust from David, then launched a void blast from his dagger. David's shield absorbed the brunt of it, but the force sent him flying back into the rubble. "These damn shields... I guess I do have to kill you first. Sorry, Death," he said, beginning his approach.

Her eyes went to Francis, hoping he would pick up on the hint without her having to ask. Launching spells all over, he was too busy defending their side while the injured Mary stood in front, barely a diversion at this point.

Despite Nyfe's slow approach, each step brought him closer. She tensed again, creating a thick crystal prison around him, which he shattered with a simple swipe of his empowered blade.

"Oh no," he said, his grin widening. "Not this time. I'm beyond such petty spells now. You know, it is nothing short of hilarious that even after everything, your fate is still to die here in Terrangus."

What else can I do? She took a deep breath. It would be a substantial risk to draw more power, but she only had a few seconds left. She gasped, tensing harder and ripping the crystal energy from inside her, then created a barrage of crystal spikes, with six smaller ones and two giants behind them. Screaming, she launched them all at once. The soreness returned, ending her glow, but she accepted the pain and stood in defiance.

Nyfe dodged the smaller ones, shattered the first giant with his dagger, then took a crystal spike straight through his shoulder, opening a violent gash that would have killed a normal person instantly.

He screamed out a horrifying shriek that nearly made her ill from causing such pain to anyone—even him. His darkness amplified, matching the intensity of her old platinum aura. The darkness flowed through the wound, healing it quickly as he stood and laughed. "You have no idea what I am capable of...and I don't either."

"FOUL DEMON!" Sardonyx yelled, tackling Nyfe to the ground from behind. He came down with an iron fist, pounded Nyfe's face, then leaned back to strike again. His fist missed, crashing into the rubble before Nyfe jabbed his blade directly into Sardonyx's lower chest. Letting out a pained roar, Sardonyx rose and stumbled back, clutching the wound.

NO! I can't shield him again. I have nothing left; if I tense anymore, I may lose consciousness. "Pyith, Zeen! Engage Nyfe! Now!" Francis was the better choice, but if he couldn't defend their flank, they would all die. Pyith shook her head in disobedience as she flailed against three crawlers, but Zeen rushed over.

David arrived first, swinging the Herald of Fear and crashing against its dagger counterpart. In a clash of fear and death, both stood strong and exchanged swings; everything met with dodges or blocks. They were equally matched veterans; two men who had taken similar dark paths, but found themselves on opposite sides.

After a sloppy block from Nyfe, David pushed forward

and spun, swinging his blade towards Nyfe's neck. Nyfe crouched under the blade and rushed forward, thrusting his dagger at the opening. David's crystal shield shattered from the strike, saving his life but knocking him to the ground.

Serenna grasped her staff until her knuckles lost all color and managed a dim shield around David that barely hummed with a faint glow. It wouldn't be enough. She finally turned to Francis, but his attention was lost on Pyith's side, desperately casting inaccurate spells of all elements to prevent Pyith from getting overrun.

No, no, no. This cannot happen. We CAN'T lose...

"Interesting," Nyfe said, almost in a disappointed tone. "I didn't expect you to die first. Farewell, Child of Fear. For whatever it's worth, I respect you the most." His dagger glowed with a void blast forming at the tip as he pointed it at David.

Zeen rushed in front, slashing downwards across Nyfe's chest before she could blink. Nyfe let out a pained scream and stumbled back as the void energy left his dagger to heal the wound. Zeen didn't follow through; he waited for Nyfe to retaliate, then dodged his dagger and slashed down at the opposite angle. Void energy healed the wound, but this time at a much slower rate.

Blood poured down Nyfe's body, his void wings and red eyes dimming. Zeen unleashed a barrage of relentless strikes, most getting blocked, but he didn't seem to care. Scrapes and gashes opened all over, and after a masterful upward slash that went completely undefended, Nyfe flew in the air and landed on his back.

"KILL HIM!" she screamed. They wouldn't get this chance again. An overwhelming joy of relief coursed through her as Zeen approached. Terrangus was in shambles, but they could fix that. Senator Reilly was dead, but they could pick up the pieces. They could fix everything once Nyfe was dead.

Nyfe's Harbinger form vanished, leaving their old nemesis struggling on one knee. "Zeen…help me… Please…I want to go back to Emily, back to the days where I didn't hear the screams. I'm so afraid to die…help me… *Please…*"

"KILL HIM!"

"Nyfe…" Zeen hesitated, taking a deep breath. "I'm sorry, but I don't… I don't think we can fix this one—"

Nyfe lunged forward from the kneeling position, ducked under Zeen's off-balanced sword swing, then stabbed the love of her life straight through the side of his neck. Nyfe casually ripped the blade out as an endless stream of blood flowed down.

The world went mute. She couldn't breathe. She rushed over, diving to Zeen and holding him in her arms. It wasn't real. Her hands felt the wound, now covered in blood. Too much blood. It wasn't real. "No…you damned silly boy…*why?*"

His mouth moved, but no words came out. He grabbed her, mouthing something incoherent over and over. His grip tightened, nearly crushing her arms with his pained desperation. It hurt, but nothing hurt more than when the pain stopped. He let go completely, closing his eyes forever.

He was gone. They would never marry. They would never make love. They would never start their family. Any hope inside her vanished, any determination, any reason at all to keep going. All that remained was a void. A powerful void, one that had always lingered inside her.

There was exactly *one* more reason to keep going.

Her sobbing eyes turned to Nyfe, who had not only regained his Harbinger form, but now hovered in the air. He let out a roar, morphing into some angelic monstrosity.

"I am no longer a Harbinger of Death," he said, his voice completely distorted. "I have transcended to Death itself. I will slay every living being, every god, even Time itself. Life cannot exist. I cannot allow it to exist."

She would face Death with Death. Even if it destroyed her in the process, even if Terrangus crumbled into the next Boulom, no price would be too high to see Nyfe dead. It was all she had left. "I am nothing. I am forever…"

Her eyes closed. For the first time in her life, the darkness was beautiful.

"I am the end."

She tensed and waited for something, anything, to happen. "I am nothing. I am forever. I am the end.

"I am nothing… I am forever… I am the end."

Still nothing. Where was his voice? The voice that had tormented her the entire year? "I AM NOTHING! I AM FOREVER! I AM THE END!" she screamed with all the energy she could muster. Still, nothing happened, so still, she screamed.

Death itself broke through the stormy clouds, the impossible dark figure with blinding red eyes. "Oh, Serenna. Serenna, Serenna. You had your chance to be mine, but this one is a miracle of despair. This is the path you have forged. I hate you. It is exhilarating to hate someone again. It will all be over soon. I will look upon your essence one last time in the void before I forget you ever existed at all."

So be it. Meet me in the void, my love.

She grabbed her staff and approached Francis, who was the only one standing against Nyfe while the rest struggled against demons. His eyes screamed condolences, but no words were said. No words needed to be said. He resumed his multiform—still vivid and beautiful, an achievement from a lifetime of service to elemental sorcery. He deserved so much better. They all did.

She tore any energy that was left from her empty body.

Tears blurred her vision; she couldn't tell how bright the platinum emitted off her. Likely not much. It didn't matter.

Nothing mattered anymore.

CHAPTER 39

THE END OF FOREVER

arkness. Is this the void? I can't move my body, but my mind still works. It's warm here. The sun beats down on my face; this can't be Terrangus. Serenna will never forgive me for this one. I just wanted to do the right thing. I'm sorry. I'm so sorry...

A warm, wet...something touched his face. *Slurp. Slurp. What the hell is that?*

Zeen's eyes opened, finding a unicorn standing above him, licking his face. A majestic being, with a bright hazel mane and a sharp ivory horn. It matched the description from the Rinso saga perfectly. The unicorn neighed and galloped off towards a distant figure with a tail.

This surely wasn't real.

Faint feelings returned to his body, allowing him to wiggle his fingers and toes, but not much else. Large green blades of grass surrounded him, about half his height if he could still stand. The sky was a welcome shade of orange, accompanied by a subtle gust of wind that balanced out the intensity of the sun. All too vivid to be a dream.

"Welcome, human," a gruff voice called out. "I observed

your actions. They were unwise, yet honorable. The gods should have crafted you as a zephum!"

The voice was vaguely familiar. Feelings gradually returned, giving him enough energy to sit, aided by both hands. "Where am I?"

"*Ah*, you have reached the destination all men seek, but none wish to find."

The wound. Zeen struggled to move his arm towards his neck, searching for blood, a wound, any indication at all of his blow from Nyfe. Somehow, finding nothing was more unsettling than if his hand had returned bloody. "This isn't the void."

"No, my boy. This is a plane of peace. The Great Plains in the Sky, as my people call it. Over time, it has developed into a sort of…waiting room for the true end. Forgive an old zephum for being blunt, but I *do* have my favorites. *You*, as fate would have it, are one of them!"

Let's try this again. Zeen pushed himself up, stumbling as he rose. A zephum stood in the distance, gazing off into the plains with his hands behind his back. The God of Strength? The voice matched, but the aged zephum showed no signs of the immortal warlord from the stories. The zephum stood about Tempest's height, with plain ragged clothes in place of armor. Even his tail was short, the green skin exposed and settled in the grass.

Still, his presence had an aura to it. Not a literal one, like a Harbinger, but something about his wise, zephum frame standing calmly in the infinite fields filled him with awe. This was the God of Strength. The first warlord. The first Guardian. His honest figure outweighed any glory from a giant statue in Vaynex.

Not sure what to do, Zeen bowed. "It is an honor, God of

Strength. Please, I must ask, how are the others? How is Serenna?"

"Hmm. Not well."

He would have preferred a gentle lie, some sort of peace, before his end came. "No...what can we do? I *cannot* be the reason Serenna dies. Please; I will pay any price, accept any sort of bargain."

Strength sighed, turning around and meeting his eyes. Long, gray whiskers hung off his snout. "My boy, do not be so quick to offer yourself to a deity."

"The words are said. I would do *anything*."

"Ah, anything. Most of the problems that plague your realm are from desperate lives willing to do anything. Relax for now, humor an old zephum."

She was going to die. They all would, and it was his fault. "*How* can I relax?" he screamed, tortured as the words *I love you, Zeen* tore through him. Nothing could be worse. For a brief moment, he wished she had never said it. No...it was better to die this way. Even if it had only been for one night, he was able to embrace true love.

I just screamed at a god...

Strength stepped towards him and, to his relief, offered a warm smile. "Shh," he whispered, stopping at his side and gazing back into the plains. "When I was a Guardian, I loved my dear Noelami. Not...in a mating way, of course, but as my human sister."

Surely, I'm not remembering this correctly. "The Goddess of Fear?"

"*NEVER* use that title in my presence again." His deep voice shook the entire plains, sending the unicorn to flee into whatever awaited beyond.

"Never again," Zeen whispered, his eyes locked on the ground.

"Loss does terrible things to a soul. As much as you love Serenna, even as much as David loves his Melissa, nothing will ever compare to how much Noelami loved her kingdom of Boulom. Her suffering grows worse each year. I try...but I barely recognize the woman underneath the shadows anymore. Ah...us gods have lived too long."

"Strength?"

"Shh. Do you remember the words, my tiny human?"

After Zeen had been covered in Vim's blood, he would not dare forget. "Yes, of course. A dishonorable life is met with a dishonorable death."

"No...no, that is not correct at all. I suppose the words do not actually matter. I only desire mortals to love each other and be happy. Death is why that is not possible. I do not blame your Nyfe or my Ermias. Desperate men need love and support. Not threats, not promises of grandeur, not...*lies!*"

Love and support for Nyfe had landed Zeen in the afterlife. He could no longer share Strength's ideals, even if he truly wanted to. "I tried to see life the way you do, but I have to admit some people are too far gone."

Strength nodded. "There is no shame in admitting that. The only true shame comes when you do not try."

Zeen had said something similar to Serenna not too long ago, and nearly smirked at the irony until reality set back in. Even in death, he would never forget the warmth of her body when they had embraced. The comfort, the love that was never given a chance to blossom. "Strength, do I have any chance of saving her? I accept my fate, but she must survive. *Please.*"

The winds gusted as tranquility filled the air. Each moment of silence stole what very few fragments of hope he had left.

"Zeen, I have been a god for far, *far* too long. Promise me you will look after Tempest. He has so much potential, but I see tears forming in the maelstrom. My only regret is not being able to see his journey."

What does that mean? "I will defend him with my life. I swear to it."

"And I believe you. I will send you back, and then I will die."

An overwhelming guilt invaded his gut. "What...why would that kill you?"

"We cannot kill; we cannot bring life back. The two sacred rules. We all...dance around the first one, but this is a *blatant* violation of my purpose."

"You would die for me?"

"The world is so marvelous, Zeen. You catch glimpses of it, but only when it threatens to end can you truly see the delicate pillars holding everything together. Death wants it all to end. If I can stop that—just one more time—it would be the greatest honor any zephum could ever hope to achieve. A final act of protection from the first Guardian."

Tears rolled down Zeen's cheeks. His actions would kill a god, likely the only honorable one. "Thank you, from the bottom of my heart. I dedicate this victory to your name. For as long as I live, the Guardians will persevere."

Strength took a deep breath, rubbing his snout before turning to Zeen. "Indeed. Now, close your eyes, my boy. And please, try to remember the words. The other gods all claim the title, but my mantra is the true Legacy of Boulom. Strength without honor—is chaos."

Zeen's eyes closed, returning him to the darkness that had led him there. The heat from the sun faded, and no more gusts of wind blew across his face. A warm, rigid hand grasped his forehead. He kept his eyes closed, repeating the mantra in his head over and over until Strength's voice came to him a last time.

"Goodbye, my little human. You are simple, pure...I will always love you from whatever existence comes after this life."

*

Zeen's eyes opened and he smiled as rain poured down from the dark skies of Terrangus. An unfathomable strength coursed through him. Strength didn't just send him back, he sent him back with the wrath of a god.

The one true god.

He rose, surveying the battlefield, but an odd red haze blurred his vision. He checked his hands to find they were glowing a dark crimson. Mary was closest, leaning against a broken pillar, holding her shield against several crawlers slashing at her.

Zeen started to run, but the first step sent his entire body flying with perfect precision. Appearing in front of her, he gave her a warm smile before slashing his sword across. Only now did he see Hope radiating the same dark glow as his body. The demons didn't just die, they *shattered* as his blade vanquished everything in their immediate vicinity.

She yelled something, but the searing energy blocked out all sound as Zeen spoke. "It's okay, Mary. Today, let me protect *you*. We're going home after all." Her mouth kept moving, but he dashed instantly towards Sardonyx and Pyith.

Sardonyx was panting, swinging his sword with one hand in pure exhaustion. Pyith used the same strategy as Mary, relying only on defense with no chance of counter attacking. With a swift swipe of Hope, the demons on this side shattered. The warlord and Pyith stared at him in awe, then knelt in reverence as if Zeen were a god. "At ease, my friends. Strength without honor—is chaos." Sardonyx glared at the skies, weeping as he screamed something over and over.

Serenna and Francis were lying motionless on the ground

as David clashed against Nyfe. Zeen closed his eyes to focus and could feel their heartbeats from afar. It wasn't too late; they both lived. Serenna rose, still not noticing him and refreshing another dim shield on David. Francis tried to stand, but collapsed to his knees, screaming some sound Zeen would never hear.

Zeen appeared next to David, blocking Nyfe's strike and pushing him back. All eyes were upon him now, and he could feel them all. He could feel *everything*. Nyfe stumbled back, and David fell and sat against a broken pillar, laughing nearly to the point of madness as tears rolled down his cheeks.

Francis met Zeen's eyes for a brief moment and squinted. He appeared almost disappointed to see him, or maybe just confused. Glancing at his staff, Francis mouthed some silent words, then collapsed.

And there was his love. Serenna stared at him, similar to the cautious gaze Francis had given him, as if she couldn't believe he was real. She dropped her staff, started to run, then fell. He appeared above her, crouching and holding her in his arms. She appeared too exhausted from the day. Too exhausted from the burden of leadership. Too exhausted from the burden of loving a very foolish man. How long did he have? Did Strength give him his life back or was he on borrowed time? Perhaps this would be his last chance to speak to her.

"I love you, Serenna. If I cannot return, hold my heart as the void takes me away to the end of forever."

He kissed her forehead and rose, refusing to linger on her silent yells and haunting eyes. Across from him was Nyfe, radiating his Harbinger glow. Death towered above them from the black skies, roaring in pure silence. Terrangus Guardian Zeen Parson looked upon them both and felt nothing.

From the infinite gaze of crimson-tinted brightness, Death is but a thing to be ignored.

He appeared in front of Nyfe, then swung Hope once to knock him to the ground. This insignificant man had the audacity to betray him. After *everything*? Had Zeen lost the chance to live a happy life with Serenna? His clash of emotions yielded to an intense rage. Rage—pure rage—the rage of a zephum god.

Nyfe lay there, terrified, as he should be. Zeen appeared on top of him, then rained down blows on his face over and over, screaming and letting out an infinity of madness from frustration, pain, and loss. For a moment, Nyfe had made him lose faith in the necessity of good. It was the worst thing you could do to anyone, but he would *never* do it again.

Nyfe's face was a vortex of violence. He still breathed, but each labored breath appeared to take a staggering toll as blood poured down his mouth. His Harbinger form ended, and his energy drifted towards the insignificant deity in the sky. That was enough. Serenna would decide his fate. All hail Serenna of Mylor, leader of the Guardians, keeper of his heart.

Zeen rose, stumbling and breathing heavily. His strength faded as everything went black. Closing his eyes, he collapsed with a smile.

CHAPTER 40

HAPPY

David leaned against his pillar, gasping for air, with a giant smile on his face. He had made some terrible choices as a Guardian, but choosing Zeen was not of them. How did he…what the hell happened today? It didn't matter. Not in the sense of his usual apathy, but in the sense that Hope had found a way. He missed his old sword, but it was in the right hands.

Serenna held the fallen Zeen in her arms, weeping profoundly. He had to be alive, but David would not dare approach them in her current state. Heavy, dark circles dragged under her eyes and blood flowed out from several wounds all over her face and body. She had likely aged several years today. David knew the feeling, and knew what a terrible burden leading the Guardians had placed upon her already. It would only grow worse.

Forgive me, Serenna. No one deserves this, but someone has to do it. I'm sorry that someone is you.

For whatever it was worth, she'd done an incredible job, although she would never see it that way. She was too similar to David to be happy. Every mistake likely played through her thoughts over and over. Even if the nightmare came true and Zeen was gone…her leadership had given the realm just a little more time. They would still lose eventually, but eventually wasn't today.

"My sweet David," Fear's voice called out from behind. "Rise. You have a job to finish."

Fear's voice sent a shiver down his back. He rose, drawing the Herald of Fear. He didn't need any further instruction as he approached the fallen Harbinger. Nyfe's broken body lay before him, with any remnants of power long gone. This wretched man… What a waste of life. David raised his blade, not bothering to offer any redemption from the void.

Essences of fear seeped through his skin. In the end, Nyfe had feared that life itself wasn't meaningless, but he made it so by being a terrible person. He feared that even with the knowledge of how it all occurred, if he went back to the past, it would be the same result. Insignificant men doing insignificant things. It wasn't the story of Terrangus; it was the story of Nyfe.

"YES!" Death yelled, causing David to stumble back. That voice. It had been so long. "KILL HIM! KILL THE FAILURE!"

"No," Fear whispered, her arms caressing David's shoulders. "Keep him alive as a mockery. Defy Death. Make him see his own failure every day of his worthless existence."

David turned to Fear, ignoring the horrific deity coming down from the skies. "How can you ask this of me?"

"It will make him suffer. And I'm *not* asking."

Dealing with threats after such a day was exhausting. He didn't bother to respond, instead, meeting the glowing red eyes of Death before him. "Why do you care if he dies?"

"YOU WILL KILL HIM, AND YOU WILL KILL HIM NOW!"

Such a useless deity. He would defy Death, not for Fear,

but for himself. And maybe somewhere, if Melissa was still watching, for her too. "Your words mean nothing to me. Be gone from Terrangus while I still allow it."

The crimson eyes had never shown any shape or emotion, but David swore there was shock in its expression. "You *dare?*"

"*Yes*, I dare. I have defeated you for over twenty years. Get the *fuck* out of my kingdom."

The dark glow of the entity amplified, chilling his skin. David stood strong, hoping the absolute terror tearing through his insides would stay concealed.

"Your Melissa suffered before she died, but her suffering will be nothing compared to what I find for you. Your ally is the empress of a dead kingdom. An empress of loss. I am nothing. I am forever. I am the end. I AM THE END!"

He...can't do anything to me. These are all just empty words. We won. We...won. "You *are* nothing; it is the only part of your mantra that offers any truth. I pity you." He turned his back towards Death and walked away. Thunderous roars tore through the air, only to be ignored.

Death was defeated, and David was the only monster remaining. Somehow, that didn't bother him anymore. Being unhappy had never been a choice, but...well, doing nothing about it was an unconscious decision he had made decades ago. No more. He would change for her and, more importantly, for himself. David deserved it. He had fought so hard to find meaning in the pain, clinging to the familiarity of despair as if it were the only choice. But he deserved to be happy.

He always did.

CHAPTER 41

THE ABSURDITY OF FREEWILL

Francis struggled to breathe, forcing himself to one knee as David walked away. Death was screaming at him, and the man just walked off as if it was nothing. How could anyone be so bold?

Once, just once, I wish it were me.

He turned to Mary, hoping to meet her gaze, but she was lost in the madness. All eyes were fixated on David, except for Serenna. She had never turned away from Zeen. True love. A feeling he had entertained, but could never seem to find. Mary should be looking at him. He had saved her. They had lain together last night. The whole affair had been so...casual? She had treated the act as something to do for fun, the way one would choose a book based on the season. How odd.

Do...I love her? I don't even know. She won't love me. Why love me when she can choose any of the fools that stumble upon divinity? I'm just a thing to be used...

A Guardian.

Francis had finally mastered the multi-form in pure desperation, an achievement only four other Guardians had ever accomplished. He could name them all—their names lay buried in the textbooks, mere footnotes below the true heroes, heroes like Zeen and David, flailing in chaos and randomness.

It's not fair. Zeen saved the day... Zeen? Really?

It was all such a joke. Where was Strength when Nyfe had murdered the Golden Scholars? Julius had believed in him, and his reward was a meaningless death in a hostile kingdom. Francis sighed; it was an easy decision. This would be his last Harbinger. *Well, Mom, I guess you won.*

A familiar voice filled his thoughts. *"Ah, Francis. I saw it all. You were a marvel."*

"Wisdom?" A surge of adrenaline gave him the strength to stand, aided by his staff.

"Indeed. Is that despair I see in your eyes? Oh yes, of course it is. This is the result of the absurdity of freewill. Boys running around playing god. Do you still challenge my perception? Today speaks for itself, I must say."

"Honestly, I don't care anymore. I'm heading back to Alanammus to begin a life of politics. I should have followed in my mother's footsteps. It will be difficult, but my name and clout should serve as an advantage."

The deity appeared before him. "Hmm. My dear Francis, may I offer an observation? Terrangus needs an emperor. A difficult job to maintain, apparently."

Francis clutched his staff fiercely. "Do not speak ill of Reilly. I will *not* allow it."

Wisdom chuckled. "Allow? My absence has made you quite bold. A grievous error on my part, I will admit. Do not mistake my words as an insult. She died so you may live, and that alone makes her a hero. A hero in the legend of Emperor Francis Haide. The one that will bring Serenity to the realm."

Emperor Francis Haide...

Is he mocking me? I should send him away for abandoning

me. *No...no, no. Don't let him leave you again. This is your only friend left.*

No one else loves you. "Please, I can't tolerate insults after today. Please..."

"I would never mock you. Turn around—look at them!" Francis gazed across the ruins, finding a wave of people drifting towards them from the military ward gates. They all appeared lost and hopeless, desperate for someone, anyone, to guide them.

It could be me?

"How do I get them to believe? I can't...connect with people in that way."

"Why, just tell them the truth! Tell them you defeated Harbinger Nyfe. You are not only the hero of Terrangus but the savior of all the realm. The closest thing to a god any mortal could ever achieve."

"But—I didn't defeat Nyfe. In the end, I made no difference whatsoever. No one will ever believe I am a hero."

"Ah, but perhaps they will. You defeated Nyfe...with the power of *this*." After a bright flash, the Herald of Wisdom staff appeared in the air and floated in front of Francis. The staff didn't glow, it didn't radiate, it just stood there floating, with the golden eye of Wisdom at the end staring directly at him.

The power was *insurmountable.*

No one else would understand. Not even Serenna. His hand reached out—

"Francis, I must warn you. If you touch this staff, you will gaze upon something no mortal is ever supposed to find: the *truth.* There is no turning back from the horrors of enlightenment. Days will come when you yearn for the warmth of ignorance. That warmth will never come. *Never.*"

Francis stepped back, his hands retreating. The way Wisdom had said *never* filled him with dread. Was life really so bad? He was a well-respected scholar and Guardian, courting a beautiful woman who seemed to return his affection. The way she had smiled at him while they'd lain naked in his bed had been the pinnacle of his entire life. But how long would it last? She would move on. They always did…

Think of how much she would love you if you became emperor. Do it for Reilly, do it for Julius. Hell, even do it for Tempest. Golden Scholars, led by Emperor Francis Haide, savior of the realm and Herald of Serenity.

And by his side, the radiant Empress Mary Haide.

He grabbed the staff. A sudden shock tore through him, sending him to his knees as a loud ringing pierced his ears. Random truths assaulted him, creating a throbbing migraine as the thoughts flooded in.

Delusion is the cornerstone of happiness. Strength is no more. The Time God soon wakes. There is no God of Wisdom. Tears form in the maelstrom. Death is not of our realm. Addison Haide was a tyrant.

There is no God of Wisdom.

He let go with a gasp, then shot his eyes at the deity in horror. "What…what are you?"

"The most beautiful lie ever crafted: a friend. Speak my mantra and hold it again… I will reveal *everything*."

"I don't know your mantra…no one does."

"Oh, but I just told you. Take a *guess…*"

"Delusion is the cornerstone of happiness," Francis said, as his hands eased to the staff. Despite the lies, the chaos, he had to know. Another bright flash, but no cacophony of words bombarded him. Darkness crept through, ending his consciousness…

Francis awoke in the middle of an unfamiliar throne room. He glanced at his hands. This wasn't Francis, but the perception was apparently the form of a man close to his own age. A young woman sat on her throne as senators discussed and observed him from their high, circular vantage points surrounding him. He had never seen the woman in his life, but she matched the textbook description of Empress Maya Noelami. *Boulom of old? Is this a trial?*

Behind Francis was a chalkboard, filled with obscure mathematical formulas well beyond his comprehension. Even after a lifetime of scholarly work, not a single equation on the board vaguely resembled anything coherent. *What... Why am I seeing this?*

The empress rose, silencing the crowd and shooting him a glance of melting disappointment. Hmm. They must have been friends before this trial. "Professor Ermias Naiman. After reviewing the evidence, my court finds you guilty of reckless supernatural endangerment. Your...'time magic,' as you have deemed it, has led to the presence of demons in my empire. *Again.* I gave you a second chance, but no one gets three. Not even you. You are hereby sentenced to death. Damn you Ermias...*damn you.*"

Anyone who had ever studied Boulom history would know that name. *Ermias Naiman. This is a flashback of the first Harbinger of Death. Why am I seeing this?*

Against his will, Francis spoke out. "Inconceivable," he said—in Wisdom's voice. "This is how we reward the pursuit of knowledge? With execution? I could have fixed *everything,* made our life how it used to be. You believed in me, Noelami. You believed in Serenity. Now...believe this. I will not die a powerless coward in a court of LIES!"

Wisdom was the first Harbinger. The destroyer of Boulom.

Still against his will, tears rolled down his face as he stared directly at the empress. "Despite everything, I will always love you. Forgive me for this. I am nothing. I am forever... I am the *end.*"

His power surged as screams filled the room. By instinct, he grabbed the staff from his back, seeing the golden eye of Wisdom staring at him again. Clutching the Herald of Wisdom—or whatever it was—he launched a blast of fire straight into a clump of senators. Essences of life flowed from the inferno, seeping into his skin. The power was unfathomable. He let out a terrible roar and then the vision ended.

"You know the rest," the deity said. "I destroyed Boulom. Then the Guardians of old eventually slayed me. For reasons I still cannot understand, the Time God offered me divinity after my death. I am the God of Arrogance."

The God of Arrogance...

Francis stood dumbfounded. "I'm lost for words. What does this mean?"

"That, my friend, is up to you. I wasn't born a monster, just a professor who wanted to learn, create progress for our people, and *maybe* fix some past mistakes. The potential of time magic was...*inconceivable.* My freewill drove me to obsession, to madness. It should have never been that way. Why would anyone be cursed with such misguided intellect? After my failure, I found my true purpose. Serenity is not just an ideal, a silly thought from the mind of a child. Serenity is the only option—the true Legacy of Boulom. Francis, the reality is that I need you more than you need me. You can disagree with my ideals, but I still prefer to have a friend on the throne."

A friend... It terrifies me how much I understand his pain. The staff was still in his hands, with the golden eye staring through him. No matter what angle he held it, the eye always met his own. "I assume you prefer the title of Wisdom?"

"Indeed. Death and Fear embrace their titles, but I prefer something a bit more...eloquent."

Francis smiled. The idea of Wisdom being flawed and not a perfect entity was—oddly enough—rather freeing. "My dear

Wisdom, let us usher in the next age of enlightenment. What shall I do next?"

Arrogance chuckled. "All mortal gods look down upon their subjects from a castle. Tap into the power of my staff. Starting now...*anything* is possible."

Francis glanced at the rubble before gazing into the eye of his staff. "How does this thing work?"

"Use your mind. Think about the task in the proper way, and it will be so."

Clutching the staff, he closed his eyes. *Castle.* Nothing happened. *Terrangus castle.* More silence. His grip tightened.

Emperor Francis Haide demands a castle, NOW!

A deep rumbling began, along with gasps of awe from the crowd. He opened his eyes to find he was floating in the air, radiating a glow of pure gold. Power coursed through him, and he closed his fist as the rubble from the ground settled into the shape of the old castle. He had no idea how, but his arms moved themselves, shifting and morphing the rubble to adjust the outline of rock and steel into the once massive stronghold he had long despised.

In his wonder, he lost track of time, but the task was done. Terrangus castle stood where it had always been with the same tower, the same doors, the same pristine glass on the east end. All it lacked was an emperor.

The morning's storm dissipated, and Death was gone. The sun's warmth tinted the streets with an amber glow, clearly a blessing for Wisdom's chosen one. Gazing through the crowds and Guardians, Francis could finally see David's deity above him. They met eyes—and by the gods, he saw fear in her expression.

Tread carefully, Goddess. You are my enemy.

Mary frowned at him from the ground. The gaze tore through him, but she would understand in time. They all would. *I must say something. These people need inspiration.*

Still floating, he raised his hand to silence the crowd, the same way Forsythe had done when he was the emperor.

"Fellow people of Terrangus. For those who do not know me, my name is Francis Haide. Rejoice, for Harbinger Nyfe has been defeated by the power of divinity. I have devoted myself to the eminence of the God of Wisdom, and together, we can rebuild our kingdom."

He paused for cheers, but most just looked up in confusion…or fear? *Dammit, what would my mother say?*

Target the desperate. "It is no secret that our kingdom has suffered greatly in the past decade. I have seen families starve in the streets, crime go unpunished, taxes that go straight to war. Answer me this: why are we at war when we cannot feed our own?" That got a few murmurs.

Create their fears, which only you can resolve. "Forgive me for speaking the truth, but the harsh reality is that Harbingers are not the greatest threat to Terrangus. We have no *leadership*! Everyone just moseys about and accepts their station because it could be worse. That isn't a life. And I can say that because, up until now, that has been my life."

Adrenaline rushing through him, he soared to the ground with a loud thud, then drifted through the crowds. People touched his golden aura in awe. "I don't want to live that way anymore… *I can't*! I want knowledge! I want prosperity!"

He finally met Mary's eyes. "I want a *family…*"

Simple promises of infinity. "After everything, we deserve to be happy. All of us, but only I can make that happen. I will craft Terrangus into a Serenity. A paradise, where each individual can be guaranteed the life they deserve. Poverty will be a footnote in our history books, a lost chapter our children will mock and say never occurred." Some clapped, some nodded, some even cheered.

He raised the Herald of Arrogance in the air, the same way Nyfe had done when he was general.

"People of Terrangus, yield your incomprehension and let my wisdom cradle you into the Serenity you swore could never be real. For as long as I reign, you will never know fear or despair again. Perfection is the cornerstone of happiness."

He lied to them, the same way his mother had done when she was the archon.

A well of near-infinite knowledge. Forgotten archons, forgotten warlords, their mistresses and bastards lost in the chapters of history no one bothered to remember. Despite it all, one unanswered question still remained, the one that had lingered since his mother's death.

How much can a person be damaged before they are considered broken?

EPILOGUE

RENSEN THE RED

Two months after the defeat of Harbinger Nyfe, Serenna drifted through the rainy Terrangus streets in her full Guardian armor with the Wings of Mylor across her back. She had hated Terrangus. She had feared Terrangus. But to pity Terrangus? That was a new one. Random townsfolk and soldiers stopped their repairs to smile at her as she made her way to the military district. They loved their Serenna of Mylor, Crystal Guardian, savior of the realm.

That was also a new one.

The castle stood in the back of the recovering kingdom, but she kept her distance. She wasn't ready to face Francis... Emperor Francis. The southern kingdoms had been outraged, with Archon Gabriel ensuring to remind Serenna the whole chain of events had ultimately been her fault. Maybe it was? No time for such debates; arguing about the past never fixes the future.

She hugged Landon at the entrance to one of the smaller black barracks in the ward, exchanged brief pleasantries, then made her way to the compact healing room that was reserved for one man.

The still unconscious Zeen lay in his bed, a brown woolen blanket covering him, while a fire crackled from behind. For all of Francis's faults, allowing Zeen to rest in his own military barracks had been a kindness. Anything to keep him away from the castle. Away from Francis, from Wisdom, away from that glowing staff with the terrible gaze.

Serenna wrote her name in the visitor's log, smiling as she noted *Empress Mary Walker, Warmaster Tempest Claw, Guardian Pyith Claw* and, of course, *Warlord Sardonyx Claw,* who had…left a note?

To my favorite human, she read, *please take care of my friend. When Zeen wakes, bring him to Vaynex AT ONCE! We will feast! It will be GLORIOUS! Strength without honor—is chaos.*
-Warlord Sardonyx Claw, son of Fentum Claw.

She put the note back on the table with a laugh.

Perhaps David had visited too, but had been wise enough to leave his name off. To most, David's legacy had become that of a monster: a champion of Fear, murdering an emperor and leaving a wake of dead soldiers in his path. For Serenna, she would always remember him as her old leader, and—more importantly—her friend. Both views were equally just and unjust. As with all perspectives, once forced to exist, they had no choice but to hold some level of truth.

She took a deep breath, pulled up her chair, then grabbed her copy of *Tales of Terrangus: Rinso the Blue – Volume I.* Zeen hadn't smiled in his sleep since the battle, but she would fix that.

"'Rain. Hard rain. Heavy rain,'" Serenna read out loud. "'Rain that pattered from the sky.'" *Gods, please get on with it.* "'Rain that dripped down the face of Rinso the Blue, the newest human Guardian of Terrangus. He quickly drew his blade, staring down his opponent: a Harbinger of Fear. Now, there are two types of Harbingers…'"

She turned the page after a particularly long exposition dump. "'Rinso charged, tightly gripping his blade, struggling to block out visions of the sultry Olivia awaiting him back at the castle. Oh, sweet Oliva, with her…'"

She turned the page after an outrageous and anatomically bizarre description of Oliva's body. "'Rinso swung his sword across, meeting the steel staff of his Harbinger opponent. They met eyes, and Rinso immediately recognized the slim man with a tanned face, blue eyes, brown hair, average human-sized nose, and of course, ragged black armor. The mage could only be one man: his *twin* brother: Rensen the Red.

"'Rensen took his staff, gripped it tightly, and quickly bashed the staff against his brother's face, sending him to the cold, Terrangus floor. The world went dark… Rinso shot up from his bed, gasping loudly. Whew, it was only a dream.'"

Serenna sighed. "Oh, come on. Really?"

Zeen continued to lay there unconscious, so Serenna turned to the next page.

MEET THE AUTHOR

Timothy Wolff lives in Long Island, New York, and holds a master's degree in economics and a career in finance. Such a life has taught him the price of everything but the value of nothing. He enjoys pizza bagels, scotch, karaoke, oxford commas, and spending the day with family and friends. The obvious culmination of the past 35 years was to write a 400+ page fantasy novel where a drunk teams up with a swordsman, two mages, and lizard-people to oppose god. Why do we write these in the third person?

Strength without honor—is chaos!

He can be reached at:
@TimWolffAuthor on Twitter
TimWolffAuthor@gmail.com

THANKS AND ACKNOWLEDGEMENTS

First and foremost: to anyone still reading at this point, I thank you beyond words. If I were an octopus, I would hug you with eight arms. My first thanks are owned to my immediate family of Larry, Joan, Danny, and Matt, who listened to a madman's ramblings about why the giant lizard-man had to kill the unicorn for *symbolism*. I can't thank my beta readers enough, particularly the ones that dredged through my early drafts. Listed in no particular order below:

Amber Lilyquist
Michelle Cerone
J. Flowers-Olnowich
Macy Lu
John North
Shelby Nesbitt
Vivian
Samantha Jordan
Jona Murataj
Chelcie Alexandra
Sasha Pinto Jayawardena
Courtney Kelly
Alyssa Kegel
Swords & Scythes Beta Reading
Rose Kolassiba

This novel was *so bad* in its first iterations, and we should all be thankful they suffered so you didn't have to. In one of my earliest drafts, I forgot to attribute a dialogue tag or any context to *"they killed my son,"* so my poor reader read the rest of the novel assuming Serenna had lost a child, only to never mention said child or the event again. Exceptional job on my part.

An enormous thanks to my editor, Jonathan Oliver. He corrected the horrors of my em-dash and semicolon usage, while pointing out plot holes that made no sense, and the fact that characters shouldn't smile if the POV-character can't see their face. It was a joy to sit on a zoom call as two professional adults and discuss why the lizard-people should say "dishonorable" instead of "honorless."

Special thanks to Hannah Gokie for going well beyond a simple proofread and correcting numerous errors that nearly made it into publishing. I added this part after her work so if there are any typos it's my fault.

My final thanks to everyone that gave my novel a chance. In a world where there are hundreds and thousands of wonderful fantasy novels to choose from, it is simply harrowing that anyone would give my work a read. It's cheesy, but I always appreciated when RPG games ended the final credits with a thank you to the player. With that being said,

Thank you.

Ingram Content Group UK Ltd.
Milton Keynes UK
UKHW012126060323
418151UK00007B/82

9 798986 765525